Suddenly, urgently, Ariel called his name, "Simon."

He swung around as she ran across the room, fleet as any horse or bird alive—flying into his arms. Her nestling head sought his breast, and she clung to him passionately, seeking the comfort of his heartbeat.

Words of tenderness he had never used before trembled from his lips. His strong arms supported her, catching her in a lover's embrace until they were almost one.

Abruptly he turned away, slamming the massive door shut in her face, thrusting the bolt home. Ariel fell to her knees, clutching the door for support, her body wracked with dry sobs...

Also by Katherine Hale
Published by Ballantine Books:

OBSESSION

MADNESS

KATHERINE HALE

BALLANTINE BOOKS • NEW YORK

To my mother and her grandchildren, Melinda and Ian

Library of Congress Catalog Card Number: 83-91244

ISBN 0-345-31144-2

Manufactured in the United States of America

First Edition: April 1984

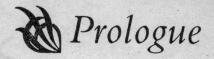 # Prologue

Be careful, my child, the old man warned, that your destiny be not fire and madness, and the stone walls. Over and over he warned me, but I ceased listening. He was too dangerous, and so I, too, came to find myself within stone walls.

Stone walls...

I remember Jacobean paneling, silken screens, Oriental courtiers, arabesque tiles, but that was long before the walls became padded. No design, just filthy splotches reeking of tears like my stone bedroom. My suite—for I am rich in rooms— three to be exact.

Will no one ever come to my tomb to save me?

Where did I lose him? As a child, a young woman, or when I went mad? For they say I am insane. I, Ariel Farjeon.

Please, help me! I am not yet dead. Don't let me die within my stone prison. I have paid for my crimes.

Come to me, my dearest love. Come to me so that I can sink my ruby lips into yours.

But give me life... Yours, my beloved.

 *One*

"*I*nsanity?" *Simon Desmond gave* a rueful smile. "No, I'm afraid that's far removed from my sphere. I'm just the local GP."

Farjeon's gray eyes narrowed. "But surely you must have had some cases?"

"Oh, the usual lot. Hysterical women, dipsomania, senility—but nothing this serious."

"I'm not saying it is serious. Weston Asylum considers her cured. All I ask is that you check her two or three times a week."

"Is that really necessary?"

"In our world, doctor, once insane, always insane. Even a cure offers no protection against malice."

"Why do you still keep her locked up?"

Nicholas Farjeon shifted behind the Egyptian motif Regency desk-table. A beautiful piece of work, Desmond thought wistfully; the mahogany top so highly polished that each precisely arranged objet d'art stood brilliantly reflected. An item of furniture in perfect harmony with the room's elegance. Linen-fold paneling climbed up to a swirl of Jacobean plaques high overhead. Immense shelves bent under obviously read books. A wool carpet of curious design—arabesques, Desmond decided, shimmered on the dark oak floor—an exotic contrast to the simplicity of the Regency furnishings.

"Why do I still keep her locked up?" his host repeated. "A

2

foolish promise made to my wife. Regina detests Ariel's presence in this house—" A spasm of emotion crossed his face. "Understandable, really. She once tried to kill me."

"Then why bring her home?"

"Because she's my sister, and I still love her. Because I cannot bear the thought of her being shut away in Bedlam—"

"Bethlem?" Simon Desmond looked bewildered.

"I am given six months' time." Farjeon's tone was biting. "If Ariel shows no sign of improvement, she'll be sent to Lambeth. And once inside—that's the end."

"This isn't my field," Desmond protested. "You need an expert. And surely there are public asylums more convenient to Norfolk. Granted, Bethlem is no longer the hell it once was, but I'd want no relative of mine incarcerated there."

"And do you think I want it?" Farjeon exploded. "My hand is forced—" Abruptly, he broke down, his voice imploring. "Get her to talk. The slightest improvement is all I need to keep her here at Bellereve."

Desmond's eyes flicked warily towards Farjeon. "You'll think me very tiresome, sir, but are we dealing with a sane woman or a lunatic? From your earlier remarks, I assumed that she was well."

"And so she is, Desmond, and has been for a decade, we think. Long ago, the attacks of mania ceased, but circumstances always prevented my bringing her home. Ariel could quite easily have spent the rest of her life in Weston Asylum. The staff was more than willing to keep her on." He sighed. "One's world hangs by such a fragile thread. My sister's was smashed by madness; mine by bad investments. No longer can I afford the luxury of housing her at four hundred pounds per annum in a private hospital. Regina has long resented the heavy expense, and as the father of two young sons, I'm in no position to pick a quarrel with her. To be blunt, I am strapped, and she pays the bills. . . ."

"Yes, I quite understand," said Desmond briskly. "May I see the patient before making a final decision?"

"Certainly." Farjeon rose, his back to a dazzling oriel window. "She's in that wing over there. Completely isolated from the rest of the manor-house, as you can see—"

Desmond snatched a perfunctory look. A door in a wall, barred windows—little more.

Nicholas Farjeon smiled. "Come with me, doctor." He stepped out into a vast corridor banked on one side by an almost continuous wall of bay and oriel windows. The library's magnificent plaster ceiling wound its intricate way to the far end of the wing. Ancient portraits hung on the wainscotted walls, jewels and pale, oval faces glistening in the afternoon light.

Stopping in amazement, Desmond gaped like a schoolboy. Farjeon laughed at his incredulity.

"Well, it had to be done after the first fire. Too much damage occurred to use it solely in its official capacity." He waved an arm. "So all these rooms were built into the Long Gallery, and one can still stroll at leisure. . . ."

Leading the way down the great Jacobean staircase, with its garlanded pattern of vines and animals, Farjeon continued his discussion as they walked through a less antiquated part of the house, where the past surrendered to the present in a series of à la mode fantasies. Garish wallpaper and paint disguised antique splendor; plump sets of furniture and brash knickknacks from London's fashionable arcades made each room a hazard; and anything that could be shot, stuffed, beaded, or draped was so displayed. It was such a disconcerting setting to the wing above that Simon Desmond winced, remembering another such house—one he'd been hoping to forget.

Sensing his unease, Nicholas Farjeon said flatly, "This is my wife's domain. . . ." and flung open a door to the inner courtyard. On three sides, the great building embraced a desolate rectangle. Withered stalks of grass and moss sprouted between cracks and broken stones. "Picturesque," some might have called it. An unexpected foil to the manor's enchantment. But nothing could have prepared Desmond for what lay beyond. A stone block three stories high, set in the midst of a charred ruin.

Farjeon turned to the younger man. "We're standing on what was once the oldest part of the manor-house." With a grimace, he surveyed the uneven brick flooring. "Twenty-five rooms destroyed by lightning early in the eighteenth century, and that"—he nodded toward the ruined wing—"was caused by a fire twenty years ago. Accidental."

Desmond asked the inevitable. "Why not tear it down?"

"Well, both my father and I hoped to rebuild. One of those dreams that die on speaking." He shrugged. "The vines do a passable job of masking the destruction. The center survived because it's stone. . . ."

"Stone, not brick or flint," mused Desmond, who didn't like the look of the place at all.

"I'll tell you about it later." Farjeon's tone was curt. Reaching a heavy iron-banded door set in the blackened stone, he leaned against it, inserting a key. "See her, Desmond. Tell me what you think——" A rumble and the great door began to move. "Sometimes she speaks, but not to me."

A foul odor greeted Desmond's nostrils as a sharp-featured woman appeared in the doorway. Under a dirty white cap, her hair hung in wisps, demonstrating a vain attempt to hide the almost pointed ears. Jagged, decayed teeth, a long skull, and a too lean body reminded Desmond uncomfortably of the loathsome jackal of the nether world weighing hearts of the dead against the feathers of truth and right.

Am I worthy? he thought numbly, and stared beyond. A creature, drooping on a couch, sat in the bed-sitting room, rocking back and forth.

At Farjeon's prompting, Simon Desmond stepped forward and raised the woman's head, astounded to find it beautiful—as lovely as a Greek statue. Classical, exquisite features, eyebrows like a bird in flight, skin like pearl, a mouth to bewitch an emperor, a porcelain, aristocratic nose, and eyes of a changeable gray, both loving and frightening, that could break a man's heart.

"What happened to her hair?"

Nicholas Farjeon ran a hand through the pure-white strands. "Something in the asylum . . . during a period in seclusion."

Cupping her slender shoulders, Desmond watched for a reaction. "When did she stop speaking?"

"About eleven years ago." Farjeon spoke distantly.

The gray eyes flicked. Unless Desmond was mistaken, she was definitely aware of them. Comprehension was another matter, however. "Is she completely mute?"

"No, she makes her needs known—briefly."

"Was she ever diagnosed as catatonic?"

A tremor ran through her body, and the brother exclaimed, "No. Never!" Backing away from his sister, he muttered to Desmond, "Let's you and I have a talk, eh?"

The Jackal saw them to the door, which was then locked from the outside. A walk across the courtyard was followed by a superb glass of brandy in Farjeon's library.

Moody and disconsolate, Farjeon threw himself into a chair, his heavy lidded eyes on Desmond. "Ariel was incarcerated when she was eighteen—"

"And how old is she now?"

"Thirty." Her brother's voice was caustic. "She had an unfortunate misalliance with a ne'er-do-well son of a good county family. When I discovered this deplorable situation, I persuaded his relatives to ship him to Canada—"

"And your sister?"

Farjeon drank deeply from his snifter, his face pale with anger. "God, I had such hopes for her. . . . Gifted with beauty, a fine mind, every accomplishment—and then she threw away her life on that bastard. How they met, I'll never know. But I caught them *flagrante delicto*. Actually committing the act in the stone room. How just!" He sneered. "The villain departed, and I was left with the consequences—"

"Which were?" Desmond raised an eyebrow.

"An unborn child and an unmarried mother." The words came thickly. "Ariel was the dearest person in my life. I would have done anything for her. So I took a cottage far away from Foulsham, where we wouldn't be known. . . ."

"And what happened?"

"She went mad and accused me of killing her child."

Desmond blinked. "Does she still accuse you?"

Farjeon's look was faraway. "Oh, no. She knows I love her."

"What happened to the baby?"

"It was overlain. . . ." The melodious voice sank. "Well, Desmond, will you take the case or not?"

He needed the money desperately but was not about to be rushed into a hasty decision. "Overlain? How?"

"She stifled it in bed." At Desmond's blank look, he added with a touch of impatience: "Ariel killed it. An *accident*, you understand. Nursing it, she fell asleep."

The young doctor frowned. "How old was the child?"

"Three, four days. . . . But she wouldn't accept it as her fault and blamed me. I was planning to have it farmed out."

"Then why let her nurse it?" Desmond asked quietly.

"She wanted to for a day or two. Like a little girl playing with a doll. I thought she'd get over it. . . ." His eyes clouded. "Then she tried to kill me."

"When?"

"After its death. First, she refused to give it up. Then, when it was taken from her, she became very ill. But her recovery was swift, and she seemed quite normal. Fit to return to Bellereve. Never mentioned the baby. . . ." He stared past Desmond. "One day while I was reading, she crept up behind and stabbed me—" Grief-stricken, he pounded the table. "What else could I do but confine her to an asylum!"

Puerperal mania, Desmond judged, dropping a few compassionate words to his distraught host. "Why is the building stone?" he asked suddenly.

"Regrettably, a streak of insanity runs in this family."

"Oh?" Desmond leaned forward, startled.

"Ariel is one of a half-dozen to be confined, and they were all lodged there. In a stone suite built like a fortress, to house our mad . . ." He swore under his breath. "Two centuries ago, the last male Farjeon died. The heiress married a Norwich merchant, who took our name and brought the poison. It struck one male; the rest were females." His face sagged. "Never did I think it would take my sister. . . ."

Desmond held out a sympathetic hand. "I'll do what I can for her, sir."

But what was he consigning her to? he wondered, driving back from Foulsham to Heydon. Would she spend the rest of her life in that mausoleum, guarded by dregs like the Jackal? In an asylum, no matter how dismal, companionship of sorts was available. Which was the lesser evil?

His depression deepened as he drove the trap the long way home, turning deliberately out of his way. Why hurry when nothing awaited him? Just his sister-in-law, Beatrice Clayton, who had financed a venture that was fast approaching disaster. No wonder the practice had been so easily obtained. The last physician couldn't make a go of it either. When Dr. Grinnell retired, his patients looked elsewhere—to Reepham, Salle, or Aylsham. No new Heydon man stood a chance.

Down winding, rutted lanes, his horse cantered. Desmond stared out dully at formidable hedges and walls shielding country houses, at woods crisscrossing acres of bleak land. Why in God's name had Farjeon sent for him? Why not Reepham's Colin Broughton? A highly respected man, he thought acidly, clattering through its market place, glaring in dislike at the frosty Georgian houses whose inhabitants cut him dead whenever he came to the village. Even the idlers loafing outside the King's Arms couldn't be induced his way.

Salle's vast, exquisite church with its awesome tower for once failed to move him. One more mile and he'd be home. To again meet the disappointment on Beatrice's face. A bit more money and he could have settled in Lynn, Norwich, or a resort town—places sure to welcome a newcomer. Instead what was he doing? Treating penniless laborers and playing nursemaid to a madwoman.

Reaching Heydon, he bypassed the village green with its enchanting straggle of houses and shops, ignoring the people who so patently ignored him. Approaching Fairhaven, he was again touched, almost poignantly so, by its charm. A small Queen Anne house, with dormers nestling in a steep-pitched roof, reddish-brown bricks and white-painted woodwork, shone in the fading light—a beacon of peace, like its name. Spring would bring a blaze of flowers set among box borders and fruit trees in the Elizabethan garden fronting the house. A glorious display, stretching into late fall, so bewitching that within a half-hour, he had fallen victim and made a fatal mistake. A penny postcard would have served him better. . . .

Beatrice Clayton, twice widowed, sat waiting for him on a horsehair sofa in the parlor. Dressed in black bombazine— which she would always wear not for her second husband but for Jedediah Desmond, her only love—she flashed her placid smile over clicking ivory needles. A ball of yarn tumbled to the floor and was swiftly retrieved by her brother-in-law from the too curious paws of a tabby cat.

"Did anyone come?" he asked brusquely, flinging down his greatcoat and top hat. A flutter behind him was Bessie, the parlor maid, whisking away his bag and garments.

"No, dear."

"Six months! Six months we've been here, and all I've managed to snare is a handful of mice," he exclaimed bitterly, strolling over to a bow window. "They feed us, but no money. How much is left, Bea?"

"About a hundred pounds."

"And that will last you how many quarters?"

"Two at least. By then you'll be settled."

Irked by her calm, he swung about. "Well, I do have another patient—Miss Ariel Farjeon." He bowed with a wry flourish.

"Nicholas Farjeon's sister?" Beatrice Clayton looked stunned. "Why, that's wonderful, Simon. Now you'll sweep up the whole family, and others will follow. The gentry are like sheep. It's a good start, dear."

But his mood rankled. "Maybe we should just pack up and leave while we've still some capital. If another fool bought the place, as I did, we might latch on to something better."

"I've never reproached you, have I, Simon?" she asked anxiously. "How could you possibly have known?"

"I grabbed it because it reminded me of Mother and Jed. Not once did I ask a pertinent question. You know how impulsive I can be when so struck." He grimaced.

Sudden, unexpected tears stung her eyes. "I've always promised myself not to ask you this, Simon, but lately I think of him more and more. Dear God! I miss him so—" Her body wilted like a neglected flower. "How did Jed die?"

Desmond hesitated, throwing her a wary glance. Under faded copper hair, pulled into a tight bun, her plain face was wracked with grief. For once the dancing brown eyes were bleak, the generous mouth crumpled into a jagged line. She looked much older than her forty-five years. Stricken, he finally saw the aching despair that she had so skillfully hidden from him all those years.

"How did Jed die?" she again asked, very quietly.

"You were in the courtroom. You heard the evidence."

A trembling hand reached out to pet the tabby. "He killed himself, didn't he?" she whispered.

"Certainly not! He'd had too much to drink and while trying to shave cut the jugular vein. You might call it a freak accident, but such events are commonplace. . . ." Desmond kept his voice steady. "My findings were confirmed by the doctors. The coroner's jury accepted it. Why you should question their verdict after seven years, I can't imagine! 'Death by misadventure' . . . What else could it have been?"

Turning on his heel, he strode off to the surgery annex, opposite the parlor, a three-room suite designed by the renowned Dr. Grinnell's grandfather, the first of Heydon's prize doctors.

Patients entered the waiting room by way of the hall or the Elizabethan garden. Beyond stretched his surgery and consulting room. Heartsick, Desmond slowly paced the empty, echoing rooms. No expense had been spared to make this area as cheerfully attractive as possible. White paneling highlighted pale lemon walls, and Beatrice had done wonders with the waiting room, making it as comfortable as their own quarters— even a children's corner was provided. Desmond had been insistent that nothing suggest pain or unhappiness.

The surgery was outfitted with the finest medical furniture and equipment from Norwich. Unused instruments gleamed like silver in a pristine walnut cabinet; the large leather table served as an examining or operating table; and all his drugs in bottles, boxes, and phials stood neatly filed behind locked glass on wooden shelves.

A soothing wallpaper design warmed his consulting room; here the furniture was as elegant as his taste and finances would allow. And what did it all add up to? So few patients as to hardly leave a shadow. Some fractures, a case of mumps, several confinements, a possible leg tumor, a death due to overwork—not much more. But they were grateful, these poor laborers, sidling up to his back door with a scrawny fowl, a bouquet of crops coaxed from a tiny plot, or a treasured but valueless trinket. The small boy who had had mumps shyly presented him with a pair of skates. . . .

"Oh, God, Jed, did I make you die?" he cried aloud, suc-cumbing to a bout of self-pity. Seven long years ago, finally he'd scraped up enough money to begin his second year at Guy's Hospital. . . . With a shaking hand, he poured a glass of brandy, studying himself in the gilded convex mirror over the marble fireplace. A ferocious eagle glared down at him, a fit companion for his mood.

The man reflected was thirty-two years old—vain, ambi-tious, six feet tall with an athletic physique, and a thick crop of honey-colored hair crowning the proud head and patrician features. Sunlight would expose the hazel eyes' bitterness, the ironic twist to the sensual mouth, but by candle or gaslight, the fierce intensity of his emotions was muted. He gave himself another few years, then the waste would show, cutting through him and everything he touched like a sword.

Strange that nothing showed on Ariel Farjeon's face. Not a whisper of the past. Except for that appalling white hair. . . .

"Oh, God, why didn't I leave him alone?" he asked his tortured image. Hadn't he scraped, humbled himself, enough to have earned that money? Months of grubbing away as a clerk in some wretched store on Oxford Street, counting up the day's receipts, entering figures into giant ledgers, eyes dimming, back wrenching from the tedious strain; sharing a squalid room with the dissipated son of a Peer whose small allowance paid for his vicious habits. A man not adverse to bringing his chippies back home. It amused him to see Simon's disgust, his desperate longing, but Desmond yearned not for the prostitute's tricks but for love. . . . And at the end of every week, his meager salary was grudgingly shoved into his hand— small recompense for all the pleasures denied him: the elegant clothes mesmerizing him from shop windows, the superb meals and fine wines he had once known, and the women he longed to bed. His passionate virility attracted many, he knew, and that was the hardest thing to deny. But detesting the idea of furtive sex, he turned aside each overture. One day, he would find the woman who would set his soul and heart on fire. Until then, he had but one ambition. Return to Guy's Hospital. And gradually, like grains of sand, the pounds mounted up into a thick wad, and there was enough.

Back he went to Southwark to apply for readmission into the medical school, battling his way by foot across London Bridge. The ice was gone from the Thames, releasing a flotilla of boats. Winter had fought its last battle. Cowed by spring's approach, the bone-chilling mists and sulfurous fogs had seemingly evaporated. Behind him, London glistened like a mythical kingdom. To Simon Desmond, age twenty-five, gripping his second chance after a promising start cruelly interrupted by his father's parsimony, it was the most beautiful morning of his life.

Reaching Southwark, he ran all the way to the hospital, greeting the porter at the gates with a joyful shout. An hour later, he was welcomed back as a perpetual pupil—a post enabling him to walk the wards and attend lectures. Told to report the next morning, he tore out to find digs in Borough High Street.

The room he took was not unlike his squirrel's hole in Soho, but to Desmond it was finer than Windsor Castle. Set in a cluster of eighteenth-century buildings, his paradise was an attic room crouched over a soot-laden garden and a battered plane tree. A second dormer window faced High Street, and each morning exotic odors awakened him from the greengrocer's shop below. Everything he needed was within arm's reach. He had only to leap out of bed, dress, down a muffin and a cup of tea, and be at the hospital in five minutes. He was, to say the least, supremely happy.

And then came the note from his beloved brother, Jedediah, fifteen years his senior. *Laddie, can we have dinner? Cheshire Cheese or your domain?*

Eagerly, Simon Desmond wired back: *I'll be off Saturday at five. Meet me at the Queen's Head.*

He loved all those ancient coaching inns, nestling under the protection of Guy's, still able to preserve a semblance of their former life despite the railways' effort to make them freight depots. The thirsty, hungry customer simply turned a deaf ear to the daily weighing in of tons of goods. Desmond's favorite was the less raucous Queen's Head. A hop merchant leased its north galleries, and on a Saturday night the only loud noise came from the taproom.

Tonight's bill of fare wouldn't be bad, he thought, studying the placard: "One shilling dinner. Cut from the joint, two vegetables, suet pudding, bread, and a glass of ale or stout."

He ordered a bottle of champagne as a surprise for his brother and dearest friend, whom he hadn't seen in months. . . . A man approached him hesitantly, and he blinked at the shabby apparition. Reaching into his pocket for a few pence to toss to the beggar, he stopped, appalled.

"Jed?" he asked incredulously. "Jed, is it you?"

"Yes, Simon, it's me—elder brother." Grabbing the bench to steady himself, he sank down with an old man's fatigue, short-winded. Yet the mischievous grin—so like Simon's in a puckish sense of humor—lit up his wasted face as he eased himself out of his coat and top hat.

Simon Desmond bit his lip, his throat tightening. Helplessly, he signaled to the tap boy to open the champagne. "How's my favorite Bea?" he asked, averting his eyes from the frayed suit hanging on the emaciated body.

Jed's face shone. "The loveliest woman I ever knew," he murmured. "God, at least, has blessed me in marriage."

Their glasses clinked. A barmaid turned up the gas jets, warming the dark wood. More and more patrons drifted in, a lively chorus to their conversation. Ripples of laughter shot out like a rocket stream. Jed mopped his perspiring forehead with a large handkerchief, then elegantly touched his lips.

No, it's not drink, Simon thought, numbed. What the hell is it? A big hand convulsively clasped his. Not wanting to let go.

"Do you know I was so jealous of you the day you were born?" Jed gave a hoarse laugh. "I wasn't about to share you with Mother. And, God damn it, you were an ugly baby—face like a wrinkled peach. But I felt I had to take care of the two of you. My duty—what with Father enriching himself in a warehouse, or in some whore's bed!"

It had always puzzled him. He could tell from his mother's attitude, no matter how loving, that he was unexpected. "How was I conceived? A reconciliation?"

"He got drunk and went to the wrong bed."

Simon's face turned ashen.

"I'm sorry, Laddie. The head housemaid—'stepmama'—was on holiday, so Father, stupefied, fell into his wife's bed. You were the magnificent result." Unintentionally, he had hurt him. The last thing he wanted. Hastily, he poured them more champagne. "'Golden Fingers,' the gentry dubbed him when he built that colossal villa to bad taste! Do you remember the old house?"

"Vaguely," Simon answered, his smile tight. After all those years the memory was still painful and now, coupled with this new information, unbearable. Gardens, a stream, and a sweeping park enveloping a Georgian house so much attuned to his mother's gentle personality that it reflected her every mood. His childhood's haven in Kent situated near one of those ancient villages packed with half-timbered houses, high hedges, and droves of sheep roaming the rich pastures.

"She loved us very much. We compensated for father's lack. Something to get up for in the morning, eh?" Jed coughed into his handkerchief, a spasm contorting his body. With a show of bravado, he recovered, smiling broadly. "What would our lives have been like if we'd gone into business with him?"

"Terrible." Simon's voice was dry, masking anxiety.

"Well, give him credit for one thing. He got the bitch pregnant and married her—"

"Lucky for him that Mother died, eh?" Draining his glass, Simon ordered a second bottle.

"Oh, there was nothing nefarious about it, Laddie. Cancer has no favorites. . . ."

Lifting a new glass, Simon examined it distantly. "Who sent us through the university?"

"Father. Mother's funds were held in trust for us when we came of age. Sadly, there wasn't much—" Again came a wracking cough and a sputter of apology. "Now, if we were boys with sense, we would have come crawling, begged his pardon—or whatever he wanted!—and be living the plush life in Tunbridge Wells."

"You forget the breeder," Simon snapped. "She's already dropped nine and is expecting her tenth. I know because I wrote Papa, telling him that I'd finally worked my way back to Guy's."

"Was he pleased?"

The hazel eyes turned black. "As he did with you, Jed, he said he wanted nothing more to do with me. His obligation was finished—" He sneered. "That if I ended up in a duke's

mansion or East London, he couldn't care less. . . ." His voice
shook. "Told me not to write again."

"Laddie. Laddie!" the older man murmured comfortingly.
"Bea and I are so proud of you."

"I remember the day he packed me off to Rugby like someone's foul linen. After that they never took me in—only you
and Bea." Abruptly, the rage dissipated, and he became ex-
pansive, less concerned about his brother's alarming appearance, remembering only the warmth of many shared holidays.

"Why didn't you ever bless the world with little Desmonds?"

Jed flinched at his jovial mood, two bright pricks of color
stinging his cheeks. "I thought you might have guessed, Simon.
Mother's legacy got me into the Middle Temple, and that was
it. You need money, boy, to succeed in this world. I had little
and had to content myself with polishing someone else's briefs—
donkey work! Time and again, I was told I had the makings
of a splendid barrister, but nothing came my way—not even
from the Old Bailey. . . ." The nails on his once fine hands
were chewed to the quick, and he stared at them in dismay.
"Only a loving woman makes failure tolerable, Simon," he said
thinly. "Bea wanted children so badly—"

"Is she barren?" he asked with youth's insensitivity.

Jed's smile was tender. "No. But we will not bring children
into a world where we can't support them. . . ." Out came the
handkerchief, muffling another hacking cough.

"Can't you scrape by on your job?"

A deep flush of shame touched the sunken features. "I lost
it, some time ago—"

"Why?" But he knew. It wasn't alcoholism or the devil
cancer. It was consumption. He had seen the spots of blood
on Jed's handkerchief. Dear God! If only he'd spent last Christmas with them, he would have caught it earlier. But he, proud
soul, wanted to return in glory, divested of Oxford Street's
stench. And he'd waited too long. . . . Hating himself for his
neglect, he gripped Jed's calloused hand.

"What can I do?"

Jed broke down. "We have no money."

"Am I right? Is it consumption?" He might have been on
ward duty from his crisp tone, his rigid face.

At his brother's nod, he said quietly, "I'm famished. Let's
have dinner and then go back to my place." Ignoring the one-
shilling plate, he ordered the most expensive meal on the menu
and chose an old bottle of wine. On the way home, he bought

a bottle of brandy. Settling Jed in his one chair, he filled two cracked glasses with cognac, then smilingly toasted his brother.

"Marry an heiress, Laddie. Then you won't ever know such hell."

Simon stretched out long legs, his mood pensive. "I'm like you, Jed. I could only marry the woman I love."

"Poverty ends a career." Jed's voice was bitter. "Still, she came to me with nothing, and I accepted her. She's never complained, but I'd like to have given her my baby—"

"Well, you're not in a fit state to do that now, are you?" He fought a growing spiral of despair. "How have you been living?"

"Bea saved, and the pawnshops oblige," he said in a slurred tone. "I found a few jobs—"

"And?"

"Once they found I was consumptive, I got the boot."

"It's difficult to hide when you're bleeding," Simon replied, weighing a decision. "You must get out of England—someplace where it's dry and not too moist. Nice, Cannes, Malta, Algiers—anywhere but London and these fogs."

"How? With no money?"

"I've a bit saved up, beyond my tuition expenses. That should do for a year. . . ."

Jed stared at him open-mouthed, dully accepting more brandy.

"It's not much," Simon said blithely, "but enough to get you and Bea away from these pea-soupers." Rummaging in a bureau drawer, he withdrew a shabby wallet. It was the end of Guy's. He felt one moment of anguish for all his expectations—the cherished dreams lost. There would be no third chance. But Jed, not once confessing his own bad luck, had been his sole emotional support all those years, and he owed him this gesture. He couldn't live with himself if he didn't make it. The precious load dropped into his brother's hand.

"A *soupçon* to boost you on your way—"

"Simon, I can't take this!"

"Oh, yes, you will! If you don't, you'll die."

And now in extremity their positions were reversed: Jed the lonely, little boy, wan face terrified. "What am I to do?" he whispered.

Simon stood before him, pale but composed. "You'll live abroad and clear up this wretched thing. Then you and Bea can come home and start afresh. ..." Eyes misting, he embraced his brother.

Jed sagged against him. "How will you manage?"

"Continue at Guy's," he lied. "And if I get in a pinch, there's lots more where that came from!" He forced a smile.

"Well, don't go robbing Garrard's and end up in a black arrow suit chipping granite at Dartmoor!"

They laughed, and Simon helped Jed don his rusty-black coat. A bit drunkenly, the two walked to the door.

"I love you," said the older man, cradling his brother's cheek. ...

God! What time had they parted? Simon Desmond wondered miserably. Shortly after nine. And in the early morning had come a wire.

Why? Why had he committed suicide?

"Yes, that's what I've always wondered myself."

Through blurred eyes, he saw Beatrice Clayton standing before him. At his bewildered look, she wiped a tear-stained face and leaned on his desk, confronting him.

"I'm sorry, dear, I didn't mean to pry, but you left the doors open, and you don't usually talk to yourself."

"Have I?" He looked dazed.

"I always felt that Jed did, but I didn't have the heart to discuss it with you."

"You heard my evidence in court—"

"A lie to save Jed from a suicide's disgrace!"

Vehemently, he shook his head.

"I found his body, Simon. There was no brandy bottle or half-filled glass on the washstand. You put them there, didn't you? And made certain other changes. ..." Her voice trembled. "You see, I went back when you fetched the doctor." She took a deep breath. "And there was all that money under my pillow. He didn't have a pound note the day before."

"Father—"

"No! He disowned you both and didn't even see his firstborn buried. You gave it to him, didn't you?" Desmond turned away. "And that's why you left Guy's again. But why did he kill himself?" she asked in agony.

"Why does anyone?" he muttered. "It could be a dozen reasons. The most obvious not the right one. For years, it's haunted me. Would he be alive today if I'd not helped him?" Rising from his desk, his face taut with anger, he began to pace. "I swore then that if ever I met Father again, I would kill him—"

"Simon!"

"There was enough to keep the two of you out of England for a year. Later, things might have improved, or Jed could have returned to the same situation—no decent job, no money—and the illness, under those circumstances, would have recurred. That's a reason, I try and tell myself," he said dully.

"That money gained me a second husband. I would have returned it to you, dear, had I known, but for a long time I truly believed it came from your father." She gave a faint smile. "Life is so strange. My second husband left me a nice bequest—enough to get you started, and here we are—"

"I'm sorry to have so bitterly failed!"

"You haven't, Simon. It always takes time. Just looking after you is a pleasure." Her eyes misted. "You bring Jed back to me. Makes the grief a little easier. . . ."

Desmond looked at her curiously. "If you loved him so much, how could you bear to marry again?"

"Security, my dear. The terrible fear of not knowing where you'll end up." She cleared her throat. "And I thought I might have a child. . . ."

Unbearably moved, he embraced her. For a moment, she clung to him, then with a shaky laugh drew herself together. "You never told me how you managed to get the funds to return to Guy's. Did you work in one of the breweries?"

He strolled over to a window, purposely avoiding her. "No, I was a draper's assistant on Oxford Street."

"They must pay well. You were back within a year."

"Oh, I'm very thrifty," he replied, trying to hide his bitterness.

"Well, let's not brood anymore about the past. I'm sure that Farjeon woman will change everything." At his distant nod, she smiled. "Tea will be ready in fifteen minutes."

Oh, he'd been thrifty, all right, he thought, listening to her rustling skirts recede in the distance. Back he'd gone to his dissolute friend in Soho, resuming the old privation routine, until his roommate told him he was being a fool.

"You may not realize it, Simon," he drawled, "but there's an element in society that is just desperate for the likes of you."

"The harlots?" Desmond asked sarcastically.

"Oh, they'd eat you up. You're a damned handsome man!"

He laughed coarsely. "No, that's not the group. We have in our midst ladies without family—spinsters and widows. Ladies who desire to go to the theater, the opera, museums, soirées, et cetera, but alas! are doomed to stay at home because they lack an escort. Now a number of my friends have done surprisingly well for themselves, accommodating these forlorn souls—"

"It's ridiculous!"

"No, my friend, it's a profitable journey! You'll be kept for a while, then turned over to someone else. Remember, these are ladies, and it doesn't look well to be seen too often with the same gentleman. In one week, if you're a success, you'll make more money than you would slaving for months at Selfridge's."

Desmond showed a spark of interest. "What's involved?"

"Breeding and a good wardrobe. You have the first. I'll provide the second. Then I'll introduce you to your first pigeon, and you take it from there. A little kindness goes a long way. Be amusing, charming, listen to their prattle, and make them forget their loneliness. They really ask for little."

"And that's it?"

"Not quite. A few may want more." He leered. "Give it to them, Simon. You'll find them exceedingly grateful."

Desmond's face froze. "You mean I'm to service them, eh?"

"Precisely."

"Be a male prostitute. Is that it?"

"Oh, don't be so self-righteous! I've seen the way you look at women in the streets. You're starved for sex. And some of these ladies are quite lively. Just close your eyes, Simon, and pretend you're with a beautiful tart. . . ."

Fighting repulsion, he tackled the new venture. A few weeks later, he was able to quit the hated job at Selfridge's. Passed around like an entrée in his new life, he bedded his clients more often than not. To blot out the odor of reeking, middle-aged bodies poisoning his mind and heart, he took to visiting brothels, always choosing the youngest, most innocent-looking whore available—one who might reflect his inner torment, his abject humiliation. And the only thing sustaining him was the thought of Guy's Hospital. . . .

Toward the end of 1878, on the eve of his twenty-ninth birthday, Simon Desmond passed his examinations and became a member of the College of Physicians, but his troubles, far from over, increased. The medical field was packed with eager young bloods—many with enough capital to buy a share of a practice or start their own. Those with influence joined the elite in Harley and Wimpole Streets. The poorer men, like Desmond, seized anything they could get. Fearing that he might be recognized, Simon Desmond avoided the escort world lest his career be ruined. A fine opportunity came his way to buy a flourishing practice in Somerset. Humbling himself, he wrote a pleading letter to his father. Total silence was his answer. So, doggedly, he labored in dusty, ill-lit rooms, working for men with dubious reputations and filthy instruments.

One day a woman died on the table from shock. Desmond, who'd had no hand in the operation, was told to get rid of the bitch. By not complying, he would become an accessory after the fact, hissed his master.

Or worse, thought Desmond, and he obeyed. Waiting until nightfall, he walked the wretched woman out, supporting her as if she were very drunk. Then, with his heart beating so loudly that he felt any passer-by might have heard, he finally managed to dump her among piles of refuse in a cul-de-sac backing Paradise Row, Chelsea. Fit resting place for the dead, he thought, weeping. Once a row of splendid seventeenth-century houses, it was now brought to its knees by decay: empty buildings, laundries, mean lodging houses. . . . No one would find this broken creature for some time. The contents of her shabby purse, along with a few trinkets, were thrown into the evil-smelling Thames.

And that was it. No one had ever come forward to claim her, Desmond mused, closing up his desk in the elegant Heydon consulting room. . . . Who cared among the outcasts when life was more precarious than death? Any bit of baggage could wear a wedding ring, and the fetus had expired so quickly, like a tiny, ill-nourished plant. No great loss. . . .

Something in him snapped that awful night. Pity. The ability to love—which emotion he didn't know. He went back to being an escort, cynically realizing it couldn't ruin a nonexistent career. His were small pickings. A stint on the wards at Guy's or London Hospital; or he might journey to Stepney to help treat Dr. Bernardo's destitute boys, for days at a time immersing himself in lice, ringworm, and every childhood malady imaginable. Whenever he ran short of money, he courted his lady friends.

And then Bea, widowed a second time, came to him during

one of the blackest moments of his life and with her offer to buy him a practice patched up the threads of his futile existence. After years in the abyss, he had at last found the ideal niche— only to see everything crumble before his eyes.

Now his sole hope was a madwoman: Ariel Farjeon. And he began to laugh.

 *Two*

Again, Simon Desmond was struck by the exotic beauty of Farjeon's estate. Planned or deliberately allowed to run wild, he couldn't tell. It was bewitching. Like a Perrault fairy tale. Aged trees—elms, oaks, and beeches—heavily embraced over the winding road to Bellereve. In the distance grew a fir plantation. Against the brick wall, clasping the wrought-iron gates, stood a double row of pleached limes. A pheasant, its ruby breast on fire, streaked suddenly across the frost-tipped grass, then rose in a low, majestic arc.

The manor-house burst upon him like an explosion of fireworks in the afternoon light. By some trick of his imagination, the reddish bricks looked golden; the sun winked from each bay and oriel window. In the moat, water lilies slept, awaiting spring. Simon Desmond felt again the ache of his young manhood: the desperate need to find his heart's darling.

Trotting sedately over the drawbridge, his horse entered the courtyard. A groom sprang forward.

"I'll be here a half-hour." Desmond spoke distantly, caught between the ruined wing and the beauty of the surviving building. Outside, shone gold. Now he saw the silver of flint darting among brick. And ahead, clutched in blackened arms, stood the stone chamber. Turning his back on its ugly desolation, he struck the great phoenix-headed knocker. The butler, Jenkins, conducted him up to the library. On Nicholas Farjeon's desk-table stood an onyx box.

"It's kept there, sir, with instructions. She is to be locked in and out when you visit her."

"Where is your master?"

"Out riding, sir."

Desmond hesitated, wondering if he should leave Farjeon a note asking if he could get rid of that damnable Jackal woman when he paid his calls. That way, his patient might relax with him.

The butler cut in on his thoughts. "A word of caution, sir. Don't turn your back on Miss Farjeon."

Simon Desmond raised an astonished eyebrow. How the devil was he to treat her? Called sane by the asylum, she was being treated like a lunatic in her own home. In such an atmosphere, how could she possibly improve? And what did his work entail? Turning her into a talking marionette?

Inserting the key in the lock, he flung back the bolt, then thumped on the door for the guardian. The Jackal appeared, her manner fawning.

Desmond stepped past her into the chamber. It felt like ice. There must be more to it, he suspected, noticing closed doors to the right and left. Patches of salt scaled one wall like a disease; a trickle of water snaked down from the ceiling to a cracked earthenware jug. The barred windows were so caked with dirt that an outside view was impossible.

"How is she today?"

"Middling well, sir."

A nimbus of white hair hid the exquisite features. Anyone seeing her would think her an old woman. Desmond felt a pang of distaste, not wanting to touch her flesh. Putting down his bag, he approached the couch.

"Miss Farjeon, do you know who I am?"

Back and forth, she rocked. He repeated his question.

The remarkable gray eyes locked with his. She looked dazed, a bit frightened. Then came an imperceptible nod.

"Who am I?"

The full mouth shut tight, and she bent her head.

As he took her pulse, she flinched. Slightly erratic. Probably due to his presence, he reasoned.

"Help me undress her, will you?"

"She won't like you touching her," the keeper whined, removing the blanket she had clutched about her shoulders.

"Why the devil is she wearing a cotton frock? This is December!"

"It's one she had as a girl. Missus said might as well get some use out of them."

"It's wool she needs," Desmond said in a cold fury. "Unless you want pneumonia!"

The crone merely shrugged and unbuttoned the shabby gown. Much too thin, he thought. "Why isn't she wearing a corset?"

"They don't want laces 'round her. No knives, scissors—"

"But she's well, I'm told."

The ragged teeth clacked together in a hiss. "Of course, she be, sir, but the Missus ain't taking a chance."

Ariel Farjeon sat before them, a look of shame on her face, the full breasts thrusting almost obscenely through the thin fabric—a voluptuous contrast to her body's fragility. Averting his eyes, Desmond pressed his stethoscope to her heart. The beat was good, no murmurs; and there was no swish of air, crackling, or bubbling sounds coming from the bronchial tubes. He ran his hands through her hair.

"No lice," he muttered, looking now for bruises or body sores. There were none, and she was remarkably clean. Sweet-smelling, like a flower....

"What's her appetite like?"

"Bad."

"What's she eating?"

The Jackal's wizened face creased in thought. "Breakfast: gruel. Lunch: broth, a bit of bread. Supper: meat or a potato, tea—"

"And that's it?" He looked incredulous.

She nodded.

With difficulty, he restrained his temper and ordered the woman to dress Ariel Farjeon. "What time do you leave?"

"Before it's dark. Back again next morning."

Closing up his Gladstone bag, Desmond again surveyed the room. No lamps. The chamber was already deepening in shadows. And no fire for warmth. No wonder the poor creature huddled in her ragged blanket. The room—the whole thing— sickened him. "I'll be back in two days," he said roughly. As he started to leave, a thin hand brushed his coat sleeve.

"Please... What is your name?"

"Simon," he said involuntarily. As the taut features relaxed, he corrected himself. "Dr. Simon Desmond."

Ariel Farjeon repeated his name to herself, then looked up.

"What are they going to do to me?" The words came haltingly, as if from a sleepwalker.

"Keep you here at Bellereve. Get you well," he replied, falsely cheerful. "That's why I've been called in."

A flicker of fear leapt across her face, and the moment of response dwindled, leaving the eyes blind.

"Ariel?" he called urgently. "Ariel?" But there was no reply. Stroking her forehead, he found it silken as a child's. She submitted with resignation, but the tremor running through her body indicated a frightened woman. He likened her to an animal not knowing whether it was going to be kicked or petted.

"Open your eyes!" he snapped harshly.

They flicked open, filled with tears.

Ashamed of his brusqueness, he said slowly, "I'm not going to hurt you, Miss Farjeon, but you must obey me if you want to get well." She blinked. An understanding, he thought, glaring at the room. "I'll see what I can do about this. . . ."

Bolting the iron-banded door, for some inexplicable reason he felt bereft. God knows, he'd seen enough misery in his lifetime, but a patient who wouldn't confide in him was an affront. A reminder of his heart's desolation. He both pitied and despised her. And a patient who aroused such emotions was a hazard.

Nicholas Farjeon stood waiting for him in the library, his powerful body formidable against the light.

"Well?" he asked tensely. "How is she?"

"Physically, I can find nothing wrong. . . ." Frustration and rage made him slam the key into its box. "But a number of things I find alarming—"

"Oh?" A satanic eyebrow rose.

"Her diet is atrocious." Desmond flung a scrap of paper onto the desk-table. Reading its contents, Farjeon's face was impassive. "She is dressed in cotton. It is December, and the room is freezing. No lamps, no fire—"

Farjeon cut into his outburst. "I didn't know about the meals or the clothes, Desmond. That was all left to my wife."

"And you took no notice, eh?" Desmond cried bitingly. "You hired me to keep her out of Bethlem, yet you confine her to quarters befitting an animal. What do you want? A corpse on your hands, a lunatic, or a recovered woman?" He paused, expecting a response. None came. Contempt flashed in the hazel eyes. "If you want her well, Farjeon, help me! I cannot do it alone. That Jackal woman is worthless—prowls like her kind. I want her out of there on my visits."

Farjeon poured them both a snifter of brandy, which Simon Desmond refused.

"You know my predicament, Desmond. My wife, unfortunately, holds the purse strings in this family. I am bankrupt. In order to bring Ariel home—Regina wanted her immediately shifted to Bedlam—I agreed to all her conditions. No lamps or fire—there might be an accident. She was to be confined throughout life in the stone suite—"

"Yes, I've heard all that before," replied the young doctor impatiently. "Why the cotton gowns in winter and the wretched diet?"

"All her old wardrobe was returned to her." Farjeon looked bemused. "And she was to have whatever we ate."

"You don't look like an easily intimidated man, sir." Desmond's voice was faintly insulting. "Fix it up, will you? Otherwise, she's better off in the workhouse. And I'll be delighted to tell them so."

The big man stirred in his chair, uncomfortable and unhappy. "Do you think I could deny that beautiful face anything? She breaks my heart each time I see her, which is seldom. . . ."

"I ask for little. Creature comforts." Desmond stood sternly before him. "But she is also afraid of something. What is it?"

"The nervousness that comes with her disease." He shrugged. "How should I know a will-o'-the-wisp's fancy?"

"Damn it! I want the truth, not a poet's answer. What frightens her?"

Farjeon's smile was tinged with melancholy. "The past and the constant fear that she might relapse. We are together haunted. . . ."

Humbled by the man's obvious grief, Desmond softened his attack. "Well, you can't expect any improvement as she's living now. It's a miracle she hasn't suffered a physical collapse. Turn that ruin into a home, and she'll respond."

"There'll be a change, I promise you. . . ."

Over the dinner table that evening, Beatrice threw her brother-in-law a quizzical glance. "What's bothering you?"

"The case bewilders me. Hysterical, perhaps, but not—" Desmond hesitated, not wanting to divulge her malady.

"I hear she's been visiting relatives in the United States. Boston, wasn't it?"

Starting to lie, he told her the truth, knowing that she could hold her tongue. "As I said, it baffles me. I see no real signs of insanity, but if she's not 'improved' in six months, she'll be packed off to Bethlem. Why?"

Beatrice Clayton shook her head, perplexed. "Money?"

"Yes, obviously that's part of the problem. He's in straits, and his wife doesn't want her."

"No, dear, that's not what I meant. Does she have an income that might revert to her brother if she went mad?"

"Presumably, if that's the case, he gained it years ago." Desmond poked thoughtfully at the dying embers in the steel grate, arousing them to a lively blaze. "No, I see nothing sinister about Farjeon. The wife is the problem."

"You should talk to someone who knows the family." Her face brightened. "Why not Peter Curwen?"

"The solicitor who arranged our valuable purchase!" His voice dripped acid.

"Don't forget, dear, you asked no questions," she gently reminded him. "Curwen's family is old Heydon stock. If he doesn't represent the Farjeons, perhaps he can refer you to their lawyer." She rang for the maid. "Don't you have a confinement?"

Moodily holding up his glass to the flickering light, he finished his wine. "Imminently..."

"Well, get some rest while you can, Simon."

Two hours' sleep, and then he was hauled to his feet by the bell's urgent jangle above his bed. Out he went in his open trap, bundled up in a blanket against a sleeting rain, an umbrella set over his head. Daintily, his horse sidestepped the treacherous ruts in the road leading to Salle.

Twins. The babies came rapidly, eager to burst into the world, and he gazed at them proudly, always moved by such a sight. Beautiful little creatures, they were, whose lives would probably be broken in the fields or some factory. Watching them nuzzle their mother's breasts, he wondered again about Ariel Farjeon. Why had she nursed a baby to be farmed out...?

Two days, Simon Desmond had said. Well, he'd surprise them and come a day early since his caseload was so light. Find out if Nicholas Farjeon had kept his word. And he had. A note to Desmond offered not only assurance that his sister had been made more comfortable but an apology for his neglect.

In the stone chamber, Ariel Farjeon still sat with head downcast, but the gown was a thick wool, and a cashmere cloak was flung over her shoulders. On a table lay the remains of a breakfast tray.

"What was breakfast?" he asked the Jackal.

"Splendid, sir. Splendid!" She grinned hideously. "Ham, egg, toast, jam, tea . . ."

Pleased, Desmond raised his patient's head. A faint blush touched her cheeks. "Do you know who I am, Ariel?" At her timid nod, he asked, "What is my name?"

"Simon . . . Dr. Desmond." She had a melodious voice like her brother's, which fancifully reminded him of a flute playing in the night.

"Thank you." And she gave him her first smile.

"Good girl," he said softly. "Just keep eating and soon you'll be strong enough to take some exercise."

A loud noise, regularly punctured by oaths and hoarse snatches of song, drifted in from an open door to his right. It was at once humorous and intensely irritating. Flicking a glance at his patient, he saw that she had slipped back into her trance. Well, it was one way of blocking out such a racket. Investigating its source, he found himself in a large kitchen. A stone fireplace stood choked with wood and cinders, grime an inch thick covered the walls, and the iron range looked barely functional. Deep in a lazy scouring of pots and pans stood the Jackal.

Over the clamor, he shouted, "I trust this is not where Miss Farjeon's meals are prepared!"

"No, sir, they come from the big house, though I used to dice up her food—"

"Can you write?" he asked, fighting a wave of disgust.

She returned his glare. "A bit."

"Good. You can keep a list of her diet. Any changes are to be reported immediately to Mr. Farjeon, and you are to take your orders only from him or me. Not from Mrs. Farjeon," he added emphatically. "Do you understand?"

The sharp features were crafty. Dipping into his pocket, Desmond dropped a crown into her crablike hand. The talons clacked together in triumph. "And you might wash the windows," he said smiling. "She needs more light. . . ."

In the days preceding Christmas, whenever possible Simon Desmond visited Ariel Farjeon. Stopping by for a brief call, he coaxed her into a halting conversation or a shy smile. Her response was his reward.

Surprisingly, he was now quite busy, his waiting room

jammed. Heydon's professional and farming classes were lining up to join his small band of laborers. A second groom and boy were employed to handle the excess carriage traffic. Calls came day and night. Mrs. Stephens, a wealthy Heydon widow who had scooped him up as her protégé, tossed out a good word and summons came from other elderly, bored ladies. Beatrice Clayton was ecstatic.

"You have circles under your eyes, Simon," she said mischievously. "That'll put you to sleep, rather than pacing."

"I'm sure they only come out of curiosity—"

"I agree. But stay because they like you. Ariel Farjeon is a gold mine!"

He thought of other gold mines in his past and winced.

She handed him a glass of champagne, which he downed too quickly. "Come with me to Midnight Service tonight."

"Why?"

"It's Christmas Eve and you need to be seen, Simon—"

"By the gentry in full force, is that it?"

"Yes, dear, it's time. They're rife and ready."

"Oh, I bet they are," he said with a trace of scorn. "Do they still believe the Boston fantasy?"

"It's unraveling, I think."

"No way to protect her, I suppose." He scowled in annoyance. "What happens if she ends up in Bethlem? Will my bounty depart?"

"Oh, no. Then you'll have them firmly hooked." Bea refilled his glass. "Simon, I'm not mercenary by nature, but Jed and I lived a very pinched existence. He was never adept—"

"Ruthless, you mean, don't you? As I am!" he cried.

"You survived. Jed killed himself. That's the difference between you. . . ." Tears filled her eyes. "But it taught me a valuable lesson. If fortune comes, grab it—"

"Where were you schooled?" he asked savagely.

"From my second husband," she whispered. "But I survived that marriage thanks only to Jed's memory—"

"Do you know how I got my money?" With a vicious gesture, he flung his glass into the flames. "From lonely, desperate women. . . ."

"Yes, dear, I thought that was the case." Mutely, they stared at one another. Then she seized his hand in a fond grasp. "Your father never gave you much choice, did he? A word or two in the right ear, some money allotted, and you would be in Harley Street today and Jed in the Middle Temple. . . ." She handed him her full glass. "I'm sure you gave them as much as they gave you—"

"But don't you see, I'm using Ariel Farjeon in the same way—" His voice broke. "I thought I'd put all that behind me when I left London, and once again I find myself involved in the same ugly dance. God, it's pathetic how her face lights up when I appear. She is still young. . . . They were old—"

"Time you were thinking of marriage," Beatrice Clayton said crisply. "Give yourself another year and you should be well able to afford a wife."

"You think I need it?" His look was sardonic.

"You need more than me to come home to. Now, give me a kiss, Simon. We're under the mistletoe. . . ."

He left Fairhaven the next morning, fragrant with the scent of Christmas, for a ride on horseback. The air, crisp as a knife, stung his face, whipped into his lungs, urging him on. Basket-laden villagers waved as he trotted by the village green. A young woman held up her child, sick the week before, now flourishing, and Desmond, laughing, took the little boy for a spin on his chestnut. Well-wishers shouted greetings. All's right with the world, he thought smugly. Beatrice had been right, of course, urging him to be seen. One would have had to be blind not to notice all the attention lavished on him throughout and after the service. First came his old patients, a bit shyly; then Mrs. Stephens and her circle, smothered in furs like a pack of ancient, tipsy bears, introduced Simon Desmond and his sister-in-law to all the "right" people. And finally the ice was broken as the gentry welcomed him into their charmed circle. Old stock and parvenu held out their hands. Many a spark of interest Desmond caught in a young lady's eligible eye; the rise and fall of a tremulous voice or an agitated bosom indicated a rapt willingness to be courted.

There was enough time to canter to Salle—even to Reepham, beyond, he thought, laughing at all the choices now available to him. But the horse had ideas of its own. As if bewitched, it flew across the flat countryside to Foulsham, and Desmond gave a sigh of pleasure, every muscle alive, his senses keen. Too good a brute to waste pulling a trap. This one would race to the stars. He must see that it got a decent run weekly.

Again, they came to the massive wrought-iron gates with black and gold arabesques entwined about the letter "F." The horse reared impatiently, frantic to get in while the keeper, with a muttered greeting, swung one side open.

Desmond didn't want this visit—today of all days. Nothing must mar the joy of his new expectations. Time to move on to the fillies not so distressingly burdened. . . .

Up the winding path, the horse galloped, sunlight dappling its body. Abruptly, Desmond pulled to a halt, breathlessly aware of that strange aura encircling Bellereve. Too quiet, he thought, looking about—not a shadow of an animal or bird, the conifers as still as the dead trees above him.

Feeling unwell, he dismounted. Too much champagne, he guessed, leaning against an oak tree. In the distance, Bellereve glimmered through the hedge—a mirage. Enthralled by its beauty, his queasiness gone, he led his now docile horse along the cobblestone path, hoarfrost crunching underfoot. Parting a thicket, Desmond gashed his wrist on a thorn. As the blood fell, he swore. Just the type of wound to get infected. Small blessing it wasn't his hand, and he whipped out a handkerchief.

Sounds of laughter and music greeted him from the manorhouse. An unusually cheerful groom took his horse; even the butler, Jenkins, normally as somber as his uniform, wafted cordiality. In the great drawing room, a large group of elegantly dressed men and women clustered about a blazing yule log. Jewels flashed amid the clink of champagne glasses and an intoxicated roar. Distantly observing the crush, Nicholas Farjeon sat, brandy snifter in hand.

Climbing the staircase, Desmond caught a glimpse into the far chamber beyond. An enormous pine tree loaded with ornaments, its trunk smothered by presents, stood at one end. Tier upon tier of candles fought a losing battle against the sun's rays streaming in through an oriel window. The effect was at once brilliant and startling—as if the great pine had burst into flames. Spinning before it, like whirligigs, danced a horde of children, their shrieks rattling the bored group of nannies and governesses planted in ladder-backed chairs.

Childish screams and adult laughter followed him up to the library. The onyx box lay waiting. In searing light, he took a good look at the key. It wasn't brass, as he had supposed, but silver, with a golden filigreed design. And there were letters: a floral "F" and some Arabic characters. Tracing the pattern, he thought of the woman beyond. How right for her. A beautiful key to lock up an exquisite woman. . . .

The windows in the stone suite were still caked with dirt. Damn! Had he been that busy not to notice before? Opening the door, he paused on the threshold. Ariel Farjeon, wrapped in her cloak, stood at a window overlooking the moat, sketching on the frosted panes. In her absorption, she heard neither the heavy door close nor his approach. Graceful fingers continued their work. Desmond made out a Christmas tree; a church, remarkably like Foulsham's; people, animals, birds. The glass was covered with tiny drawings.

He spun her around. "Have they left you alone?" he cried sharply.

"Yesterday—" She looked bewildered.

Cruel to frighten her. He relaxed his hold. "She left yesterday, is that it?" The beautiful head nodded and tried to turn back to the glass world. Desmond let her be, searching the chamber for signs of a tray. Nothing.

"She has a home. She would want to be with her family," the melodious voice said, and then she laughed. "I have such trouble drawing the animals. But the tree is not bad—"

"When did you last eat?"

"Breakfast."

"Yesterday, eh?" he asked grimly.

"Yes." A swift fingernail sketched in a star and a bird in flight.

"It's enchanting, my dear. You show much talent." He strode off into the kitchen. Dirt. Grease, everywhere. Blasted woman hadn't even swept the floor.

For a long moment, Simon Desmond was tempted to walk out and never set foot in those quarters again. In East London, he had sneered at the Harley Street physician's delicacy, fastidiously avoiding the miseries of poverty. But he coveted their pristine life, dreamt of it, and now saw it looming in his future. A glorious image to be crushed by a poor madwoman. He would never be free of his wretched past while in this rotten building. Her hell wasn't his. . . .

Get out of here. Get out of here fast, he told himself. This is the last bad moment you'll have at Bellereve. Leave her.

As he stepped into Ariel Farjeon's sitting room, a shaft of light burst through the grime, illuminating her magical village. Birds in vast numbers soared; a blazing star shone in the sky over the heads of grazing animals and parishioners hurrying to church.

A stricken Desmond hesitated, feeling the ugly mood vanish. Humbly, in silent gratitude, he kissed her cheek.

"Merry Christmas, Ariel," he cried softly, ashamed that he

had nothing to give her. No small gift. It had never occurred to him. "I'll bring you something to eat," he said brusquely.

In the middle of that packed drawing room reeking of liquor, perfume, and smoke he shot out a challenge to Nicholas Farjeon, managing to hold his temper by a supreme effort until they reached the library. Then he exploded.

"At Christmas! How dare you leave her so wretched? Without food or water. No warmth. The place is a charnel house—"

"My wife runs the household. After I made the necessary changes, I assumed that everything was under control...." Exhausted gray eyes met his. "What do you want me to do? Station myself outside her door?"

Still pricked by bad conscience, Desmond snapped, "No, just treat her with compassion—not barbarity—or, I warn you, Farjeon, I'll notify the authorities. They're always keen about neglect." He leaned on the Regency desk-table. "If dinner isn't ready, then I'll take her something else, and from now on I want her to have a glass of sherry at luncheon and a glass of wine at dinner."

Farjeon sneered. "Why? To make her an alcoholic?"

"No, sir. Just to make that stinking place more bearable!"

Armed with a tray loaded with Christmas fare, Desmond returned to his patient. Ariel Farjeon was still at the window, preoccupied with her sketching.

"I have something for you." He swept up the cover from the silver tray. "Have some sherry." She took a sip from a crystal goblet, a tear running down her cheek. Embarrassed, Desmond looked away.

"I'll be back tomorrow," he said, heading for the door. Oppressed by its bulk, he muttered, "I don't like to lock you up...."

"That's your duty," she whispered, and then suddenly, urgently, she called his name, "Simon!"

He swung around as she ran across the room, fleet as any horse or bird alive, flying into his arms. Her nestling head sought his breast, and she clung to him passionately, seeking the comfort of his heartbeat. Words of tenderness he had never before used trembled from his lips; his strong arms supported her, catching her in a lovers' embrace until they were almost one.

Abruptly, Desmond tore away, slamming the massive door shut in her face, thrusting the bolt home. Ariel Farjeon fell to her knees, clutching the door for support, her body wracked with dry sobs. . . .

Out of pity, Simon Desmond came the next day, Boxing Day, and this time he brought her something. Not to make too much of it, he handed his patient an unwrapped book.

Ariel Farjeon smiled. "I once had a copy. At one time I think I knew all of Browning by heart." Reverent hands caressed the leather. Opening it to the title page, she looked up, bewildered. "This is your book!"

Jed had given it to him years before. He could easily have bought another edition, but for some reason it was important to him that she have his volume. "Your name is on it now. See?" And then he rather stiffly presented her with a second gift, a woolen scarf. "Knitted by my sister-in-law."

Eyes misty, she buried her face in the soft wool. "I wish I had something for you—"

"You gave it to me yesterday—those charming drawings."

"Still here!" She laughed, pulling him to the window. "I stood on a chair for the top row."

A choir of angels hovered over the village. He shook his head, amazed. All that glory behind bars.

"I am getting better, aren't I?"

"Yes, very much so."

Kissing his hand, she pressed it to her cheek. "When you go, I feel so desolate—as if my soul were being cut out. . . ." Her voice was low. "Are you married?"

Desmond could still feel her body against his and his frustration at not being able to kiss her, but they were moving in dangerous waters, and he knew too well that look of infatuation in her eyes. Easier to hurt her now than later.

"Yes."

She flinched, then spoke dully. "Do you have any children?"

"No."

Ariel Farjeon drifted away, the scarf trailing on the stone floor, her eyes on the dead fireplace. "I had a baby. At night"— she touched her breasts—"sometimes I wake up to feed it, but I can't find him. . . ." A look of terror darted across her face.

Desmond stared at her. Such was her intensity that if pushed, she might very possibly break down. From impatience with Farjeon he moved to sympathy, watching his sister on the razor's edge.

"Where is he?" she cried.

"You don't remember?" he asked cautiously.

She shook her head, dazed.

"Perhaps, it's only a nightmare—"

"A nightmare to drown out the day's sorrow," she whispered. "Perhaps." Again came the stilted tone. "I hope one day you will be blessed with children."

"That is my gift—your wish."

"She must love you very much."

"I suppose so," he said flatly, hating the lie.

Despite her self-control, she looked crushed. He couldn't leave her like that. Not after yesterday.

"Keep on at this rate and one day you, too, will marry."

Her laugh was brittle. "Have you forgotten, Dr. Desmond? I'm insane. . . ."

A day later, Simon Desmond was again back at Bellereve. The wretched Jackal crept to the door, and he yanked her into the kitchen, almost lifting her off her feet in fury.

"Why the devil didn't you tell Mr. Farjeon you were leaving? Was he supposed to be a mind reader? If I hadn't stopped by, she would have gone two days without food—"

"I did tell him," she whined, cringing under his wrath. "Well, I had a word with Jenkins. Told him to pass it on—"

"And I gave you orders to go directly to Mr. Farjeon or to me. Don't you understand? He never got your message." A fist pounded on the wood dresser, making the cracked set of Willow-ware dance alarmingly. Undoubtedly, the communication had been intercepted by Farjeon's wife. And what if Desmond spoke to her? Pleaded for compassion. Might it not rebound against Ariel Farjeon? If the husband had so little influence, what chance had the physician? No, it was too great a risk.

"How much are you paid a week?"

"Six days—six shillings," she slobbered.

"You're off on Sundays?" At the sly nod, he sneered. "Leaving Miss Farjeon to fend for herself, eh?" The Jackal sniveled. "Well, I'll tell you what I have in mind. You come every day until June, when there may be a change of plan. I'll double your salary and add a shilling, but if you abandon her again—out you go!"

She gave a cackle. "You seem mighty interested in a poor madwoman!"

Desmond's voice was steely. "All my patients interest me. She's no different—" He stormed out to the sitting room. Ariel Farjeon stood by the window, his shawl wrapped about her throat, an arm resting against the bars. The frost had melted, obliterating her village. Only pools of water on the stone floor gave evidence of its existence. Outside, there was nothing to see except blurred images of trees and the moat. None of these windows had been washed in years, he thought angrily.

Something about her pose distressed him. "Miss Farjeon!"

She turned around, the book of poems at her breast. "Dr. Desmond." Her face was tear-streaked, the beautiful eyes had that blind look he found so upsetting. The wall he had thrown up between them yesterday was as stout as the brick wall surrounding Bellereve. God! If only he'd caught himself in time. An engagement might have been easier for her to accept. A gracious way of keeping them at arm's length. But by making it a *fait accompli*, he had smashed any pitiful fantasy she might, in her loneliness, have lavished upon him. Later, a blow could be withstood; now he wasn't so sure. She was too vulnerable.

"You've not slept?"

"No, I have my bad nights."

"Would you like me to give you a sedative?"

"No. No, I beg of you!" she cried urgently.

"Were you often medicated in the asylum?"

Her glance was wary. "I don't know. . . ."

"Do you remember much about it?"

"No restraint," she said dully. "Don't give me . . . anything—"

Baffled, he dropped a few banal remarks to soothe, his eyes sweeping the room. Near the iron-banded door stood a smaller one. Closed.

"What's beyond?" he asked, pointing in its direction.

"Destroyed by fire."

"But there's another room to this suite, isn't there?" Ariel Farjeon nodded, her expression stubborn. "May I see it?"

"A bedroom—that's all," she replied tightly.

"I'd like to see it."

With great reluctance, she led the way. It was very small, about a sixth the size of the sitting room. One barred window high up in the wall and a pallet covered by a worn blanket. Nothing else. Behind him, her voice was barely audible, and he wheeled about, remembering the butler's warning: "Don't turn your back on Miss Farjeon. . . ." The delicate hands still clasped the book.

A shiver ran down his spine. "You don't use this room?"

Vehemently, she shook her head. Returning to the main

room, he carefully shut the door, knowing that was her wish. To shut out whatever unpleasantness it contained. The larger room was scarcely better with its shabby furniture. Nothing to warm the heart. Only the woman.

Pity overwhelmed him. "My marriage shouldn't make any difference between us," he said huskily, determined to repair some of the damage. "Don't shut me out—"

"I was the fool, Dr. Desmond—not you. But it's not been the first time."

Her voice sounded high, unreal. Alarmed that she was slipping away, he said tensely, "Confide in me, Ariel. You must. If not for me, then for your brother."

"For my brother Nicholas," she echoed, meeting his eyes for the first time. He smiled encouragement.

"What happened to your wrist?"

Desmond had pocketed his gloves, and the bandage was visible. "I caught it on a thorn from one of your thickets."

"Is it infected?" she asked gravely.

"Yes."

"I have something that might help. A salve my family has used for generations. I found some the other day in one of my dresses. Perhaps, you might like to try it?" Her look was wistful. "May I give you some?"

Touched that patient was becoming doctor, he ripped off the bandage. "I should be honored!"

She took a small tin box down from the mantel. He caught a glimpse of its contents: a shell, comb, a broken piece of mirror, and a jar. "My treasures!" and she laughed. "Let me wash my hands." Vanishing into the kitchen, she reappeared a moment later and tenderly examined his wrist by the feeble light. Fascinated, Desmond studied her. Engrossed in her task, she worked with deft precision, her fears and sadness dissipating over a thorn scratch. Desmond found it as moving as the few possessions in her battered tin box.

"Leave it on overnight," she instructed. "The inflammation will be gone by morning." Her face was luminous. "Do you have a clean handkerchief?"

Delighted that they were heading back to the old footing, he gave her one, saying, "You have a gift for healing, Ariel."

She blushed with pleasure.

"Thank you, sweet friend." His voice was low, intimate, and he left, still smiling.

Desmond awoke, sun streaming in through a silk curtain. Hiding from the chill, he buried his face in the pillow by his side, arms outstretched. The throbbing in his wrist had stopped. At one point during the night, convinced that the ointment was increasing his infection, he nearly tore off the bandage. Now in daylight, unwrapping the handkerchief, he blinked and sat up. The wound was almost healed. Only a minute scar would be left.

So that I never forget you. . . .

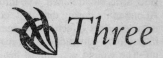 *Three*

"*I hope you don't* mind this intrusion—"

"Not at all, Desmond!" A beaming Peter Curwen handed him a glass of sherry. "And you'll stay to lunch?"

"Thank you, yes."

"Good. I hate dining alone, and the wife and girls are on a shopping spree in Norwich. You'd think Christmas would suffice!" He sank back into a fireside chair, waving his guest to the mahogany one opposite. "The bills these women run up— over trifles, as they say!"

Desmond smiled at the rumpled figure before him, complaining but obviously content with his lot. And a rich lot it was. One of the biggest Georgian houses in Heydon, a dozen servants, and a house chock-full of valuable possessions. Rather like Regina Farjeon's busy domain, but unlike Bellereve, there was warmth here.

"What can I do for you?"

"I'm trading on your time," Desmond muttered, wondering if any violent emotion had ever shaken this comfortable room. The thorn incident had given him pause. Studying the wound, he had felt Ariel Farjeon's body as keenly as if she'd been in bed with him. A feeling so shameful, he determined to turn over her case to someone else. Instead, he rushed out and bought her an ivory comb, brush, and mirror, breathlessly awaiting her reaction, and when he saw it in her glorious eyes, his heart wrenched. Prudence made him cut down his daily visits to twice weekly. Still, her image haunted him—in the long, cold hours when he couldn't sleep, in his surgery, out on rounds.... He felt bewitched by her beauty and pathos. Curwen's help he now sought, out of desperation because his normally cool self-possession had deserted him.

Forcing a smile, he asked, "Do you represent the Farjeons?"

"No, and with great regret. My family has always looked after them, but we lost them to Regina when she married Nicholas. A Norwich firm handles their affairs."

Desmond leaned forward. "You know that I'm treating Ariel Farjeon?"

Curwen's bushy eyebrows shot up over gold-rimmed spectacles. "All central Norfolk knows." He stretched out plump legs to the fire. "By God, she was the most beautiful wench any man in these parts ever set eyes on...."

His host was mildly intoxicated, face flushed by the fire's warmth. At the butler's summons, Desmond steered him down a long hall into the dining room, set with a feast such as he knew only on special occasions. Curwen settled down to enjoy his gargantuan meal, a quizzical eye on his guest.

"How are you getting on?" he rumbled.

Desmond grimaced. "The practice is picking up—amazingly so. Less and less, people tell me about Grinnell's expertise."

With a hearty chuckle, Curwen speared a squab. "We were waiting, Desmond, to see what you'd be like. The last man was no good. No feel for his patients."

"Ariel Farjeon opened the doors, eh?"

"Yes, you take on a Farjeon, you get the countryside."

Desmond's finger restlessly circled his wineglass. "Can you tell me something about them?"

Attacking his plate with gusto, Curwen shot his companion a confiding glance. "When I joined my father's firm, one of my first tasks was to acquaint myself with every client's history. The Farjeons were of Saracen origin—"

"Saracen?" Desmond looked astounded.

"Yes, from Spain, which they fled in 1492, when the Inquisition began." He poured them more wine. "As I recall, they came to England, like the Jewish émigrés, via Holland, and settled in London. Somehow managing to escape with money and jewels—enough to set themselves up as merchants. They prospered. So much so, they were able to outfit several ships for the Armada. An appreciative Elizabeth rewarded them with Bellereve."

"Has it always been called that?"

"No, the first family possessing it was annihilated during the War of the Roses. It was a crumbling ruin when the Farjeons took over. They rebuilt and grew even more wealthy."

"How did the insanity begin? A Farjeon heiress married a Norfolk merchant?"

Peter Curwen blinked. "Good heavens! Where did you hear that? No, two cousins married—first cousins, mind you, and the illness came from their union."

"Farjeon told me the males died out."

"Oh, of course, he would say that. No one likes to talk about madness in their family."

"How many were struck?"

"About half a dozen. Perhaps eight or nine."

"Women or men?"

"Mostly males, though a female or two suffered. An imbecile child, an hysteric . . ." He faltered. "Is it true she's afflicted?"

There was genuine grief on his face. Desmond said gently, "Yes, but her brother now thinks her cured."

Curwen's eyes glistened. "How is the poor woman?"

Desmond shrugged. "I really can't tell. That's why I came to see you. I want to know what she was like before—"

"Exquisite, refined . . . a joy! Every man was captivated by her, each of us hoping to claim her for a bride." He gave a rueful laugh. "And didn't Nicholas know it! Clung to her as if he'd never let go."

"What's the age difference between them?"

"Ten years or so—"

"He looks older."

"Well, with Regina, who wouldn't?" Curwen snorted. "Dreadful, common person. A wealthy draper's daughter dragging her affectations about like stale perfume. Was there ever such a mismatched couple!"

Desmond smiled. "How did they find one another?"

"Farjeon went through his fortune and his expensive tastes needed replenishment. Regina seethed to enter the gentry—"

"What are those tastes? Gambling, liquor, a mistress?"

Curwen hunched over his wineglass, warming it with fat hands. "No one knows, Desmond. Howland told me he was withdrawing increasing sums of money over the years. We warned him. . . . Could get nowhere. Then he married Regina."

"What about Ariel Farjeon? Did she have her own income?"

"Her grandfather—the one who burnt down the wing—left her a tidy sum, to come to her at age twenty-one, unless she went mad. In that case, it would revert to Nicholas."

Desmond looked bewildered. "You say the second fire was set deliberately?"

"Well, no one knows exactly what happened. The old man was senile. A lamp could have been overturned—accidentally or deliberately—but he was confined to the stone suite for the rest of his life."

"For whom was it built?"

The dishes had been cleared away. Dessert, cheese, and fruit were set before them. Curwen cut into a treacle tart. "The first lunatic—the one who set the original fire."

Desmond raised an eyebrow. "Farjeon said that one was caused by lightning, and the second was an accident."

"Insanity is a very painful topic. Naturally, he'd put the best light on it possible." A shaking hand spilled some wine on his cravat. "How is she?" he again asked, wiping his eyes.

Desmond hesitated. "I see no overt signs of madness, but she lives in appalling conditions—enough to drive any sane person mad. . . ."

The older man sighed, speaking almost to himself. "Well, you don't need to put two and two together to see that I adored her. But as a widower with children, I felt it unfair to press my suit. Let the younger men do that."

"And was that affection returned?"

Curwen handed him a glass of port, then cut some cheese. "How could it with her brother at her side? An introduction to Ariel always included a chat with Nicholas. He was more protective than a duenna. We only saw her at Foulsham's church, or at Christmas parties—the rest of the time she lived secluded with him at Bellereve, as isolated as a nun, pursuing her studies. Finally, one of our young bucks guessed that she was being groomed for a London season. That what he had in mind was marriage to a Peer's son. Our Norfolk lot wasn't good enough for her. And then she vanished—a trip to the continent, we heard, followed by the Boston visit to relatives. . . ."

"Did she have a romance with a local boy?"

Curwen shook his head. "Not that I know of. Getting past Nicholas was like running the gauntlet. Still—" and he laughed, "beauty of that sort stops no one. An infatuated man would have found a way to her side."

Desmond toyed with the idea of telling him the truth, then decided against it. Liquor loosened his friend's tongue, and he didn't want that poor creature suffering more than necessary.

"Does she still have that bewitching raven hair?" Curwen sat dreaming. "I saw it once unbound, falling like a mantle down her back."

The young doctor winced. "No, it's white now, shoulder length. Something that happened in the asylum, I gather."

Peter Curwen gave a hissed intake of breath, deeply shocked. "Let's go back to that fire, eh? It's damned chilly in here." And he led the way, now briskly efficient, fortified by that splendid meal and looking forward to a steaming pot of coffee.

"Just a few more questions, sir." Desmond said amiably. "How long have Farjeon and Regina been married?"

"Seven years—at least."

"His sister was incarcerated for twelve years. Where was Farjeon earlier?"

"Traveling mainly—in America, then Europe."

"So that in five years, he lost all his money?"

"Not all of it, Desmond—he made inroads. I assume there was enough to court Regina. Whatever the case, she wouldn't stoop to marry a pauper. Howland, who was his banker then, could help you on that point, and you might try Foulsham's vicar."

"What about their father? Any problems?"

"No, not a bit."

"Just the grandfather?" Desmond mused.

"Among the immediate family—yes!" Curwen's smile was painfully tight.

Simon Desmond stood up to take his departure. "Would you think she would go insane?"

"She was like the sun, lighting each heart she touched." He shook his head sadly. "No. No, I saw nothing wrong. . . ."

Not the parlor maid but rather Beatrice Clayton opened up Fairhaven's door to him, her face anxious. "Did you learn anything?"

"No, not much," he replied, shedding his hat and ulster, removing his boots for more comfortable shoes. "Just that Ariel Farjeon seems to have been every man's Circe."

She blinked, then leaned over to whisper. "The waiting room is full, Simon, but I put a woman and her children into the surgery. Frankly, I don't like the look of them. I'll be here if you need me." She returned to the parlor.

With a reassuring smile, he crossed the waiting room and entered his surgery. One little girl was dragging her rag doll about the floor. A second girl sat on the table, supported by her mother—one of those aged-looking women of the fields whose beauty faded after the first childbirth. Already her face was permanently bronzed by a pitiless sun, her fingers gnarled like poor vegetable roots. Trying to keep her composure, she clung fiercely to the child on the table.

"Do you have a sore throat?" he gently asked his small patient.

She shook her head, but her face was feverish, and a membrane had already covered the tonsils, pharynx, and crept into the nose. A racing pulse accompanied the stentorian breathing. Swiftly, he turned his attention to the child on the floor, lifting her up onto a chair. "How do you feel, puppy? Swallowing a bit prickly, eh?" At her nod, he felt her glands—a slight swelling, but she was cool, thank God. He faced the woman, one of the laborers' wives, who were annually expecting another baby. A glance revealed that she was infinitely worse than the child perched on his table.

"How long has it been going on?" he asked wearily.

Her breath came in a hoarse sob. "Three, four days."

Desmond's face was rigid "I'm sorry, it's diphtheria. Did you come by cart?"

"Walked."

"My groom will take you home in the trap, and I'll come see you when the clinic closes. Is anyone else sick?"

Tears welled in her eyes. "My boy, sir. Too sick to walk."

"Any other children they've been playing with?" He sounded almost angry.

"Yes, sir. The whole row plays together. . . ."

Desmond sighed. "I'll give you some perchloride of iron now. How are you for eggs, milk, beef, tea—things like that?"

She studied her filthy, hobnailed boots. "It's been a bad year, sir. Crops poor. Animals dying." Anguish filled her expression. "We can't pay you—"

"Yes, you will," he said softly. "Just get well. . . ."

Moments later, he tackled Beatrice Clayton behind closed parlor doors. "Have you had diptheria?" he asked anxiously.

"Yes." She paled. "Dear God! Is that what it is?"

Desmond nodded. "Now listen. She's from Cottage Row, and there's a good possibility that we have an epidemic on our hands. They live like rats down there. I want this family taken home, and these staples, plus ice, are to be ordered daily." He handed her a list. "The amount will increase as cases rise. I'll pay all expenses. After clinic, I'm off to the row. I doubt if I'll be home tonight." Clasping her hands he added, "Please screen all oncoming patients for me. It's dangerous, Bea. One can get it again, but it must be done. If things get out of hand, refer people to Colin Broughton. Hopefully, I can stop by once a day—"

"You sound as if you'll not be sleeping for weeks!" Her laugh was shaky.

"That goes with the profession. . . . Oh, and another thing, Bea. Give Nicholas Farjeon a message—personally. Tell him I'm staying away from his sister until this thing is over. She's frail enough without burdening her with diphtheria. I don't like leaving her, but I can't risk the threat of infection. A few weeks won't make that much difference. . . ."

Cottage Row lay on the outskirts of Heydon, far removed from the green's charm—a miserable collection of lopsided hovels, each one propping its neighbor. These people had been his first patients, and Desmond bore them a special affection. Not even abysmal poverty could blunt their generous spirit. Food and clothing were shared in bad times, and the doctor was paid with whatever produce flourished in the narrow patch of gardens. At such moments, a humble bunch of beets or turnips meant more to him than a sovereign.

His lean years had been rich compared with this lot. Out of a dozen chimneys, smoke drifted from only four. Sadly in need of repair, thatched roofs sagged over broken flint walls. Inside, humans and animals huddled in the communal room, the older children bedding down below while the adults and youngsters crept up a rickety ladder to the loft.

Desmond found his three patients lying in bed together. In a corner, wrapped in a ragged quilt, lay the boy—dead, his thin body still warm. Tears stung Desmond's eyes as he turned back to the bed. The little girl was still playing with her doll, but the mother and older child were in serious condition. An ominous note was the obstructed nasal breathing. One of them would die—of that he was almost certain.

Swiftly, he examined the rest of the family. No sign of

disease, and he forbade any mingling of the two groups. A quick survey along the row disclosed eight more cases.

By the next morning, the youngest girl had almost recovered, while her sister was showing a flicker of improvement. Still, there was the obstructed breathing—a clear sign that the relief was only temporary. Desmond sent an urgent word to Bea for more medical supplies, food, and blankets, then settled down for a long stay. During the next twenty-four hours, he dosed the child with brandy, hoping to aid her prostration. To no avail. Helplessly, he watched her die, cursing his failure.

Removing the little body from her mother's side, in alarm he noticed the parent's gross deterioration. Feverish and delirious, her face was turning blue as the windpipe clogged. Unseeing eyes bulged in a frantic effort to breathe. The pulse was almost negligible. There was no time to waste. Whipping out a scalpel from his bag, Desmond slit into her larynx and performed a swift tracheotomy. Minutes sped by. After what seemed an eternity, a breath of air was drawn into her lungs. The diaphragm's convulsive contractions lessened. Gradually, the bluish tinge faded, the pulse grew stronger, the exhausted eyes opened, and she managed a faint smile.

His patient lived, but with every success came defeat— diphtheritic paralysis or death. Desmond lived on Cottage Row for a month, only leaving for an outside emergency. Fortunately for Heydon, the outbreak confined itself to that one poor area. On his first trip home to collect additional supplies, he conferred with Beatrice.

"Did you give Nicholas Farjeon my message?"

"No, dear, he was in London, but the butler took it." Her hands fluttered in apology. "Did I do wrong? Shall I try again?"

Desmond frowned. "No, I need you here. If I have time, I'll send a note, but they must know what's happening in Heydon. Anyone that concerned about his sister would realize why I haven't been around." Closing his bag, he roamed the surgery to see if anything had been overlooked. "Poor woman! Death by diphtheria would be infinitely more merciful than that tomb she's immured in—"

"Simon!"

A warning note in her voice steadied him. "Sorry, Bea. I've been on my feet so long, I'm a bit stupid."

"Call in Broughton. You need a rest."

He flashed his charming smile. "I'm Heydon's doctor, and after fighting so hard to gain that position, I'm not about to relinquish it." Heading for the hall, he called over his shoulder, "Miss Farjeon will manage." Together, they stood at the front door, gazing out at the dead Elizabethan garden. "God! Will it ever bloom again?" he whispered.

"I could visit her," she urged.

"No, don't bother. A bit of benign neglect never hurt anyone. . . ."

Regina Farjeon had long awaited this chance. For almost two months, a madwoman had lived under her roof, and not once had she seen her. But with Nicholas in London and Simon Desmond's note in hand, what could be more natural than to pay her sister-in-law a visit? Cheer up the unfortunate! With a sneer, she went upstairs to change her morning gown for a more appropriate costume. Ringing for her maid, she leafed through her wardrobe, deliberately choosing one of her most elegant ensembles. An Oriental blue damask gown with matching velvet bodice and a border of sea otter. A splendid gown, highlighting her eyes and tawny hair, and she laughed like a woman in love.

Thirty-five years old. Well, she'd kept her figure, she thought, inspecting herself in the cheval glass. The extra weight gained from two pregnancies enhanced her beauty, her admirers claimed. Only what did it matter to Nicholas?

"Get my cigarettes!" she yelled to the maid. "And I'll wear the fur satin pelisse." She grimaced at the outdoor wardrobe, the next moment hissing, "Not that hat, idiot! The blue plush with ostrich plumes!"

Through a smoky haze, she studied her image in the dressing table mirror. A faint suggestion of a double chin, but her complexion gleamed, and lines of anger and discontent, seen alone, had not yet marred her face.

Snuffing out the cigarette, she lit a second. He hated her smoking—a small pleasure that she could so annoy him. But how dare he complain when they met so infrequently! Lodging in separate wings, they met *en passant* in the rooms below— strangers more than husband and wife. Perhaps it was the odor of smoke, and she swept to a window, kicking back the heavy velvet curtains to glare down at the ruined wing. Impossible to escape it. All the courtyard rooms overlooked that abomination. Tear it down! she thought bitterly.

The bravado spent, she felt that prick of uneasiness gnawing away. Why had he married her? At twenty-eight, the only child of a Norwich draper whose fortune had tripled in real estate, she had met Nicholas Farjeon at an assembly ball. All the other men in her life—and many courted her—were eclipsed by this dark-haired giant. Her father protested, but Regina, caught in the spell of her dashing new admirer's wooing, persisted. His every glance suggested the most forbidden delights; passionate words teased her ears; his full mouth bruised hers, tantalizing; his hands at her breasts drove her wild with desire.

At her dressing table, hunched in a pool of light, she lit a third cigarette. After a month's courtship, they were married. So enraptured was she, he could easily have bedded her at any time; Nicholas, however, preferred to wait. A gesture eventually known to her father, which impressed him. Not once in her life had he been able to deny her a thing. Now, in the waning years of her youth, he was willing to grant her her heart's desire—a man he considered most unsuitable. True, the family was old gentry stock and reputably wealthy, but something about Farjeon disturbed him. Dark, powerful, with a streak of melancholy running through that Greek god's face— not the soothing husband for his stubborn, strong-willed Regina. Against his better judgment, he relented, giving her his blessing and assuring both of his continuous support and devotion. With tears in his eyes, he watched them depart on their honeymoon.

And what an odd night it had been, she thought grimly. Better, perhaps, than the horrid tales learned from schoolmates at Cheltenham Ladies' College. In a vast bed, Nicholas was considerate: a few caresses, mumbled words, then the deep painful thrust, but no more. Expecting fire, she found ice, and an unexpected shame on her part. In the moments following as they lay awkwardly entwined, in an act which ironically impregnated her, she still felt his latent sensuality—the hopelessness of a man born to be a lover, whom she had wedded and could not arouse, not to the ecstasy he demanded. Daily, she saw the contained passion in his handsome, brooding face, the conflicting emotions, but she couldn't reach him. A single touch and he flinched. It was as if he were enchanted, but by then she was too ill to care. Months were spent in bed fighting nausea, and when she was finally on her feet, she and Nicholas were emotionally and spiritually estranged.

Their child was born in her father's house in Norwich. Afterward, the baby was hustled over to a wet nurse, and three months later Regina Farjeon again found herself pregnant. But never again had Nicholas come to her bed. . . .

Of course, she had taken lovers, she thought spitefully. What woman wouldn't in the face of such indifference? Undoubtedly, he knew of her affairs, less did he care. At one point, she had seriously considered unburdening herself to her father, but the prospect of failure was hateful. She, a woman who had always succeeded, didn't even know the word. Could she live apart from her husband? More to the point, how could she endure the social ostracism? And so she kept quiet.

During her second, less debilitating pregnancy, Regina made two alarming discoveries. Whenever Nicholas traveled, she opened their mail. Thus, she learned that he was in precarious financial difficulties. No one could be more explicit than the Bank of England. But the most terrifying incident occurred in a visit to her son's nursery. Pausing on the threshold, she overheard the nurses in deep conversation. One sat holding the little boy on her lap, drying his naked body with a soft fleeced towel. The second stood nearby, dangling a rattle before the baby's laughing face.

"Poor wee one! You think he'll get it?" she asked.

The other woman sighed, fluffing up the infant's hair, which made him chortle. "Who knows? But if I was the missus, I wouldn't be dropping them so fast. Not with the mad streak in this family. There be over a half-dozen took . . ."

Regina Farjeon, seven months pregnant, turned away. Dazed, sick with fear, she stumbled back to her suite. Gradually, the terrible hurt turned to fury, and fortified by hot tumblers of brandy and milk, she retired to her cold bed. Several days she waited, until word was brought to her of Nicholas Farjeon's return. By then she felt sufficiently in control of her raging emotions.

Coolly dressing, as if for a soirée, she headed for his studio—a room always kept locked. Well, today he would have to open it for her. Many explanations were due.

Knocking on the door, she called sharply, "Nicholas!" There was a long pause. Then she heard his voice, harsh, staccato, telling her to come to the library. Angrily, she strolled down the Long Gallery, made eerie by the Jacobean frosting and the reek of worm-eaten oak. If only she'd had her way, it would have been ripped to pieces.

Nicholas Farjeon flung open the library door.

"Why do you keep that place locked?"

"You're not interested in paintings, Regina. Much of my work is unfinished. I don't like prying eyes—"

"Not even from your wife?" she spat, sitting before his desk-table.

"What can I do for you, my dear?" he asked politely.

Exasperated by his tone, she glared at him, somewhat disconcerted by his obvious strain and another emotion she couldn't define. But she'd always been impatient with other people's emotions. . . . "Where have you been?" she muttered.

"In London, Regina. Business affairs—"

"Your investments have been falling alarmingly."

"I'm sorry, my dear, there are good years and bad. Unfortunately, I seem to have hit a slump."

Her lips curled in scorn. "Quite a slump, I gather."

"How long have you been reading my mail?" He smiled.

"Only when you're away—out of necessity, Nicholas. What are you going to do about it?"

The gray eyes darkened. "Rely on your—as yet untouched—dowry. That should keep us going for quite a while." She flushed. "And it is my right, you know, by law."

"Yes, Nicholas, by law!" Her angry defiance snapped. "Damn you! Couldn't you have told me about the insanity in your family?"

He blanched. "Would you have married me if I had?"

"Certainly not!" Her laugh was shrill.

"I knew that. That's why I said nothing." Sadness etched his face. "Nor would I to any woman. I had every hope our marriage would succeed—"

"Did you?" she asked curiously. "And has it?"

"We have one child and are shortly expecting another—"

Enraged, she leaned across the table. "How many went mad?"

"What do you want—a divorce?"

She gaped at him. "You dare to ask me that! You, who have given me one child who may go insane and a second awaiting the same fate. Divorce is no answer!"

"I'm like other men," he said distantly, turning his face to the oriel's brilliance. "I have my dreams. . . ."

Barely able to hide her fury, she rose. "Why did you marry me?"

"One always hopes for the best, Regina. I had simply come to that age in life when I felt I must marry—"

"Must marry! If not me, then someone else, eh?"

His voice was flat. "I needed, I wanted, a wife—yes."

"I see, anyone could have done. . . ." Her hands shook. "Did you ever love me?"

"I don't know," he answered quietly. "But did you . . . me? All I saw was lust."

She looked bewildered.

"On our wedding night, you offered yourself to me like a harlot."

"What was I supposed to do?" she cried.

Now his eyes were cold, half-closed. "I'm not even sure you were a virgin."

She crouched in her chair. "Oh, God, what did you want?"

"The miraculous—but it died years ago. . . ." Wearily, he searched her pale face. "You should be in bed, Regina. This is upsetting both for you and the child."

"How nice that you now show me compassion!"

He bowed his head.

"I won't divorce you, although you deserve that and worse," she said between clenched teeth. "You have my dowry, but I'll see that my inheritance goes only to our children."

"An excellent idea."

Unsteadily, she rose to her feet. "Do you keep a mistress? Visit brothels?"

"No, I can't stand such filth."

"Is there anyone else?"

"Only the dead." His face sagged.

She closed in, relentless. "Do you have any relatives now insane?"

"My sister. . . ."

"Where is she?"

"In a private asylum outside Norwich." He topped her out-cry. "Don't worry, you'll not come in contact with her."

Her voice trembled. "How can I live with this?"

"Help me." He held out his hand. "Together, we'll manage." His smile was ironic. "We can, at least, try to be friends. . . ."

"Friends!" Regina Farjeon sneered into her toilet mirror. His words still rankled. Ashes littered the dressing table. Shouting for her maid to clear up the mess, Regina jammed a hatpin through the plush felt hat balanced gingerly on her elaborate coiffure, then reached for a Georgian silver-gilt flask kept hidden in a drawer. The sting of brandy eased the tension of too many memories—of a second son born two months later and her subsequent six-year estrangement from Nicholas. . . . Lust, yes, she had to admit he had been right about that. . . . Love eluded her. And why not? How could she help her inability to respond or to offer it. An alien emotion, which she despised, turning people into fools, making them miserable.

During one of their steely altercations, Nicholas had carefully pointed out that the selfishness was not one-sided. "I have your money, Regina; you have my social position, which is what you wanted, isn't it?"

Furiously, she had to agree. Not understanding his complexity, not even caring. All her attention was riveted on his finances. Week by week, she studied his accounts, watching in awed dismay as her dowry dipped lower and lower. And then on a twilit evening, he came to her suite, his face ashen.

Without preamble, he asked, "Can you get an advance from your father on your inheritance?"

Now at last she had the upper hand. The blue eyes opened wide in innocence. "For what?"

"Certain obligations that I cannot meet."

She purred, rejoicing in his humiliation. "Cards, the Turf? What is it, Nicholas?"

"I'm not a betting man, Regina, you know that. But my luck has been damnably bad of late. Please, my dear, help me. It's my sister—"

"Your sister!"

"I need two hundred pounds more for the next year. Give it to me and I'll repay you as soon as possible."

"With what? Air?" she jeered. "What have you usually done with the afflicted?"

"Incarcerated them in the stone suite."

The concept fascinated her. "Wonderful! Bring her back to Bellereve for a rest, then we'll ship her on to Bedlam."

His face darkened. "Why Bedlam?"

"Why not the best for the mad?" Regina's eyes sparkled. "My cousin is on the management committee. I'm sure he'd be most solicitous of her welfare."

Nicholas Farjeon looked at the black hairs on his hands— hands that a loving woman had once adored. How low he'd stooped.

"She is not now insane."

"Then why keep her at such great expense?"

"She tried to kill me. . . . I had no choice."

"What about our sons? What risk is there to them?"

He looked surprised. "Nothing. How can she harm anyone miles away in Weston Asylum?"

"That's in the past. I think it time she came home. I can't keep shoveling out money on a madwoman when you have such splendid facilities available."

"I don't want her shut up in that tomb—"

"I'm afraid you have no say in the matter. Certainly, you wouldn't want my father to learn our awful secret." She daintily wiped her eyes with a lace handkerchief. "Think of our sons. . . ." The bitter anger she felt toward him was masked by a triumph as heady as champagne. "I'll make a pact with you, Nicholas. If she doesn't prosper at Bellereve, off she goes to Bedlam." He was silent. "Well?"

"I beg of you, let me have the money. She'll be out of sight then—"

"No! It's enough that I allow her to return. . . ." Unexpectedly, she found herself standing opposite him, on the far side of the ornate half-tester, dripping with satin and velvet, a bed so enticing to her lovers, but not to this enigmatic man—her husband. "Why won't you sleep with me?" she mumbled.

"Don't you think two children enough for us? Besides, my dear, I wouldn't dream of interfering with your amours. . . ."

Thoroughly rattled, she reached for a cigarette. "For God's sake! Why the charade? Why not divorce me?"

He looked amused. "A solution I once offered you. Now, I say, why should I? You're the mother of my children. We're each content in our own way." He folded his arms with a wry smile. "Agreed, Regina. I'll bring Ariel home on your terms. You need never see her. I ask only one thing. That you accept an outsider's opinion—a doctor—as to her state of mind. Whatever he says will determine whether or not she goes to Bedlam."

"Agreed," she echoed in cold fury. "Six months, I give her."

"So be it, my dear. . . ."

Regina Farjeon stared at her hands. A faint yellowish tinge was discoloring the pale flesh. She was smoking much too much. Silly to lose control when she had Ariel Farjeon at her mercy. Only four more months, and if today's visit was successful, there would be others. Many more. No one would ever think to tell Nicholas. And such a frail woman should topple easily.

 *Four*

Loud pounding on the door brought an unpleasant-looking creature to the threshold. Greasy hair and filthy apron, a wisp of bad breath delayed Regina Farjeon only momentarily. It was the woman beyond who caught her attention, sitting like a schoolgirl on a kitchen chair, a book in her hands, lips moving silently as if in prayer.

"Leave us alone!" the visitor hissed, walking into the chamber. Five feet from her quarry, Regina stopped. So it was true, as the servants whispered. She was still beautiful despite the white hair. Pity overwhelmed her for a moment, then disgust and hatred spurred her on. The thought of madness housing itself in such a body was more repugnant to her than the miserable being in the kitchen.

"Do you know who I am?" she asked acidly.

The gray eyes, so like her husband's, regarded her gently. "You're my brother's wife."

"Regina Farjeon," the older woman spat.

"Regina Farjeon."

"*Mrs*. Farjeon."

Ariel closed her book. "Mrs. Farjeon."

"I came to tell you that Dr. Desmond has dropped your case." A tremor shook her victim's body, her face was expressionless. "He considers you incurable—"

"Incurable," she echoed.

"Yes, damn it!" And she stamped her foot. "The asylum

was no place for the likes of you. A woman who murders her baby should be hanged!" At last she had hurt her. The beautiful face turned white, her book fell to the floor as she blindly sought the dirt-encrusted window.

"I lost it. . . . I don't remember what happened."

"You killed it, bitch!"

Still, she hadn't broken her. There must be other visits. Angrily, Regina Farjeon retrieved the book. "What's this?"

"Browning's poems."

"Poetry, eh? Why should a madwoman read poetry? Much too exciting for an overwrought brain. Who gave it to you?"

"Dr. Desmond."

"Dr. Desmond, eh? In a whimsical moment, I suppose. Well, so much for him and this atrocious influence." Breaking the book's spine, she ripped the volume apart. Shreds of paper scattered to the floor. Ariel Farjeon stood by the window, rigid. Unmoved.

Outraged by her failure, Regina drew herself up proudly. "I'll come again," she purred. "You must be lonely with only that old crone to talk to. Expect me any time. . . ." Now she saw it. Fear in the dazzling eyes. "You'll be with us for such a short time, we should get to be friends. Sleep well, my dear. . . ." and she swept out the door.

Chilled and frightened, Ariel Farjeon awaited her return, growing stiff with fatigue. Realizing that it was at last safe to move, she located the broken spine, then sank to her hands and knees, collecting paper scraps. When she found the piece bearing Desmond's name, she wept in silent misery. . . .

February, and the diphtheria epidemic was over. Too many had died, but more had lived. Depressed and out of sorts, Simon Desmond resumed the familiar routine at Fairhaven. By now his practice had doubled. Seldom did he catch an unbroken night's sleep. So busy was he that a groom now delivered medicines while Desmond concentrated on rounds. Even the surgery hours were extended.

Beatrice Clayton, catching him napping at his desk, offered a mild protest. "Don't you think you're overdoing it, Simon? You have a punishing schedule."

"No more so than Colin Broughton. I hear we're running neck and neck." On his feet, he ran a hand through rumpled hair and straightened his necktie. "Well, I'd best report to Bellereve before they think I've forgotten her."

"Have lunch first. I don't want to have to summon Broughton for your collapse," she said smiling.

"No time," he snapped, wondering why he was so irritable. Fatigue, probably, or something else. Time to make one of his furtive visits to a select brothel in Norwich or King's Lynn. Get it out of his system. Despising himself for his weakness, yet unable to go a step further and take a mistress. The idea was repellent. A nasty little house with vulgar furnishings and a nondescript garden. Consigning his life to a poor shopgirl or some slut; always living in dread of discovery or the unwanted bastard. At least he could give his father credit. He married the fecund bitch. Legitimized all those offspring. Dressed them in gold. . . .

"I hate my father," he said coldly. "Living in Kent in that glass monstrosity. He broke Jed's heart. As good as put the razor in his hand."

Beatrice Clayton blinked in dismay. "It didn't embitter him, Simon. Not until the end, I think. . . . Jed gave me love. The kind of love I hope you will know. It makes up for so much. . . ." The pause between them was too long, uncomfortably so between old friends. She reached for his hand. "Simon, this is neither the time nor the place to discuss such a delicate matter, but soon you should think about getting married. You are too lonely."

Desmond flushed.

"There's now quite a bit of money. You're in a good position to court a woman."

"I can't court just any woman," he said brusquely and left.

Pausing restlessly on his chestnut outside Bellereve's gates, Simon Desmond wondered if he had done the right thing. He had deliberately stayed away two extra weeks so that whatever emotion Ariel Farjeon felt for him at Christmas would have evaporated, and he could now treat her with cool dispassion.

Confronting Bellereve's master in the spacious library, he asked, "You did get my messages, I trust?"

Bewildered, Farjeon offered him a chair. "I had no word. Frankly, I thought you'd dropped her case."

"We had a diphtheria epidemic in Heydon," Desmond replied, irked by the misunderstanding. "I didn't want to expose your sister to the risk of infection."

"That was considerate of you, Desmond. For one who has so greatly suffered, such an illness would be devastating." His

smile was gentle. "Now go to her, please. We've six weeks
lost—"

"May I have your permission to take her outdoors, sir?"

"My wife is afraid of her—that she'll harm the children."

"I'll be with her. You have acres we can walk in. No one
will come in contact with her, I promise you." Annoyed at the
man's hesitancy, he snapped, "For God's sake, is it so much
to ask? A breath of fresh air. The woman has nothing to keep
her going!"

"Do you think it's easy on me?" Farjeon's eyes flashed. "I
long for the day when she'll talk to me, yet I live in dread of
precipitating a collapse."

"We both want the same thing—her well-being," Desmond
retorted, strolling over to a bay window for a glance at the
stone building. "Would you object to my visiting the asylum?"
Farjeon swung around in surprise. "I'd like to learn more about
her treatment. What their prognosis was. . . . You and I differ
on a crucial point, sir. If she spends the rest of her life in such
isolation, it might provoke the very catastrophe you fear. But
there is an alternative." Smiling, he returned to his chair. "Have
you ever considered placing her in a private home? There are
people who specialize in such cases—"

"Money is my problem, Desmond, as I've said before."
Farjeon's voice had an edge. "Within reason, I'll do anything—" He shrugged. "But that suite has always housed our
mad. Ariel will survive like all the others."

"You said mainly females were afflicted?"

"Yes." Peter Curwen had stated just the opposite.

"Here's the address." Farjeon scribbled on a sheet of paper.
"It's the Weston Asylum in Bracon Ash, south of Norwich.
I'm sure you'll find Dr. Portman quite helpful. . . ."

As the bolt shot back, the Jackal sidled into view, teeth
bared in welcome. Across the room, Ariel Farjeon sat with
bent head on the shabby Regency couch, which doubled as a
bed. Back and forth she rocked in the old attitude of despair.

"How long has she been like that?" Desmond asked in an
angry undertone.

"Weeks, sir."

He could have throttled the wretch. "I told you to report
any change to Mr. Farjeon."

"I thought you meant food and clothes, sir. Her clothes is
warm. She eats, and the missus said she'd take him word."

Holding her back fee, Desmond's hand poised in mid-air. "Mrs. Farjeon came here? How often?"

Like a dog eyeing a bone, she slobbered in anticipation. "Once, twice, sir—not much." Knobby fingers grabbed for the coins. "I swears it. They just chats a bit."

He dropped the money into a greasy palm. "Leave us!" With a grimace, she slunk off to the kitchen.

Six weeks. Six long weeks. Painfully busy to him, intolerable to her. He ought never to have left her so long. Hesitantly, he touched her shoulder. She gave a whimper of fear.

"Why do you shrink from me?" Receiving no answer, he raised her head. She showed no sign of recognition. "Did you think I'd left you?" Still no reply. "Speak to me, Ariel. I want to help you...." Her continued silence was getting on his nerves. Yanking her to her feet, he brushed against her body. The feel of her breasts at once aroused and alarmed him. Acute shame mingled with a fierce need to make love to her. God, how he craved it! His eyes darkened with passion as he pulled her closer. All he had to do was to get rid of the Jackal. Then he could feast in this beautiful woman. Take her again and again, as he had dreamed of doing. Who would believe her— a poor madwoman—if she damned him? He very much doubted that she even knew who he was at that moment.

Tears fell on his wrist as she wept, a mournful, pitiful cry in that awful room. Lust turned to compassion. The caressing hands attempted to soothe. But she cried out, now terrified of his advances, and he promptly left her alone to her misery.

Upset by her deterioration and his vile conduct, Desmond decided not to tell Farjeon about her relapse. Time enough to do that later—if necessary. If he stepped up his visits, she might improve. Yet any doctor with sense would immediately summon another physician. All those nights of wanton dreams, pretending the woman was unknown.... He, the hypocrite, was no better than his father—a filthy libertine. The damned calling the other damned.

The least he could do for her—to make amends, to appease *his* conscience—was to visit the asylum and learn if the withdrawal was part of a pattern. Armed with that knowledge, he could then decide whether or not to call in Colin Broughton....

Thatched, tiled-roofed, cream-walled cottages, some heavily creepered with ivy or sleeping flowers, lined the road to Bracon Ash. In the distance, lime trees and pink mays huddled

around a towerless church. Shops clung to a few side streets;
two large parks hid ancient halls; and then on the outskirts,
lonely and formidable, stood the gigantic building Simon Desmond was seeking, set well back from the main road. Presenting his credentials at the main gates, he leaned back as his
carriage drove through a park so sparse that nothing inflamed
the mind or warmed the heart.

He wasn't surprised to find the institution built along the
lines of Hanwell Lunatic Asylum, eight-and-a-half miles outside London. There were the three massive rotundas: the central
for reception, the left and right crowning male and female wards
and all their attendant facilities. Separate airing courts and yards
clutched the formal garden at the rear; beyond that lay out-
buildings, kitchen gardens, orchards, and the isolated burial
ground. But the section he was most interested in undoubtedly
was off limits.

Hanwell had been constructed by the well-meaning for pauper lunatics. Weston Asylum was obviously designed for the
wealthy. Nothing jarred. Entering the massive doors of the
central rotunda, he might have been stepping into Norfolk's
Holkham Hall. A marble floor and columns greeted the nervous
eye; no despairing shrieks wafted down the long corridors. The
matron, who greeted him from her office, was relentlessly
cheerful, her uniform crackling with immaculate precision. A
hum of voices on his left told him he had probably arrived at
the end of luncheon. Behind closed oak doors, he caught the
swish of chairs being thrust against tables.

Matron's whispered commentary ushered them through the
rotunda into a rectangular wing containing dispensaries, a study,
and the committee room, where the medical superintendent
awaited him. Desmond, used to the stark, carbolic-smelling
atmosphere of Guy's and London Hospital, looked about in
astonishment. It was a captivating room in the style of Adam.
A bank of windows overlooked the park; blue, the color of a
twilit sea, stained the walls; the classical motif in the white
marble chimneypiece was picked up in the plaster ceiling and
frieze. Any feeling of oppression was muted by the gaiety of
stuccowork and the room's elegance.

Dr. Cecil Portman, tall, lean, with an ascetic countenance,
exuded cordiality. Offering his guest a chair and a snifter of
brandy, he swept off to rummage through a bulging walnut
file. "Ah, yes, Ariel Farjeon," he sighed, extracting a thick
folder from its mates and slamming the drawer shut. "A tragic

case, Dr. Desmond. The first year, almost totally mad; the next eleven years—quite sane."

Simon Desmond had a hangover. A vicious one. He had spent the night in Norwich, bedding not only one but two whores in a violent attempt to forget Ariel Farjeon. All he remembered of those disgusting hours was the stench of over-powdered, cologned flesh, and the boring mating with un-wanted bodies; sheets damp with perspiration; and his feeble efforts to shave in tepid water. The haggard face that looked out at him in the mirror was even more desperate than hers. And as he shaved, he hoped that he was hacking away at her image. . . .

"Tell me about the first year," he mumbled to Portman.

The superintendent leafed through the pages. "She was brought here by her brother, Nicholas Farjeon, in 1870, at age eighteen. Apparently, she had had an illicit affair with a young man of the county, who was packed off to Canada. A child was born—"

"Overlain?" Desmond stifled a yawn.

The heavy lidded eyes registered surprise. "Overlain? No, it was stillborn."

"Who told you that?"

"Farjeon, on her admittance."

"I must have misunderstood. . . ." Desmond ran a finger across his mouth, frowning. "Was she violent?"

"Only in the presence of her brother. On two occasions, she attacked him—"

"Physically?"

"No, verbal abuse. Punishment followed in a padded cell."

"What did that entail?"

"Seclusion, reduced diet, and mechanical restraint—if necessary."

Desmond was snapping out of his lethargy. "Is this the usual procedure?"

"Well, you know the dangerous patient requires discipline. Occasionally, an ice-cold bath suffices." He consulted his notes. "In Ariel Farjeon's case, the first offense called for a week's seclusion. After the second attack, she spent a month in a padded cell. The third incident was more serious."

"What happened?"

"The wardress stepped out to bring in tea, and Miss Farjeon lunged at her brother—"

"He's a big man. Surely, he could have turned her aside single-handedly?"

"That's not the point, Desmond. With a weapon, she might have killed him. As it was, she went for his eyes."

"And how was she punished?"

"Six months in a padded cell."

"With the usual?" Desmond could barely keep the sting out of his voice.

"No, this time she was put in a straitjacket for extended periods, which necessitated her being hand-fed."

"What did she eat?" he asked after a pause.

"Oh, the usual slop—gruel. They all resist initially. But a period of self-starvation, followed by forced feeding, brings results."

God! Is there no end to this horror? Desmond wondered. "And this is how you conquered her insubordination?"

"Yes, the forced feeding does it." Portman smiled thinly. "That tube is not only damned unpleasant, but sometimes lethal." He leaned back expansively in his chair. "After that bout, she was as docile as a lamb. Never gave us any trouble, though she rarely spoke."

"How did she communicate?"

"Oh, she always made her needs known. Questions were answered simply and to the point, but there was no reference to her past life."

"Not even to her baby?" Desmond looked skeptical.

"Only in the first year when her brother came visiting. Obviously, it was part of her insanity. She persistently blamed him for the child's death." He grimaced. "Of course, she was then in an acute state of mania."

"Was she ever withdrawn?"

"According to her file—yes. Those episodes usually occurred after her periods in seclusion."

"What were the symptoms?"

Portman flipped through the notes. "She didn't speak. Appeared to be unaware of her surroundings. Was frightened if anyone touched her—"

Desmond interrupted: "Catatonic?"

"Outwardly, yes, but we never felt it a true case. I think she heard everything said but for some reason wouldn't respond."

"I don't understand. Why the pretense?"

"Why did her hair turn white? Shock?" For the first time,

Portman's clipped voice faltered, a blush lighting his high cheek bones. Then he said dryly, "But this bizarre conduct was only confined to the first year. As far as I'm concerned, from then on it was a waste of time and money. . . ."

The brandy was easing his throbbing head. Desmond thumbed through his notebook. "Where was Farjeon during this period?"

"Traveling. After the last episode, we advised him to stay away for a while. Obviously, he was an irritant. But by the end of the second year, she was sufficiently improved to encourage a visit. He wrote back, however, asking that the meeting be delayed."

A flash lit the hazel eyes. "Why?"

"He loved her, Desmond, and the thought of a relapse was too painful to bear. Many relatives feel that way," Portman added, studying a letter. "The next year we wrote again, but he was in Europe, as he was the following year. When she had been with us for five years, we learned he had married and was reluctant to take on the burden of his sister. A year later, he informed us that his wife refused to have a lunatic in the house."

"She's still of the same opinion." Desmond's retort was icy. "But you think Miss Farjeon now well?"

"As well as anybody, Dr. Desmond."

"They're shipping her to Bethlem unless I can effect some kind of miraculous cure—"

Portman's official face dissolved in concern. "But we released her as sane."

"Nicholas Farjeon said, once mad—always mad. Would you agree?"

"Few people will give them a second chance. Yes, they're branded for life, I'm afraid."

"I see only a lonely, vulnerable woman." Desmond spoke quietly. "Once, she mentioned her baby, saying 'she lost it.'" The two men stared at one another. "That disturbed me, and she's had two periods of withdrawal. Hopefully, she'll snap out of this one as quickly as the first. . . ." Abruptly, he switched topics. "Who paid the bills?"

Portman ran a pen down another sheet. "Nicholas Farjeon did. Then when she was twenty-one, her trust fund reverted to him, and that took care of her for some years. You know she left because of his financial affairs?"

Desmond nodded. "How did she receive him after all that time?"

"Well." Portman gave a wry smile. "But then she was heavily sedated." He stirred restlessly, suddenly anxious to terminate the interview, but Simon Desmond wanted more.

"Would you show me the seclusion cells?" The older man looked startled, and Desmond rose, his voice charmingly persuasive. "A room in her suite upsets her. It occurred to me that it might be similar to this one."

With a shrug, Portman stood up. "Very well, Desmond. It's off limits, but I'll take you, if you insist—"

"Thank you, yes! I want to see it and everything used to discipline her."

"That's a bit unorthodox, doctor."

"I'm trying to keep her out of Bethlem. I must know what frightens her. Something—or someone—causes these relapses."

Portman led the way back through the rotunda, up a spiral staircase to the gallery above and a locked oak door. Beyond lay a short passage and a metal door, heavily bolted. Three keys were inserted into different locks, releasing the gigantic bolt. An ominous clang sounded as they stepped into a long windowless corridor. Down one side ran a row of doors, each with its own peephole and massive bolt.

"We're directly above the female ward. A similar unit runs over the men's unit." Portman shook his head in laughter. "Some of these ladies can throw quite a tantrum."

"Show me the exact cell," Desmond whispered, feeling his stomach tighten.

"Here you are, doctor—safe and soundproof!"

Desmond peered in through a peephole. A dribble of light slid in from a window. Again came the key ritual and the thunder of a bolt being unleashed. The room was small, pitifully so, a mirror image of the one at Bellereve—even the window occupied the same position. Padded material coated with a nauseating brown-gray fabric lined the walls and floor.

"How do they see?"

"Daylight does well enough. We can't have oil or gaslight. They'd set themselves on fire."

The room stank. In all his career, working with the poor in Southwark and East London, Desmond had never smelled anything like it.

As if reading his mind, Portman gestured towards a filthy mattress. "That's where it comes from. Amazing how they foul themselves. Worse than animals. Seem to take a delight—"

"When was she here for the six-month stint?" Desmond interrupted, his mind reeling. At least the padding was gone from Ariel Farjeon's stone prison. . . .

"Winter."

"May I see the mechanical restraints?"

"You're a persistent man, Desmond."

"I'm not here from the press," he cried fiercely. "I'm trying to keep a *sane* woman—and we both agree on that—out of Bethlem!"

"Very well, sir," came the aggrieved sigh. "Everything is kept here."

Desmond's eyes focused in the gloom. A metal cabinet, bolted to the wall, stood next to the door. Out came another key. One by one the grisly implements were displayed: hand and foot manacles, chains, a rubber tube, and the straitjacket.

"Was she subjected to all this?" he asked faintly.

"Not at first. The manacles were put on during her second incarceration."

Very gingerly, he touched them, feeling her warm flesh. "For how long?"

"Until her wrists and ankles started to ulcerate—"

"Dear Jesus! On a gentlewoman! Why?"

"We're here to discipline, not to pamper," Portman replied in mild reproof.

Desmond's fingers brushed the straitjacket. "And this, too, was used?"

"Yes, in the six-month confinement. It was the only way she could be handled. Silly fool kept tearing off all her clothes. Finally, we left her naked. At the rate she was going, she would have stripped us of all our uniforms."

Simon Desmond knelt beside the reeking pad on the floor, fighting to control his fury. "Was she ever abused?"

Portman's voice was prim. "I don't know what you mean."

Desmond bowed his head. He had desired her. Passionately so. Others must have wanted her. . . . On his feet, he faced his guide. "Sexually attacked in this room—"

Even in that murky light, he caught Portman's strained expression. "As a man of the world, Desmond, you must realize such things happen. Some of these insane females are incredibly lewd—deliberately so, to their own destruction. A man, in such circumstances, might be tempted. . . ."

"Did it happen to Ariel Farjeon—in this room?"

"We think so, yes."

"When she was manacled or in a straitjacket?" Desmond stared at him in horror.

"Probably, the latter. Easier to get them. Unless they're chained to the wall, shackles can always be used as a protective weapon."

The young man looked again at the nightmare on the floor, the thick malodorous padding on the claustrophic walls.

"No one would hear her, of course," the superintendent replied casually, lips still pursed.

"And when did you first learn about this appalling incident?" Desmond mopped his forehead with a handkerchief.

"A bit later, when she was in the infirmary after her release. It came out gradually. . . . Although the man—a warder—denied it, he was sacked."

Simon Desmond had wanted to rape her. Yes, he must use the word. Admit his guilt. What right had he to be outraged? "Don't you watch them?" he asked dully.

"Most custodians don't want this wing. The people working it—men and women—are brutalized by what they see. Frequently, they're drunkards, or worse." He raised a cynical eyebrow. "We've had women assault women. Because the pay is minimal and the work so unpleasant, we take what we can get. Usually, the turnover is swift."

"But to leave her in the dark, so helpless. . . . Dear God!"

Portman's voice softened. "Forgive me for making an assumption, Desmond, but aren't you forgetting your professional obligation to Miss Farjeon? An objective distance is absolutely necessary between doctor and patient." The young man's eyes were stricken. "I had two doctors taken off Ariel Farjeon's case because they lost their perspective."

He forced out the words. "Are you saying they fell in love with her?"

A trace of malice tinged Portman's laugh. "You know the woman. She's still lovely. But you should have seen her years ago. Even mad, she was ravishing. I'm certain many men who came in contact with her had their fantasies. But we doctors are above that sort of thing. . . ." Returning the disciplinary tools to their cabinet, he led his visitor outside. "I'm just warning you, Desmond. She's Medusa without the snakes—"

"You make her sound still insane!"

"Oh, no," Portman hastened to reassure him. "She gave us no trouble after the first year, and she developed a rather remarkable gift. . . ."

They strolled down the windowless corridor to the multi-locked metal door. As the heavy thing rumbled shut behind them, Desmond asked, "What was it?"

"She had an amazing affinity with some of the older women patients—many of whom were quite difficult to control. She would sit with them by the hour, holding them in their griefs.... We gave her greater freedom after she saved a wardress's life."

Back in the Committee Room, Desmond buttoned up his ulster. "Then it's your belief that she's been sane these past eleven years?" He faced his host.

"Clinically so—compared with the lot we have here."

"What pushed her over the edge?"

"An unhappy love affair and an illegitimate baby."

Crossing the rotunda, Desmond hesitated. "Why should she mourn a stillborn, unwanted child?"

Portman shrugged. "Perhaps she wanted to marry the chap. Women are mysterious creatures—half-fact, half-fancy—and this one's doubly crippled by hereditary insanity." He blinked out at the drive stretching in a wide arc beyond the portal. "You've been asking all the questions, Desmond. Now I have one. Are you married?"

Desmond blushed, too vulnerable in the sunlight. "No."

"Ah, that's your trouble," replied the older man affably. "Get yourself a good wife in bed and a few babes in the nursery, and you won't have time to brood on the enigmas of people like Ariel Farjeon...."

Arriving back in Reepham on a late afternoon train from Norwich, Desmond fetched his trap and set off—not for Heydon but for Foulsham. He was profoundly shaken by his experience at Weston Asylum, intellect fighting a losing battle against emotion. If the stench of that horrible room haunted him, God knows what it had done to Ariel Farjeon!

As he strode through Bellereve's black and white tiled hall, an impasse in yellow chiffon barred his way—Regina Farjeon, escorting a group of women into the drawing room for tea. At sight of Desmond, she confronted him as one might a cobra.

"Simon Desmond!" she hissed. "Dr. Desmond?"

He bowed stiffly.

It took only a moment, and she recognized in Desmond a kindred spirit of the flesh whose rage and frustration matched her own. The sensual mouth, the yearning in his eyes made her bored heart quicken. Waving her guests ahead, she leaned against a pillar, her bust rising provocatively. As he threw her a lingering glance, she smiled.

"I thought you had left us, Dr. Desmond."

He was polite but cool, well aware of her ploy. "You knew what detained me, madame. A diphtheria epidemic."

The blue eyes were insolent. "She's not worth it, you know. Mad like all the rest. Nicholas sees nothing!"

Flattery might gain him an inch. She wasn't unattractive, if one liked the type, but too heavily perfumed, which only made him more poignantly aware of the sweetness of Ariel Farjeon's body. Without any artifice, she walked in an aura of spring flowers.

Desmond's voice dropped suggestively. "I know what troubles you, Mrs. Farjeon—"

"You should come to me." Her look was blatant. "I pay the bills, and I can be very generous," she teased, allowing him a glimpse into her overly tight bodice. The pink and white coloring of too plump flesh reminded him of last night's orgy and of a hundred other nights spent with such overripe fruit.

"She won't hurt you or your sons," he said tensely.

Seizing his hand, she ran it across her bosom. "We'll talk about it again, eh?" With a sly laugh, she rejoined her companions.

Controlling his anger, he climbed the staircase and found Nicholas Farjeon entrenched in his library, sitting subdued before a roaring fire, a pile of books beside him. Did the man never move from that room? Desmond wondered. No, how could he with that hyena lurking below?

He began without preamble. "Was the baby overlaid?"

Farjeon stirred, his thoughts miles away, then leaned back against the couch, his gray eyes the color of an overcast sky, his pale features a dramatic contrast to his raven hair. "Yes, of course, Desmond," he said distantly.

"Then why did you tell the asylum it was stillborn?"

The question drove Farjeon to his feet. Curtly directing Desmond to a chair, he poured them some brandy. "A stillbirth is seldom questioned, but the overlaid child is another matter—"

"I don't understand the lie."

"Sometimes, Desmond, you seem very dense. I did it to protect Ariel. The child was overlain accidentally—at least, I assume that's what happened," he added dully. "I was downstairs, and when I returned, I found her lying on the baby, asleep. The child was dead. I can testify to what I saw, but others might be skeptical. Some might call it murder—"

"Murder!" Desmond exploded. "With your evidence?"

"Madness runs in our family." Farjeon's voice was icy. "A love affair terminated and an illegitimate baby overlaid. Now was she really asleep? I thought she was."

"How long were you away?"

"A half-hour. . . ."

"Did you call a physician?"

"I called no one!" He pounded the desk-table in fury. "Don't you understand? I wasn't there. I don't know what happened. Overlain means one of two things: accident or murder. When I left, she was nursing the poor brat, but even then her state of mind was shaky. She wanted to keep it! Can you imagine? Keep a bastard!" His voice trembled. "Who is to say what really happened? Call in a doctor, and if he refuses a death certificate, where do you end up? Before a coroner's inquest. A step more—if you're unlucky—and you're bundled off to the Norwich Assizes. And what of the verdict?" he cried grimly. "Guilty but insane. Sentenced to Broadmoor for life. Or that other—death by hanging."

Chilled, Desmond whispered, "What did you do with the child?"

"I buried it that night in the garden."

"And your sister?"

"Awoke about an hour later wanting to feed it. I told her the baby was asleep, but she didn't believe me. I had moved its bed away from her, and I remember. . . ." His eyes glistened with tears. "How feebly she struggled against me, trying to get out of bed. She began to weep, breaking into those awful shrieks of her labor. . . . I had only whiskey to quiet her. In desperation, I simply poured it down her throat. Anything to stop those inhuman cries!"

Badly shaken, Desmond asked, "Did she know what had happened?"

"I told her," Farjeon admitted brokenly. "Grief, prostration, and alcohol soon reduced her to a stupor."

Something jarred in Desmond's mind. "Earlier, you said she refused to give up the child, and when it was taken from her, became quite ill—"

"I meant that in a figurative sense, Desmond. Emotionally, she couldn't accept the baby's death. Why, I don't know. We had been hoping for a miscarriage." His laugh was very bitter.

"Twice, she awoke, enacting that same pathetic scene. . . . By morning, she was desperately ill. Finally recovering, she appeared to have forgotten its existence. Or so I thought until she attacked me."

"How could you hide it?" Desmond mumbled, unable to get that foul room out of his mind.

"Easily. No doctor attended her confinement. The midwife came from a distant village. A half-witted woman cooked and cleaned while I looked after Ariel. No one inquired. There was no interest in us at all—" Sensing disbelief, he cried, "I wasn't about to shout my sister's disgrace to every man jack in Norfolk! I had hoped that once the child was farmed out and Ariel recovered we could return to Bellereve as if from a trip abroad. But because of her wretched labor, I made a fatal mistake. . . ." Refilling his glass, he drank morosely, his handsome face dark with emotion. "Now you see why I misled the asylum."

"I think I should tell you—" Desmond faltered, not wanting to hurt this deeply wounded man further. "Someone abused your sister there."

"Abused?" The gray eyes flashed.

"Raped." At Farjeon's appalled reaction, he apologized. "I thought it best you know. It might account for the lack of speech."

Anguish contorted the proud features. "When? How often?"

"During her six months in a padded cell."

Farjeon stood up, enraged, and Desmond spoke urgently, "I know your agony, sir, but you mustn't blame her. She was totally helpless—in a straitjacket." He stared at his brandy, trying to keep his voice under control and his hand from shaking.

The brother turned away in dismay. "Any consequences?"

"No." Awkwardly, Desmond sought for the right words. "I never had a sister, but from what I know of Miss Farjeon, she is virginal in spirit, in heart. . . . Whatever her future, her life is virtually over. Don't turn against her. Perhaps she is just too beautiful. Who knows? The first man may also have raped her," he added wearily.

Farjeon wheeled on him, sneering. "Are you, too, falling under her spell?"

Desmond's eyes narrowed. "She's my patient," he said coldly, on his feet. "I know my place." His tone softened. "To be honest, I had thought of getting a second opinion. She's slipped a bit, but the worst thing to do at this point would be to introduce a new doctor. It would only frighten her. We were building up a feeling of trust before this epidemic—"

"Were you, now?" Farjeon sounded embittered. "How the hell do you think I feel? She's only a few yards away and I can't go near her!"

"Help me and you'll soon be with her." Their eyes met. "I want that abode"—he spat the words—"made palatable. Carpets, clean windows, draperies, decent furniture. . . ." He glanced around the splendid room. "A few paintings to lift her spirits, books. . . . And I intend to take her out walking—"

"Next thing, you'll want to court her!"

"You mock me, sir," Desmond said angrily. "Do as I say, and I'll give her back to you—well." He reached for the onyx box. "I'm going to her now." At the door, he hesitated. "Be merciful, Farjeon. She wasn't to blame. You love her. I'll bring you together. Don't ruin two lives. . . ."

Dully, he pushed the key into that oppressive iron-banded door. There was no mistaking her look of terror at his entrance. Delicate hands clung to a chair for support.

"Who else has been visiting you, Ariel?" he asked gently.

Her lips tightened in mute protest, one hand clenched in a feeble show of defiance. Grasping it, he felt her resist, then it opened. In her palm lay two scraps of paper. One of Browning's poems.

"Regina Farjeon tore up the book?"

Her eyes shut. He knew. He understood what had happened.

"Don't be frightened. I won't say anything. Are you alone?" She nodded.

"I never meant to leave you so long. We had an epidemic—" His voice shook. "I sent a message to your brother. It was intercepted, wasn't it?" Their eyes locked. "I will come to you whenever possible. Often, I don't know my schedule from day to day, but I'm not leaving you, Ariel. . . ." It had been too long a day, filled with too many horrors, too much sadness. Blindly, he caught her in his arms, pressing her head to his shoulder.

"You're unhappy, aren't you?" she whispered, holding him fast.

He kissed her forehead. "Not when I'm with you."

"Be careful, Simon." She raised her head. "Be careful."

Simon Desmond stroked her face, smiling. "You heal me."

He laughed. "Just as you did with that thorn scratch. I touch you and I feel cleansed."

He had forgotten the fantasy wife, his determination to keep a distance between them. In his joy at holding her again, it never occurred to him that she was too willing.

 *Five*

Away from Ariel Farjeon, Desmond felt again that sense of despair that had been plaguing him since his damnable visit to Bracon Ash. Thus, he arrived at Fairhaven in a temper, berating his groom and snapping even at Beatrice Clayton.

Not bothering to shed his dripping ulster, he stood muddied and rumpled in the parlor, leafing through Bea's detailed notes, muttering to himself, kicking the cat aside when it sniffed his boots. Finally, he announced, "I'll see these three now."

She fussed over him as she had when he was a boy, but he retreated into a mulish silence, glaring at her ministrations. "Was it so bad?" she asked, laying a fond hand on his shoulder.

"Yes." Unexpected tears filled his eyes, and he wiped them away roughly, ashamed of his emotion. "It's a miracle the poor woman survived. And whatever I say will condemn her to a lifetime in hell!"

"She is only one patient among many. Why make so much of her?" Bea asked, perplexed.

"I make nothing of her!" Angrily, he stalked into his surgery with Bea following breathlessly at his heels.

"You worked on the lunatic ward at Guy's. Is she so different from the others?"

"Yes, God damn it! She's not mad!"

Ignoring his outburst, she said reasonably, "You're still exhausted from that epidemic, Simon. What's in order is a week's rest—"

"That's the last thing I need!"

"Well, you might be interested in this." She gaily handed him a buff-colored envelope.

He slit it open with marked impatience, running a hand through disheveled hair. "Supper and a ball at the Howland's. On Saturday—" He shot her a look. "You're invited, too."

"Yes, I know." She beamed. "Mrs. Howland told me at the church bazaar."

"What's the catch?" His voice was cold.

"Simon, dear, you're accepted—no more than that."

"He has a marriageable daughter, doesn't he?"

"Yes, surrounded by admirers. No need to worry." She laughed. "But there is one thing, dear—money. We need it rather badly. The contractor called while you were away. It's going to cost over a thousand pounds to make improvements. We have money, but not enough for you to advance socially— as you must—and to refurbish the house. Howland will give you a loan."

"And what do I have to do? Court his daughter?"

"No, just flatter him," she said mildly. "He's a pompous little man, but feed him a crumb and he'll be amiable." She stared into space, dreaming. "Think what it means! Gaslight, hot water pipes, a new kitchen—"

"And for this I sell my soul?" At her startled expression, he grimaced. "I'm sorry, Bea. I'll play the fool or whatever's required of me. It doesn't matter, does it?"

"I've not known you in such a mood since Jed's death," she said tensely. "What is it, my dear?"

"I'm at the crossroads of my life, and I very much fear"— he faltered—"that I've already made the wrong turn."

"Nonsense! I see only a man, Simon, still young and very lonely. That's your problem."

"Is it?" he said mockingly. "Accept the Howlands' invitation. But just explain that I may be called away."

Mounting the chestnut, he rode away to keep his appointments, his way lit by a brilliant moon. Three rich old ladies with trifling ailments—more bored than sick. A harmless tonic, a chat, and a squeeze of the hand worked wonders. Riding from one grand residence to another, he grimly wondered if he would have to bed Regina Farjeon in order to protect Ariel. As her lover, he might have some influence over her, but once he was dismissed, the hated sister-in-law would be carted off to Bethlem. Of that, he was certain. He must get Farjeon to place her in a home where she could be cherished.

Cherished. The very word disturbed him. Yet never before had he known any woman whose physical presence held him in such thrall. And there was only one remedy for this dangerous infatuation. Get married, as everyone was advising him to do. But first he would have her—take her by force, if necessary—or spend the rest of his life in torment. . . .

Shame drove him the next day to Foulsham's vicar, the Reverend John Duncan, a gentle man who patiently answered more questions about the Farjeons. In every respect, he confirmed Peter Curwen's account, but to Desmond's alarm, he went a step further, siding with Regina Farjeon. Smiling at his guest over a glass of port, he quietly asked, "Would you want her in your house, Desmond? Could you ever trust her? Wouldn't you always be waiting for another breakdown?"

At a loss for words, the young man rose unhappily to take his leave. His host escorted him to the door, his voice low. "There's a rather ugly story circulating that she had a baby. Is it true?" Desmond nodded. "It's also said that she killed it!" Duncan whispered in shocked tones.

Desmond found himself protecting her, as had Nicholas Farjeon at Weston Asylum. "No, it was stillborn. Tell people the truth. Her life is pitiful enough without her being branded a murderess. . . ."

Turning his back on the temptation to visit Bellereve, he drove home in very low spirits. Most likely Regina Farjeon had initiated that gossip. Damn the woman. He would have to do something about her very soon. . . .

During the next few days, his caseload was so heavy that he found it impossible to leave Heydon. Emergencies erupted like mice evacuating a burning building. Beatrice Clayton, observing him, said nothing. The heavy schedule, the ceaseless activity, cut down on his irritability. Thriving in such an atmosphere, he seemed to be his old self, the tint of melancholy gone. She even heard him whistling as he shaved on Saturday morning before he bounded downstairs to breakfast.

"You're in a happy mood!"

"I'm taking a few hours off," he said, smiling, as he helped himself from the sideboard. "God willing, I can fit in everyone later."

"Don't forget, we're due at the Howlands' at eight."

"Ah, yes, I'm to perform my begging-dog bit—"

"Simon!" she muttered reproachfully.

"Sorry, Bea." He sat across from her, trying to contain his nervous excitement. "I'll behave."

Her expression was curious. "Where are you going?"

"I'm taking the chestnut out for a ride." He dove into his meal with relish.

Beatrice looked down at her plate. "You're going to see Ariel Farjeon, aren't you?"

"I might, if I'm out Foulsham way." He poured himself more tea. "After all, I'm paid to do so."

"By whom?"

"Nicholas—the lord and master!"

She kept her voice even. "He has no money. It's all his wife's. . . . I wonder if they'll be there tonight?"

"Regina might," he said vaguely, pulling back his chair. "Must run, love." He gave her a peck. "I'll be back for lunch. Hold the fort. . . ."

For a long time she sat at the table, ignoring the maid, who worked around her. As if oppressed by a bad dream, she tried painfully to remember what her emotions had been like with Jed. Rocky—until they finally married, and then such happiness. The tabby came, twisting around her ankles like a fur boa, purring loudly, and she petted it.

"He's had so little . . ." she whispered. "Maybe Sally Howland will be the answer." Well, they were almost through February. Three more months. And then it would be over. . . .

Catching his ebullition, the horse tore down winding paths, crossed blackened fields, shallow streams, and thick hedges. For an hour, Desmond gave him his lead, then, unable to control his impatience, directed the chestnut to Bellereve. Conifers were getting a new growth; the other trees stood thickly furled with buds. Winter's bleakness was slipping away, and the Farjeon park, normally so still, seemed alive with expectations of spring. A chattering of small animals reached him from the hedgerow; high overhead came the loud booming of a male bittern winging its way to the Norfolk Breckland.

Still, Desmond's pleasure was marred by a tinge of apprehension. How would he find Ariel Farjeon—remote or responsive? And what was he really offering her under the guise of healing physician? A sordid passion, if he wasn't careful. An emotion particularly dangerous to one so fragile. In June, he could walk away with his money, leaving her imprisoned, her heart broken either by tenderness or seduction. But if his infatuation by some miracle changed to love, there was salvation. In love, he wouldn't touch her. It was too cruel. . . .

Approaching the manor-house, his spirits were subdued as he threw the reins to a groom. Softly, he climbed the staircase, hoping to avoid the meddlesome Regina. Not a glimpse of her. Farjeon, too, was away. Again, in the rank courtyard, he saw that spring was even reaching the vines stretched over the ruined wing. Farjeon was right. They obliterated most of the damage, making it oddly romantic except for the horror clutched in its heart.

Ariel Farjeon stood by the moat window, her back toward him. As the door opened, she wheeled about, stricken. Desmond consulted with the old hag, who came scrambling out of the kitchen. A decent carpet had been put down, and odd pieces of furniture—Sheraton and Chippendale—had been added to the room's stock. Rejects from Regina, he thought, smiling. Well, with the drapes, it was somewhat improved.

"Why weren't the outside windows cleaned?"

"Master says no. Don't want her being stared at."

That had never occurred to him. He flicked an anxious glance at his patient. A faint blush touched her cheeks.

"Have you had any trouble?" he asked the Jackal.

"Everybody likes to look at a loony." She smirked. "They caught a local sniffing around the other night—"

Desmond slipped her a few coins. "Go up to the house for tea. I'm taking Miss Farjeon for a walk."

The Jackal gave a loud sniff. "She's not allowed out."

He hurried her on her way. "I'm her doctor. She's perfectly safe with me. Come back in a half-hour," and he slammed the door shut. Turning, he faced Ariel Farjeon.

"How are you?" he asked, crossing the room.

She avoided his eyes, her voice stiff. "Well, thank you."

"Trouble sleeping again, eh?"

She was tense, very nervous. "Yes."

"It's time I gave you something—"

"No!" The anguish in her voice made him pause. With an effort, she controlled herself. "I'm sorry. . . . I know you were responsible for these changes. Thank you."

"I only wish I could do more." He smiled. "Let's take that walk, shall we?"

"We'll be seen!"

"What if we are? I'm taking my patient for an airing. You

need exercise. Who can criticize that?" Reaching into her wardrobe, he pulled out a cloak, moved as always by her out-of-date gowns and the elegance with which she wore them. Helping her into the garment, he let his hands rest on her shoulders. She flinched, and he took her arm. As the door opened, she gave a breathless cry, shielding her eyes from the glare.

"Ariel, forgive me! How long has it been?"

Against him, she sagged, blinking at the golden building opposite. "Months. I was brought home at night. . . ."

Touched, he walked her slowly past the ruined wing, interested to see that she ignored it. Not trusting her body's strength, she moved like an invalid, alert to any pitfalls. In soothing tones, he coaxed her along to the moat.

The grass, brown and withered, fascinated her. She fondled a few blades as if they were precious jewels. "In the spring, it becomes a velvet carpet, thick and soft like moss. Tiny, wild flowers grow all around that wing." She nodded at the ruin. "And the moat is more beautiful than a Constable, with its cloud of water lilies. . . ."

A red squirrel frisked across the far side, stumbling over the weight of a pine cone. Ariel Farjeon watched, enthralled, her face wet with tears.

Desmond looked around. No one in sight. Very gently, he murmured against her brow, "I don't want to leave you."

The gray eyes grew sad. "But you do and always will. . . ."

A shadow passed across the sun, bringing with it winter's chill. Loathe to return to reality, he whispered, "How lovely you are!" And he took her back to her stone prison and locked her in. . . .

Standing in Edward Howland's lavish conservatory, Simon Desmond was uncomfortably reminded of his father's country house in Kent. Both of these irregular mock castles were built in the Picturesque style, every room against its park setting a hymn to Gothic taste. All show and little substance underneath the opulent glitter but a fitting backdrop for a nouveau riche gentleman with expectations of knighthood.

Footmen circulated through the packed rooms, carrying goblets of champagne on silver trays. In the conservatory, cathedral windows lined the walls—moonlight vying with candles and fairylights twinkling from columns and arches. The long room was redolent with perfume and hothouse flowers. Desmond had taken refuge by a far window where he could observe the

guests. Many were his patients, and he had been greeted with
a dash of malice.

Malice in watching eyes whenever he and Sally Howland
talked. At odd moments, he wondered whether he had joined
her throng of admirers or was being used as a wedge to separate
her from a too ardent suitor or to spur on another, because he
certainly found her readily available.

No one could fault her charm. At age twenty-three, with a
mass of light-brown curls; amber eyes dancing under wisps of
eyebrows; a saucy nose, dimpled cheeks, and a mouth that
turned from pout to laugh in a second—she was captivating.
Skillfully, she kept some of her beaux at arm's length; others
were encouraged with flirtatious looks.

Now she stood gazing up at Simon Desmond, an impish
gleam in her eyes. "Aren't you having a good time, Dr. Desmond?"

"Very much, Miss Howland. Just catching a moment's rest.
I've been on my feet for three days running—"

"Well, I know the perfect tonic for keeping you awake."
Seizing his arm, she swept him off to the octagonal drawing
room. Candles glimmered in crystal chandeliers, the rich oak
shone, and a large group of musicians burst into a Strauss waltz
as they glided onto the floor. Her evening gown was white and
gold, as ornate as the room's floral design. Around and around
they spun, her chatter amusing him, the great pier glasses
catching their animated reflexion.

Abruptly, she stopped her banter. "I hear you're treating
Ariel Farjeon. . . ."

"Yes," he said warily.

"They say she's raving mad!"

"Nothing of the sort! Where did you learn such rubbish?"

"Oh, everyone knows it," she cried lyrically. "Is it true that
she had a baby?"

"Dear Miss Howland." He bent over the elfin face. "I never
discuss my patients. It's against professional ethics." His smile
was charming. "Where did you hear that story?"

"It's common gossip. Now we're all trying to guess the
baby's father!" Her eyes shone. "They say she was a great
beauty and could have married a peer. Imagine, ending up like
that!"

"Well, pity her, then," Desmond said, trying to still his
emotions. "And stop the talk. It's kitchen prattle. . . ." Glancing
across the room, he spotted a group of people drinking by the

marble fireplace. Among the party surrounding the diminutive
Edward Howland were the Farjeons, Nicholas and Regina.

Noticing them, Sally giggled. "Speak of the Devil!" She
dragged Desmond through whirling couples to her father's side.

"Ah, Desmond, isn't this more fun than attending sickbeds?"
Howland asked with a chuckle.

"A splendid gala, sir!"

"You know Nicholas Farjeon, of course?"

The two men muttered the expected pleasantries, then Howland winked at Regina. "But I don't believe you've met the
beauteous Mrs. Farjeon!"

"Just once," Desmond replied, aware of Farjeon's surprise.
Taking Regina's hand, he bowed. She was the only woman
dressed in red, but with her coloring and too ample figure, a
more subtle hue might have tantalized and won her the admirers
she sought. Now all but the most blatant avoided her. A very
odd match indeed, Desmond thought.

"I saw you walking today with my unfortunate sister-in-
law." She smiled, her voice unnecessarily loud. "Isn't that
dangerous? What if she turned on you?" Cold blue eyes flashed
in Farjeon's direction. His face was ashen.

"I see no danger. None whatsoever," Desmond replied.

"Good heavens, sir, you sound infatuated!" Others joined
in her coarse laugh.

He stood his ground. "She's no more mad than I am. And
many things have been said about me, but not that—"

"Dance with me," Regina said on impulse.

Many women had he danced with in his life, and he knew
instinctively how they wanted to be held. As he pulled her to
him roughly, she caught her breath in pleased surprise. Still
smiling, Desmond argued quietly, "She's not crazy, I tell you.
You've nothing to fear." Farjeon was watching them, an ironic
smile on his lips. Take the risk, Desmond thought. It may be
the only chance. "She belongs neither in Bethlem nor that stone
atrocity. I'll find a family—"

"That costs money."

"Money well spent. Do you want her misery on your conscience?"

She tossed her head angrily. "My conscience is concerned
with other things, doctor. The welfare of my children—"

"She's incapable of harm!"

Her cry cut like a knife. "She killed her bastard!"

Around them rose a hum of voices, rippling across the room to the conservatory beyond. A shocked Desmond exploded.

"That's a lie. Wanton cruelty to force her back among the insane!"

Sally Howland and her father appeared with discreet speed. Separating the combatants, Howland whispered in Regina's ear, and she laughed. Arm in arm, they drifted out of the crowded chamber. The younger woman stared at Desmond.

"I didn't know you cared so much—"

"I care nothing about her," he tensely interrupted. "But I will not have any of my patients maligned."

"I like loyalty in a man." With a thoughtful smile, she held out her arms for another dance.

At midnight came a supper that would have undone King Henry VIII. Wine flowed endlessly with each course. The musicians played from a gallery. Desmond found himself seated next to Sally Howland. At one point during the long meal, she whispered to him behind her fan, "You must apologize to Regina."

His face went livid. "Whatever for?"

Toying with a piece of fruit, she smiled at his naïveté. "It just might help your patient, Dr. Desmond. She can be quite vicious when crossed."

"I'm surprised to see Farjeon here." He glanced down the immense table. "I heard he was a recluse."

"True, but he always wants money from Papa, and our invitations are seldom refused." She winked at Desmond. "And do you, too, seek a loan, sir?"

"No," he lied. "I came for a pleasant evening."

"Has it been?"

"Yes—superb," he admitted, trying to block out Ariel Farjeon's heartbreaking face. . . .

More dancing and champagne followed. Couples disappeared to the great rooms' shadows. Women's soft laughter floated over the music. In the early morning hours, Desmond, more than relaxed from champagne, made a charming apology to Regina Farjeon.

She accepted it with a slow smile, her eyes and mouth hungry, but an escort stood beside her. "Perhaps, Dr. Desmond, we might discuss this at greater length at Bellereve. . . ."

He met her frank look with one equally as bold. "I should be honored." He gave her hand a lingering kiss. Afterward, he sought out Farjeon, finally locating him in the library, a pretentious room filled with expensive sets of unread books. Ariel's brother stood at a Gothic window, gazing out at the park and the great oaks marshalled before the house. Hearing footsteps, he turned, his brooding face etched in sadness.

"Now you see what I'm up against, Desmond."

"Yes, sir, I do, but I felt I must speak out. Best to contradict her if your sister's tragedy is on everyone's tongue. I only hope I've not made things worse. I have apologized—"

"Ah, yes, she likes people crawling to her. That gains you a point, Desmond. I am grateful to you. . . ." He returned to his study of the landscape, the interview over.

On the way home to Fairhaven, Beatrice sighed, "Such a lovely party. I think you made a hit with Sally Howland."

"Nonsense. She saw no more of me than anyone else."

She shivered, huddling in her pelisse, hands clasped over a warmer in her muff. "I only wish Ariel Farjeon's name hadn't come up. That was unfortunate."

"Why?"

"Well, I understand, dear, but some people were astounded at your championing her."

"Dear God, she's my patient! Was I to stand idly by and let that virago spew out her poison? It's time these gentry knew the truth."

"And will that keep her mouth shut?" Wearily, she shook her head. "How will it all end, Simon?"

He flicked the horse lightly with his whip, an ache filling his heart. "I don't know. . . ."

Five hours to sleep. It had been the most exhilarating night Desmond had spent in a long time. Not since London had he seen such largess, but here there was no sense of disgust, except for that wretched encounter with Regina Farjeon.

Sally Howland was a pretty little thing, he thought, turning restlessly on his pillow. Adored by her father, she would bring her husband a magnificent dowry, and he laughed out loud. How would she like being a doctor's wife? The bell jangled sharply over his head. Swearing, he felt for the box of Lucifer matches on his bedside cabinet and lit a Wizard lamp. Overhead, silence. Throwing on his robe and carpet slippers, he padded quietly downstairs so as not to awaken Bea across the hall. No one stood waiting at the door. Baffled, he went to each one in turn. No sound of horses, no hurried footsteps—nothing. A dream, he thought dully, his eyes trying to pierce the still night redolent with boxwood.

Slowly, he climbed up to his bedroom. Yes, he was certain Sally Howland would resent such interruptions, the petty annoyance of always being at someone's beck and call. Now if he were a Harley Street physician. . . .

Someone was waiting for him in the large brass bed. Naked, lying on the coverlet with legs spread wide—Regina Farjeon. "Give me what I want," she hissed, "and I'll play your little game. I knew what you were the minute I saw you. . . ." The lamplight quivered over her flesh. She laughed as he turned down the wick.

"You'll leave her alone? Not torment her?" he cried urgently, fumbling for her body. Grasping air, he awoke with a start, alone in the bed, weeping against the pillows. . . .

Someone was sitting beside her, bending over her face. She caught the stale whiff of perfume, powder, perspiration, liquor, and smoke. Smoke. If she lay very still, pretending to be asleep, she might be left alone. Wreaths of smoke drifted about her bed, making her gag as the building was engulfed in flames. Smoke coiled about her, and she threw off the worn blanket, arms outstretched in terror. A flash of fire shot into her eyes, and a gloating face emerged—a goblin peeping from a hedgerow.

"Ariel. Ariel!" called a sly voice. "I came to share my evening with you. . . ." The hideous face grimaced, and she recognized Regina Farjeon.

"Ah, that's better," said the older woman, pinching her cheek. "I like an audience when I speak. . . ." She sighed. "Poor thing, how bored you must be."

Ariel Farjeon sat up, muscles aching from the rude couch. "You are kind to visit me," she said in the old voice used to address a governess, the tone that so amused Nicholas. "I want no more of these mincing manners," he had chided her, laughing. "Answer me from the heart. . . ."

"Yes, aren't I?" giggled her visitor. "Well, we went to a ball at the Howlands', and guess who was there?" Not waiting for an answer, she shrieked in glee, "Simon Desmond, of all people! Your doctor, my pet. Goodness! Away from his patients, he loses that dour look. The man's quite passionate. We danced together several times, and he held me so close—" Ariel's face was expressionless in the lantern's glare. "So tightly, I was embarrassed. From his manner, I think he fancies me!"

Again, came a raucous laugh. "Later, he caught up with me in a room where lovers drift. And his hands—" She was breathing hard.

"Yes, Mrs. Farjeon?" Ariel's voice was flat.

"In the dark, his mouth seized mine, and his hands clasped me here—" She stroked her plump bosom.

Say it. Say it. She wants it said. . . . "And he made love to you, Mrs. Farjeon?"

"Would have, I know, but others were present. So we'll just have to wait for another occasion." She yawned loudly. Wrapping her fur-lined cape more tightly, she rose. "I thought you'd like a little chat." She kissed Ariel's forehead. "Enjoy him, too, while you can. He's probably the last handsome man you'll ever see. He's going to certify you. All this coming and going—mere pretense. Had to do that so Foulsham can't say we abandoned you. . . . Well, good night, my dear. How nice that we're getting to be friends! People think me very brave."

Ariel covered her face. "I do appreciate it."

"Look at me." There was no response. "Look at me, damn it!" Stricken eyes looked into hers. "How could you do it?" Regina Farjeon asked in horror. "Kill your baby?"

Tears ran down the younger woman's cheeks, and Regina smiled. "Weeping won't bring the poor little creature back. Nor will a lifetime in an asylum—"

"He's going to send me to Bedlam?" Ariel cried fearfully.

"Yes, dear." She hesitated. "Of course, you could save us all a lot of bother. Why don't you kill yourself . . . ?"

Abruptly, Simon Desmond found himself in a frantic social whirl. During the next few weeks, a flurry of invitations descended on him and Beatrice Clayton. Dinners, soirées, balls, musicales—the list was endless. Whenever free he went, if only to distract himself from Ariel Farjeon. His visits to her of late had been somewhat disconcerting. She seemed unhappy, ill at ease, at times clearly frightened. No longer did the beautiful gray eyes light up with pleasure at the sight of him; now her glance was wary. Desmond, confused and shamed by his emotions, probed no more deeply than necessary. It was enough if she received good food, warm clothing, and an infrequent outing. The tremor of her hands when they touched, the occasional slovenliness in her appearance, failed to impress him. Not once did it occur to him that she might be grieving. A state of affairs normal in a man seeking to rid himself of one woman while courting a second. A jewel had dropped into his lap, and he'd be a fool to let her escape. Ariel Farjeon was beautiful and had touched his heart, but for all human purposes she was as good as dead. The visits were cut to a minimum.

So Desmond concentrated on the living, amused to find Sally Howland glued to his side, as persistent as a burr. If she missed him at a party, she made a trip to his surgery, popping into Fairhaven at all hours. The least thing—a sliver, a broken fingernail—served as an excuse for ministration, or she would take tea with Beatrice and be mischievously pleased if Desmond joined them. Several times, she even accompanied him on horseback while he made rounds.

Still, there were days at a time when he didn't see her, and he found, to his perplexity, that he never once thought of her. The prattle, which had charmed, now bored him. A caustic band ran like a knife through the skittish wit. Beneath the fawn lay a fox.

One day, he realized that he disliked her. Yet he had for a month paid such court to this animated doll that he was taken seriously, to his chagrin. Forgotten were all her rabid beaux, still pursuing her assiduously. All of Heydon, watching with breathless, spiteful interest, had Desmond and Sally Howland yoked for life. Beatrice Clayton secretly congratulated herself on her matchmaking efforts, and in the grandiose mansion the banker and his daughter waited for the suitor's proposal.

"Are you sure you want this man for a husband?" her father asked in a quiet moment.

"Yes, Papa. He doesn't scrape like the others, but once he's mine, I'll bend him like a willow." She trilled with laughter.

Still, Desmond made no move. . . .

A package came for him from a Norwich bookseller. He put it aside to be delivered later.

A second came for Ariel Farjeon at Bellereve. One that she refused to open.

The voice was speaking rapidly with suppressed excitement, words biting in the dark. "Someone sent you a package, dear. Who was it?"

Wearily, she turned her head on the couch. "I don't know, ma'am. I know no one who would send me anything."

Regina Farjeon gave her a familiar nudge. "I bet it's a secret admirer! Maybe that chap who got a peep at you. Everyone knows you're back. Perhaps it's one of your lost loves, pining. . . . Let's open it, shall we?" Ripping apart the frayed string and brown paper wrapping, she gave a feigned shriek of dismay.

"God, who would send such a thing!"

Ariel Farjeon began to rock backward and forward in dumb grief.

 *Six*

Closing his surgery door on his last patient, Simon Desmond strolled into his consulting room, his mood pensive. It was time to call in a second opinion. Ariel Farjeon had slipped disastrously. He, who had deliberately closed his eyes to her changed condition, was reawakening. How could he not notice when he was perhaps the cause? Holding out a hand and then brutally withdrawing it when she most needed him.

He penned a swift note to Reepham's Colin Broughton—once his rival, now a close friend. Two days later, a message came.

> *I see no evidence of a mentally well woman. On the contrary, she is extremely unstable and, I fear, close to a breakdown. I strongly recommend incarceration.*

Desmond stared at the letter, dumbfounded, then tossed it into the fire. How long had it been since his last visit? A week. What had happened? Dr. Portman's voice rang in his ears. "A Medusa without the snakes . . ." Had he been so bewitched that he imagined a sick woman well? Impossible! Portman thought her cured. Yet these withdrawals always coincided with his prolonged absences.

Very much on edge, he returned to Bellereve. The guardian of the stone suite sat grumpily in the sitting room. Desmond saw no sign of Ariel Farjeon.

"Where is she?" he asked coldly.

Wiping her nose on her apron, the Jackal ambled over to him. "Very strange, she's been, sir. I don't like being around her."

"What do you mean by 'strange'?"

"Won't talk. Won't eat. Don't dress proper."

He forced a smile. "And I ask again—where is she?"

She jerked her head toward the small room. "In there. But I'd stay out if I was you. She's been so queer—"

Desmond slipped into the miserable room. Against the far wall stood Ariel Farjeon, barefoot in a shabby nightgown, her back toward him, not gazing longingly through murky panes but at something held in her arms. Softly, he called her name. A slight movement of her body indicated she had heard him, but there was no reply.

As a medical student studying insanity, he had been repelled by a drawing in Taylor's *Medical Jurisprudence* of a woman in a fit of mania: hair standing on end as if shot through with bolts of electricity, teeth bared like a wild animal's, eyes ready to kill. The contrasting sketch of the same patient in a lucid interval, with its sickly sweetness, was equally devastating. He didn't want to touch Ariel Farjeon and find such horror.

"Please speak to me. . . ."

She stood mute.

"Speak! Don't hide from me," he cried, his fear increasing. "Each time, I promise not to be away too long. Always, something happens. How can I undo this hurt?" He touched her shoulder, but she was deaf to his pleas. Taking a deep breath, he swung her around. The face under the disordered hair was as remote as when first they met. Against her breast, she clutched something wrapped in his shawl—a bundle that she surrendered without protest. Slowly, he unwound the soft purple wool. A doll lay revealed. A baby doll.

"Jesus! Where did you get this?" No answer. "Who gave you the doll, Ariel?"

At his wits' end, he began searching the room, finally locating a cord and some brown paper stuffed underneath the thin mattress. By the feeble light, he saw that the postmark had been washed out. He flicked a glance at Ariel Farjeon, still locked in a dream, her face begrimed, then he walked out to the sitting room.

"Who gave her this?" He waved the doll at the Jackal.

She gaped in genuine astonishment. "No, I ain't never seen it before. My, what a wonder!"

"It didn't walk in here. Now think!"

She made an effort. "Five days ago, a package came—"

"Yes?"

"But she wouldn't open it."

"Why not?"

"Said she didn't know anyone who'd send a package."

"When was it opened?"

"Well, I ain't seen it 'round her for a few days—"

"When did she start going in there?"

Her look was baleful. "Think you owe me something, sir."

"You'll get your pittance when you tell me why Miss Farjeon went into a room she so detests!"

"I don't know what fancies creep into her head. She went in"—there was a laborious counting of knobby, sticky fingers—"when the package went."

"Has she been in there continuously?"

"As long as I'm here, sir." She fawned. "Don't know what goes on at night."

"When did she stop dressing?"

"Well, she got very careless several days ago. All wanton, she was!" She grinned at him lewdly.

"Who sent it to her?" Desmond asked, fighting impatience.

"Lord knows, sir. Ask her. Ask the loony!"

Controlling his repugnance, he tossed her a sovereign. "She's not crazy," he whispered. "And I'm counting on you to take good care of her." Hurrying back to Ariel's cell, he found her still transfixed. "Who sent you the parcel, Ariel?"

She winced, obviously hearing him.

Desmond waited, tapping a boot on the rough stone floor. The bars on the window began writhing. His nerves felt strung out. "Who sent it, damn it!" No reply. His patience snapped, and he slapped her across the face, hard. Like a broken statue, she toppled to the floor, weeping. Bereft, he clasped her to his chest.

"Hush, my dearest. Hush. . . ." He ran gentle hands through her hair. "Tell me who gave you the doll?"

Her breathing was labored. "You did. . . ."

A pounding on the door interrupted them. In a cold fury, Desmond opened it to the fawning Jackal.

"Beg pardon, sir, but this came." She thrust out a grimy slip of paper. An urgent summons to attend a Cottage Row woman in labor. With an oath he returned to Ariel Farjeon, still on her knees.

Warming her icy hands in his, he said urgently, "I didn't give you that doll, Ariel. I gave you a book of poems, which was destroyed. Now, *who* opened the package?"

She looked stunned, as if pulling out of a trance. Beads of perspiration dotted her forehead, her face was translucent. "By night . . . Regina—"

"Regina opened the package?"

"Yes." Her expression was terrified. "Don't tell!"

Stifling his anger, he soothed her. "No, I won't say anything. Not now. Don't be afraid. But I want you to bathe, get dressed, and leave this room," he added softly. "I must go now, and I'm taking this 'thing' with me." Thrusting the doll under his arm, he raised her to her feet. "Tomorrow I'll be back—" A shy smile illuminated her face, and he stroked it, murmuring, "You are sane, Ariel. I would stake my whole career on it. . . . I've not abandoned you. If Regina Farjeon comes tonight, remember that I'll be with you tomorrow."

"Come soon," she whispered. "The pretense is hard. . . ."

Pretense. The word haunted him. Sanity or insanity—to which did it refer? Fortunately, for his unquiet mind, he faced a rough confinement: a breech birth, no sooner successfully concluded than he was greeted at three in the morning by a frantic call from another cottage. A youth of fifteen, repairing a thatched roof, had fallen and broken his leg. Out of the torn, bloody stretch of ragged skin stuck a piece of bone.

Desmond winced. "I'm sorry, it's got to come off—"

"What? The bone?"

"No, the leg—"

The boy screamed, frantically trying to escape. Grasping him in a vise, Desmond addressed the parents in tired anger. "This is a compound fracture. His chances aren't good, but they're much greater if I amputate."

The mother's face, gray with hunger and despair, was pleading. "Nothing else to be done, sir?"

"No, the bone is too badly splintered. It's not a clean fracture."

Strapped down on a rickety kitchen table, with his parents standing nearby in horrified suspense and his siblings crying against dirty whitewashed walls, Desmond cut off that young leg. Mercifully, he was able to drug the boy with chloroform.

Tying off the vessels with long silk threads, he said a silent prayer, then quietly packed up his bag.

"He's strong and will make it. Soon he'll outhop you all!" He smiled at the cowering youngsters. A giggle came from one, and he drew the grieving parents over to the prostrate body. "You understand, I had to do it! If it doesn't get infected, he'll live."

Stupefied with sorrow, they nodded, searching for his payment. The mother held out a Blue Willow pitcher.

"Thank you," Desmond whispered gently, "but it's your crops I look forward to. Bring me some. . . ."

Returning home to Fairhaven, he caught the scent of flowers in the Elizabethen garden, and the sweet song of a nightingale. On his pillow lay a note from Edward Howland.

> *Will you join me for luncheon today at the Green Dragon? I'll be at my usual table.*

Desmond sent an acceptance, then shaved and changed his clothes. After a Spartan breakfast in his bedroom, he sauntered downstairs to the surgery. Waiting for his first patient, he glanced at the cottage garden tumbling between brick walkways. It, too, was beginning to bloom. Thinking of Ariel Farjeon, he smiled. Then his face went grim. Today he would have to tackle Farjeon, show him that loathsome doll. Put an end to Regina's mischief.

Shortly before one, Desmond joined banker Howland in the timber-framed Green Dragon, once an ancient inn, now a flourishing public house. He found Edward Howland seated at a table in the eating parlor, next to a bow window where he could oversee the village green's activities. The lunch was standard but of surprisingly good fare, a superior bottle of wine—one stocked for special customers—replacing the usual beer or ale. Trivialities were discussed until coffee arrived, then Howland settled down to business.

"Well, Desmond, I think you know why I invited you here!"

"Not really, sir."

In a penetrating voice that shook every ear in the room, Howland began, "What are your intentions toward my daughter?"

Desmond flushed. "Can't we discuss this someplace else? It's much too public."

"Chosen deliberately"—the banker smiled—"to force it into the open. Now, just what are your intentions, sir?"

"I think of her as a friend."

"No more?" The older man looked staggered.

The sharp pain in his heart told Desmond what a fool he had been, dallying with one woman while turning his back on the only woman he would ever love. A love that could never be reciprocated or consummated, because his heart's darling might be a madwoman. Somehow, in the dark, lonely hours of sleepless nights or in dreams, pity and lust had turned to love. . . .

"We thought you sincere." Howland fumed over his coffee cup.

"I was. I still am. We are friends."

"Oh, no, you're not, Desmond." Heads turned curiously in their direction. By evening this tête-à-tête would be all over the village, his guest thought grimly. "We thought you something else, and now you'll make my daughter the laughing stock of Heydon—"

"I hardly think that, sir. She has many admirers. Had we discussed this in private, few people would know."

Howland leaned forward, his face purple with anger. "We picked you as the most promising young stud in the area. What Norfolk needs is new blood and vigor, and you have both. Too many milksops among these gentry. You've a rough background, I warrant, as rough as mine, but with my wealth and influence, we might push you into Parliament."

"You want your daughter married to a man who doesn't love her?" Desmond asked in disgust.

The banker sneered. "Love! Is that what you want? I thought you ambitious, not a lily-livered, sentimental fool."

"I'm as ruthless as they come and have never hesitated to take what I want—when I wanted it." He smiled coldly. "Sally is charming, but not for me."

"You have compromised her, sir."

"If so, it was not a deliberate deceit. Your daughter, I think, cares no more for me than I for her."

Howland's fury changed to a purr. "You're a brothel habitué, aren't you, Dr. Desmond?"

"Rarely." The hazel eyes flashed. "My practice and social life keep me fully occupied."

"I wouldn't bank on having either much longer, doctor!"

"You can't frighten me, Howland. It's not the first time I've been knocked down and climbed up again."

"I don't doubt it. That's what I liked about you. A pity we can't do business." He rose, a small venomous figure. "But this time, Desmond, you're staying on the bottom. . . ."

"I don't want to worry you, Beatrice," Desmond explained at the close of the second clinic, "but I'm afraid I've made a rather dangerous enemy—Edward Howland. I turned down his proposal to marry Sally."

She stared at him in open-mouthed astonishment.

"I couldn't bear a night, let alone a lifetime with that woman—" He faltered. "Things may get rough." In the sunlight's harsh glare streaming in through the parlor windows, he was suddenly aware of tiny lines, like a spider's web, crossing her face. For once her gaiety failed her.

"The fault is mine, Simon. I pushed you into it."

"It doesn't matter. We are completely incompatible. So there's an end to it."

"But you must find a wife, my dear." She sniffed into a handkerchief. "You can't keep visiting those . . . houses!"

"I am discreet. Am I hurting anyone?"

"All right, keep doing it!" she said with sudden vehemence. "Other men do it, too. Not your brother, but my second husband had his doxy—" She took a deep breath. "As a bachelor, Simon, such conduct is suspect. Marry and few will question your peccadillos. If you can't abide Sally Howland, plenty of eligible young women roam these pastures. . . ."

"I need love," he cried passionately. "Don't deny me my chance for happiness." He strode out into the hall. "I'm off to Bellereve."

She followed him out to the cottage garden, watching as he picked a posy: jonquils, hyacinth, and impatiens.

"They say she's still very beautiful. Is she?"

Caught off guard, he laughed. "Yes, a face to rival an angel's." He set off jauntily for the stable.

Ariel Farjeon was waiting for him, radiant in a lilac mohair walking dress, her hair tied back simply. Shooing the Jackal up to Bellereve's kitchen, Desmond set down a package on a tripod table, then gave Ariel his bouquet.

Her eyes shone. "How beautiful they are!"

"Only the most simple from our garden. Just to remind you that spring is on its way. Impatiens was my favorite as a child.

We had a great bank of them in Kent, and I used to roll in them like a sultan on his cushions."

A faint shadow darkened her expression. Burying her face in the flowers, she quickly asked, "What were you like as a little boy?"

"A scamp! Naughty and bedraggled as a puppy. I got into so many scrapes it's a wonder I ever survived." He smiled ruefully, remembering. "Father administered the cane; Mother and my brother Jed gave me love. He was the one who took me in hand after her death. Father had packed me off to Rugby— I was interfering with his backstairs romance." He sneered. "Jed saved my life. Convinced me to make something of myself."

Her smile was sympathetic. "And so you became a doctor?"

"Yes. You haven't opened my gift." He cleared his throat.

She winced. "I'm not allowed scissors or a knife."

Making light of an obviously embarrassing moment, Desmond drew out his pocketknife and cut the string.

"Shakespeare! My favorite!" With disbelief, she saw that there was something else: a sketch pad and a box of watercolors.

"Now that should keep you busy for a while, eh?"

Her eyes brimmed with tears. Trying to control his racing heart, he gently embraced her.

"I don't know how to thank you," she said in a muffled tone.

"Just continue on as you're doing."

"How many months do I have left?"

"A little under three."

Against him, she trembled. "He's going to send me away, isn't he?"

"No, Ariel, he wants you here. It's Regina who's fighting it." He picked up the bouquet. "Best put these in water or they'll wilt." Hand in hand, they strolled out to the kitchen. Smiling at him, she filled an earthenware jug from the tap. Watching her arrange the flowers, he was charmed by her grace. "You know I'll do everything possible to help you." His voice was husky. "Did she come last night?"

"Yes, she seldom misses a night."

Desmond grimaced. "I'm proud of you, Ariel. You met me as if nothing at all was the matter." Their eyes locked. "Why does she come?"

"To bait me." Her face was pinched with strain. "She comes

at any hour. I think she's trying to drive me mad. If I have a relapse, I go. And she wants me in Bedlam."

Desmond walked her back to the sitting room. "That won't happen, not if I have a say in the matter. I know—your brother knows—that Weston Asylum considers you now sane. Eleven years of sanity pitted against one year's madness. Surely two individuals and an institution can protect you."

"But my lapses!" she moaned.

The withdrawals, the long periods of silence. Some might call it insanity, as Broughton had. Desmond, however, was beginning to see another side to the picture. Self-protection, perhaps.

Ariel Farjeon sank into a chair, overcome with grief. "She said I killed my baby!"

Simon Desmond hesitated. "Do you remember doing such a thing?" he asked cautiously.

She looked at him in horror. "Did I have a baby? I can't remember. God, why can't I remember? Even when she gave me that doll, it meant nothing. Nothing!" She wept.

"Why did you take it into the other room?"

The gray eyes were dazed. "I thought I might remember. Somewhere I've been through that before . . . in some other room . . . Fire burning. . . ." She shuddered. "What's the matter with me, Dr. Desmond?"

"Nothing," he murmured, deeply moved. "I'll talk to your brother. We'll put a stop to these damnable visits." He stroked her face. "Oh, my dear, had you been mad, you would have suffered a breakdown by now. . . ." In another moment, he would kiss that full mouth. Pulling away from temptation, he fetched her cloak. "Let's go for a walk. . . ." He took her out to the moat. "What else does she talk about?" he asked as they strolled up and down.

Her body went rigid. "My lovers," she shamefully confessed. "She says there was more than one. That my brother kept no young manservant at Bellereve, because my conduct was so notorious. . . ." In despair, she searched his face. "I don't remember, Simon. Only one man—"

Mastering his fury, he cried, "Look! Just look about you!" Every branch crackled with life. Birds, small animals, leaves— the park was awakening. Arms entwined, they stood rapt, gazing out at the great forest encroaching upon the moat.

"You've given me back my life. Hope. Thank you!" she breathed.

"Your hair in this light is almost blond. Flaxen, as mine was as a child."

She laughed delightedly. "Little scamp!"

"Read. Draw a picture for me everyday. Fill the pad."

Her eyes glowed.

"Promise?"

She nodded.

He wanted to say it. To tell her what she meant to him, but he couldn't. "I must see your brother now, but I'll be back tomorrow, even if I have to skip clinic."

Fear clouded her eyes. "What if Nicholas confirms Regina's accusations?"

"I doubt it, Ariel. Everyone I've talked with calls your previous behavior irreproachable. But should there be one iota of truth in her remarks, remember that you were once very ill and certainly not responsible for your actions." He smiled tenderly. "I believe in you."

The storm left her face. She was again the most lovely of women—radiant in her innocence.

What did she think about in the dark, lying on that rude couch in her stone prison? Desmond wondered, fetching the doll from his trap. Did any of the horrors surface? The banished lover, the dead baby, the later atrocities... Did they come as dream fragments, frightening her in the eerie stillness, the dirty, rough walls still reeking of smoke from the ruined wing? And did day bring forgetfulness, so that the bewitching face relaxed into its exquisite perfection?

A dazzling sun streamed in through the library's oriel and bay windows, each one overlooking the ruined building. Uneasily, Desmond peered out, trying to learn just how much Farjeon could see. Nothing inside—the grime-encrusted windows took care of that—but he would be aware of all comings and goings. And what of the small patch of ground where Desmond and Ariel walked? Was he privy to that as well? No, he thought with relief, alarmed by a violent stab of jealousy. Whatever happened during the next months, he must be very, very careful. His objective was to lodge her in a home. Damn it! He'd gladly pay her expenses, if necessary. Anything to keep her out of Bethlem's hell or the loneliness of life at Bellereve.

A noise behind yanked him out of his reverie. Nicholas Farjeon stood before him in rolled up shirtsleeves, the black matte of hair on his chest blatantly exposed. Again, Desmond was awed by the man's powerful physique. Examining his face, he was touched by the startling resemblance to Ariel. Both shared those peculiar gray eyes—silver with a touch of gold about the pupil, so in certain lights they seemed to glow with feline grace. But the delicacy of her features was coarsened in her brother's. The ethereal became sensual. Still, as a young man, he must have been remarkably handsome.

"All sane Farjeons have watched the sick through those windows. You understand the burden . . . ?" Nodding in sympathy, Desmond took his usual chair.

"How is she?" the brother asked softly, frowning at the unexpected parcel lying before him on the desk-table.

"I find her greatly improved. She speaks with intelligence and vigor." He took the proferred glass of brandy. "But there is something distressing—" Farjeon raised an eyebrow. "Apparently, your wife has been visiting Miss Farjeon."

He looked baffled. "Whatever for? She hates Ariel."

"Your sister fears she's being baited—that it's a ploy to send her to Bethlem. A breakdown now would be disastrous—" Desmond broke the string on the parcel, exposing the doll.

Farjeon drew back, appalled. "Dear God, where did you get that?" he finally whispered.

"It came to your sister about five days ago. She didn't touch it. It was your wife, paying one of her visits, who unwrapped it."

"Of course, Regina would think of such a thing. Anything to get rid of Ariel." Scooping up the doll, he bent over it. "How long have these visits been going on?"

"For some time, I gather—nightly."

With a furious movement, Farjeon flung the doll across the room. "What has my wife been saying?"

"Well, the doll represents the dead baby—obviously. She's been told she killed it—" At Farjeon's outraged cry, Desmond added mildly, "I am only repeating your sister's words. There's talk of her lover, and other affairs." The brother grimaced. "But the extraordinary thing is that she seems to recall none of it—"

"I don't understand!"

"The last twelve years of her life have been horrific. Years too painful to bear, and so she forgets."

Nicholas Farjeon leaned forward, fascinated. "Then you think she remembers nothing?"

"Oh, bits and pieces, perhaps—unless she's a facile liar,

which I doubt. She can't explain the past, can't put it together. That's why these visits are so harmful. She must be awakened very gently."

Farjeon lounged in his chair, running a finger across his mouth. "If that's the case, would she still blame me?"

Desmond shrugged. "I think not."

The older man began to pace the room in growing excitement. "Then might it be possible for me to see her?"

"Yes, I think so. I'd risk it if you would, but just give me a few more days. She's still quite apprehensive, and there's something about that small room—" He studied his host. "Why does she so dislike it?"

Farjeon's look was grim. "All our mad relatives slept there. A fact Ariel has known since childhood. Grandfather died in that room. Others before him. A suicide, two raving. . . . Even with scant memory, she can sense its grief."

Desmond looked away at the doll. Its head had been bashed against the marble fireplace, and the sad little face was now pitifully indented, its skull smashed like an egg. A way to kill used by some distraught mothers. But Ariel Farjeon's child had been overlain. . . . Taking out a handkerchief, he dabbed his brow. "Did Dr. Broughton discuss his findings with you?"

There was a long pause. Farjeon, clearly upset, stood gazing out the oriel window. "Yes, Desmond, he did. . . ."

His body tensed. "And your wife? Does she know?"

"No."

Simon Desmond was on his feet, urgently speaking. "I'm convinced his visit came after she saw that doll. Yesterday she was in a bad state—withdrawn, frightened. But the woman who met me today was completely different—" So touched was he by the memory that he faltered, then in the next moment, plagued by doubts, he wondered if she had guessed his secret. "She has great strength—" he added distantly.

"What am I to do, doctor?" Farjeon's voice bridled.

Desmond took himself in hand. "Forget Broughton," he ordered. "Not knowing her case, he jumped to the wrong conclusion. So would I in such a situation. Her behavior, for a while, was erratic. I'll have a word with him, and perhaps you would be good enough to speak to your wife."

For the first time, Nicholas Farjeon smiled. "Rest assured, Dr. Desmond, that will be done. . . ."

Driving away from Bellereve, Desmond found to his annoyance that he had forgotten the doll and his pocketknife.

Hopefully, Farjeon would destroy the blasted thing, and the knife was of no great importance—an unexpected prize for the Jackal.

In Fairhaven's drive, he checked his pocketwatch. A quarter of an hour before the second clinic. As the trap was led off to the stable, he turned and made a slow survey of the cottage garden. How long ago had it been? Only two short hours—no more—when he'd stepped out with a light heart to pick a bouquet for a lovely woman under a sky more blue than a crush of sapphires. Now earth and sky were gray—as gray as London's streets. On such days—soul-killing, he called them—he disliked Norfolk, finding no comfort in seared fields, washed-out pebbled cottages, and bleak church spires glistening in the rain, turning their backs on the lost. It reminded him too much of his life's failures.

He loathed the color of gray except in her eyes, where it became as touching as a rainbow. Dully, almost as an after-thought, he stuck a jonquil into his buttonhole and went inside. Bessie, the parlor maid, took his hat, coat, and bag, her brown corkscrew curls dancing like sausages under a rigorously starched cap. Desmond glanced into the darkened parlor. "Where's Mrs. Clayton?"

The young thing dropped a curtsy. She was one of the Cottage Row girls, frantic to please, a bit rough on the edges, but would be a gem in a few years. If she lasted and didn't succumb to the wiles of some poor bloke who offered nothing more than a bite of passion, too many babies, and a lifetime of poverty. In the kiss is the dream . . . is disaster, he mused wryly.

"She's in the study, sir."

"See to the fire in here, will you?" he said brusquely, sur-prised that it had not been stoked. Bea spent hours in this room immersed in his business affairs and her own projects. Over a smell of beeswax came the aroma of Indian tea. With a happy sigh, Desmond strolled down the hall to his favorite retreat. Technically, it was his domain—as the parlor was Bea's—but they had tacitly assigned this room for tea. It had an aura of warmth lacking in the more formal parlor. Beatrice, too, basking in a male kingdom of pipe ash, brandy, bay rum, and perpetual clutter, cherished this closeness. With his back turned, blond hair tousled, sometimes he looked so much like Jed her heart almost stopped.

"You're going to have to have a word with those girls," he

said with mock severity, warming his hands before a blazing fire. "We've a cold front coming through, and that parlor's like ice. They know better than to let it die." Behind him, she sat slumped on a couch, drooping over a bountiful tea. Studying her in the chimney glass, he noted her pallor. "What's the matter? Are you ill?" Removing the tabby from a leather armchair, he settled down in concern.

"Well, you warned me!" Aimlessly, she twisted a serviette. "I just never believed he'd be so vindictive. Silly, pompous man—" Abruptly, the tears began flowing as she searched feverishly for her glasses and a letter, which she handed to Desmond. "Stupidly, I thought it an invitation and opened it."

Accepting a cup of tea, he deliberately drank half before examining the terse contents.

> *Dear Sir:*
>
> *Your request for a loan of £1000, recently granted, is hereby revoked. The first installment, made to you in February 1882, is to be refunded, plus penalties, within one month.*
>
> *Edward Howland*

Desmond's eyes flashed. "Well, he'll get his pound of flesh first thing in the morning."

"We don't have it, Simon. It's been spent," she sobbed.

"Here . . . here, don't panic, Bea!" He reached for her hand. "I've that much and a bit more saved. We'll manage, and I'll get a loan someplace else."

"Howland has all of Lynn and Norwich in his grip," she cried. "He knows everyone."

"So?" Desmond coolly refilled his cup and helped himself to a scone. "I'm not beholden to his cronies, and I'll find someone less intimidated by that bloater." He laughed, exhilarated by the prospect.

"A message came from Squire Hedley's wife. You're not to stop by this evening. She's consulting an Aylsham man."

Desmond flushed. "Well, he moves fast. Turning the gentry against me—"

"But don't you see, dear? If they go, others will follow, and the poor don't pay—"

"No, they only feed us!" The scone tasted like ashes in his mouth. "Cheer up, Bea. I've been in worse scrapes before.

We'll muddle through. After all, I still have the Farjeons in my pocket."

Beatrice Clayton clenched her hands, fighting a mixture of emotions. "The family is tainted, Simon, with no money. Only Regina keeps them afloat. . . ."

He felt suddenly chilled, thinking of a wrinkled hand on his thigh—his first London conquest. And she had been generous. Very. Fine clothes, money—until she felt it more prudent to push him on. And they had passed him around in a saraband of sex, destroying his young, passionate dreams of love until he became as vile as any guttersnipe. Would he end up in the same dance with Regina Farjeon? Yes, if he gave her the chance. Their mutual corruption drew them together. . . .

Turning away from his ravaged expression, Beatrice winced. "Simon, if you certify Ariel Farjeon, Regina will reward you— handsomely, no doubt. She's terrified of the creature. But thwart her and you'll end up with nothing—"

"I can't condemn her to such hell!" he cried vehemently.

"She killed her baby!"

"I really don't know what happened—"

"Then what's your alternative?" she argued. "She's a terrible liability. Scrap her and you may be able to dig out from this Howland fiasco."

"I've no proof yet that I've become a pariah in Heydon. If that happens, I'll make a decision." Icy contempt shone on his pale face. "In the meantime, Bea"—and there was a warning note in his voice—"Regina may control the purse, but Farjeon has the final say, and he's on my side."

"Why make such a sacrifice for a deranged woman?" She shook her head in dismay, self-control crumbling. Hurrying out of the study, a storm of words came angrily over her shoulder. "If I didn't know you better, Simon, I'd think you'd gone daft over her!"

"Daft over her, am I!" he muttered, wryly amused, running a quick eye over Howland's note. As long as everyone thought that, and no deeper emotion, he was safe. No threat would force his hand. Not until he was ready to move. Crazy or sane? What did it matter when just being with her gave him peace of mind? And for that blessing, he would take her into his own home, if necessary. Surely, Farjeon would agree to such an arrangement where he could see her frequently. No man professing such devotion to his sister could condemn her to a lifetime in that monstrous stone building, for Desmond was certain that was to be her fate. Bethlem would lose, he thought grimly.

Cramming Howland's note into his pocket, he stepped out into the hall, arrested by the sound of low weeping. Behind closed doors in the dining room, Beatrice Clayton sat, head buried in her hands.

"Come, dear, it's going to be all right." He put a comforting arm around her shoulders. "It'll work itself out." But fear gnawed at her as it hadn't done since Jed's death, and she stiffened in protest.

He kissed her cheek. "You had enough faith in me to give me a start, didn't you?" She nodded through blurred eyes, her mouth quivering.

"Then hold on, Bea. We'll make it. I'll not fail you." He marched off to his surgery.

 *Seven*

He sat for a long time after Simon Desmond's visit, engulfed by bruising shadows. The snifter was long drained, but unlike his usual habit, he made no move to refill it. In front of the fireplace lay the miserable doll, but Nicholas Farjeon saw nothing. He heard only the sound of splashing fountains and a lone voice singing in the orange-drenched night. Before him danced a woman so beautiful that she tore apart his soul. Helplessly, he watched her by moonlight, his blood on fire, his heart mad with love. Closer and closer, into his waiting arms, she slipped like Salome, naked against his body. . . .

Youth and love. Lost so many years ago. And now, jaded and dispirited, he must not only assume the crushing burden of his sister's madness but the double tragedy of watching her grow old. Never would he send her to Bedlam! If Desmond spoke the truth, she might learn to accept him and not hold him responsible for her terrible folly. As wretched as she, he had a bounty of tenderness to bestow—if only she had indeed forgotten her lover and the dead infant.

Unexpectedly, he broke down and wept. Once he had dreamed dreams, as she had, and it had all come to ashes. The failed artist . . . the beautiful child—so extraordinary in her grace that even the coldest eye was moved. The perfection Farjeon sought lay not in some exotic city or obscure corner of the world but at Bellereve. Like a soul possessed, he wanted only to sketch and paint that youthful beauty before maturity ruined it. To his amazement, watching her grow, he saw that the fragile loveliness instead of fading was developing into something quite remarkable. Even their father, the most prosaic of men, studying his son's work, had once exclaimed, "Good, Nicholas! You've certainly caught her." But on a later occasion, the normally caustic voice had been tremulous. "You must watch her, my son. She has a dangerous beauty. A fatal love affair. . . ." The pause had grown too long, and Nicholas had cut in impatiently.

"Would do what?"

"Might destroy her. Promise me that you will find her a good husband, an older man, who will be considerate. I despair for Ariel. She will bewitch and be abandoned."

Shaking his head in disbelief, Farjeon burst out laughing, but his father had turned on him, deeply angered. "The child is pretty, but the woman will be astonishing. Soon you will have to assume the responsibility of being her guardian. It will only be for a few years. Just pray that she doesn't go mad. It has skipped a generation—"

"And may yet another. . . ."

They were standing in the courtyard, the proud old man an exhausted image of his handsome, virile son. Skin bronzed by the sun stretched tight over high cheekbones; a Roman nose, grizzled hair, a bitter slash of mouth—but the features were blurred by illness, the body emaciated with suffering. Before the ruined wing, with its stone heart, they distantly watched the endless pacing of the poor madman within. Back and forth, he walked on twisted legs, keening to himself, beating his head against the walls; hands, like jelly, fluttering impotently on the barred windows.

The lunatic's son, Nicholas Farjeon's father, had whispered, "Ariel is tempestuous in spirit. These emotions must be curbed, not ignited by a great passion. At seventeen, she'll be ripe for marriage. Children should calm her. . . ." He faltered. "But if my hope is crushed and she ends up there, don't let her be seen. I beg of you. It's not been easy on me to watch. Still, in our family, it's considered an object lesson for the sane—at least for those who can bear it. . . ."

Many suitors came wooing—some fatuously young, others lustful and greedy, and the remainder, the more stable element, his father had recommended. Nicholas Farjeon was in the process of choosing her a mate when his exquisite sister betrayed him. Still, he could have salvaged her life—despite the bastard's death—if only she hadn't attacked him. Then it was too late. In terror, he saw what his father had dreaded. Madness in those wild eyes. Beauty turned into a monster.

If the years of her incarceration had been agony to her, they had been an even greater torment to Farjeon. It was his failure, and he had to live with it. Hourly, he asked himself the same question: how had Ariel slipped through his grasp? She, who was so gently reared, had run wanton by sun and moonlight, wrecking his family's honor without shame, jeering at his misery, and then made him her Judas. . . .

He didn't know which was more painful—that grotesquerie or the lifeless woman who met him years later in the asylum when he came to take her home. Still with the face of a houri but crowned with a death's head shock of white hair. Out of pity, windows were left uncleaned. No one could taunt her at Bellereve, mock her ravaged beauty through twelve years of filth. But Nicholas Farjeon kept up the watch, as had his father and other haunted relatives before him. . . .

The doll still sprawled on the floor, head askew, arms and legs stiff like a corpse in rigor. Refilling his brandy glass, he picked up the damned thing, his mouth curving in disgust. The thickly coated wax face and shoulders were melting in the fire's heat, exposing a papier-mâché composition. A stench of charred matter and stuffed cotton body fouled the air. Cramming the wreckage into its wrappings, Farjeon flung open a casement window, his mind on Desmond. A fortunate choice, that. And thank God, the man had sense enough to demolish Broughton's report. A lethal document if it fell into Regina's hands. He was very much in debt to Simon Desmond. Somehow he would be properly rewarded. Now he had to attend to his wife. After all, she, too, must learn to keep the watch. One of their sons might be so grievously afflicted.

Made melancholy by the thought, he downed his brandy, then went in search of Regina. At this hour of the day, the pretentious tea would have ended, and she would be dressing for the evening's cheerless ritual of dinner. Leaving the austere magnificence of his wing, he descended the great staircase and found the drawing room bare of sycophants. Two parlor maids, one wheeling a dumbwaiter and the second balancing a heavy tray of sherry and madeira decanters, were disappearing down the vast black and white tiled hall. Following their labored progress, he glanced in rage at a chamber—once so startling in its Jacobean beauty, now only an advertisement for Regent Street.

Regina Farjeon, after wedding and encountering marital difficulties, had vented her wrath on Bellereve. The rot must go, she declared, stripping, plastering, and papering all the ancient wainscotting she could lay hands on. Ornate ceilings were flattened, their incredibly rich texture and design beaten into submission. Velvet drapes shrouded the glorious expanse of bay and oriel windows. Ferns, stuffed animals, and bric-a-brac fought one another amid a forest of the latest craze in furniture. Farjeon could never walk through these rooms without flinching, but he had yielded to their renovation as a means of keeping her quiet. What Regina called "a small recompense" for the duplicity of their marriage.

Cornering his wife making her toilette, he dismissed her maid with a snap of the fingers. Husband and wife glared at one another in the gloom of lowered gaslight.

"Nicholas!"

Too many teeth flashed in a false smile of welcome. The blue eyes steamed, and she tossed a tawny mane of hair made limp by its loss of rats and false curls, her voice rattling inanities with bulletlike precision. On the rare occasion when she found herself alone with Nicholas in her boudoir, she lolled before him, dishabille, hoping to entice him back to her bed—not for love but for conquest's sake. A cheap trick, and he knew it. Farjeon preferred his women to be subtly passionate. The temptation of the hidden always excited him more than brazen charms. His models were painted clothed. Rarely had he found one whose nakedness so inflamed him that he had to paint her nude. But then he was much younger, and such perfection should go naked.

Why had he ever married this dreadful woman? With his lineage, despite money, he had had his pick. Had he been drunk or sober when he proposed? He couldn't even remember, she meant so little to him. Just being in the same room with her made his skin crawl. Yet he had been able to bed and impregnate her twice. Poor little boys...both sickly. But he no longer had the stomach to mount her again in the hope of rejuvenating his stock. Her absurd posturing and her mannerisms were a mockery to the memory of that lovely creature who had once—so easily and with such love—given him her heart and soul. How many men were lucky enough to know such joy? he wondered. And why, in God's name, had he never found it again?

Regina's teeth clacked together, anticipating a coming tiff. If she couldn't arouse him sexually, a good quarrel was second best. "Well, Nicholas, what brings you here? Has the lure of brandy and paint worn thin?"

"Simon Desmond tells me you're seeing Ariel—nightly."

Under her coating of powder, she flushed—a great blotch spreading from her face to her chest, mottling her complexion. "You don't go near her. Someone should keep her company!"

"I'm forbidden, and you loathe her. So why go, Regina?"

"A social call, husband," she drawled.

His eyes glittered like flint. "And does that include telling her about her lovers"—he spat the word—"and her poor dead child?" Tearing off the wrapping, he tossed the mutilated doll onto her lap. Caught off guard, she screamed, then pulling herself together, she flung the thing into a wastebasket.

"How could you do such a vicious thing?" he cried.

"What proof have you that I sent it?" She looked bored.

"You have motive. That's enough for me."

Long fingernails drummed on the satinwood dressing table. "A court of law would demand more, Nicholas."

"I know you have no pity, Regina. An emotion foreign to your poverty-stricken soul, but I ask so little. Ariel is well now. Both the asylum and Desmond concur. All she needs is a refuge in that dwelling. I'm not asking that she live with us!" He sneered. "Even I know that's impossible. . . ." Ignoring his plea, she began brushing her hair, counting each stroke aloud to deliberately annoy him. "Regina, she's greatly improved," he added softly. "Leave her alone."

Pulling out some hairs from the silver brush, she eyed them coolly. "She's anathema—"

"Leave her alone, bitch! That's all I ask. Have mercy—"

"And if I don't?" she hissed.

A spasm of despair crossed his face. "I'll kill you if you go near her again! She has hurt no one in her life."

"What about her baby?"

"An accident!"

She turned on him in fury. "Then why, Nicholas, did you call it deliberate?"

The gray eyes were weary. "Foolishness said in a drunken moment. After all, I didn't witness the event. But she is my sister—my only sister—who once caused me a great deal of grief."

"You speak in riddles, Nicholas, of an evil, profane woman. I have the money—"

"We made a bargain, Regina. Insane, she goes to Bedlam. Well, she stays—in that building!" Farjeon shouted. The doll caught his attention, and he dangled it in front of his wife's alarmed face. "You sent this charred mess. This hell's doll!" Finally, he saw a tear on her cheek and pressed his advantage. "Desmond and I will know if you hurt her again. But if she still evokes no sympathy from you, Regina, think of your sons. One day, you may have to mount a guard over them, my dear," and turning on his heel, he left her alone. . . .

Simon Desmond stood on the threshold of Edward Howland's smart Heydon office. When his name was announced, he sauntered into the room towards Howland's desk. The little banker looked up in irritated surprise.

"Here you are, Mr. Howland. Two hundred and fifty pounds, plus penalties. My obligation is met." Coolly, he spread out a wad of notes on the richly varnished mahogany.

"Damn your insolence!"

"Come, come, Howland!" Desmond said laughing. "Surely you appreciate a prompt return, though you've lost a customer! I'll be banking in Aylsham—"

"Bastard!" Howland leapt to his slippered feet, huffing with rage. "Out of here!" It was one thing to make a fool of Sally, but another to cross him. Had Desmond not flaunted himself but paid his debt with a proper show of humility, Howland's anger might have dissipated. Instead, a vitriolic flood was unleashed. Out flashed wires to all the banks in central Norfolk warning them against one Simon Desmond, M.D. Character and background, unsavory. Credit, suspect.

Then Howland moved on the home front, convincing his reluctant wife to spark a scandal. With heads together, they came up with the igniting match: Regina Farjeon, who was delighted to oblige. Denied access to Ariel, she now saw a way of destroying her through Desmond. Besides, she bore the man a grudge. Not once had he come to visit her.

Out came her list of grievances over tea with a dismayed Mrs. Howland. Nicholas Farjeon had been ruined, Regina confided—as would her darling boys—by the futile care wasted on the madwoman. As for Simon Desmond, he was totally unscrupulous. Not only were his medical ethics dubious, but he had cruelly used her desperate husband and crazed sister-in-law to gain entrance into Norfolk society.

Then Regina, with many blushes and a heaving bosom, woefully unburdened herself. On the night of the Howlands' ball, Simon Desmond had positively flung himself at her, subjecting her to sly caresses while vile suggestions had come tumbling from his lips. Hadn't anyone noticed? she plaintively asked her hostess. There had been some fuss, Mrs. Howland recalled. And from not liking Regina Farjeon, she became her staunch ally. That night the poison began to spew out. . . .

Simon Desmond seemed oddly indifferent to the clouds storming above his head, but Beatrice Clayton, handling his accounts, privy to gossip, watched him with a sinking heart. Why didn't he see the change? Or did he notice and not care? Happy—that's what he was, she decided. Intoxicated, perhaps, with the coming of spring, or with something far worse.

Another uneasy bystander was Nicholas Farjeon. Obviously, Desmond's career was in jeopardy, he reasoned, and a defamation of him hurt Ariel. . . . Damning his wife—Regina had to be involved in such a mess—Farjeon moved swiftly. Over a week had passed since that disgusting incident with the doll. Daily, from his studio, he observed Desmond's visits, waiting until he felt himself on sure ground. Prepared for an outburst or the enormity of a rejection. Even if the worst happened, they still had two months to ready her. Desmond, who had her interests at heart, would keep such disaster a secret. If the man didn't lose his moorings over the Howland business.

Simon Desmond reached for Ariel's key in the onyx box.

"I have it, Desmond," Farjeon said, appearing behind him. "Don't you think it time I paid her that visit?"

Suppressing a stab of disappointment, Desmond agreed. "By all means. It's the only test." Aware of the other man's nervousness, he added, "She'll pass it, I'm sure."

"I want to walk in with you. Catch her unawares. That way, we'll know how she really feels." Tension etched his face. "What if she breaks down?"

"Leave! But if today is successful, I hope you'll come as often as possible. All we have to do is rid ourselves of the Jackal!" Both men laughed, in good spirits, but outside the iron-banded door, Farjeon hesitated, torn by doubts.

"I never meant to hurt her," he mumbled. "I only did what

I thought best—" A strong hand gripped Desmond's shoulder. "Help me! If she turns against me—"

Simon Desmond had his own fears haunting him, too. After all, he had a great deal at stake in Ariel's recovery. But it wouldn't do to let her brother see his vulnerability, so he hastened to reassure him. "Never have I seen any signs of derangement. What I have encountered at times is a badly frightened woman who withdraws, perhaps in self-protection...." Broughton had not agreed with his findings, dismissing them as poppycock. Desmond was in no position to provoke an argument, so it remained a difference of opinion between two physicians—not additional fodder for the gossip mills. If Farjeon kept his mouth shut, all would be well on that score.

"Hurry, man!" Farjeon's voice was harsh with anxiety.

The heavy door had become warped over the centuries, so it opened with a protesting groan—a signal alerting the Jackal, who popped out like a spiteful jack-in-the-box.

"Go up to the manor-house," Desmond said brusquely.

Oozing past him, she gaped at Farjeon, dropped him an unsteady bob, then bolted across the courtyard.

Simon Desmond's hungry eyes were seeking Ariel Farjeon. He found her bathed in a shaft of light at one of the moat windows—a pillar of fire. And she, for a long moment, saw only him. A slow radiance spread across her face like a rose opening to dawn. She held out her hands, his name on her lips. Then she saw Nicholas Farjeon. Her reaction was slight—only wary curiosity. Another doctor, perhaps?

Desmond, with heart pounding, broke the awkward pause. "Ariel, this is your brother, Nicholas."

The gray eyes widened. A flash of gold illuminated the irises, then they dulled and a lovely smile appeared. With becoming modesty and grace, she curtsied, her white hair spilling around her shoulders.

"Nicholas!"

It was too painful for Farjeon. He clutched her to his heart in a desperate attempt to erase the memory of those hideous years. Finally, when he could speak, he muttered huskily to Desmond, "When I first brought you here, she didn't know who I was. Does she now?"

"Judging from her reaction, I would say so," Desmond replied, ashamed of his jealousy.

"I have lived for this moment!" Farjeon whispered, kissing her forehead, on the edge of weeping.

"I think this is enough for today, sir." Desmond held out a restraining hand. "Come with me tomorrow. Too much emotion distresses her." He walked him to the door.

Nicholas Farjeon looked dazed, his great strength a shadow. "Will she be all right?" he asked tremulously.

"I think so—if you can keep Mrs. Farjeon away." Desmond smiled. "She received you well, don't you agree?" Farjeon nodded, too moved to reply. "And tomorrow will be even better!" Closing the door, Desmond turned back to his patient. She stood where her brother had left her, silent and remote, as if still caught in his embrace. The pose was at once uncanny and profoundly touching.

"I have no flowers today," said the young doctor. "Will my hand do?"

Very gravely, like an obedient child, she took it in hers. The touch seemed to awaken her. "Help me, Simon!" She held on to him tightly. "Promise me something."

"Anything. . . ." Indulgently, he cupped a silken cheek in his hand.

"If they come to take me away, give me fair warning—"

Startled, he jerked away, a smell of carrion in his nostrils.

"You don't have to pretend with me." Her smile was almost maternal. "That's what she wants, and Nicholas can't oppose her."

"He will if I'm here!" Desmond cried vehemently. "Your brother and I are in complete accord—"

"You don't understand!" Tears filled her eyes. "She'll win. I'm a madwoman. . . ." Images of a thousand flowers, fountains, and gardens by moonlight whirled through her mind, and she reached again for his hands' security, her lips barely moving: "That moat can drown a dozen men—"

It was the hardest moment he had ever spent with her. Not to take her in his arms. He knew her terror, and he ached to comfort her. . . . Why was he hesitating? God damn it! And then he remembered that incredible lie and the urgent need to keep it spinning. Without that barrier, he might destroy her.

"You're not going to Bethlem," he said roughly. "Any move in that direction, and you'll come to Heydon with me. I—my wife and I—will protect you—" Clearing his throat, he made himself look her in the eye. "Do you trust Nicholas?"

"Of course." She seemed surprised by his question.

"Good. . . ." Impulsively, Desmond ran a hand through her hair, noting with deep pleasure its softness. "Someday I'd like to take you on a real outing."

"What about your patients?" She stared at him in wonder.

"Oh, doctors take holidays!" He grinned. "I'll have a 'medical meeting' in Norwich or Yarmouth. Have you seen the Rows?"

"Yes, once, as a child. I had a very fat nanny, and she could barely squeeze through!" Laughing, she added, "I thought them intoxicating—even more than champagne—"

"A child drinking champagne!" Desmond gently teased her. "Who so indulged you?"

"Well, it couldn't have been Father," she said slowly, trying to remember. "He was much too fond of it to share, and Grandfather disapproved. So it must have been Nicholas. He introduced me to the world. . . . My tutor—my poet, I called him."

Enchanted by her shy enthusiasm, he asked, "Didn't you have a governess?"

"Oh, yes, half a score! But when I was fourteen, Nicholas came home from one of his jaunts and took stock of my progress. With only tatting credentials, he said I'd never amount to a thing, so he tutored me himself—" She faltered. "Why are you smiling?"

He could never tell her the truth—only whisper it to walls and dark night. "Because you are so charming." He kept his voice light. "Did you prosper under your brother's tutelage?"

Her eyes glistened like stars. "Oh, yes, he was the most patient of teachers—" A tremor shook her body, and she hid her face. "He would be so ashamed of me. . . ." Tears spilled between her fingers. "God! How much does he know?" She fell to her knees. "He cared about me more than anyone. Father was always too busy, and Grandfather—" Back and forth, she rocked, clearly very upset. "Nicholas became my guardian. . . . It was always Nicholas!"

And it will probably always be Nicholas, thought Desmond sadly. "He loves you, Ariel, and your recovery has given him much hope for the future. No harm will come to you through him, my dear. . . ."

As he was leaving, Ariel timidly touched his arm. "If one day you don't come, Simon, what am I to do?"

He kissed her hand. "I'll be here. Don't worry." The radiance of her smile stayed with him through the day and into the evening, made bearable the loss of patients and Bea's anguished look of concern....

In the early hours of the morning, Nicholas Farjeon entered the stone building—not by way of the iron-banded door—its grating noise would have awakened Ariel, frightening her. He came through the detested small room from a door leading into the second half of the ruined wing. Smoke clung to his hair, skin, and clothes, and he grimaced. Aided by a bull's-eye lantern, he had clawed his way through perilous wreckage to reach his sister. She lay uncomfortably on the couch, her hands twisted in mute appeal against the night's cruelties.

Until dawn, Farjeon sat by her side, watching her sleep. Deeply moved. No insanity here, he thought, only the fretfulness of a disturbing dream. At the end of that long watch, as a sliver of red shot across dirty windows, he left, satisfied that she was in good hands. Simon Desmond would be well rewarded.

For several weeks the two men saw her together, and her conduct was exemplary, her manner charming. The smile for one passed to another. Farjeon, of course, knew nothing. Only Desmond, jealous of their few precious moments alone, seethed with unhappiness.

Ariel Farjeon grew and strengthened as did the spring flowers. Even the meanest soul could see that she was recovering.

"I am well," she said softly to her brother. "Well." And he kissed her.

 *Eight*

April, that year of 1882, was exquisite. Hawthorn hedges burst into bloom—a shower of white, pink, and red. Ivy glistened like jade against cream-colored or red-brick walls, and Simon Desmond walked humbly but with profound delight in his box-bordered Elizabethan garden or more freely amid the confused glory of the cottage garden. Fairhaven's comfortable rooms were filled with flowers, Beatrice needing little inspiration for a new bouquet.

Heydon's common had come alive with heather and the gold of gorse. Children dashed about like frolicking puppies while their indulgent mothers watched and chatted under an umbrella of beeches, limes, and oaks. Even around Ariel Farjeon's wretched building an army of wild flowers sprouted. On the ruined walls wisteria mingled with English ivy, turning the monstrosity into a place of enchantment, Desmond thought.

Thanks to his dwindling practice, he had not missed a day—a situation he refused to discuss. Not even Bea was privy to his thoughts these days. He lived only for the moment when he saw Ariel. Neither gossip nor Farjeon's presence deterred him. It was enough if she smiled at him or gave him her hand. Deliberately, he brought her flowers and small gifts, just so they might touch. On the brink of ruin, he was incredibly happy.

Farjeon was nowhere in sight, so pocketing the key, Simon Desmond sped away to his sweet love. To his surprise, he found the sitting room empty, except for the Jackal, who came shuffling towards him, her manner unusually furtive.

"Where is your mistress?" he asked in bewilderment. The creature grunted in the direction of the small room. Desmond hurriedly opened the door. Ariel Farjeon was lying on the pallet.

"Don't know what happened. Found her like that," the Jackal whined.

Five o'clock in the afternoon. With an oath, Desmond shoved the keeper into the courtyard, then returned to Ariel. She was conscious, but her eyes had that blind look he so dreaded. The worn shift had been ripped to pieces, and she lay naked, legs stretched wide apart, arms crossed on her bosom, tears flowing down her cheeks.

"Oh, God. . . . Oh, God! What happened, my darling?" He pressed his face to hers, but there was no response.

A thousand times had he dreamed of seeing her naked. Now he examined her not with a lover's but with a doctor's eye. The bruises and abrasions around the vaginal area were multiple, the bites on her body hardly the passion of a loving man.

Wrapping her in a shabby blanket, he stroked her face, grieving. "Ariel, tell me what happened!" Still the arms remained locked, her eyes faraway, reliving the horror.

"I wouldn't waste too much time on her, Desmond," Nicholas Farjeon snapped from the doorway. "Obviously, she's had a relapse. Let her be. . . ." His voice sounded old and tired. "It's happened before. My sister, with her astonishing beauty, has always caught any man she wanted. Time and again, I found them sniffing around Bellereve like rutting bucks, and her like a bitch in heat."

A shocked Simon Desmond rose to his feet. "A number of men in these villages speak of your sister's beauty, admit they were infatuated—some longed to marry her, but so tight was your hold they couldn't get near her—"

Farjeon laughed. "Oh, the she-devil was clever. Her tastes were low. She preferred the coarse lovemaking of gypsies and servants to the gentry! Why do you think I dismissed all the young male servants from my estate? My God, she went through them faster than a Messalina!"

"But the love affair? The baby!" Desmond was appalled.

"I don't even know who the father was. Nor does she!" Farjeon cried in a passionate whisper. "But a scoundrel adds to her pathos—"

"Damn the past!" Desmond retorted in fury. "This woman has been brutally raped!"

"She likes it that way." Farjeon's eyes were icy. "I caught her once in the act, and I couldn't believe the way she teased and tormented the poor bastard. It was not a gentle coupling. Many's the time I've seen her body like that."

Beside himself with anxiety, Desmond exploded, "You just find the bastard who did this, and then we'll ask her how much she liked it!"

"I can't question my staff without letting all of Foulsham know. It's too risky, Desmond. I always kept her conduct secret, and I'm not about to expose it now."

Simon Desmond shook his head in stunned disbelief. "Can you at least get her another shift?" He held up a rag. "This one's been torn to pieces."

"Oh, she likes being naked. Don't you, Ariel?" her brother jeered, stripping off the blanket. "Still a lovely body despite its abuse, don't you agree, doctor?" A glint of amusement crossed his face. "Did she never attempt to seduce you?"

Furiously, the younger man pulled up the blanket.

"I'm surprised, Desmond. You look like a highly skilled lover. You're often alone with my sister—has she made no overtures? In her own way, she's quite expert. Madness has its compensations. She's completely uninhibited. Could teach any bawd a few tricks. . . ." His voice shook. "Do you know, she even tried to seduce me? I was painting her dresses in a kimono, and she stepped out from behind the screen with the belt so loosely tied that the gown fell open. She was fifteen. . . ." Anguish contorted the proud features.

"That's not my concern now," Desmond said dully, trying to stifle the ugly image. "She hates this room." He looked around, dazed. "Why is she in it?"

"No one would hear them in here." Farjeon said dryly.

Desmond winced. "Help me, please. I want to bathe her and put her back to bed, then get some food in her if she'll take it. I'm afraid she's in shock, and if this is a woman who takes pleasure in rape, I see no evidence of it."

Farjeon turned on his heel. "I'll call the Jackal—"

"Just a minute, sir! How many people have keys to this suite?"

"There are only two, Desmond. I have one, and the second is kept in the butler's pantry."

"Does your staff know about that key?"

"Of course. They have to, in case of fire."

"So anyone could have taken it," Desmond mused. "See if it's been returned."

"I don't like being ordered about in my own home, Desmond."

On bended knee, beside the pallet, the young doctor flushed. "I'm sorry, but this attack will set her back. You realize we have little time—"

"I'm aware of it." Farjeon spoke distantly.

"Why did you lie to me?" Desmond asked in a very low voice.

"Look at that face and you'll understand. I love her. She can't help being what she is. . . ."

"I have a room in my house used by patients without family or those too ill to travel. Would you consider it presumptuous if I took Miss Farjeon home with me?"

"Under the circumstances, doctor, since your reputation is on the wane, a move like that would undoubtedly finish you and cast aspersions on my sister's already tainted character." His tone was scathing. "You've lost all your important patients, haven't you?"

"Yes, the hypocrites, hypochondriacs, and drunkards—all the *crème de la crème* of the countryside!" Desmond spat the words. "But the faithful laborers remain—"

"Be careful, doctor. Don't make an enemy of me!"

"I have no intention of doing that, sir. If I sound peremptory, it's only because of my deep concern for Miss Farjeon. You don't want her in Bethlem, do you?"

Farjeon hesitated, heartsick. "No," he said finally.

"Then help me," Desmond urged. "I need a change of linen and more blankets for her bed, and some fresh nightclothes." He looked up, worried. "Will the Jackal talk, do you think?"

On his way out, Farjeon leaned against the doorjamb. "Oh, nothing she says here would be taken seriously. She's not the problem—it's my staff. They must be handled with great delicacy. If word of this reaches my wife—"

"Is there no way she can be protected? A guard at night?"

"That's drawing attention to her—the one thing I cannot permit."

Simon Desmond studied Ariel's pale face, embarrassed to find himself trembling. "If it happened once, it can happen again—until her assailant is caught," he said uneasily.

"I assure you, Desmond, I'll do everything possible to find

him. . . ." Farjeon's voice was thick with emotion. "But I very much fear it's the end for her."

"We'll see. Just get the devil, that's all!" Desmond turned back to Ariel. Still she lay in that awful position so reminiscent of those days in seclusion. Where was she now in her terror? Back in that hideous room? Stroking her livid face, he whispered, "I'm not leaving you, sweetheart."

Working speedily, he gave her a sponge bath, covering her body against drafts and his own too fervid imagination. From the sitting room came sounds of her bed being remade. A nervous young maid knocked timidly on the door, a bundle of night-clothes in her arms.

"I brought a light supper, too, sir."

"Good!" Desmond smiled, taking a brandy flask out of his bag. As the outer door banged shut, he forced some brandy down Ariel's throat, trying to relax her. Still, she resisted. Another dose was given with words of loving encouragement. And a third. The clasped arms loosened; the rigid legs moved feebly. Hoarse sobs broke from her as she tried to hide her face. In a few moments, he had her dressed. Carrying her into the other room, he tucked her into fresh, sweet-smelling sheets— fine cotton, he noticed, not the rough muslin she usually had, and the nightgown and peignoir were made of silk. Items pinched from Regina's voluminous stock, he thought grimly.

No food would she touch. Not even broth tempted her. So he simply cradled her against his chest, hoping that bodily contact might ease her misery. Toward one o'clock in the morning, by lantern light, she spoke, "Simon? Is that you?"

"Yes, my dear. Now try and sleep." His lips brushed her forehead.

"What . . . happened . . . to me?"

Arranging the pillows behind her, he wrapped a comforter around her body. "A nightmare, Ariel. No more—"

"Where am I?" she moaned. "In the asylum?"

"No, you're at Bellereve, in your sitting room."

"How dark it is," she sighed. "Now I understand what Grandfather meant. That dawn and the loved one are so slow to appear. . . . Why do you come by moonlight, my dearest? Are you afraid to meet me in the sun's glory . . . ?"

"I love you," he whispered, but she had fallen asleep, her cheek damp against his hand.

A half-hour more he waited, then, taking the lantern and his bag, he stole out of the room. A faint sickle moon lit his way across the courtyard, illuminating cracks in the bricks like darts of flame. Ahead stretched the great house—in darkness a monolith. From the hall shone a Cylops' eye; a second shot from Farjeon's library and a more distant one glimmered from an area beyond—his bedroom, perhaps, Desmond thought wearily.

Nicholas Farjeon, imposing in a black velvet dressing gown that enhanced his pallor, opened the door. "How is she?"

"Sleeping peacefully, and I'd let her stay that way until she wakes. She wouldn't eat and she's disoriented, which is to be expected.... Have you had any luck?"

"No, but I have an idea who it might be. Hopefully, we can fish him out without an uproar."

"I'll be here about noon tomorrow. Keep her as quiet as possible, and don't see her until I come—" He apologized for his abruptness. "She's terribly frightened, and if pushed, she may go overboard. It's a case of her leading us—"

Farjeon's face was a mask in the flickering shadows. "Will she recover?"

"I don't know," Desmond wretchedly confessed.

Driving back to Heydon, distraught and utterly drained, he felt hemmed in on all sides—at last awake to his perilous situation. So much so that his mind was painfully alert to Bea's anxious inquiries. Obviously, Howland and Regina Farjeon had launched those damning stories, the two of them banding together in a brash attempt to destroy him through a helpless woman, who in turn would suffer. Dismayed by such cruelty, he unburdened himself to Beatrice over a late-night supper.

"As far as I'm concerned," he said bitterly, "she was totally vulnerable in that building. An apt victim for any man!"

She shook her head in dismay. "Has Farjeon been shielding her all these years? Is that possible?"

"Oh, to a certain extent, yes. Witness the fabrication of the Boston years, and its reality—an insane asylum. But I just wish I could get him to be honest with me," he added worriedly.

Beatrice offered him another slice of meat pie, which he refused. "Is it lies, Simon, or a matter of pride? For him or for both of them?" She searched his stricken face unhappily. "Is she really worth such heartache, dear?"

A flash of anger glittered in his eyes. "I've not seen a madwoman, nor the slut Farjeon described today. Every man I've talked with calls her chaste."

And now she finally asked the question that had been nagging her for weeks. "Are you in love with her?"

"One would have to have a heart of stone not to be moved—"

"You're not answering my question, Simon!"

"Of course I'm not in love with her," Desmond answered flippantly, and with a loud yawn, he went up to bed. . . .

Someone was kissing her face. Kissing her face, her throat, her breasts—sucking on them until she wondered if it was her baby. The insistent pull, the fondling, making her body aflame until she moaned in the night, and the heavy mouth found hers, parting her lips with searing kisses. A hand spread apart her thighs, pulling up the nightgown. Words of passion rang in her ears as his hard body covered hers, and he took her gently— not ruthlessly, as he had the night before. The act over, he was again at her breasts, and she pressed his head tightly to her warm flesh, feeling the sudden flow of milk released as it had with her baby. Now the thrusts into her body were harder, more painful, but his mouth was a gag. After the second rape, she was only dimly conscious of the ravenous mouth, the agony of bruising hands, the invasion of her body. The baby was taken away. She held out pleading hands, and a straitjacket was thrown over her and wrapped so tightly that she could scarcely breathe. A burning pain caused her to faint. . . .

Simon Desmond had barely closed his eyes when a shaft of sunlight exploded in his face, and Beatrice Clayton's alarmed voice pierced his exhaustion. Grumbling he sat up, his head pounding. "What's the matter?"

"It's Cook, Simon. She's scalded her arm. Pulled a full kettle over herself!"

He fumbled for robe and slippers. "What time is it?"

"Ten after six."

"What do you want to bet, Bea?" He grinned. "Today's going to be a real hell-raiser!" But one look at the woman's badly blistered arm, and he was immediately awake. In a corner, hunched and miserable, sat the scullery maid with a red, sniffling nose and a towel wrapped around a bleeding hand.

"She cut herself in the excitement," Bea whispered, handing Simon his bag and fetching some ice.

Enmeshed in ointments and gauze dressings, Desmond was

greeted by a new crisis. Bessie came flying in with a note. "Beatrice!" he snapped, still working on Cook's tender arm.

She read it over, then looked up, her expression grave. "It's Mary Henley, Simon. She's dying and wants to say good-bye to you . . ."

"Poor old soul!" He sighed. "Well, she's had a good, long life."

"No family?"

"Oh, yes, but they're seeds replanting in Canada and America." Tying the bandage, he said, "Rest it. I don't want a failed breakfast tomorrow!"

Cook beamed, and Desmond spoke sotto voice to Beatrice. "Send word to the vicar, please. And bring some flowers from the garden. She always liked them. . . ."

Bessie fled from the scene of disaster, summoned by a frantic knocking at the front door. Minutes later, she appeared, gasping, "You're wanted at the Hall, sir. Lady Symonds is in premature labor. . . . Her doctor is in London!"

"I am not her physician," Desmond answered coldly, turning his attention from the scalded arm to the cut finger. "Hmm . . . that's nasty. Wash it carefully. I'll have to take a stitch or two—" She groaned, and he said gruffly, "Don't faint, girl! Hurry up. I'll be in the surgery." He marched down the hall, followed by a nervous Beatrice Clayton.

"What about Lady Symonds?"

"She can go to the devil for all I care—"

"Simon! You were once her doctor—"

"Yes, and they abandoned me at Howland's whistle!" he said angrily. "You think I now want to humble myself groveling at her bedside?"

"The woman's in labor, Simon, and needs help. If you safely deliver her, he'll be grateful. Very!"

"And suppose the child dies? Then I'll be held doubly accountable, eh?"

"You have no choice!" she cried. "Take the risk. I implore you. Otherwise, we might as well pack up and leave today."

"Are things that bad?" he asked, shocked, eyes misting.

Beatrice ran a hand through his rumpled hair. "Simon, it will work out. I've prayed for such a thing to happen so that you might regain your foothold—" Turning, she saw the scullery maid hovering in the surgery doorway. "Come here, my dear. Let's give you a sip of brandy to ease the pain." She helped the girl to a chair. "I'll see Mrs. Henley, Simon, and you come when you've finished at the Hall."

Desmond, sewing up the girl's finger, said nothing. Finishing, he smiled. "That wasn't so bad, was it?" He went to collect his Gladstone bag.

"So, everything's all right?" Bea asked hesitantly.

"No, it's not, Beatrice, but as you so wisely reminded me, what other option have I?"

Lord Symonds graciously condescended to spend a few moments with Desmond at his wife's bedside. She was his second Lady—a good thirty years younger and the successor to a woman who had died worn out after bearing her husband six daughters.

"I can't stop her labor," Desmond said hurriedly, drawing his lordship over to a recessed window. "How old is the baby, m'lord? Between eight and nine months?"

"Correct," drawled Lord Symonds.

"She's too small to be delivered vaginally. I'll have to do a Caesarean—"

"Rubbish, man! Our doctor indicated no such thing."

"Is he here now? What would he say?" Desmond's eyes were flat with suppressed rage. Raising his voice to be heard over her ladyship's screams, he added, "You want her to live? It's the only way."

Lord Symonds's pink, fleshy jowls trembled. "And the child?" he gasped. "What about the child?"

"Will be all right, I trust."

There was a long pause, punctuated by frantic cries. Desmond strode back to the bed, shouting over his shoulder, "Perhaps, you should call in another opinion!"

"Damn it! Do what you will," Symonds hissed. "But so help me, Desmond, I'll run you out of Heydon if one of them dies!" He stormed out of the bedchamber.

"Get her ready." Simon Desmond spoke coolly to the attendants, washing his hands and arms vigorously in hot water. From his bag, he plucked a bottle of chloroform. Boiled instruments and gauze were laid out on a covered table near his reach.

"Soon it will be over," he said, comforting his anguished patient. "Take a deep breath." One by one, drops fell on an open mask covering her face. Gradually her cries sank to low moans, then stentorian breathing. Desmond reached for his scalpel, and the knife slashed in a steady line across the swollen abdomen. In the midst of a wash of blood, the child was born. A strapping little boy, healthy and robust, and his mother was doing nicely, Desmond thought, tying the final stitches.

"His lordship is so pleased, Dr. Desmond! He wants to see you," whispered a maid excitedly.

Not until he was packing up his instruments was he fully conscious of his intense strain. The back of his neck ached, and he had a throbbing headache. Luck, bloody luck, he sighed to himself. So far it had dogged him most of his life. He'd always been able to bounce back. Why then did he feel so uneasy?

Putting a gold-embossed leather purse into Desmond's hand, Lord Symonds, wreathed in smiles, raised his goblet of champagne, and the two men drank a toast to the heir.

"You should try marriage, Desmond. A moment like this is worth all the disappointments!" said Symonds ecstatically.

"I rejoice for you, m'lord."

"Now you'll be back with us, won't you?"

"An honor, sir. Yes!" Simon Desmond stepped out into the sunlight, heaving a profound sigh of relief. Down the wide Palladian steps he raced to his waiting trap. Now he must bid farewell to his old friend—his first patient, Mary Henley. She and Desmond, both lonely, had instantly taken to one another. On many an occasion when he dropped by for a chat—old age was her only ailment—she lit up his face with her wit and spry gaiety. In return for that warmth, he was grateful to be with her at her life's close. For both, it made the passing easier. . . . Luckily, he reached her tiny, wisteria-covered cottage in time to plant a gentle kiss on her forehead and to hold her hand.

"I was waiting for you, Simon," she said, smiling, faded blue eyes dancing like little stars. "You are the flower of my old age. Thank you, my son. Be happy. . . ." The old head sank to one side, a frail white curl fluttering in the breeze coming from a casement window.

Desmond closed her eyes, his throat constricting as he knelt by her bedside. After a long moment of silence, he rose and conferred with Vicar Martin. "I'll take care of the funeral and headstone."

The cleric looked bewildered. "She wasn't that poor, Desmond."

Beatrice Clayton opened her mouth in silent protest, but Desmond, flashing her a warning look, pressed Symonds's purse into her hand, then turned back to the vicar. "I know that, but her children could use that money, and she was good to me. . . ."

At the afternoon clinic, as his patients trooped in with their maladies and domestic woes, Desmond mended and listened patiently, his mind preoccupied with only one thought. Soon, my darling. Soon, I'll be with you. . . .

Tempted to go by horseback, at the last minute he decided to take the trap, driving the chestnut at a merciless gait to Bellereve. Tossing the reins to a groom, he ran up the steps to Farjeon's library—only to find the man himself slumped at his desk-table, a decanter of brandy by his side. Quite obviously, he had been drinking heavily.

"Have some," Farjeon mumbled. "You're going to need it."

Desmond halted, key in hand. "What's happened?"

"Judging by her appearance, I'd say Ariel has taken a lover."

Simon Desmond wheeled about and tore down the great staircase. No sounds came from her suite. Apparently, the Jackal had gone home. With his heart in his mouth, he opened the door to the small room. Ariel Farjeon was lying on the pallet, her nightgown torn, legs obscenely parted, hands clasped across her breasts. At his alarmed approach, she began to whisper, "Not the fire. . . . Please, not the fire!"

Under his touch, she shrank, eyes blind, her body trembling violently. Desmond seized her in a convulsive embrace. "My God, Ariel! Who hurt you?" But she turned from him, sobbing bitterly.

He made the decision in a split second without any regard for the consequences. Rummaging through her wardrobe, he pulled out linen, a dress, her cloak, and shoes. Dressing her was like robing a manikin, but at last he had her ready. And he carried her out of that loathsome building.

Nicholas Farjeon stood waiting for him in the courtyard, his expression grim. "What the hell do you think you're doing?"

"Removing her until you find that villain!" As the older man tried to block his way on unsteady feet, Desmond tightened his grip, his voice cool. "Shout more loudly, Farjeon, and you'll bring out Regina and the entire household!"

"You have no legal right—"

"She's of age—"

"She's insane!" Farjeon muttered brokenly. "Can't look after herself. . . ."

"Find that monster, and then we'll discuss it." Desmond's

hazel eyes flashed. "I'm taking her to my home. My sister-in-law and I will tend her while you solve this mystery." With difficulty, he restrained his temper. "Good God, man, I'm trying to save her! Don't you understand? I'll send word when she's fit to receive you."

"You ask me to expose my sister's tragedy to the world?"

"Bring in the police if you feel you can't tackle it. But get it done! Remember what's at stake." He stalked past the unhappy man and crossed the drawbridge. The groom would see them. Well, it couldn't be helped. Others undoubtedly had witnessed that courtyard scene, and word would spread like brushfire. Frankly, he didn't know if he did have a legal right to remove her. Such power was probably invested in her brother. Luckily, the man had been drunk, and he'd gotten away with it. The more fool, he.

Exhilarated by his success, he ignored the groom's startled leer. Nothing mattered except Ariel Farjeon's freedom from that hell-hole. But his mood plummeted as the damnable shadows crept around them, engulfing them like mist. Flicking the chestnut lightly on its flanks, he urged it down through Bellereve's park to the ornate iron gates. A second astonished face gaped at them when the keeper appeared. Another tongue to wag. . . . Ah, well, he had her now.

Hoping to avoid inquisitive stares, Desmond kept to back lanes. The hood of her cloak partly shielded her face, but there was no mistaking the exquisite features and white hair. By tomorrow, gossip would run rampant. As they rode and her frail body sagged against him, he whispered his love. But Ariel Farjeon, drowning in a stupor, heard nothing. Long before they reached Heydon, she had fainted.

Arriving at Fairhaven, Desmond carried the unconscious woman inside, calling softly for Beatrice Clayton. The hall was in semi-darkness, but a sliver of light and a sound of voices came from the kitchen. Hearing him, Beatrice appeared in the doorway. He braced himself for an outcry, but she approached quietly, picking up an oil lamp on the way.

"Simon?" At sight of the woman in his arms, she paused. "Ariel Farjeon! Is that who it is?"

His face tensed. "Yes." Any protest she might have evoked was stifled at the sight of the bruises around the young woman's mouth. "Help me!" he cried urgently. "We're going to nurse her back to health, and you'll be my witness in case my conduct in this affair is ever questioned."

"I'm your sister-in-law, Simon," she said, frowning. "Won't people think I've lied for you?"

"Others have seen these wounds. You simply back me up and act as our chaperone." He started up the stairs. "Tell Bessie to bring hot water, towels, linen—"

"Wait!" She held out an imploring hand. "Are you absolutely sure of what you're doing?"

"Yes. I've never been more confident. Now hurry, Bea. . . ."

Down the first-floor hall, he walked to the bedroom next to his—large and bright, it would awaken her to new life as it had others. Placing her on the brass bed, he stood nearby in raging despair, making no attempt to touch her until his witness rejoined them. After all, nothing would happen with Bea present. . . . She came, efficient and composed.

"Help me undress her," Desmond ordered. Dutifully, she complied, not liking it.

"Oh, dear God!" Her eyes swept the ravaged body.

"Nicholas Farjeon says she likes this kind of treatment. Courts it. I disagree!" he added savagely. "And I say she will suffer a breakdown or even die if left at Bellereve while this sadist prowls." He tucked a blanket around her. "When I'm in the surgery or on rounds, I want you to sit with her. A warm, sympathetic woman will do wonders, Bea. Listen to what she says. Write down anything that sounds odd or significant. Get any scrap she mutters in her sleep. But don't question her. She mustn't feel forced or frightened. We've barely six weeks to bring her 'round."

"You think Farjeon will let her stay?"

"Yes, because he wants her at Bellereve—well. If I can convince him she didn't instigate this horror, he'll welcome her back and might be amiable to my suggestions."

"Brother and sister reunited, and you lose Regina's money!" she sighed, unable to keep the sting out of her voice.

"Lord Symonds was generous, and I've still a bit cached in Aylsham. I'm not at the workhouse yet, Bea!" He glanced thoughtfully at the still figure lying on the bed. "Do you know, something just occurred to me."

"What?"

"Regina desperately wants her sent to Bethlem. Word must have reached her about Ariel's steady improvement. Perhaps this was her idea of a solution. Hire an outsider or one of the servants to assault her—"

Bea looked horrified. "Can you prove it?"

"No, but someone attacked her. You saw it. You attest to it!" His glance was piercing. "Farjeon thinks she's reverting to former behavior when she was ill. Not knowing enough about that period, I question it."

A knock sounded on the door; it was Bessie with two heavy cans of hot water. Taking them from her, Beatrice closed the door firmly. "What happens if this . . . gets known?" she asked uneasily. "Is she mad or not, Simon?"

He stroked a silken cheek. "No."

"You're in love with her!"

Simon Desmond laughed. "Does it show?"

A despondent look crossed her face. "Yes, my dear, it does. Very much. And that must be kept a secret, or it will ruin us. Doctors don't fall in love with their patients, and certainly not their mad ones! Does Farjeon or his wife suspect?"

"I think not, and she, poor darling, knows nothing."

Beatrice shook him in desperation. "Be discreet. I beg of you. Keep it quiet, love. . . ." Against his shoulder, she began weeping. "I've always wanted you to know the happiness Jed and I shared. But not this, dear. This woman is not your future. She can only bring you grief!"

"No one knows that better than I," he dully conceded. "But feelings die, don't they, Bea? It will pass." His smile was cynical. "All I want is to find her a safe refuge. If I fail, and the meddlers can't appreciate compassion, then we'll leave Heydon and seek our fortunes elsewhere—"

"And all for a lunatic!" she moaned. Then a whisper: "Will you continue to visit the brothels?"

"Would you rather I kept a mistress, Beatrice?"

For once, she was brutally honest. "Yes, rather than a mad love!"

"You make too much of it." His tone was biting. "Help me bathe her." She balked. "You are my witness, Bea," he said in cold fury. "I depend on you as you once depended on me!"

"Why don't Bessie and I do it?" she urged. "It's only fitting."

"I'm her physician. It's not the first time I've seen her naked," he cried angrily.

"Oh, my dear, I meant no criticism, but that way no one can fault you."

"We've been constantly alone together at Bellereve, and I have yet to violate her!"

"Simon!" Tears filled her alarmed eyes. "I want you to be happy—you know that. But this love will destroy you."

"No," he replied in an icy voice. "I will abandon her when the time comes. Any truth I let fall will be a lie later on. After all, I care about my self-preservation!" He sneered. "Just let me stay here now. With two women present, she runs no risk, does she?"

"I'm sorry," she muttered, wringing her hands. "Forgive me."

His headache had returned, stupefying him. "No, you're right to be so concerned. I lost my wealthy clientele because they thought me intimate with this 'mad' woman. Should have taught me a valuable lesson!"

Beatrice Clayton, head averted, said nothing. She had, in her anxiety, gone almost too far, and she couldn't bear the hurt, stunned look on his face.

"Well, call her up, then!" Desmond snapped.

Under his supervision, the two women bathed and dressed Ariel Farjeon while he made himself stand aloof, his mind feeling his darling's body. Then, in their presence, he applied the necessary salves. Now she slept, arms at her side, her face tranquil.

"I'll take the night watch," Desmond said casually as Bessie left the room with towels and water cans. At Bea's startled look, he exploded, "I don't want her waking, thinking she's back in the asylum. You can relieve me in the morning unless there's an emergency, and we'll keep the doors open to avoid temptation, eh?"

Disregarding his outburst, she asked quietly, "How will she accept me, Simon?"

"I'll have her up when you arrive. Hopefully, we'll have no problem."

"You spend one night with her, Simon," she shook her head ruefully, "and you'll lose your heart forever...."

 *Nine*

Forever. Less than six weeks. A prudent man would coolly analyse his position, and Simon Desmond, amorous and desperate, took such a step that night. At the most, they had two weeks together at Fairhaven, and as long as she lived under his roof, he must be very circumspect. Well did he know Beatrice's argument: it was his own. Ruination of his career, and something far more deadly. The kindling of any affection that Ariel might feel for him was not only heartless but a peril. Should he keep up the "wife" pretense? Bea might endorse that. His missing "spouse" could be visiting relatives in Dorset—or some such nonsense. The idea sickened him. No, he must handle it himself. Be gentle with her, yet aloof. No more would he ever touch or kiss that delicate skin, and so thinking, he caressed her cheek. With a sigh, she nestled against him, and he was at peace.

Beatrice had brought him dinner on a tray and a decanter of wine, and they sat invitingly nearby on a walnut polygonal table. But time was too precious to waste on food and drink. These moments with Ariel must last a lifetime. Her brass and and iron bedstead stood against the same wall shared by his. Tomorrow he would fill her room with flowers and flood it with sunlight to make her smile. And he would dream by day of sleeping with her at night. . . .

Distraught, he saw that it was nearly eight o'clock. "Ariel!" he called softly. The gray eyes snapped open in terror; her body

froze into that alarming position. Forcing apart her rigid arms,
Desmond cradled her so that she couldn't lock them again. He
felt her scream, but it never came aloud. Just ran silently through
her body, almost shattering it.

"Who am I?" he asked gently.

A thousand faces flashed in her mind: leering, obscene,
jeering at her degradation. A few were kind: a tiny child's, the
lover of the dark nights, and someone else who was holding
her now. Enemy or protector? She couldn't tell and braced
herself against his assault as lips like a spring flower brushed
her forehead. Deceiving her. Frantically, she tried to push him
away, but his arms tightened, imprisoning her against a racing
heartbeat. In endless padded rooms, she heard his mocking
voice, felt his foul caress.

"God! Put out the fire!" she moaned, waiting for the hot
mouth on hers, that searing kiss of destruction. Instead, she
felt only the powerful arms and sheltering body of this stranger.
A tear slid down her cheek, matched by one of his. Turning
from the abyss, she stared at him in wonder.

"Simon. Simon Desmond . . . ?"

"Yes," he murmured. "And you're in my home, Ariel, safe
from anyone or anything that harms you."

"But your wife!" she protested weakly. "Won't she object?"

Desmond winced. "I lied to you, Ariel. I'm not married.
Never have been. That was only a foolish bit of deceit because
I thought—" Hesitating, he fumbled for the right words. "I
thought we were . . . becoming too close."

"You mustn't, Simon. Not with me!" she cried in deep
alarm. "Everything I touch dies—"

"Nonsense!"

Almost too quickly, she changed the subject. "Why did
Nicholas let me come?"

"He had no choice. I simply carried you out of there and
drove off." A tremor shook her body, and he searched her face,
attempting to decipher her mood. It was now less fearful but
extremely wary. "You know I'll do anything to help you, Ariel.
With luck, I'll keep you out of Bethlem and that wretched stone
building, too."

She stared at him in disbelief. "How?"

"There are families who take care of people like you—"

"Loonies?" she asked sadly. "God! Will I ever be well?"
She began to laugh, on the edge of hysteria.

"I think so. . . ." She was becoming unduly fatigued, and it was almost with relief that he heard Beatrice's soft knock on the door. For an uncomfortable moment, the two women silently regarded one another, each apprehensive. As Beatrice Clayton came forward, her faithful shadow, the tabby, darted ahead. Always curious, the animal sprang onto the bed and daintily sniffed the new patient. A smile broke through Ariel's exhaustion. Bea looked amused.

"I think you've made a friend! Do you mind?" she asked as the tabby settled down, folding up its paws under a plump body.

"No, its been so long since I've seen one. We had a few at the asylum—" She blushed. "But they were rat-catchers, not pets."

"What about some breakfast and then a nap?" asked Desmond.

"Yes, please. . . ." Then her eyes swept the room in astonishment. Beatrice had flung back the chintz curtains and light poured onto gleaming white woodwork, a dark oak floor, highly polished Georgian furniture, gaily painted wallpaper, and a garlanded plaster ceiling.

"It's so lovely—" She covered her face in a futile attempt to hide her tears. Tenderly, Desmond stroked her hair.

"I'm off to my surgery now, but I'll be with you for lunch."

"Aren't I inconveniencing you?" Their eyes locked, and he smiled.

"Not at all, Miss Farjeon. It's a pleasure." He left, deliberately avoiding Beatrice's look of concern.

At luncheon, he insisted on being left alone with his patient. Dinner they would all have together, but this brief time he wanted only with Ariel. "And the door will be left open!" he added savagely.

Beatrice Clayton had also done some hard thinking overnight. Practical by nature, unlike her tempestuous brother-in-law, she knew her days with Simon Desmond were limited. Eventually, he would take a wife, who would want to be mistress in her own home and not share it with any in-law. Thus, she now schemed, out of love for Simon, so that when she left to fend for herself, he would treasure—not dislike—her memory. No quarrel over a deranged woman was worth a breach, and a man that infatuated wasn't about to listen to reason. Not in his state. But an opportunity might arise where he could confront his folly and save himself. So she controlled her fears.

"There's no need for that, Simon!" Her reward? A swift hug—his joy so painfully obvious, it wrenched her heart. . . .

Ariel Farjeon was a model patient, touchingly grateful for their solicitude. Only her waking moments gave trouble. Clearly, she was frightened—but of what, neither Desmond nor Beatrice Clayton could learn. She seldom spoke in her sleep, and the words were always the same: mumblings of "fire" and "baby." Desmond found her more reticent. Nothing alarming, he judged. In time, she would come around. How much she remembered of her attacks, he had no idea. Little, perhaps. Violent memories to be locked away like the years in Weston Asylum. . . . All in all, he found her progress most satisfactory. In four days' time she was able to leave her sickbed, and Desmond wrote a second letter to Nicholas Farjeon, asking for his renewed support. There had been no reply to his first appeal, but on this occasion the brother appeared at Fairhaven. Desmond was in his surgery making up a batch of medications. In pleased surprise, he welcomed his visitor.

"So she's much improved, eh?"

"Greatly!" Desmond smiled. "I'd say forget Bethlem—"

"Something in your note distressed me," Farjeon curtly interrupted. "A comment about Regina."

Desmond corked and labeled the bottle he was holding, setting it down on a table. "Have you found the man?"

"The police weren't called in."

"I didn't expect them to be," Desmond said mildly. "I was just curious if you'd discussed it with your wife?"

Farjeon sank down heavily on a wicker chair, nervously tapping his walking stick. "Yes, she was terribly upset—"

"Naturally."

"Is such a thing possible?" He looked stricken.

"Well, someone brutally assaulted your sister on two occasions. Those weren't love's marks."

The man was tense, unhappy. "May I see her?"

"Of course, sir, she would be delighted." Desmond's voice softened. "Just don't remind her of those events. She refuses to discuss it." He led the way upstairs.

Ariel Farjeon was sitting in a wing chair next to a bow window overlooking the wild glory of the cottage garden. Before her stood a mahogany embroidery frame holding a screen panel. She worked easily, fingers dancing over multicolored threads. Opposite her, Beatrice sat knitting a scarf. The tabby stretched lazily between them, basking in the sun. Kindness had transformed the patient. Dressed in one of Bea's morning gowns, she looked the picture of contentment. At the sight of her brother, she froze.

"No, darling, I've not come to take you back to Bellereve. Only to see how you are."

Ariel held out a hand in greeting. "Well, thank you, Nicholas." She smiled shyly at Beatrice and Desmond. "They've been very good to me."

Kissing his sister's cheek, Farjeon cupped her face in big hands, examining it fondly, then muttered to Desmond, "You've done a superb job! When will she be well enough to leave?"

He had prepared for the moment but found it almost more than he could bear. "When you've discovered her assailant . . ." he whispered tensely as they withdrew to the doorway.

Farjeon's face was taut with strain. "I think I have. The older servants I trust implicitly, but this man is new to the staff—a rough, young groom Regina picked up at a hiring fair. Naturally, he'd know the whereabouts of the second key. Regina, I'm sure, had nothing to do with it!" Fury shot from the gray eyes. "For one thing, she knows it would end our marriage." He stared past Desmond's shoulder at Ariel. "I want so much to bring her home—"

"Get the man out, but make sure he's the right one," Desmond replied with a heavy heart. "Then give me a week or more. She's barely convalescent. . . ."

That evening, Regina Farjeon, through a haze of cigarette smoke, powder, and scent, saw her husband stride across her boudoir to the dressing table. So angry was his manner that she slammed down the swansdown puff, inadvertently upsetting a tortoise-shell box of powder. Brushing off the mess from her feathered peignoir, she gave him a baleful glance. "What's the matter now, Nicholas? More financial woes?"

"You promised me not to disturb Ariel again! What the hell have you been doing?"

From side to side the blue eyes flicked, searching for an escape route should his mood turn violent. For once, she regretted the cluttered chamber. Not a straight path anywhere. Impossible to reach the bell-rope, and that wretch of a maid was too far along the corridor in the sewing room. Remain calm, she told herself, her gaze still stony.

"I swear I never had contact with her again, Nicholas. I gave you my word. . . ."

On a tulip wood stand stood a jewel case. Farjeon picked out a ruby necklace from the top tray and held it up to the light. It glimmered like a splashing fountain at dusk. A beautiful thing it was, very old, long in his family, having once graced an exquisite neck. Deftly tossing it into the air, he whipped it about his wife's throat, tightening it slowly.

"I warned you to leave her alone—"

"And I did, Nicholas!" she frantically gasped. "I never went to the suite again—"

"But you sent someone else!" he shouted.

"No!"

He bent down, his face ugly by gaslight. "I know how much you hate Ariel, but by God, this is too much! What did you do to her?"

Regina Farjeon's mirror reflected an appalling image. A dumb show of a man calmly strangling his wife. The whitened face, splotched by rouge, turned purple. The chain was very strong, and he gave it another wrench, rubies spilling into his hands. Lights flickered before her eyes as she fought for breath; imploring hands scratched at merciless ones.

With an oath, Farjeon released her, and she collapsed onto the powder-strewn dressing table.

"Well?" he asked, after a long pause.

Tears mingled with powder. "My groom saw her out walking with your precious associate, Dr. Desmond. He made a comment, and I told him about the key—"

"Bitch! How much did you pay him for this rape?" The chain had snapped, and he tossed it in her face, raging as he stormed out of the chamber. "You're the one who's crazy!"

Regina Farjeon, tearful and begrimed, covered with rubies, sat huddled in a paroxysm of terror. . . .

"Well, what do you think of her?" Simon Desmond asked his sister-in-law.

Beatrice Clayton, arranging a spray of flowers for the dining-room table, hesitated, afraid of making a mistake. Overhead, steps could be heard: Ariel Farjeon moving about, dressing for dinner. She had only to appear in the simplest frock and Simon found her bewitching, whereas Beatrice, a plain woman, had to charm to be noticed. It still hurt that in Jed's eyes she had been beautiful—but that was love's miracle. Once admitted, the pang of jealousy died in shame. Ariel had so little, poor soul. And so she said quite honestly, "I have to admit,

Simon, that she's not only lovely but a delightful companion. Not a burden at all. Tries so hard to please. Hardly the mad-woman I was expecting!"

"Yes, that's what troubles me." Accepting a glass of sherry, he knocked his pipe against the pine mantelpiece and relit it. "Oh, the family is riddled with insanity, but my informers tell me the victims never recovered."

"Do you know so little about her childhood, her youth?"

"Not much. Too many different stories, and her brother in shielding her has been far from helpful!" He frowned.

Yet you wouldn't want the truth, would you? Beatrice thought sadly. Of all the women to have crossed your path, it had to be this one! Placing the vase on the table, she asked, "How long can we keep her? It's been nearly two weeks. Farjeon will want her back—"

"In time. When he's found that devil!" Desmond replied irritably. "What are people saying?"

"Nothing!" Her face went scarlet.

"Don't play the innocent with me! They chatter like mice in the kitchen. Shut up the minute I appear. As does everyone else. . . . What's the word?"

"That you're infatuated with her," Bea whispered. "Took her from Bellereve deliberately—"

"Dear God, did they see her poor body?" he lashed out. "No! Yet they vilify me because I'm young—"

"And in love," she muttered, eyes misting. He threw her a haunted look. "Simon, she's well now. You were right to bring her to Fairhaven, but can't she go now?"

"Not yet!" he snapped in fury. "And don't you try to take her away from me. One day I'll let her go. . . ."

You won't be able to, she thought in anguish, a plan forming in her ever efficient mind as she busied herself about the table, fussing with the silver and china. "Would you mind if I spent this weekend in London, dear?" At his blink of surprise, she forced a laugh. "An old friend of mine who emigrated to Aus-tralia is here on a visit. I'd so like to see her," she finished brightly.

"And so you shall." He smiled. "I'll get you some money tomorrow. Where are you staying?"

"Oh, not the Ritz! Nothing so fancy." She gave him a gentle hug. "Friends?"

"Always." He laughed happily. Then she felt his body tense,

saw his rapture. Ariel Farjeon stood in the doorway, smiling at them. . . .

Desmond waited three days, counting the minutes until he saw Bea safely on her way. Returning to his surgery, he breezed through the second clinic, then wired Colin Broughton, requesting emergency help. His acceptance came speedily. Next, he left instructions for the staff: early Saturday morning Dr. Desmond had a meeting in Norwich; he would return late Sunday. Miss Farjeon would be at Bellereve. Having spewed out the lies, he sought his patient, finding her in the cottage garden. As he came down a path, Ariel laughed, arms dripping with snowdrops, sweet william, irises, lilacs, daisies, and poppies.

"There's so much! I don't know what to choose, Simon."

"Come inside," he whispered. "We must talk."

Patiently, he waited while she arranged her bouquets with loving attention, tackling each arrangement as if it were a rare painting. But halfway along, unable to contain himself, he stopped her hand in midair.

"Simon?" she questioned, a sprig of lilacs at her breast.

"I'm taking the weekend off, and I want you to join me. Time we got you out into the world." His voice was low, urgent. "How about a jaunt to Norwich? Or something smaller, like Lynn, Cromer, or Yarmouth?"

She looked bewildered. "But your patients?"

"I'm overworked and need not only a brief holiday but a charming companion. Will you do me that honor?"

The gray eyes searched his, two spots of color touching her cheeks. "I'm mad, Simon," she said finally. "Mad as a drunken ride in the mists. And you want me to accompany you?"

He kissed her hand—desperate for her mouth—aware of approaching footsteps: a maid come to lay the table. "You need it as much as I. It will do you good," he finished curtly.

Over dinner, both were unaccountably shy. For appearance's sake, he had Ariel sit in Beatrice's chair at the table's end so that any intimacy was impossible. More to the point, he was nervous, not quite certain what she was thinking, and he, in such a turmoil, didn't trust his instincts or emotions. Dreaming . . . praying for such an opportunity, he sat on pins and needles, hoping she wouldn't fail him.

"We mustn't be seen together," she said softly. "It might hurt you—"

"I should be distressed if you didn't come with me. . . . Now, where shall we go?"

"Simon, I have nothing to wear," she added lamely.

"I brought you to Fairhaven suitably clothed. We're not running Regent Street's gamut!" he replied in a gently mocking tone. "Now, what's it to be?"

Ariel looked at him with shining eyes, radiant. "Yarmouth."

Very early the next morning, while the hedges and grass were still wet with dew, Simon Desmond and Ariel Farjeon drove to Aylsham. From there, they caught a train to North Walsham, which took them via Caistor into Great Yarmouth. Not once did they have the carriage alone, but no stranger marred their intense pleasure at being together. So touching was her joy of the countryside with its many churches, its wealth of flint and cobblestone cottages mingling with brick or reed-thatched houses, and its flat black fields ripening with spring crops that he almost wept.

Boats of every description lay at anchor as they entered Great Yarmouth, bounded by the North Sea on the east and the Yare River on the west. Disembarking at Beach Station, near the northern end of town, he drew her to a secluded corner on the platform and removed her left glove.

"Just for the weekend, my dearest, so that no one will think it amiss if we hold hands or occasionally touch—I want you to wear my mother's wedding ring." A circlet of golden flowers. Tears filled her eyes. Desmond smiled, triumphant. "A little pretense never hurt anyone." He took her arm.

The sky was magnificent, covering them with a great blue-gold veil. In the sun, her white hair might have been mistaken for the Norfolk flaxen. Ecstatic, they rambled down lane after lane of curving rows—some six feet across, others dwindling to a yard's width with houses so close together, neighbors could shake hands from an upper story. Fishing nets drooped from hooks, and his darling, as in her childhood, found the atmosphere so enticing that she hugged him joyfully.

In a daze of happiness, they strolled through the riches of the Yarmouth marketplace past gaily covered stalls where they lunched on bloaters, sausages, cheese, and strawberries. Later, poking among piles of second-hand goods and stacks of mildewed books, they laughed over some oddity in an hour's contented browsing. Desmond was delighted to see that the bustling throng—cart drivers, marketing women and their hordes of screaming children, sailors, fishermen, and hawkers—neither confused nor alarmed her. Ariel Farjeon moved like a dancer, eyes alert, captivated by everything.

In the cross-shaped parish church of St. Nicholas, which dated from the reign of King John, Desmond watched his beloved kneel in prayer. As she rose and genuflected to the altar, she blinked back tears, her voice husky with emotion.

"I pray for my baby—"

The building was deserted. Not even a sexton shuffled about in the shadows. Deeply moved, Desmond embraced her, awed that she still had faith after twelve years of horror. As he helped her up the aisle, she leaned against him heavily, spent and dispirited. But once outside, enveloped in brilliant sunshine, her grief evaporated and Desmond, who badly wanted to question her about her dead child, couldn't bear to reopen the wound. Not yet. The time wasn't right. Instead, he lovingly kissed her ringed hand, as a husband.

Tracing the old town wall, they then walked along the mile-long stone quay, which was fenced in by a fleet of boats, a double row of giant elms, and tall, graceful houses reminiscent of Vermeer.

Next they went to the newer part of town, the watering-place. Too many people cluttered the piers and marine parade, he thought, and the aquarium would be choked with families. Best take her to the beach. Hopefully, it would be relatively deserted. And it was, except for the fishing boats that were drifting in, sails crackling in the wind.

Hand in hand, they strolled on the beach until Desmond could wait no longer. Drawing her close, he pressed his cheek to hers, tasting the salt of her tears.

"I'm sorry, but it's been so long since I've seen the sea!" Spellbound, she faced the endless vista of the North Sea, where sky and ocean met in a lovers' clasp—the sky dominant in its fiery colors, the sea melting in opalescence.

Desmond looked around. No one in sight. His lips brushed the corners of her mouth. "You must know how I feel about you, Ariel. I've never been able to hide it, have I?"

Against his shoulder, she laughed. "No, but tell me. . . ."

"I want to make love to you tonight." She trembled, and he tightened his grip. "We can return to Heydon or spend the night here—" A sudden gust of wind made her take shelter against his chest. Overhead, the sea gulls screamed.

"I am so very much in love with you, Ariel."

"The ring is on my finger." Her face, with a flicker of pain, grew calm as she met his eyes. "I am no virgin. . . ."

Simon Desmond spent the next hour outfitting her at a modiste's, not caring if he was throwing away a fortune. For this lovely woman, nothing was too much. An evening gown was purchased and a spring costume for the following day. Delicate lingerie, shoes, a straw bonnet topped with roses and an ecru ostrich plume, and a velvet mantle found their way into various boxes. . . . Yet not once in his happiness did it ever occur to him that she had not spoken of love. Her love.

Then a suitcase was obtained so that they looked to be a respectable couple when presenting themselves at a hotel. Desmond chose the Star, located on the quay, an Elizabethan house once graced by Nelson and one of the judges condemning Charles I to death. The lovers were given a first-floor suite with a fine view of the Yare. Ariel unpacked while Desmond ordered dinner.

Neither of them could have described the superb meal, the wines, or the suite. They saw only each other, the tension between them so great that it was like lightning. Never had she looked so beautiful. Her hair, now long enough to be twisted into a knot, was threaded with tiny pink roses. The evening gown with its quarter train, bouffant sleeves, and bodice modestly raised to the throat, was elegantly simple, the color of a violet, and showed off her figure to perfection.

Desmond, pale and handsome in evening dress, waiting tensely for the waiter to clear the table, was attacked by bitter feelings of remorse. Finally, when they were alone, he strolled over to a bow window, pretending to study the dancing lights coming from the boats.

"I can't force you," he whispered. "It was all planned. . . . I brought you to Yarmouth for only one reason. To sleep with you—"

"No, Simon. To make love to me." Her smile was dazzling as she headed for the bedroom. "Will you help me, darling? These buttons are so very trying."

Touching her, Desmond was embarrassed to find his strong hands trembling. Ariel stirred against him, and overcome by emotion, he buried his lips in her fragrant hair. With a low cry, she faced him, her mouth taut with desire.

He kissed that full mouth gently, and then harder and harder, tearing at her clothes in his urgency. As the garments fell to the floor, her passion grew, matching his. In the back of his mind, a nagging thought stung him. Either she was starved for love, or she was the wanton her brother had described.

Ariel Farjeon stood before him, proud and unashamed, luminous in her naked beauty, helping him to undress, and then she led Desmond to the double bed and a rapturous night of lovemaking. They were bewitched with one another. Anxious not to waste a moment. She exceeded every fantasy he had ever lavished on her, craving him with a wild ardor as burning as his own deep thirst. Once she slept in his arms' security, and he studied her face by lamplight. "A bitch in heat," Nicholas Farjeon had called her, and it haunted Simon Desmond.

His distress awakened her. "Give me the baby," she begged, her eyes blind. "It needs to be fed—" Such was her anxiety that he started nursing at her breasts.

"Fire! Oh, God, the fire is too hot. . . ." she moaned, but soothed by his touch, she fell asleep.

Desmond awoke at dawn to find the bed empty. In panic, he cried her name, and she answered from the window, standing in her satin peignoir, her face radiant by dawn's light.

"I'd forgotten how beautiful it is," she murmured, nestling against his naked body as he wrapped her in a quilt.

"Come back to bed, my darling."

She laughed softly. "Simon, you're insatiable!"

"No, I'm not," he muttered. "Just deeply in love." His mouth hovered over hers as the curtains closed. "I feel like a very young man on his wedding night. . . ." And they came together with a wellspring of tenderness uniting them with such ecstasy that it was very difficult to part.

"I can't get enough of you," he breathed. Buried in her sweet body, he heard the words he had been longing to hear. Finally.

"I love you, Simon."

"What?" He laughed joyously. "I didn't understand you!"

Slowly, savoring the words, she repeated it. "I love you, Simon Desmond!" She slept against his heart, her fingers entwined in the hairs on his chest.

As daylight flooded the room, he mulled over their future. If he had made her pregnant, he would lease a cottage for her. *Cottage.* The very word chilled him. His one desire was to spend the rest of the day making love, but a crucial task lay before them. Rising quietly, so as not to disturb her, he shaved and dressed.

"Darling!" He kissed her awake. "I've ordered breakfast."

She stretched lazily, languid with passion. "Come back to bed, my darling," she gently teased him.

Desmond caught her in a fierce embrace. "I want you—

only you! But there's something we must do today." Her smile was intimate, but he was not to be dissuaded. "It's our one chance. We must find that cottage."

The gray eyes were flat. "Cottage? What cottage?"

"Where your baby was born—" She twisted away as if in pain.

"No, please!"

"Where was it?" She struggled under his hands' pressure. "I must know to help you!"

"I beg of you, no!"

Upset at hurting her, Desmond's face sagged. "Where was it, Ariel? In Norfolk?"

"Nicholas could tell you," she cried weakly.

"I want you to tell me."

Her breathing was labored. "Outside Sheringham—"

"Would you recognize it if you saw it again?"

"No, my darling, I implore you!"

"I want to marry you," he said fervently. "But I must know the truth of this child's birth and death—who its father was."

Ariel's face turned ashen. "What difference should that make to us?"

"So that when I touch you, you will know it's your husband, not your lost baby." He held her tightly as she broke into low weeping. Again, he asked, "Would you remember the cottage?"

"After twelve years—perhaps."

"Ariel, I love you. Nothing will harm you. I will be so close to you, sweet darling. . . ."

 *Ten*

She was quiet, much too quiet, and Desmond knew that he was being perverse, forcing her. Would any knowledge gained really make that much difference to their lives? He doubted it, and then in the next moment ruthlessly decided that it would. The ghosts must be exorcised.

Once more, almost pitifully, she tried to stop him. As they were about to leave their suite, she flung her arms around him, nuzzling his cheek. But Desmond, obsessed with his plan, somewhat impatiently cast her off. Forgotten were the glories of the night. Now he was off on a new hunt, another fox.

"Hurry, sweetheart!" he cried, annoyed as she dawdled over her gloves. "We'll miss the train. . . ."

Avoiding his eyes, Ariel pinned on her straw bonnet and snatched a final glance at the quay. Not even Sunday could halt the seaward trek. Church bells rang to deaf ears. Fish must be caught, money earned, while a prayer could be mumbled over a lugger's net as well as in a darkened pew.

"I'm ready, Simon." She preceded him out the door, head held high.

Constable's astonishing sky had died. Occasionally, a faint splash of gold charged ominous gray clouds, some black-tipped—swift-moving phantoms subduing the spirit. Anxious, careworn faces battered by salt and the sea's cruelty scanned the horizon for shelter. From lofts, drying nets danced crazily; auctioneers and fishsellers braced their booths against the com-

140

ing storm's onslaught while raucous gangs of working women loitering on the fringe awaited the herring boats' arrival.

Safely on the way, Desmond assumed his loving, protective role, sitting beside Ariel in the railway carriage, solicitous of her every need, painfully aware how much he had hurt her. All he could offer now was a handclasp. Caistor, as they rattled through, was a hodgepodge of dykes, windmills, and odd-shaped patches of water; a vivid splash of poppies in murky swamps; bronze, purple, and emerald-green pastures; and a vast expanse of reedy flats. A breathtaking view suddenly obliterated by an *eynd*—the Norfolk water-smoke—which crept across land, sea, and sky like an evil beast.

As the mist spread, it clung to them all along the coastline, hiding the massive Perpendicular Church and Lighthouse and the cluster of resort hotels at Cromer. Ariel Farjeon shivered, and Desmond whispered, "Give it an hour or so, and it should be gone. And a few more hours for us, my love...."

Neither of them was hungry for one of Cromer's famous crab or lobster feasts in High Street, so Desmond hired a hack to drive them west, the four-odd miles to Sheringham, another ancient fishing hamlet captured by a resort. On high cliffs overlooking a large shingled beach, breakers, small boats, and the North Sea, the older pebbled houses and cottages nestled in a tangle of nets, barrels, fishing gear, and lobster pots. Meeting no success, they left the flint-built village and plunged into the turbulence of the resort area.

Still and cold, Ariel Farjeon sat, recognizing nothing, not even warmed by a sip of brandy from Desmond's flask. As they headed inland, the reddish fossilized cliffs gave way to the heavily wooded section of Upper Sheringham. Every possible road was explored to no avail, until, darting by a forest of rhododendrons flanking a great hall, they dipped into a vale hidden by a mass of ferns and woods. Flint winked at them through a hedgerow.

Ariel's voice was shot full of alarm. "That's it!"

For the first time, he felt a passionate wish *not to know*. Two stories about this baby's death had been told to him. Quite possibly a third existed. He knew Ariel Farjeon's peril—as well as his own. If anything happened to her, he would never forgive himself.

Obviously, it was no fisherman's cottage, he thought, gazing at the rows of vegetables crisscrossing the black earth and at the blaze of flowers behind. In style, with its gabled, pantiled

roof, it looked like any Norfolk flint and brick cottage. Two
terriers lazed in the sun; a dovecot and a cow shared a noisy
enclosure with some chickens and ducks. Grunting and squeal-
ing from the building's rear indicated a family of pigs. Smoke
trailed from the chimney, making it a cozy domestic scene.

"Are you sure?" he asked, almost wanting her to say no.

She was staring at a great bank of hollyhocks. "I don't
remember any animals. Food came from the outside, brought
in by our servant. But I'll never forget those flowers. That's
where I walked, because it hid. . . ." Gingerly, she touched her
abdomen.

If she could recall that, other things might leap into her
mind. Hurriedly, he pulled her from the carriage, up the pebbled path to the front door. A face had been observing them
through a window. Now its owner, a plump matron of uncertain
age with the withered nut-brown skin of a long-time toiler in
Norfolk fields, flung open the door.

"What can I do for you, sir?"

Desmond turned on the charm. "My wife"——and he patted
Ariel's arm——"spent a few months in Sheringham as a very
young woman. She thinks she might have leased your cottage.
Is that possible?" he added, his stomach sinking. God, how
incredibly stupid! What if the woman recognized Ariel? There
was bound to be some gossip. But her face was a blank, and
the couple was politely ushered into an immaculate kitchen, as
sparkling as the proud array of brassware and crockery stocking
the oak dresser shelves.

A kettle was put on the hearth for tea, and their hostess
joined them at a round table. Instinctively, Desmond liked her,
reminded of Mary Henley's warmth. A ring on this woman's
finger spoke of marriage, but there was no evidence of a mas-
culine presence. No smell of tobacco or spirits over the sweetness of flowers decorating every bright nook. No smudge of
dirty footsteps or messy gear by the back door. A widow or
deserted. The former, he soon learned over a piping hot cup
of tea and a plate of buttered bread and cake.

"I've only lived here for seven years." She smiled at the
pale, lovely woman opposite. "Mrs. Larkin, before me, went
to stay with her children in Lower Sheringham, and she's been
dead four years. Most likely, you took it from her. . . ."

Obviously knows nothing, Desmond judged, or isn't saying
anything. Wiping his hands on a crisply ironed serviette, he
sighed, "That was nice. Thank you! Could you show us about?"

She beamed and led the way into a sunny parlor stuffed with overplump furniture and cherished mementoes. "Now, mind the stairs," she cautioned as they reentered the hall. Triangular-shaped, like thin wedges of meat pie, he decided, wondering how a very pregnant Ariel had ever managed it. She followed silently behind, cold fingers clutching his hand.

A spare room to the right, and then across the hall they gathered in a large bedroom. Intent on the woman's pleasant chitchat, Desmond glanced at Ariel. She stood apart, staring at the fireplace in terror.

"Oh, God! Is it still burning?"

"No, dear," he said in some surprise. "It's out."

The gray eyes widened, taking in the width of the bed and its proximity to the fireplace. Then she fainted.

She regained consciousness in the parlor, lying on a horsehair sofa with Desmond sitting beside her, bathing her forehead. Of the woman, there was no sign.

Ariel's lips barely moved. "Did I say anything?"

"Just a few words. 'Not the fire.'" Changing the compress, he stroked her face. "Ariel, how did the baby die?"

A tear ran down her cheek. "Nicholas says I overlay it. . . ."

He was very gentle. "Do you remember seeing it dead?"

"No," she said thickly, eyes bleak with distress. "He didn't want me . . . to see . . . it . . . like that—"

"Were you ill after the baby's death?"

"Yes, I was quite . . . uncomfortable. Pain!" she said sharply. "A terrible pain. . . ." She could still feel it. "And that's when I became afraid—"

"Of what, darling?"

"Fire." She went white to the lips.

"The fires of Bellereve never alarmed you?"

For the first time, she met his glance, smiling with faint irony. "No, why should they? The first one happened in the eighteenth century and is hardly noticeable."

"Who set the second?"

A flush of shame sparked the high cheekbones. Her voice turned oddly childlike. "Grandfather. . . . Father confined him."

"In a madhouse?"

"Oh, no! In the suite where all the mad Farjeons sleep—"

"Where was your baby buried?"

"I don't know, Simon." She looked bewildered. "Nicholas took care of it."

"Wouldn't you want to see your child's grave? Know where it lay? You prayed for it yesterday."

"Yes! Yes. . . ." she moaned, her body arching in a spasm, one hand clenched. "But something happened—"

"What?" Silence. Baffled, not understanding, he shook her in impatient desperation.

"I . . . tried . . . to kill Nicholas—"

"With what, Ariel?"

"I can't remember. It was so long ago. . . ."

"Scissors, a knife, a poker?" he asked roughly.

Grieving, she turned away, and he kissed her, ashamed of his relentless pursuit.

"Who was the baby's father?"

She flinched. "How should I remember?"

"You forget a thing like that!" He was incredulous.

And the beautiful face changed, hardened with contempt. "It could have been any one of a dozen men, Simon!" She laughed. "Hasn't Nicholas told you about me?"

Desmond stood up, white with shock. "You are chaste . . ." he muttered. "You came to me last night like a bride!"

She sneered. "Who was the seducer, my darling?" Delicate fingers caressed his groin.

Flinging away her hand, he hissed, "How did the child die?"

"*I* killed it!"

"I don't believe you!"

Again she laughed, a hard, brittle sound, delighting in his agony. "Why not ask my brother? Nicholas is a great spinner of tales. He'll give you all the facts—" Abruptly, she began to weep, hiding her face.

Heartsick, Simon Desmond concocted an excuse for their hostess, attributing his wife's collapse to her being with child.

"Ah, I know what it's like, sir." She smiled. "I had a parcel of them myself. Is it her first?"

"Yes," Desmond replied, tight-lipped.

"It'll get better, dearie, as the months go on." She waved them on their way.

"I'm . . . so . . . sorry—" Ariel wept as Desmond assisted her to their carriage. She was now very frail, leaning on him for support, her dazed eyes searching the garden, clutching her abdomen as if protecting her unborn child. All emotion had drained from her face, leaving it lifeless and wet with tears. Desmond had a vision of her at Bethlem, sitting out her life with that same vacuous stare. For that was where she must go, obviously. Her brother had shielded her long enough, and he—Simon Desmond—poor fool, still in love, found her appalling. And possibly extremely dangerous.

Back in Cromer, they had a dismal, silent meal in a run-down public house. So blackened was the paneling and dim the room, he could scarcely make out her features. She sat stunned, eating little of what was a surprisingly good repast, her eyes downcast in deep humiliation. Desmond, coldly furious, finished his crab platter, then attacked hers, washing it down with several mugs of beer. Not a word would he say to her. In that awful cottage, in some mysterious way, he had lost not only his beloved but all sense of proportion. Years of medical objectivity had not prepared him for so devastating a personal blow. Glancing at that beautiful, remote face, he wanted to kill her.

Outside, in the chilly dusk, he had half a mind to abandon her. A woman with so little knowledge of the world could hardly find her way back to Foulsham or survive amid the hurly-burly of a resort town. What would she opt for in her plight? Prostitution or suicide? It was a perfect out for him. No one had seen them leave Fairhaven. He could state blandly that she had run away. Unfortunately, mad people are subject to such bizarre fits. . . . Instead, in blind grief, he tossed the suitcase with its glittering clothes onto an ash heap and pushed Ariel Farjeon into a railway carriage bound for Aylsham.

Ironically, they were alone. No fat cleric, fluttering spinster, or busybody to interrupt their lovemaking. On fire for her mouth, he stripped the glove from her hand and yanked off his mother's ring. That gesture told her everything. In lonely terror, she huddled in a corner, watching him drain his flask, his mood growing more and more violent.

The ride from Aylsham to Heydon was a nightmare. So recklessly did he drive that the chestnut almost overturned the trap in a ditch. A brush against a hedgerow tore off Ariel's bonnet and slashed her mantle. Desmond, in torment, cursed himself for scorning Sally Howland. Not one more night would he spend with Ariel Farjeon under his roof. The thought of her sleeping against his bedroom wall was anathema, but it was too late to return to Bellereve. He would have to wait for the morning.

Reaching Fairhaven, he hitched the exhausted horse to a post, then used his latchkey to enter. No need to arouse Bessie's curiosity. Later he would run Beatrice's gauntlet, but his fertile mind could cope. Moving swiftly, he dragged Ariel upstairs. Before she could turn around, he had locked her inside her bedroom.

Not once in his house had he so imprisoned her, and it sickened him. He had caught her imploring glance.... Distraught, he went in search of his sister-in-law and ran into Bessie.

"Where's your mistress?"

"Oh, she's not coming until tomorrow, sir. We had a wire. Midday, sir." She trotted back to the kitchen.

One more night—alone with Ariel Farjeon. Uneasily, Simon Desmond glanced at her locked door. Torn with love and hate, he retired to his own room, finding sleep impossible. Maddened by her proximity and baffled by the evil that had so inexplicably seeped into his mind and heart like one of those damned *eynds*, he dosed himself with a brandy and chloral. Two hours later, still painfully awake, he went and stood like a thief outside her door, listening. No sounds came from within. Inserting the key in the lock, he hesitated, then dropped it into his dressing-robe pocket. He couldn't trust himself alone with her.

Desmond spent a wretched night in his study reading back issues of *The Lancet*, praying for an emergency call, but none came. Good health reigned. He drank continuously, but his brain was as lucid as crystal while his heart remained like ice. Only once before had he felt so alone—when he walked that poor dead woman to her foul resting place in Paradise Row, Chelsea.

"And now I am walking a second dead woman to her rest. ..." he muttered to the gray dawn.

Nicholas Farjeon stood waiting for them in the dew-drenched courtyard, little diamonds of light glistening in ragged shoots of grass. Silently, the two men escorted the white-faced woman back to her prison. She moved stiffly, hands clasped before her as if manacled. Behind her, the door clanged shut with a noise that rocked the building. Farjeon wheeled on Simon Desmond.

"What the hell happened?" he asked in suppressed rage. "I thought she was 'progressing splendidly.' Those were your words, weren't they?"

Desmond's body was taut with fatigue. Had he not pushed her, she still might be all right. How she had begged! But the madness, simmering, would only have broken out some other time. Another man might have snapped her, but not he. . . .

"Yes, they were, but I'm afraid she's taken a turn for the worse. . . ." The hollow voice sank. "I told you, it's not my field. Best if I gave up the case."

Farjeon looked stunned. "Desmond, you can't! Who else can I call in at this late date? Broughton thinks her crazy. We've four more weeks!" he cried passionately. "Just give me proof that she isn't dangerous so that I can keep her here and not in some foul cell in Bedlam. See her once, twice a week—"

"No!" Desmond's voice was too sharp.

"Ah, she made a play for you, is that it?"

With an oath, Desmond looked away, too mortified to speak. Too hurt by the memory of that ecstasy in Yarmouth.

A flicker of sadness darted across Farjeon's face. "Are you, too, in love with her, Dr. Desmond?" Receiving no reply, he added dryly, "Well, if it's any comfort, you're only one of many. I told you that. I warned you. Did you really expect a virtuous woman with that body? No man satisfies her. . . ." Their eyes locked in joint dismay. "I want her to live at Belle-reve," Farjeon pleaded. "She deserves some dignity."

Better I had left her to die in Cromer, Desmond thought grimly, getting into his trap. "Very well, I'll stay—" His lips moved with difficulty. "Until you get someone else." A shaft of sunlight, like a knife blade, shot into one of the filthy windows. From the burnt wing drifted a stench of smoke. Nothing else came to mind, so he asked, "Tell me, sir, what did you say caused that fire?"

Farjeon flung back his head, obviously torn by some inner tormet. "Time you knew the truth, Desmond. . . . A ten-year-old child. Beautiful as the devil—my sister!"

"Oh, my God! She said it was your grandfather—"

"Well, naturally, she'd hardly own up to a thing like that. Father himself was speechless. He stood next to her while it was burning, and he told me the look on her face was extraordinary. That she kept saying, 'Oh, how beautiful it is! How beautiful!' Days later, when he finally admitted to himself that no one else could possibly have set it, he couldn't bear disciplining her—"

"Why not?" Desmond cried in agony.

"He would have had to put her away, wouldn't he?" Farjeon jeered. "Imagine a ten-year-old pyromaniac! So he chose

Grandfather for the scapegoat. No one questioned it. The old man was doddering.... Two years later when Father died, I inherited the 'problem,' but Ariel's remarkable beauty was some compensation for the heartache."

He had to ask it. "How did her baby really die?"

"Do you really want to know, Desmond? You seem to be quite emotionally involved with her."

"Rubbish!" Desmond snapped, coloring faintly. "But as her physician—if I am to remain so—I demand facts, not fantasy. How did the child die?"

"She killed it."

"Overlay it, yes."

"No, my friend. She strangled it."

Simon Desmond, his legs like water, slipped down from the trap. "She did what?"

"Strangled it with her bare hands—a four-day-old baby. I heard its cries and came running in."

Desmond shook his head in horror.

"It was dead when I reached them." His voice trembled. "Imagine my predicament. I loved her. When sane, she had immense gifts, but crippled by that terrible curse, she became not only a harlot but a killer. As had my father before me, I made a decision. No one knew about the baby's birth except an alcoholic midwife who lived in Cromer. She wouldn't cross our path again. And a bit of gold shut up the maid—"

"For God's sake, what the hell did you do?"

"Buried the child in the garden under a bed of hollyhocks." A despairing look passed between them. "Obviously, Ariel was still in a state of mania. Wanted to nurse the poor little bastard—" His eyes dulled.

"Why not go to the police?" Desmond cried.

"You know what they would have done!" Farjeon almost shouted. "Madness is no protection against the law. In three months, they would have hanged her at Norwich Castle or sent her to Broadmoor for life. Don't you understand, fool! She, in her frenzy, knew nothing...." Glancing up at his wife's shrouded suite, he seized Desmond's arm, lowering his voice. "I have spent years shielding Ariel, and that bitch would destroy everything with a breath of venom. A lifetime against a minute.... Help me, I beg of you! In that building, locked and bolted away, how can she possibly harm anyone?" The bitter features softened. "After all, were our positions reversed and I the lunatic, Ariel would so protect me!"

"Yes, I've no doubt," Desmond wearily admitted, wanting to be rid of that beautiful, doomed creature once and for all. "I'll do what I can. If I find a family—"

"No!" Nicholas Farjeon cried in a fierce whisper. "Ariel belongs here. At Bellereve, where she was born and where she will die—a Farjeon. . . ."

Alone, in those hated quarters, bereft of even the Jackal's unwelcome company, Ariel Farjeon paced as she had not done since her early years in Weston Asylum. Walking to keep alive, to try to stifle a flood of memories. Why had Simon Desmond forsaken her? Don't prick the memory too much, shrilled the warning voice. You remember how he looked at you. . . . But where was it? In a lover's embrace in Yarmouth? A Sheringham cottage, or in a railway carriage? *Don't remember*. And she grieved. Grieved, as she had only once before in her life. But Nicholas came to her. He came not judging, held out his arms, and swept her to his heart.

"I'm so sorry," she wept.

"Desmond's a bastard like all the others. I asked him to stay on as a pure formality. Officially, he'll square things away. But I'll be the one taking care of you, Ariel."

Wiping away tears, she stared at him. "Why did it change, Nicholas?"

"The baby. You know that."

"But what did I do? I can't remember!" she cried brokenly. "Moment by moment it changes. What happened?"

He led her into the small room toward the pallet. "Do you remember, when we were much younger, how we sometimes spoke of the madness in the family?" A ripple of fear ran down her back. She nodded. "I told you there was a strong likelihood it might hit one of us, and we both agreed—swore to it—that if one were stricken, the survivor would look after the other for life." She was weeping again, very frail in his arms. "You are the one, Ariel. You bear the curse, and I am your protector. . . ."

"And Regina?" she asked sadly.

"Regina will find what she seeks." He smiled. "An evil, stupid woman who has played mischief-maker since she entered Bellereve."

"I'm so tired, Nicholas," Ariel said plaintively. "Where is my baby?"

"Go to bed, sweet sister." Swiftly undressing her, he helped her into the cot.

"My baby! Give me my baby," she implored.

Tenderly, he placed a small pillow against her breast. "Here's the baby," he crooned, watching her kiss and fondle it. Behind him, the Jackal appeared, mouth agape. "She'll be all right," Farjeon said dully. "These episodes don't last too long. Once, many years ago, she thought she bore a child. . . ."

Beatrice Clayton had been waiting throughout the day for a word with Simon Desmond, but he proved alarmingly uncommunicative. At luncheon, a tray was delivered to his surgery while he made up medications, and following the close of the second clinic, he departed on rounds. Hoping to beard him at tea, she was again eluded; at dinner, he was nowhere to be seen. Finally, late in the evening, she cornered him in his consulting room. He was deplorably drunk.

Distressed, she ran a hand through his blond hair, wet and tousled like a small boy's. "Do you want to talk about it?" He shook his head. She kept her voice light. "We must. Is Ariel Farjeon back at Bellereve?"

"Yes."

"There's something you should know, Simon. I had no visiting friend in London. I simply spent the weekend in Lynn." He looked up, red-eyed. "It was all a ruse . . . hoping you would realize your folly"—ashamed, she gave a small sigh—"and send her back home. You see, there's still a chance to pick up the pieces. The career, which you worked at so hard, need not be ruined. Symonds and others will help you—" She shrugged. "Granted, she has the face of an angel. I suppose not many men could resist such beauty?" At his brooding glare, she asked softly, "And how many did?"

"Not many." Desmond's face was rigid. "I gather she was the village whore. Lusting after the dregs of society. . . . Oh, Farjeon did tell me earlier. I simply chose to ignore it. Closed my eyes and pretended—"

"Well, you're awake now and must forget. I, too, was taken in. She was so enchanting. But the gossip, my dear—you must have heard some of it—has been devastating."

"What is said?"

"That you brought her deliberately to Fairhaven to be your mistress."

Desmond threw back his head and laughed.

"Who . . . attacked her?" Beatrice whispered, her cheeks pink.

"Farjeon said she likes it that way," he drunkenly replied.

"Dear God!"

He took another swig from the brandy bottle, sneering. "And what remedy have you for the besotted swain?"

"Concentrate on the living. Ariel Farjeon was lost long ago."

Unsteadily, he lurched to his feet. "How am I to forget?" he mumbled. "Am I to stamp her out of my dreams—my very existence—as if our lives had never crossed?" Again came a haunting image of being buried in her body, of taking her so many times that his soul engulfed hers. If only he had made her pregnant, then she would be completely full of him. . . .

"You must forget if you want to save yourself," the practical voice droned on. "Admit it, Simon, she's insane, isn't she?"

Stirring the dying fire's embers, he muttered, "I know only one thing. That I love her."

"An infatuation!"

"We made love," he said quietly, staring at his hands, still feeling her body's response. "We had one night in Yarmouth, sleeping together as man and wife."

Beatrice Clayton shook her head in dismay. "I was afraid that might happen—"

"She gave me her love as sweetly and passionately as if no other man had ever touched her."

"Simon, the fact that she would lie with you clearly shows her depravity!" she argued vehemently. Hiding her deep shock, she led him to the convex mirror. "Look at yourself, my dear. You can have any woman you want. Find another Howland and forget this crazed beauty!"

"How can I when I must see her twice weekly?" he cried, beside himself with raging grief.

"Something happened between you. Why did you take her back to Bellereve?"

Shadows hid his face. "I was thinking of marriage, and then I lost her—" She blinked, not understanding. "The woman I loved vanished. I no longer knew what she was. Sane or insane. . . . A killer or not. For months, I've felt bewitched. Now I'm frightened, Bea. My sanity so close to hers—"

"Tush! All the more reason to forget," she muttered. Then very gently, she said, "Have you eaten?"

"No."

"Well, I'll fix supper, and then you get a good night's

sleep—" At his muffled protest, she said sharply, "Your patients come before personal grief. Each day will get better."

"I seem to have heard that before."

"You said it to me after Jed's death."

Desmond's smile was ironic. "But you never got over him, did you, Bea?"

"No, but I'm alive and haven't done too badly." Taking his arm, she picked up a small oil lamp. "Now, leave the shadows and come back with me. . . ."

Outwardly, Simon Desmond was his old self, tending his faithful patients and wooing back the deserters while trying to ignore his dwindling savings. Twice a week, he went to Bellereve, subjecting Ariel Farjeon to the most perfunctory treatment. Always he dismissed the Jackal, not because of her irritating presence but because he wanted to hurt his lost darling by his continual silence and icy contempt. Her misery appeared not to bother him at all. In reality, so great was his despair, he could hardly bear to be in the same room with her. One day, in cold fury, he kissed her.

At her loving response, Desmond led her into the ugly little room where, oddly, he now so often found her. Locking the door, he returned to the cot, a look of passionate yearning on his face. She stood shyly before him in a worn, carefully patched chemise.

"Lie down," he ordered softly, kneeling beside her. She complied, trembling at his excitement. Through the thin material, his eager mouth sought her breasts, strong hands caressed her body. Ariel Farjeon stared at him in bewildered pleasure, yielding with joy.

Simon Desmond studied her face. She was ready. Very ready for him.

"Bitch!" he shouted.

Shock, terror, and pain crossed her face. Feebly, she tried to push him away, but he laughed, pulling the garment up around her waist, tearing open the bodice.

"How many others have you had?" he asked savagely. "Have you seduced with your 'innocence'?"

Amused by her struggles, he waited a moment, feeling her frightened heartbeat under his hand. Then he plunged into her with heavy, vicious thrusts, delighted to hear her low cries, her pleas for mercy. And his violence muted the searing memory of Yarmouth's tenderness. Taunting her, he again nursed at her breasts, then brutally took her a second time. And she said nothing. Until the very end. Finishing with her, he rose from the bed.

"Why, Simon? Why?" she asked, eyes filling with tears.

He glanced at the defiled body and wept. "I loved you, Ariel. You broke my heart." Sinking down beside her, he cradled her in his arms. "In Yarmouth, I have never known such happiness with a woman—"

"Nor I with any man," she whispered. "You must believe that."

"I know you no longer. Perhaps I never did.... Today I have obliterated Yarmouth. You are not my love—my heart's darling. You are merely a whore I bedded...." He left her alone.

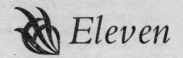 *Eleven*

She heard the outer door slam—a giant reverberation that always made her wonder why the building didn't collapse. Sometimes she felt its foundation shake, but that might be in dreams when the ancient wing burned and burned repeatedly and the great beams fell.... Next the iron bolt was driven home. That meant the Jackal's return, but the creature wouldn't disturb her. The cramped room with its history of pain was too intimidating for a superstitious mind. Nothing would make her step inside. Trays were left outside the door with a clatter and there deposited by the madwoman when finished. Only rarely did the two meet. An observer noting them would have seen a subtle change of position. Since her abrupt return from Fairhaven, Ariel, once the weaker, now dominated the crone. Had something been said? Ariel Farjeon wondered bleakly. Had she committed an act so despicable as to frighten her wardress? But Yarmouth had washed everything away. A block against past and present, and nothing fit together anymore. Not even her body, which belonged to someone else.... Once, a man had loved her. No, there were two men, among so many.... In shame, she huddled deeper into the muslin sheets. And a tiny face, like a flower, pressed against her heart.... Diamond tears fell onto her fingers.

Her brother stood in the doorway, staring down at her. Nicholas Farjeon, handsome as a Moorish prince, a man of such promise, whose life she had ruined.

"Simon Desmond left in an unusually great hurry...." Strolling across the room, he pulled back the sheet. After a long moment of silence, he covered her up, his hands trembling. "He'll pay for this, Ariel. Desmond will pay!"

"He thought himself... in love... with me—" She fixed him with great wondering eyes.

"A mistake others have made, too, eh?" He wiped her tear-stained face with a handkerchief. "And you, my pet, are you in love with him?"

"No, Nicholas," she said with a terrible smile. "It only pleased me to toy with him."

"But one man you did not play cat-and-mouse with. Who was your lover, Ariel?"

"So many years ago... so many years—" she moaned.

"Who was it?" he cried passionately, shaking her.

Equally vehement, she stood her ground. "Damn you! It certainly wasn't Simon Desmond! So leave him alone, Nicholas. He's not worth a farthing. Only one... only one." She broke into grievous sobs.

"Hush, my dearest. I'll protect you now. No one will hurt you," he crooned, rocking her as he might a little child.

"Will I be sent to Bedlam?" she asked in a still voice.

"I really don't know, Ariel. Not if I can help it, but it does depend on your behavior. Sadly, both Regina and Desmond think it best—" At her shocked cry, he gave her a pitying look. "Ah, so he played you the fool! Misled you into thinking otherwise. Teasing his way into your bed...." Her gray eyes were very angry. "Tell me, Ariel, who was the better actor?"

"We deceived one another. Does it matter?" she icily retorted. "Besides, if I'm to go to Bedlam, where am I to find such a man again?" She laughed. "The sun and the moon don't come to lunatics' cells...."

"How many have there been?"

"Myriads, you know that. But only *one love*."

"And was he dear to you?"

"Yes."

"Good! I'm glad you remember."

"Oh, I remember—" Their eyes locked. "My sins! I never forget...." A spasm shook her body, and she collapsed against him. "I'm so tired, Nicholas. Let me sleep now, please...."

"One day, we'll have him," he said slowly.

"Desmond?" She sneered. "He's nothing...."

Ariel Farjeon the child, and Ariel Farjeon the woman, was

a survivor. Having witnessed so much in her life, she had
become adept at deceit. A lie sprang more readily to her lips
than the truth. But there was a strange twilight period when
she herself was lost—bedeviled by dreams and memories: fire
in a small room, reeking padded walls, and a man's strong
arms. Among such a host, how could she remember which one
had been her lover? *Lover or love?* One man she was in love
with, and she wept, silently despairing. . . .

Nicholas Farjeon brought her dinner that evening. "Why do
you weep?" he asked coldly. "For Simon Desmond?"

"No," she whispered. "Oh, God, Nicholas, I'm so frightened! Don't let them send me to Bedlam—"

"We have three weeks, Ariel." Derision turned to gentle-
ness. "Remember I have the final say in the matter."

"Help me leave this room!" she begged. "Grandfather died
here, didn't he?"

"Yes."

"Dead three days. . . ." Panic edged her voice.

"Ariel!"

"Help me!"

"How can I if you talk like that?"

"I get things very mixed up, Nicholas. You know that. If
you turn against me . . . I'm doomed!"

"Once, I abandoned you. It won't happen again. You will
sleep in this room. Live in the other. For the rest of your life.
If you behave."

Behave. An act of forgetting. Easy enough during the day
in the Jackal's presence, or with Nicholas, who was now a
steady visitor, spending hours in her company, sketching her
as of old, reading to her, taking her for long walks in the park.
Years slipped away as they regained the old closeness. Two
minds, one thought. Once, she made him laugh, and he caught
her in an embrace.

"You are the only one who can make me laugh! Sweet sister,
even as a child you lightened my heart."

Ariel stroked his face, and they gently kissed, loving friends.

Behave. An act of forgetting. Impossible at night or in those
rare daytime moments when she was alone, desperate for Simon
Desmond. Sobbing with abandon because she so longed for
him—the soft, sweet touch of his blond hair, his mouth passionately hard on hers, his hands brutally possessive, and the
intoxicating pleasure of his lovemaking. Not understanding the

breach—what had caused that last terrible moment between them, for they were as strangers. . . .

One day, as Nicholas sketched her while she read, with the Jackal absent, he asked quietly, "Ariel, could I do a nude study? With such a body, you should run naked. Not even pregnancy marred it."

She smiled.

"Clothes are not for you. I always told you that—"

"But Nicholas, I'm so much older now!" she protested.

"I have seen your body, and it's beautiful. Even more lovely, I think, than years ago." His eyes darkened. "Take off your clothes."

Slowly, the garments fell, and she stood before him, naked. Farjeon studied her with a painter's detachment. "You are exquisite, Ariel." Then he frowned. "Only the hair is wrong. Why did it go white?"

"I don't remember," she replied, very frightened.

"Another sin, eh?" He raised a cynical eyebrow.

She stiffened and threw a blanket over herself. "Yes, I have greatly sinned."

"These last years haven't been easy on me either. You had your purgatory to go through, but I had my own hell. Can you imagine what it's been like married to that bitch?"

Ariel Farjeon laughed. "Yes!"

"No one!" he cried suddenly, very moved. "No one will ever part us again. . . ."

Hand in hand, they renewed their trust. Once, out walking, she asked Nicholas why she was so afraid of fire. "Have you forgotten even that?" He looked stunned. "Standing with Father and me, watching the wing burn?"

"Yes!" She cringed. "Only a shadow running across my path as I fell, and a great burst of flame." She wept.

Farjeon draped a protective arm around his sister's shoulders. "You mustn't distress yourself, Ariel."

But today she was weak, incapable of forgetting, the pretense exhausting. Simon Desmond had paid his visit, and his indifference left her distraught. And always nearby, waiting for the session to end, stood Nicholas Farjeon, eyes smoldering with hatred.

"Have I really only one more week?" she asked fearfully.

His voice was distant. "Yes."

Bellereve shone in the afternoon sun like a palace, reddish-gold in the glittering light. She fell to her knees in supplication.

"Have mercy on me, Nicholas! Don't send me to Bedlam. . . ." Feebly, she tugged at his sleeve. "It will kill me. I can take no more."

He spoke in a harsh whisper. "You are an evil, wanton woman. Not even twelve years in an asylum has broken you—"

"I died years ago with my baby. . . . Dear God, is there to be no end to my suffering!"

"You will be good? Resist temptation? No more Desmonds?"

"No! No," she gasped, her heart tearing.

"He will pay, Ariel." He pulled her to her feet.

No emotion crossed her face. She stood mute.

"Say it!" Farjeon gave her an angry shake.

"He will pay," she echoed dully. "Desmond will pay. . . ."

But Simon Desmond was already paying. Paying bitterly for a foul act committed by a violently jealous man. Yet the attempt to destroy, ironically, had only made him fall more deeply in love. Humbly acknowledging his guilt, he sought to atone, but there was no way of reaching Ariel Farjeon during those pitifully brief visits held under Farjeon's steely vigilance or the Jackal's leer.

One week more and then quite likely he would never see her again. Seven days, and still he agonized over his decision: one minute tempted to send her to Bethlem, the next favoring the hideous stone building while he weighed the alternative in the shattered recesses of his soul. Take on the responsibility himself. Lease a cottage and hire someone to look after her. What matter if the countryside thought them lovers and his career ended in ignominy? What matter if they never again slept together? His reputation's loss and the death of her love equaled the devastating hurt he had inflicted on her. No amount of tenderness could ever make up for such cruelty, but it might be a start. . . .

Someone else had been marking time. Regina Farjeon, whose life had so drastically changed since that dreadful encounter with Nicholas. Sitting numbed and frightened at her powder-strewn dressing table, with rubies in her hands and a welt around her throat where the necklace had bitten deep, her first impulse had been to rush her sons back to her father's house. Confess the fiasco. But such a repugnant step would admit her failure to a man who had never wanted the marriage and make him privy to the awful legacy attacking the Farjeons.

"One of your grandsons—or both—may go insane. Help me, Father!" She had never begged for anything in her life. Good fortune dropped into her lap, and it still might if only she could rid Bellereve of her hated sister-in-law. And so she watched daily, her pale face and vacuous blue eyes framed in mullioned windows, observing brother and sister strolling in the vast park, hands clasped, heads bent together in conversation, an echo of laughter rippling through the air. Regina watched, missing nothing. Nicholas, who barely gave her five minutes of his day, lavished hours on his mad Ariel.

On this particular afternoon, Regina was following their progress from the bay and oriel windows in the Long Gallery. Ariel Farjeon's head rested against her brother's broad shoulder, his arm encircled her waist. It they took their usual course, they were not likely to come in for some time. One more week, Regina thought grimly, and by God, she'd have her shipped off to Bedlam! If Nicholas fought, a monetary trick might bring him to heel. Or something else. . . .

An odor of paint wafted into her nostrils, and she hesitated outside her husband's studio. It still struck her as remarkable that never once over the years had he offered to show her his work. On impulse, she went and tried the bronze handle. Locked, as she thought, but she might get in through the library. Again, she crept up to a bay window overlooking the park and drawbridge. Water lilies, like dead fish trailing weeds, floated on the surface of the moat. A vivid splash was a carp. The whole damn thing ought to have been filled in—not just two sides— but Nicholas was infatuated with the picturesque, and so they lived with it, stench and all.

Brother and sister were far away, heading toward the fir plantation. That gave Regina a good hour at least. Ducking into the library, she hurried to the studio's second entrance, which fortunately stood unlocked. The room was a blaze of sunlight. Here, the wainscotting had been painted white to match the dazzling ceiling. Regina Farjeon, not a poetic or fanciful woman, had a moment's unpleasant impression of being caught up in a bolt of lightning, punctuated by great spurts of color. Minutes disintegrated . . . a half-hour, an hour. . . . Fascinated and appalled, she looked through stacks of canvases, folios, and sketchbooks, feeling her age for the first time. It was a shattering experience and drove her back hastily to her suite, subdued.

Many cigarettes were consumed that evening, and dinner

on a tray was ignored while she dipped into a bottle of brandy, plotting her next move. Should she ask her father to Bellereve? An unlikely idea, since he found its ancient beauty pretentious. Well, then go to her husband. Talk to Nicholas. Now was the perfect moment. . . . She began ransacking her wardrobe for the most seductive peignoir available. Satins, lace, and a great froth of silk tumbled into her arms. No, the tactic was too obvious. He would have dined with Ariel and must think that she—rejected—had gone out.

Arranging an elaborate, jeweled coiffure, Regina powdered, rouged her cheeks, carmined her lips, then put on a diamond necklace and matching dewdrop earrings. Next she eased herself into an overly tight ruby velvet dinner dress with a heavy, cumbersome train. An hour of suffering was worth it, she thought, buttoning up long kid gloves. Only an opera cloak was needed to complete the brilliant effect.

Satin slippers clacked on the oak floor as she swept imperiously down the Long Gallery. For a few moments, she stood frozen outside his suite, then knocked with a twinge of anger. A low voice responded, and she opened the door. He was reading in the massive Jacobean bed. Once, in the early days of their marriage, they had slept here. The exact occasion was obscure in her mind, but Regina had never forgotten the painting hanging over the marble fireplace, and that was what she had come to see.

A portrait of a young woman, naked, whose exquisite body was partially concealed by a wave of long black hair falling like the midnight sea. Regina had detested it because of its blatant sexuality, the face so beautiful, the body so lush that any man seeing it would be aroused. Now in its presence, she felt chilled. Again and again, Nicholas had sketched the same woman. A few months before, Regina wouldn't have known the subject. Now she did.

Planting herself at the foot of his bed, she waited until she had his full attention. "How old was she when you painted that?" she asked coldly.

The vellum-bound book snapped shut. "How old was who? My model?"

"Ariel!" his wife hissed.

He smiled as if at a simpleton. "Don't be absurd, Regina! Would I subject my sister to such abuse?"

Off came the cloak in a defiant swirl. Her voice rose shrilly. "Yes, Nicholas, you would. Today I spent an hour in your studio. Only one model have you ever used in your sketches, your paintings—Ariel!"

"I know you loathe her, Regina, but this is despicable."

Hands on hips, she screamed, "You even painted her nursing her bastard!"

"No," he said acidly. "That was a sketch made on the Continent, where women frequently feed their babies publicly." Farjeon sneered. "As someone who has never shown the least curiosity in art, I find your accusations staggering. You realize what you're implying?"

A look of fear darted across her face. The reply was a long time coming. "Improper...."

"Incestuous." Gray eyes flicked toward the canvas in its heavy gilt frame. "Since you've shown such keen interest, let me tell you about my studies." He leaned forward, an arm outstretched on the mound of pillows.

"Sometimes the artist may occasionally see a person or object so beautiful that the heart is forever ensnared. 'Bewitched' might be a better word. Such a face was Ariel's, when young ... haunting"—his voice sank to a whisper—"and it is hers above the mantelpiece. I admit it. Also, she does appear in a number of my works, as she often sat for me before her breakdown. Fully clothed, however!" he added in a scathing tone.

"That body." Throwing back his head, he regarded the portrait with half-closed eyes, "belonged to a young woman I found in Spain. A Gypsy I saw dancing one night in Granada underneath the shadows of the Alhambra. Like America's romantic Washington Irving, I, too, had taken rooms in one of the palace buildings, and I spirited her back to my suite as model and mistress...." Regina flushed, and he laughed at her discomfiture.

"By day, I drew that voluptuous body, and by night, she danced only for me to the accompaniment of guitars, castanets, and splashing fountains, and I quenched my fire...."

Husband and wife stared at one another bleakly.

"That, Regina, is her body in the paintings and sketches. But being only a Gypsy, she lacked my sister's patrician features, so I decided to combine the two." He frowned. "I think the results quite good, don't you?"

It took her a long moment to gather her wits together. Nervously fingering straying jewels in her hair, she finally managed to mumble, "I don't believe you!"

Farjeon raised a sardonic eyebrow. "What?"

"I don't believe you, Nicholas. No one in his right mind seeks such bizarre perfection."

His eyes flashed. "No ordinary man does, you mean, but an artist—"

"No!" she shrieked. "It's Ariel's body in these rooms, not some Gypsy whore." Grabbing her cloak, she ran for the door. "Tomorrow I'll see Father!"

Instantly, he was out of bed, the rich folds of his dressing gown cascading about his powerful body. "You are my wife. I've told you the truth. The face is Ariel's, and it's all I have to remember her by. Beauty, like flowers, withers overnight."

Regina blanched.

"The whore's body is probably dead by now. . . . Why be jealous—*and you are*"—he said in a furious crescendo—"of the few visits I pay my sister! She is only a poor, demented creature—"

"Poor . . . demented?" she echoed, visibly shaken. "That's why she should be put away."

"No, my dear, I can't do that. Not one of my relatives was ever put away. They lived out all their long lives in that stone building—mad but completely harmless, like Ariel."

And now she was the incredulous one. "Two Farjeons were pyromaniacs. You dare call them not dangerous! What are we waiting for? A third fire?"

"One of our sons might be so afflicted." He held out his hands in a gesture of appeal. "Would you have them incarcerated in Bedlam's hell or safely lodged in their own home?"

Regina began to sniffle. Too many cigarettes and too much brandy had sapped her strength. She ought to have arrived clear-headed. The fire blazing away was much too hot. Drops of perspiration broke out on her forehead.

Through a fog, his voice reached her softly. "I take the blame unto myself. You know that, Regina." Shadows darkened the handsome face. "Just let her stay. She has so little—"

"Each day you walk like lovers!"

"Come. . . . Come, you're overwrought! Let's have a brandy and talk about it reasonably."

"Tomorrow I'll tell Father—"

"And what will you say?" he asked coolly. "I've told you the truth. You can't embroider it like a valentine!"

She drew herself up, outraged. "I'm going to seek a legal

separation, Nicholas. What I've seen here today justifies it."
Her smile was malicious. "How will you and your dearest Ariel
live then?"

"She needs less than a child," he muttered. "I wronged you
once, Regina, but in recompense, I gave you a place in society
and allowed you to take as many lovers as you pleased. I've
paid. Now it's your turn," he added huskily. "She remains at
Bellereve—"

"No!"

"Since you won't join me in a snifter of brandy, why don't
we talk in bed? I still remember what you like!"

As he sauntered toward her, she saw that he was naked
under the robe. Her pulse began to race, and she smiled at his
desire. Amazing, after so many bitter years, that she could still
feel lust for a man she despised. Still, he was the most fasci-
nating man she had ever slept with, and it would be a double
irony if she captured his emotion in some feverish embrace
and the next day managed to loose his sister into the ditch she
so richly deserved. . . .

Water trickling down stone walls. Hearing it distinctly, Ariel
Farjeon sat bolt upright in bed. It was cascading in rivulets
down the walls, sprinting towards the numerous drains littering
the icy floors. Curiously, her tiny bedroom had expanded from
a rectangle to a square shape. All trace of a window had vanished, along with the few sticks of furniture. Stone benches
ran the length of two walls. The thick oak door had metamor-
phosed into heavily armored metal with its sly peephole.

Utterly baffled, she tried to slip out of bed but was arrested
by the sight of struggling figures in the distance. A young,
unknown woman was flailing at shadows, her face contorted
with rage and grief. Two burly, uniformed men closed in on
her, imprisoning her in a vise, while a third clamped a pair of
manacles over frantic wrists. The writhing creature was dragged
into a second room, one closer to the watching Ariel Farjeon.

Thrown onto a chair, she was quickly strapped down, thick
leather thongs biting into her flesh. A stranger appeared, bran-
dishing a shining instrument with wicked teeth. Yanking down
the mass of raven hair, a foam of lustrous coils that fell below
her waist, he laughed at her cries of alarm and set to work.
Great soft curls were hacked to the scalp, leaving only a ragged
edge. Silently, the woman wept, trying to touch her head, but
the guards restrained her. Two new figures loomed in sight:

women with craggy, ugly faces and thickset bodies, smiling at the victim's suffering. The male warders shuffled out, and a macabre procession formed around the madwoman.

Now Ariel could hear the wardresses mocking the lunatic as they pushed her into a stone room. Jeering at her anguish, they stripped her naked, then chained the shrieking woman to a wall. In stepped a man carrying a large hose. Behind him, the door clanged shut. With a leer, he took very careful aim. A blast of water hit her in the face, then ran up and down her body like icy flames. Drowning against a stone wall, the captive screamed and screamed. Mercifully, she fainted, but was brutally revived by a burst of water against her temples. Twisting in agony, every bone in her body splintered.

As suddenly as the torture began, it stopped. The three accomplices disappeared, leaving the dripping woman still manacled to the wall.

Ariel Farjeon wept, now recognizing the woman, knowing the horror to come next.

Left to dry for over an hour in frigid temperatures, the wretched woman prayed for death . . . madness . . . or oblivion—anything to forget the nightmare her life had become. Back came her tormentors. Too weak to resist, she was hauled along a stone corridor into a padded room and, still naked, was encased in a straitjacket. Bruised and bleeding, one eye swollen shut, her face puffy, lips split open—an object of disgust—she was nevertheless found desirable enough by a warder who raped her that night.

A fractured rib and the solicitous care of a horrified young doctor—was it Simon Desmond? Ariel wondered, despairing—kept her safe from predatory attacks until he vanished, and the assaults began anew.

God! Will it never end? she cried to padded walls, barred windows, and locked doors. . . .

Someone was sitting on the edge of her pallet. The stink of the cell receded in watery darkness, and the tiny bedroom reappeared in gray light. Hearing her name called urgently, Ariel's eyes flicked wide open. A sting of light shattered her face. Strong hands shook her to consciousness.

"Nicholas!" Dazed, frightened, she leaned against his shoulder to escape the lamp's blinding glare.

"Listen to me, Ariel," he muttered tensely. "Regina and I have just had a violent quarrel. She came to my suite, insisting that you be sent to Bedlam. That she wouldn't stand for anything else! I tried everything to change her mind, but she was adamant and left in a blind rage, swearing that you would go—" His sister began to moan. "She's threatening to get a legal separation unless I agree, and she's got two doctors on her side ready to commit you—Colin Broughton and that bastard Desmond!"

"No, I don't believe it!" It was unbearable. Simon Desmond, whose lips she still tasted, whose arms still comforted her in the dreaded night. Simon Desmond, betrayer.

"You promised to help me," she said feebly. "What is it, Nicholas? What went wrong? Is it money?"

"Yes, damn it! If she leaves, I'll be bankrupt. . . . But there's something else. . . ."

"What?"

He hesitated, trying to still her trembling. "You know. . . ."

Ariel stiffened. "Why tell me?"

"Because I think she's coming to see you, and I want you to be prepared—"

"For what?"

"Perhaps the worst."

The dream had exhausted her. Her head felt like lead. "What am I to do?"

"I just told you, darling. She hates you. . . ."

In the dim light, their faces touched, and she pulled back, startled, running her hands up and down his back.

"You're wet, Nicholas. Soaking wet!"

"It's pouring outside." He ran his hand through her hair. "Poor darling, now I've gotten you all wet. Shall I fetch a dry gown?"

She shook her head and clutched her knees, thinking. "You're sure she'll come in this weather?"

"Yes, if only for the pleasure of tormenting you. . . ." Rising from the bed, he ran the light across her stricken face.

"Is there no way you can protect me?"

"Not if she goes ahead with a separation. Today she's off to her father." He looked crushed, at his wits' end. "God knows, Ariel, I've tried! Hard. Very hard. But it hasn't worked out. Pity Desmond turned against you. . . ." He headed for the door, his breathing labored. "Perhaps you can think of something. . . ."

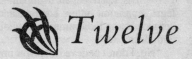 *Twelve*

The shrill jangle of the bell over Simon Desmond's bed rudely broke his sleep. Fighting the summons, he burrowed into pillows and blankets. Wide awake in the next moment, he fumbled for the match tin on his bedside cabinet, but night had given way to dawn. Flinging on his robe and slippers, he padded across the carpet to a window. Through vapors flooding the Elizabethan garden came pink rays of sunrise. Desmond winced, remembering another such glorious moment at Yarmouth. Below him, the flowers twinkled like jewels, dew-drenched. It would be a lovely, balmy day, he thought, hurrying down the stairs to answer the frantic appeal.

The man waiting for him on the porch sagged in exhaustion. One of Farjeon's grooms, Desmond realized, pulling him into the hall's warmth.

"Please, sir. . . ." he gasped. "Come to Bellereve. . . . The mistress has had a fall—"

"Down the staircase?" Desmond blinked.

"No, sir—" He went dead white, and Desmond, pushing him onto a chair, fetched a glass of brandy. With a grunt of thanks, he tossed the liquid down, rubbing his mouth with the back of a hand. "She fell into the moat—"

Astonished, Desmond asked quickly, "Is she dead?"

"Don't know, sir." The reedy voice quivered. "Master was working over her when I left."

"I'll be ready in five minutes." He grasped the man's shoulder. "Now, off to the kitchen with you, and get yourself some breakfast—"

Ten minutes later, Simon Desmond was on his way to Foulsham. As the sun rose, lush grass stood up like velvet tipped arrows; the hedgerows sprang alive with bird song and the chatter of squirrels. Down rutted lanes his chestnut tore, alarming an occasional deer, which sprang away into the forest's safety. Laborers at work waved as he galloped by.

The wrought-iron gates at Bellereve stood wide open. Of the keeper there was no sign, and no smoke came from the chimney. Obviously, he and his family were up at the manor-house, Desmond surmised, whipping his horse onward.

Bellereve, magically golden in sunlight, now had a sunken appearance, its walls a dusky red. Clattering over the drawbridge, Desmond halted in the courtyard. Dismounting, he surveyed the scene. Servants huddled together in gossip or shuffled about aimlessly, stunned looks on pasty faces.

"Where is she?" Desmond asked the groom.

"Over there, sir," and he pointed to the back moat. A small crowd clustered on the stretch of lawn where he and Ariel had so often walked. Desmond hurried forward, striding carefully across broken brick and moss-tufted cracks. By early morning light, the charred wing looked like a monster sleeping in a shroud of vines. As he approached, the group silently parted, to reveal Farjeon kneeling over Regina.

Desmond bent down, then sniffed, surprised to detect a strong aroma of brandy emanating from the body. For she was quite dead. Water lilies and pieces of reed lay tangled in her tawny hair, in the sodden folds of ruby velvet and lace. The face, brazen in life, bore a faint look of surprise, and the blue eyes were filmy. Desmond, examining her hands, saw that some of the fingertips were macerated. The body did not feel cool—an indication that she had been submerged less than five hours. There was no sign of rigor. Closing the vacant eyes, he turned to the husband.

"May I have a word with you, sir?"

Farjeon winced, his face gray with fatigue. As if snapping out of a dream, he nodded, and the two men walked away from the crowd, the ruined wing an unpleasant setting for their discussion.

"What happened?" Simon Desmond asked tensely.

Nicholas Farjeon held up a hand against the sun's glare, then shook his head in disbelief, thoughts reeling. "I really don't know," he said with effort. "Regina and I quarreled late last night over Ariel. She came to my suite—drunk. Gave me an ultimatium. Ariel must be sent to Bedlam. I pleaded our cause...." He smiled faintly at Desmond. "Keep her at Bellereve. She took that badly. Stormed out of the room.... And that is the last I saw of her."

"Go on," Desmond demanded after a pause.

Farjeon glanced over his shoulder. A servant was covering up his wife's body. "It's my custom to read until early morning. Apparently, I dozed off, because shortly before dawn I heard a scream—"

"From your bedroom?"

"Yes, a casement window was open. It came from this direction."

"What time was it?"

"Desmond, I don't know." Farjeon looked wretched. "I didn't look at a clock. I simply judged it to be near dawn by the light. I came down immediately but saw nothing...except over there—" He nodded toward the body. "Marks in the grass near the edge of the moat where, presumably, she slipped and fell, or was pushed—" The melodious voice trembled. "And there was something else...a wheelbarrow."

"A what?" Desmond asked stupidly.

"A wheelbarrow" was the brittle reply. "Listen to me, Desmond. Regina was in such a rage that it's quite likely she went to see Ariel—"

"My God, why?"

"Another taunting. Who knows what went on in that vicious mind! She made threats against Ariel and in her raging state could easily have paid her a visit." A spasm of grief touched his face. "There's something you must know. My key was in Ariel's door. It was unlocked...."

Desmond's heart skipped a beat.

"Come, see her." Farjeon headed for the stone suite.

"Now? In front of all these people!" He was appalled.

"Yes, now," cried the other man urgently. "It's probably nothing, but I want you to judge for yourself."

"The police—"

"Not yet!" Farjeon snapped, halting before the iron-banded door. "See, now it's locked. A precaution I took after checking here this morning." Withdrawing his key, he spoke in a whisper. "My first thought, I'm afraid, concerned Ariel. Had anything happened to her? But she was alone...." He sighed, easing the door open, making as little noise as possible. The two men stepped into the desolate sitting room. "Regina was nowhere in sight—"

"An autopsy will disclose whether or not she was alive when she entered the water," Desmond interrupted, nervously impatient.

"Ah, but will it reveal if it was accidental or murder?"

Faint color touched Desmond's cheeks. "Hopefully, yes," he brusquely replied. "Now, may I see Miss Farjeon?"

"Of course."

In the little room, Ariel Farjeon sat on the edge of the pallet, wearing only a nightdress, her delicate hands clasped together, great eyes fixed on the door. At their sudden appearance, she flinched, then lapsed into her rigid attitude.

Simon Desmond, battling turbulent emotions, took her face in gentle hands. Again she seemed to be caught in an unreal world, but he felt her tremble, and her eyes, meeting his for an instant, were lucid. Stroking her hair, he froze, then quickly ran a hand over her gown, backing away in horror.

"Dear God, she's wet!" he muttered to Farjeon, who hurriedly examined his sister.

"Damp now, I'd say. Earlier she was soaked through. That's what I wanted you to see."

Heartsick, his companion stumbled out to the sitting room. Behind him Farjeon closed Ariel's door. "Well, what do you think?" he asked.

Desmond mopped his face with a handkerchief, overwhelmed, his voice barely audible. "Who found the body?"

"I did. Ariel's state was peculiar—to say the least. Sitting there like that, waiting and watching for God knows what!" A bitter laugh broke from him. "I went back to the moat and examined the grass. Something... was caught in the water lilies... bumping back and forth. I returned the wheelbarrow to its shed and came back with a long hook.... What I fished out was Regina—" He faltered. "I'm sorry. It wasn't a happy marriage, but one doesn't like such an ending.... I tried to revive her, without success, then called the servants and had you summoned."

Desmond was strolling restlessly about the chamber, seeing nothing except that haunted face in the next room. "You say she was drunk?"

"Oh, yes."

"So she could have tripped and fallen in?"

"Easily, I would think." His eyes flashed. "But how do you explain Ariel's condition?"

Desmond faced him. "Farjeon, look at her! Regina was a big, vigorous woman. Your sister is frail. No match for your wife if she were conscious. And had she been insensible, I cannot imagine Ariel imbued with enough strength to drag her body all that distance away from this building."

Nicholas Farjeon smiled painfully. "You're forgetting a few things, doctor. Surely you must have learned in your student days that the mad possess not only great cunning, but extraordinary strength if needed."

"Yes." Desmond reluctantly concurred.

"Here's a woman—my sweet, beautiful sister—who killed her child and tried to murder me. . . ." The young doctor's face sagged. "Perhaps now you see the wheelbarrow's significance."

"Dear Jesus!"

"Yes, Desmond, a frail woman could push a dead or unconscious person in such a cart and easily tip it over. . . . That would give her quite a soaking, wouldn't it?"

Turning on his heel, Desmond strode to the front door. "I don't want to hear any more. This is police business—"

"Just a minute, sir!" Farjeon's tone was insolent. "*You* are going to sign the death certificate."

"I wasn't your wife's physician, Farjeon," Desmond protested. "Nor am I privy to the exact cause of her death."

"An accident. She fell into the moat in a drunken stupor."

"And what of Ariel Farjeon?" His voice sounded unreal.

"Sign the certificate. Call it accidental death from drowning, and I'll spend the rest of my life looking after Ariel. She'll never harm anyone again, I promise you."

"Do you realize what you're asking?" Desmond exploded. "You want me to shield a possible murderess!"

Farjeon sauntered over to him, grimly amused. "No, Desmond, your mistress. . . ." Horrified eyes met his. "I know about your romantic interlude in Yarmouth. Ariel keeps no secrets from me. . . . Tell me, doctor, are you in the habit of raping your beautiful patients?"

Simon Desmond caught his breath in anguish.

"Perhaps you were the villain assaulting her before and the groom was a dupe," Farjeon sneered.

"I fell in love with your sister months ago. That I won't

deny!" he cried passionately. "I even thought of marriage.
... But something came between us—"

"A rape!"

"No, damn it! Not that,..." he added wretchedly, trying
to blot out that awful moment in the Sheringham cottage when
he saw so frightful an image in Ariel Farjeon's eyes. As if a
preying animal lurked... "Still, she is to me the dearest person
in my life—"

"And so you raped her?"

Choking on the words, he shouted, "Yes, I took her and in
so doing killed our love!" In despair, he stared at the grime-
encrusted windows where she had beguiled him with frosted
sketches on Christmas Day. "Did she tell you that, too?" he
asked, unbearably moved, still hearing her cries.

"No, she didn't have to," Farjeon drawled. "Now, are you
going to sign that death certificate?"

"You realize you're asking me to commit a crime?"

"Not necessarily," Farjeon replied, laughing. "Ariel might
have been taking an early morning bath."

"What if I refuse?"

"If you refuse, Desmond, I'll press charges against you. I
see you managed to stay afloat after Howland's blow, but you
can't survive me. An immoral doctor is anathema to the public,
particularly when he abuses a helpless lunatic. I'll see that you
never work again."

"If I agree to this abomination"—Desmond's voice shook—
"will you continue to let me see her?"

"But of course, Dr. Desmond. My sister is ill. And I hope
you'll remember that and control your lust."

"I am paying for that act, Farjeon.... Now, I beg you,
give me a moment alone with her. It may never come again."

"One minute?" Farjeon's smile was derisive.

"One minute," breathed Desmond. "You can time us, and
I shan't hurt her," he added thickly.

The brother strolled over to the door and flung it wide.
"Very well."

Simon Desmond started to walk in... to catch her in a fast
embrace, to pour out his agony. Instead, he stood transfixed.
She still sat in the same uncanny position, but the hands that
had once so lovingly caressed him were like talons on her knees,
and he turned his back on her, his heart torn.

"What did you see?" Farjeon leaned against the doorjamb,
weary eyes studying Desmond's shocked face.

"I can't explain. . . ."

"Perhaps you've finally glimpsed my torment. Years of it . . ." said Farjeon, surprisingly gentle. "The angel hides the devil, my friend. She is very cunning and took you in as she roped all the others, with her exquisite charm and abandon. Ariel is worse than any London slut. Yet I cannot blame her, because nothing registers in that deplorable mind."

"I love her," Desmond whispered, grieving.

"So you will protect her," Farjeon replied evenly. "No one need know. Together we can shield her. . . ."

The examination of Regina Farjeon's body took a little under an hour. Nearby stood her husband, tensely alert to Desmond's every move. A thinned-out crowd of servants still loitered in the distance, their shadows flickering against Bellereve's walls.

"What time is it?" Farjeon asked his valet.

"Past seven, sir."

"See that my sons are told nothing. Just that their mother is ill. I'll attend to them later."

"Very good, sir."

On his knees beside the corpse, Simon Desmond raised a beckoning hand, and Farjeon hastened to join him.

"I see no evidence of foul play, sir." Desmond's voice rang unnaturally loud in the courtyard. "It appears to be a tragic accident." Farjeon shook his head, dazed. "I'm sorry, sir. Your wife was drunk. . . ." Oh, they'd caught it, all right, the scavengers who always lingered at scenes of disaster, huddling together like a pack of ravens, whispering, whispering. . . .

"Quite drunk, I'm afraid. She reeked of brandy." Every inquisitive ear heard it. Poor woman. Defaming the dead. Not a task he usually indulged in, he thought drearily. Still, she did smell of the stuff, and without the benefits of an autopsy, it would be difficult to prove otherwise. Only in thoughtful or tormented minds would doubts linger.

"I can't sign it," he muttered, staring at the ground. "Someone is bound to question her death. If not the villagers, what about her father?"

"I'll handle them." Farjeon's voice took on an edge. "Just sign the certificate. Otherwise, Desmond, it will fall on your darling's head. She'd be lucky then to end up in Broadmoor."

"I can't do it!"

"Do you wish to see her with a rope around her neck? Is that what you want?" Anger suffused the satanic features.

"Damn it, I want the truth!" Desmond hissed. "If you think her guilty of murder, what will stop her from killing again?"

"I will." Farjeon glanced back at the ruin, then at the young man kneeling before him. "Are you with me or not?"

Bitter lines etched Desmond's face. "I have little choice. You know that, Farjeon. . . . But are *you* to be trusted?" He flicked his adversary an icy look.

"As much as you, sir." Nicholas Farjeon smiled. "Ariel binds us together. If you fall, she will, too, and I can't risk that. You can count on me. Sign it!" he said with sudden vehemence.

"Twice a week, I'll visit her—maybe more often. That is my due."

"No fee then, eh?"

Desmond flushed. "Precisely." He signed the death certificate with his usual bold signature.

Nicholas Farjeon watched Desmond ride over the drawbridge, the slump of his back clear evidence that he would cause no trouble. Between them, Ariel was safe, and he hurried across the emptying courtyard to the stone suite. Quietly reentering, he studied the sitting room with bleak eyes. Like his sister, Nicholas had spent hours peering through dusty windows at the pathetic figure of their grandfather. God! How many miles had he walked in his despair? Around and around in endless circles. In and out, out and in through kitchen, sitting room, and bedroom, his body twisted by arthritis, his heart broken by his son's treachery. A gentle old man who wanted nothing more than to spend his last years contemplating Bellereve's splendors. His life was decent; he had harmed no one, and then he was imprisoned in three stone rooms because of a ten-year-old child's outbreak of madness.

The burden was too great, Nicholas thought. Day and night, she had haunted his thoughts since those unnerving interviews with his father nineteen long years ago.

"I have neglected you," the elder Farjeon said on one occasion. "And now we both suffer. A sensible man—particularly one in my position—would have remarried. But I couldn't. I still mourn your mother. Don't make that mistake," he added harshly. "What we had together was rare, but it's possible to compromise and find a different kind of happiness."

Looking at him with the cool eyes of a stranger, Nicholas saw a man laboring under great strain, whose vigor and exotic good looks had been totally defeated by his life's tragedies and the disease that was so soon to claim him.

"You must watch her, Nicholas—very carefully. Don't be fool enough to think you can relax your guard. Last year's tragedy may never happen again. I pray not." He laid a trembling hand on Nicholas's arm, grasping it urgently. "Be gentle with her. . . . After all, it might have been you." A spasm of pain shot across his ravaged features. "Marry well, Nicholas. Breed sons. Some will be healthy. . . ." Worn out, he rested at a bay window in the Long Gallery and caught a glimpse of a dancing maenad in the park. With a sad laugh, he murmured, "She dances like our Saracen ancestors. One day, you will look into her face and see the Alhambra. All the Farjeons will be caught in those wondrous eyes," he said in an ominously husky voice. "Be careful, my son. Find yourself a placid wife who will keep your feet on the ground—not a rainbow like Ariel!"

"I am not a stud, Father," the young man icily retorted. "When it pleases me, I shall marry."

"Oh, that's the way it is, eh?" His father's eyes glittered with emotion. "Then to both my children I say, the ordinary will not spark fancies. . . ."

In the sitting room, Nicholas Farjeon's desolate glance swept over shabby pieces of furniture and Ariel's poor possessions: a few books, limp flowers in a cracked vase, a mirror so dim that it could scarcely reflect her beauty. . . . How he hated this place. Stones pressing against his heart, cutting off his life.

I took on the charge, Father. Suitors came by the score, bearing lavish gifts, frantic for her hand, but none of them pleased her. Each and every one offended her tempestuous nature. Hours were wasted laughing over their foibles. It was fire she craved. And she found it. . . .

God, how much more can I bear? Nicholas Farjeon cried silently, opening his sister's door. Still she sat on the pallet as Simon Desmond had left her. At sight of her brother, she shivered.

"Nicholas, I'm still waiting," she said plaintively. "Regina hasn't come. Where is she?"

"She's dead, Ariel. Drowned in the moat."

His sister gazed at him in terror. "Oh, my God!"

Farjeon cradled her protectively in his arms. "Hush! Don't be frightened. Everything's going to be all right now, thanks to you and Desmond. He's calling it an accident." She held her hands over her ears, trying not to hear. "I know she came,

Ariel. You can't pretend with me. The key was in the door—"

"No! No—" She broke into wild sobbing.

"I'm not blaming you," he crooned. "You were provoked, weren't you, darling?"

"You'll send me to Bedlam!" she cried, hysterical.

"No, sweet. All the mad Farjeons have lived out their lives within these stone walls. This will be your home until you die."

She fell on her knees before him, clasping his hands to her heart. "I can't bear it, Nicholas. I feel their presence. Kill me. I'd rather be dead—"

"But you won't be alone, dearest," he replied, infinitely patient. "I'll not abandon you again, and friend Desmond will be our chief supporter." Abruptly his mood changed, the gray eyes narrowing with contempt. "You fancied him, didn't you?" His sister shook her head, dazed. "Trying to get yourself another baby, eh?" He jeered.

"No," she cried, fighting a dull surge of anger. "He pleased me—"

"Oh, my dear, there have been so many, and you've enjoyed them all!" He sighed at her show of defiance. "Petulance is not called for. A little discretion would help, Ariel, although Father used to say no man would bring you peace. That your soul is too restless."

"Not my soul. My body!" She spat the words, rising gracefully to her feet. The sun's rays filtered through the small barred window, exposing her figure through the thin fabric of her nightdress.

"You always flaunt yourself, don't you?" Farjeon drawled in amusement. "I've just saved your life, and you toy with me as if I were one of your victims. You'd tempt even the devil, wouldn't you?" A flicker of fear touched her expression. "I thought you'd be grateful, Ariel. Desmond, poor bastard, swallowed the story without too much prodding, but then he's enamored of you—or so deludes himself," he added bitingly. "Now we just pray that no one comes snooping—"

"But I don't remember, Nicholas!" The great eyes welled with tears. "What did I do? When did she come?"

"After my visit, I suppose. . . ." His look was curious. "You always manage to forget, don't you?" She nodded. "A fire . . . a lover . . . a baby . . . and now this. Quite remarkable!" He smiled. "You're not the first Farjeon to kill, so don't upset yourself. In a few weeks' time, hopefully, Regina will be a dead item."

"And your sons?"

"Will live with their grandfather." He stood up. In despair, she twisted her hands, her face as white as her gown.

"Nicholas!"

"Yes?"

"Forgive me!" She wept.

"Have I ever blamed you?"

"Yes," she whispered, wiping away tears.

"All that was so long ago, Ariel, even I can't remember," he said softly. "So you see two can forget." He took her by the shoulders. "Just think. Bedlam is no longer a threat. You are forever safe at Bellereve!"

Slowly her arms encircled his waist. "You will marry again. . . ." she said wistfully.

"That's a thought." He laughed, lightly kissing her forehead. "Be careful of Desmond. He's a Janus. You know why I have him in my pocket, Ariel?" She blushed. "If you're a good girl, I may set you loose upon him one day. Would you like that?"

Ariel Farjeon flung back her head arrogantly. "I might."

It was not the response Farjeon had expected. His face flushed with anger. Pushing her away, he shouted, "You are twice a killer. And once attempted to murder me. . . . Now do you remember?"

A spasm shook her body, but she stood fast. "No," she breathed.

He struck her and she reeled, making a grab for the pallet. Missing it, she fell to the floor, hitting her head. Farjeon crouched beside her, gathering her to him, muttering incoherent words.

"I'm afraid, Nicholas. I'm so afraid. . . ." she moaned.

"We need one more week, Ariel. If we survive that—everything will be fine. The way it was . . . years ago." Again she was weeping, a low, broken sound. "I swore to Father to cherish and protect you—" He kissed her cheek. "But this time, no blackguards in the bed, eh?"

"No," she sobbed bitterly. "I will be good. . . . I will be good!"

Farjeon drew back the worn blanket and sheet, helping her into bed. As he tucked the blanket around her, she held him fast in surprisingly strong arms.

"Promise me . . . whatever happens—don't send me to Bedlam!"

His voice was chilly. "I told you, Ariel, you will spend the rest of your life in this suite."

"And Desmond will come?" she asked faintly.

"Certainly, darling. You're a very sick woman. . . ."

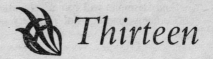 *Thirteen*

Five days. Simon Desmond, counting every anguished second since Regina Farjeon's death, waited in suspense for the dreaded visitor. A sharp-eyed constable, her physician—dear God! Who would it be? he wondered. Her grieving father, an inquisitive friend or lover? But no one came. All he met was gossip.

The poor woman, disliked in life, was pitied in death, the vulgarity forgotten or glossed over. Everyone despaired for her sons with their awful legacy and sympathized with her husband—such a tragic figure! Still, questions remained. Regina Farjeon was not known as a drinker. No one ever remembered seeing her intoxicated. The thought grew to a whisper. Who might gain by her death? And the words were spoken: Ariel Farjeon.... Now she would never be sent to Bedlam. Nicholas was too kind-hearted to commit her.

Simon Desmond, breakfasting with Beatrice Clayton, stared at her in dismay. "And this filth is making the rounds?" he asked, appalled.

Bea hesitated, hurt by his distress: the fine features pinched, the hazel eyes bruised from lack of sleep. "People can be terribly cruel...." She shrugged helplessly.

"Damn them! I wanted an autopsy. Farjeon refused," he said wearily. "But she'd been drinking heavily according to him and was saturated with the stuff. As for Ariel Farjeon—" His voice was laced with irony. "She is always imprisoned, and unless she possesses the miraculous ability to

178

float through stone walls and locked doors, I'm at a loss as to how she escaped. When Regina Farjeon fell into that moat, Ariel was safely locked up. You can tell that to all the busybodies. . . ." He stormed out of the dining room to his surgery.

But Bea's remarks had seriously alarmed him, and he wasted little time confronting Nicholas Farjeon. Brother and sister had just finished luncheon in Ariel's sitting room. Examining her with a professional eye, Desmond saw that her appetite was poor. Lunch had scarcely been touched. Dressed in one of her old gowns, her hair falling softly around a wan face, she seemed more specter than living human being, her face a mask. Only once did she meet Desmond's eyes, and he found her expression baffling. Shame, fear, and some other emotion that eluded him. Perhaps she only mirrored his own torment, he thought sadly. As for Farjeon, he was anything but the grieving widower. Regina's death appeared to have taken years off his life. He was positively affable as the two men walked back together to the library, leaving Ariel in the Jackal's company.

"Can't you find someone else?" Desmond irritably demanded as he settled down before the Regency desk-table.

Farjeon reclined in his chair like an emperor bathed in a swath of light from the oriel window behind him. "No, the woman does what's required of her, and if she chatters, no one listens. You can't have anyone too sharp in that position."

Desmond winced. "Is your sister not eating?"

"Little, since the—accident. . . ." He smiled. "But a reaction was bound to set in. Thank God, it's not mania!"

Desmond leaned forward. "I think you should know that gossip is rife in Heydon—probably the other villages, too. Curiosity as to why your wife reeked of brandy when she wasn't known to drink much—"

"Well, we all have our little secrets, don't we, doctor?" Farjeon's heavy-lidded eyes narrowed. "Unfortunately, Regina was a secret drinker. She went through long periods of abstinence and was always careful not to drink excessively in public. These bouts only occurred at Bellereve. Rarely was I privy to them as she confined herself to her suite. The night she died, she came to me, intoxicated. Hoping to calm her down, I plied her with more brandy. Sadly, it had the reverse effect. . . ." Studying Desmond's rigid face, he asked quietly, "Perhaps you'd like to see her cache?"

"We should have had an autopsy," he muttered. "Each day I expect the police. Who was her doctor?"

"Nigel Williams in Norwich. She never used any of the local people."

"Did her father say anything?"

"Well, yes, he did question her drinking," Farjeon heavily admitted. "I told him the truth. That we were not happily married, and these episodes had been going on for some years. Poor man, he got rattled. It seems Regina had been feeding him a pack of lies about her idyllic marriage."

"How did it end?"

"I think he accepted it, and returning home with his grandsons mitigated the pain. . . . Don't look so down, my friend. We couldn't risk an autopsy, and you know that damn well!"

Simon Desmond looked haunted. "Has she said anything?"

"No. As with all the other ghastly events in her life, she's conveniently forgotten."

"Conveniently?" Desmond felt numb.

"Yes." On his feet, Farjeon said, "Let me show you Regina's stock. It might ease your mind."

"Nothing will. I'm not happy living with a crime," he said bitterly. "It ought to have been reported."

"You love my sister, don't you?" Farjeon's voice was icy. The younger man nodded, distraught. "Well, she's safe now—"

"Jesus, she could be innocent! This way we'll never know."

"You really are crazy about her, aren't you?"

Their eyes locked, and Desmond replied shakily, "If she were any other woman, I would be now asking for her hand in marriage—"

"Such devotion should be rewarded," Farjeon mused. "How would you like to be her guardian? That will draw us even closer. Should anything happen to me, you will take on the burden—not as a husband or lover, you understand, but as her concerned physician. . . ." He had the satisfaction of seeing an agonized look in the other man's eyes. Finally came the almost inaudible reply.

"Agreed."

"Good." Farjeon led the doctor out of the library. "That's a matter to be kept quiet," he cautioned. "It might be misunderstood."

Desmond said nothing, and they walked the rest of the way in silence. Unlocking the door to Regina's shuttered suite, Farjeon turned up the gaslight, then headed for a satinwood wardrobe. Following him Desmond detected a faint smell of powder, cigarettes, and musky perfume. Farjeon pointed to the wardrobe's bottom. Row after row of shoes hid a half-dozen bottles of Napoleon brandy. He held one up to the light.

"This bottle is almost empty."

"How did she get them?"

"From my stock. An arrangement we worked out when I realized I couldn't control her." Returning the bottle to its hiding place, he added, "It might be a good idea to let this be known. A word or two dropped and it will spread like a bonfire. Then you can stop brooding about an autopsy!"

Impossible to argue with the man, Desmond thought wretchedly. And every time he looked into those beautiful eyes, he would always wonder. . . .

"Did you check here that night?"

"Not until the following morning, after your examination. I found a glass smelling of brandy and a flask, but she'd replaced the bottle. Even in her worst moments, she always remembered things like that—"

"I'm sorry, sir," Desmond said curtly, oppressed by the cloying atmosphere of the chamber. Dust covers hid the furniture, draped the dead woman's clothes, even the chandeliers. Velvet curtains the color of rotten plums were tightly drawn against the sun's glare.

"Some jewelry is missing. . . ."

"What?" Desmond frowned.

"The diamond necklace and earrings she had on that night. In the moat, the earrings might easily have been wrenched off, but not the necklace. It had a tight clasp."

"You've searched these rooms thoroughly?" Desmond's voice was harsh with anxiety.

"Yes. Not a sign. . . ." For the first time, Farjeon looked uneasy. "I couldn't bring myself to explore Ariel's suite—"

"Don't you think you should?" was the stinging reply. "She's not been spared much, has she?"

"Hard to spare her when it all points in her direction." Farjeon laughed grimly. "And if I know my sister, she would know where to hide such booty. After her infant's murder, before she was taken to the asylum, I found a nest of baby clothes squirreled away under her mattress, and she with blood still under her fingernails!"

Simon Desmond began to pace, anxious to leave, to escape this frightful house. "My remedy for you, sir, is to stop dwelling on the past," he suggested. "As soon as your mourning is over, I hope that you will take a new wife."

Farjeon stared at him in disbelief. "I cannot sire strong, healthy children as you can, Desmond, and I'm not attempting that cruel travesty again. Already, my oldest son shows signs of instability, and his brother is physically weak—"

"Not every Farjeon is so afflicted!" Desmond's patience snapped. "You yourself are proof of that. I would guarantee that most of your children will be healthy."

"And Ariel? What am I to do with her?"

"If you remarry, think about confining her elsewhere." He felt a stab of pain at such treacherous thoughts. "At Bellereve, she's a constant reminder of your family's tragedy. If you seriously believe that she killed your wife, there's only one place for her—Broadmoor."

Farjeon disagreed. "I can't desert her because she's unfortunate enough to be cursed with this malady! And, as her guardian, you will have the same dilemma."

"Is that really wise—knowing how I feel about her?" Desmond asked, his heart chilled.

"One day, you will no longer love her, Desmond, when you can fully appreciate what lies behind that bewitching mask. Looking after her then will cause you no pain. . . ."

In the courtyard, Simon Desmond waited for his trap. Behind him, Bellereve glittered in brilliant light, pieces of flint and red brick sparkling like jewels, mocking the grim ruin. *Jewels.* And something else teased his exhausted brain. A phantom he couldn't place. That tawdry suite, with its remnants of the dead, and his conversation with Farjeon had unnerved him. *Jewels.* One more thing to forget if he was ever again to gaze peacefully at that ravishing face. Two murders. . . . He strolled over to the moat, not giving a damn if Farjeon was spying on him from the library.

The distance between the stone building and the moat was a long one. She might have done it, aided by a wheelbarrow, but how did she kill her? There was no ligature mark around Regina Farjeon's neck, no head wounds, and the abrasions and contusions on the body were consistent with a dead weight hitting the sides of the moat.

In deep thought, he walked along the moat, eyes alert for anything unusual in the water, but a mass of water lilies and weeds obstructed his vision. Turning, he found himself opposite the grime-encased windows in Ariel's sitting room.

Something white stood against the panes. It had to be her, he thought, his heart racing—no trick of the sun. Hurrying forward, he made out her figure—forehead pressed to the glass, arms raised beseechingly—an attitude he knew so well.

Deeply moved, he lifted his hands to meet hers, and she backed away in alarm. Softly, insistently, he called her name. Returning slowly, she touched his hands, her face pressed tightly to his glass image.

"I love you, my darling. I love you with all my heart," he cried. "God, can you hear me, Ariel?"

A second later the white figure vanished, and the nagging thought surfaced. Certainly, Ariel gained from Regina's death, but so did Farjeon, heir to his wife's property, unless she had left her fortune to her sons. Quite likely, he had spent his due, but it was an idea worth considering. . . .

Damn the jewels! he thought in fury. What the hell had happened to them? A prudent man would have gone no further, but Desmond, lovesick and rashly impulsive, took a strong course of action. Violently impatient, he thumped on the iron-banded door.

Silence within. Silence without. Shaken, he again pounded on the door, cursing the Jackal for her laxity. At long last the door screeched open, and the crone peeped out at him, sniffling with excitement. Before she could decide what to do with him, he was in the room, filling her hands with coins. Her feeble mind reeled: on orders from the master, Dr. Desmond was never to be left alone with the patient.

Ignoring her grumbling, Desmond glanced at his darling, who stood rooted by the window. "No, I've not come to see your mistress," he snapped. "I left a syringe in the other room—" He strode off to the tiny bedroom. Closing the door, he approached the pallet warily, a hand caressing the pillow and worn blanket. His body tensed as he flung back the mattress. Nothing. With a sigh of relief, he let the thing fall back and, in so doing, felt a hole. It was quite small, well away from the edge. Only room for three fingers at the most. With a feeling of dread, he probed gently, felt something, and then extracted a handkerchief tied in knots. As the little bundle tumbled into his hands, he was tempted to put it back. But official business always precluded the personal. . . . On his knees, crouched like a supplicant, he knew what he would find. Diamonds flashed in the room's drab light, falling into his hands like beads of water. A necklace. A pair of earrings. . . .

Beside her bed, he broke down. He couldn't tell Farjeon.
Not yet. Not until he had some control. . . . A noise behind
made him wheel about. Ariel Farjeon stood in the doorway.
As the Jackal loped forward to play duenna, her charge slammed
the door shut. Desmond was caught with the jewels in his hand.
More swiftly than he would have believed possible, Ariel bore
down upon him. Bracing a knee against his back, she clawed
at his hand, tearing it open. Awed by her strength, he yielded,
solely intent on her expression.

"Oh, God!" she cried. "Where did you find that?" Her
beautiful face, flushed with exertion or some other emotion,
turned white. Picking up an earring, she stared at it, bewildered,
eyes filling with tears.

"Don't you know?" he asked coldly.

Dazed and frightened, she shook her head, and he snatched
back the jewel. Stuffing it into the handkerchief, Desmond slid
the bundle into its hiding place, then rose breathlessly to his
feet. Either she was innocent of this theft or a consummate
actress.

All he wanted was to crush her in his arms, to taste that
ardent mouth under his, but he knew if he were to touch her
once, it would be his undoing. A lifetime spent shackled to
that infernal beauty, lying and protecting her in a demon's
embrace until one of them was dead.

"Simon!" She took a hesitant step towards him, arms clutching her waist as if in great pain. "How did you know where
to look?"

Ignoring her plea, he backed away. "I don't know what you
are," he said thickly, "but you frighten me. I wish to God I
had never laid eyes on you!" He flung open the door. Behind
him, as he left the building, came the sound of low, desperate
sobbing. . . .

She was dry-eyed that evening when Nicholas Farjeon came
to dine with her. As he sauntered into the sitting room, she
put something into his hand.

"What's this?" he laughed. "Child's play?" Untying the
handkerchief, he stiffened at the sight of its contents. Brother
and sister stared at one another.

Nerves on edge, Ariel Farjeon snapped, "Simon Desmond
found that under my mattress—"

"When?" Farjeon looked mystified.

"This afternoon," she cried angrily. "How did he know
where to look?"

"Don't stress yourself, my love." A warning note crept into his voice. "From something I told him." Her eyes blazed. "Baby clothes—remember, Ariel?"

She shook her head, her body crumpling in fright.

"Ah, another convenient forgetting." He smiled indulgently. "Well, better here than in a carp's stomach, eh?" He poured them each a glass of sherry. "Curious about Desmond. He didn't report this to me. You're incomparable, Ariel! The man's so infatuated he'll do anything to shield you." Silently, he toasted her. "I have so much on him now that any one of a half-dozen things can ruin him. Do you know, I think the damn fool would even marry you if given the opportunity...." Two spots of color touched her cheeks, and she broke into a fit of coughing. "Regina did leave me some money, after all. Isn't that nice? It should tide us over for some time. Now, come and eat."

She sat opposite him at the round table, fingers picking at the linen cloth, her manner subdued. "I'm not hungry."

"You've hardly taken a bite since Regina's death. Don't tell me you've finally had an attack of conscience!"

"The mad have no conscience, Nicholas. Don't you know that?"

Diving into his pheasant, he looked irritated. "You're beginning to sound like Grandfather—"

"We share something in common." Irony pricked her voice.

"Petulant, aren't you?"

"Not really," she answered quietly. "But it never ends, does it?"

"No, it doesn't," he drily agreed. "Eat. I don't like emaciated women...."

Sooner or later, he would have to tell Nicholas Farjeon about the jewels, Simon Desmond thought, pretending to read *The Lancet* in his study. Yet after one week, he still couldn't do it. It was too final. Proof of theft—yes, but not murder. He wasn't willing to go that far.

The curtains were open to night breezes and the intoxicating aroma of flowers from the cottage garden. A soft glow rising from several oil lamps warmed the room. At his desk, fortified by a cup of tea, sat Beatrice Clayton, deep in monthly bills, checking each one against her ledger.

"Will you be getting payment from Nicholas Farjeon?" she asked over her shoulder.

"Perhaps," he lied, stalling for time, knowing damn well he'd never see a penny.

"Are you still treating his sister?"

"Yes." He sounded bored.

She put down her pen, affecting a casual tone. "Isn't this the ideal time to turn her over to Broughton?"

"I know the case. It's of no consequence."

"That's not true, and you know it—"

"Beatrice, this was to be a quiet, peaceful evening," he said, slamming down his periodical on a footstool and disturbing the dozing tabby, who glowered at him. "If I choose to play the fool, that's my affair!" He sighed heavily. "How are the finances?"

"Not too bad," she replied with reddened cheeks. "Climbing to the level we were at when Howland withdrew his loan. Another few months and we might start making improvements—" She faltered. "I don't mean to hurt you, Simon. . . ."

"I know, Bea." Putting a comforting hand on her shoulder, he flipped through the ledger. "What's the word on Regina?"

"I'm afraid she's reverted to her old unliked status." She managed a smile. "People pity Farjeon more than ever."

"Yes, he has a lot to bear" was the wry comment, and Desmond stepped out through French windows into the moonlit garden. Slowly, he paced the uneven brick paths, inhaling a heady fragrance of roses, jasmine, and lilacs. During his convalescence, he had walked here with Ariel Farjeon leaning on his arm, her face radiant, gray eyes dancing as they talked.

She permeated his soul like a disease, he thought miserably. This woman who had smashed his dreams, humbled his pride, and mocked his once proud ambitions. Yet such was his perversity that if he couldn't marry her, he would take no other woman for his wife—a decision bringing its own grim hazards: years of loneliness and, if he wasn't careful, alcoholism or suicide—two nightmares besetting his profession. And there was no comfort in knowing that his darling shared a similar fate when they could only meet as strangers. Never to be left alone. Never to touch. . . . And in the world, he must walk a tightrope of deceit, ever vigilant against the person or thing set to destroy him.

Is she worth it? he asked himself bitterly. But what say had he in the matter? His destiny lay in Nicholas Farjeon's hands. And now he was afraid. Acutely afraid to stand with his back to her.

Turning to go in, that little worry festering in his mind stung again. Farjeon had heard a scream—something that couldn't have come from the stone building. Every windowpane had been long sealed. Now, this suggested an accident or a murder committed outside. Unless Ariel had a wheelbarrow on hand, she would have been hard pressed to kill Regina, strip off her jewels, dump her body into the moat, and smuggle her prize into a mattress. Jewels knotted in a handkerchief, hidden in an obscure spot, indicated some foresight, yet she'd not had time to change her nightdress before her brother came down.

A scream . . . jewels . . . a damp nightdress. Farjeon, deep in sleep, might have imagined that cry, or Ariel—cunning Ariel, he thought, grieving, remembering her brother's warnings— could have done it after disposing of Regina.

"Simon!" Beatrice called from the study. "You have a patient. The Miller's baby is due."

"I'm coming. . . ." If only it were possible to confide completely in Bea, but this time he'd gone too far; even she, with her loving tolerance, couldn't condone his latest actions. Everything pointed to Ariel Farjeon's guilt. The damning feature was the cache of jewels. . . . Without it, the case against her was considerably weakened.

Jewels, and a brother's weakness. For truly Nicholas Farjeon did love and yet defame her. A curious combination for a protector, Desmond thought, entering Fairhaven with a smile for the prospective father.

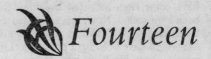 *Fourteen*

Nicholas Farjeon opened the iron-banded door to Simon Desmond the next afternoon. From the kitchen, Desmond heard the Jackal's tuneless song. Ariel Farjeon sat listlessly on the couch, eyes downcast, hands clenched together. The draft blown in with Desmond's entrance sent her into a violent fit of coughing. One glance and he knew she was ill. Swiftly approaching, he took her pulse—much too rapid. She looked feverish, and he ran a hand across her forehead.

"Do you have a headache? Any tension or fullness?" His eyes darkened with anxiety.

"Yes, my throat is sore, and I ache—" Her voice was unusually husky, the words came with effort.

"Take a deep breath," Desmond ordered. She obeyed, and he heard a distinct wheeze. "How long has she been like this?" he asked Farjeon.

"Not long. Why make so much of it? It's just a summer cold."

"No, it isn't. It's bronchitis." He glanced at the grim room with distaste. "Is there no place else you can put her? This suite is much too damp. She needs a decent room with fresh air."

There was a long silence. "Desmond, I can't bring her into Bellereve. My staff would walk out en masse!"

"I'm giving you fair warning, Farjeon," Desmond snapped. "Your sister is frail, and living in conditions such as this pest-

188

hole could endanger her life. She needs warm bedding and clothes, 'round the clock care—" A deafening crash came from the kitchen. "And get that blasted woman out of here!"

Farjeon's tone was icy. "No one else will come near her."

"I and my sister-in-law will," Desmond's temper rose. "Give me the second key, and we won't have to bother you—"

"Dear God, after what you did to her!"

The young man flinched. "Then at least take her into the manor-house, where she won't have to breathe this foul atmosphere! The walls drip, and I'm certain those are rat holes—" Swearing under his breath, he pointed them out. "If you neglect her, you're going to have a desperately sick woman on your hands." The two men glared at one another in loathing.

"I'll get you the key," Farjeon spat, striding out of the chamber.

Alone with Ariel Farjeon, Desmond cradled her against his chest, trying to soothe her. "Soon, my darling, we'll have you well again. . . ." A spasm wracked her body. Avoiding his eyes, aloof to his tenderness, she began rocking back and forth in the old attitude of despair. Farjeon reappeared in cold fury.

"You just can't keep your hands off her, can you, doctor!"

"You know how much I love her," Desmond muttered. "I'd take the risk if you would give her to me."

A flicker of emotion touched the brother's face. "You really would marry her, knowing her history?"

"Yes," Desmond answered humbly, on his feet. "As a doctor, I think I can take better care of her than you, Farjeon."

He laughed. "You took her on once and endangered your practice. Are you trying for a second round?"

"I can't bear to see her in such abysmal surroundings. When she was with us, she flourished."

"Capped by the trip to Yarmouth, eh?"

Desmond flushed. "We were in love—"

"You think Ariel capable of genuine love for one man?" Farjeon sneered. "Haven't I told you how many she's bedded?" He ran an appraising eye over his sister. "Here, watch this!" Moving like lightning for such a big man, he caught her in his arms, a large hand caressing her breasts. She moaned, and bending down slowly, he kissed her full on the mouth.

Simon Desmond looked on, appalled.

Farjeon raised his head, his breath quickening. "And I'm her brother! What do you think of this beautiful woman now? Is this what you want for a loving wife?" Desmond stood speechless, rooted to the spot. "Watch her face," Farjeon ordered. Whipping off his jacket and shirt, he stood before Ariel naked to the waist. And she stared mesmerized at the heavily muscled torso, the thick matte of hair on his chest.

"She wants me, Desmond, always has, ever since she was fifteen," Farjeon shamefully confessed. "Naturally, I turned her down, and so she lusted after others, but the embers still smolder. . . ." He threw out a challenge to his sister. "Kiss me, my darling!" And she came, her body languid, eyes feverish. Behind them the door slammed as Simon Desmond fled.

Laughing exultantly, Nicholas Farjeon took Ariel into her bedroom and locked the door.

"Take off your clothes."

"No, please!" she begged.

Ripping the garments, Farjeon stripped her hastily, reveling in her naked beauty. As layers of once fine fabric tumbled to the floor, he forced her down on the bed, a heavy arm across her body.

"My lovely, lovely harlot," he said thickly, his mouth covering hers. . . .

Simon Desmond still had the key. Damn! thought Farjeon, cursing his mistake. But after that last bit of playacting, he very much doubted if Desmond would ever again set foot in Bellereve. It had been worth it just to see his horrified face. Still, one couldn't predict the emotions of a lovesick man. The fool was so drunk with Ariel he was capable of anything. Unless the last episode had broken him. Hopefully, yes. And there were other things to keep him in line. . . . Farjeon laughed softly.

But she was ill. Even Nicholas had seen that. Her face damp to the touch, and the tears sliding down thin cheeks fell from weakness, not shame. An emotion unknown to them until that interloper. . . . Best bring her back to Bellereve, and he opened up a long neglected boudoir that led from his wainscotted chamber to a second bedroom beyond.

All the married Farjeons who could abide one another had shared this great suite: the master sleeping in Jacobean splendor while his wife slumbered in a more au courant room. Their mother, rebelling against nineteenth-century excesses, banished Egyptian and Greek motifs for the fairy-tale elegance of Early Georgian, fashioning her suite in the Chinese style.

On handpainted wallpaper, exotic trees supporting a menagerie of birds and animals hovered over a group of lords and ladies locked in everlasting gossip and amorous words. Nearby, a starchily dressed quartet of musicians, playing antique instruments, defied the night mist sweeping in from a lake, its vapors covering the great houses on the hillside opposite. Slivers of moonbeams shot through, avoided by the lovers; only a bevy of retainers, preparing a gigantic feast, sought its fitful light.

Around the walls, this fanciful world swept, a fitting backdrop to the porcelain, jade, screens, and japanned and gilt-lacquered furniture. But the room's glory was its bed—a richly carved affair surmounted by an oriental half-testor and delicately woven Chinese silk hangings in a floral pattern repeated on the satin bedspread. Ariel laughingly called it her "gondola" when Nicholas installed her in the room at age fifteen. She and her brother had been born in that bed; it had witnessed her mother's tragic death five days after her birth, but nothing dampened her enthusiasm for the suite. She adored it, proud that Nicholas thought her adult enough to live in it.

"It must be redecorated," her brother remarked. "The decor doesn't suit you." But he kept putting off the chore, wishing to undertake it himself after their European tour. Then the hell awaiting them eclipsed all other thoughts and projects from his mind.

Flinging back gold silk curtains from a bank of dusty, cobwebbed bay windows overlooking the courtyard, he opened up some casements to air the suite. Three or four maids could clean it in a few hours, and by nightfall, he would have Ariel reinstated, surrounded by every luxury. Of course, she would be locked in, he informed his alarmed staff, personally vouching for their safety.

A bewildered Ariel Farjeon was carried back to Bellereve by her brother. Bathed and dressed in rich linen, she was put to bed between satin sheets, and then joined by Nicholas for dinner, which she refused to touch.

"Try!" he urged. "You need strength to get well."

Stupefied with exhaustion, she glanced around in disbelief. Twelve years of hideously ugly rooms, broken only by a brief stay in a charming bedroom at Fairhaven—now to be returned to a chamber she had once loved and never thought to see again.... It was too painful, and she began to sob piteously.

"No tears, sweet," he whispered. "It drains you too much."

During the next few days, Nicholas Farjeon was in constant attendance: the adoring brother who kept her company by the hour, read to her, drew her amusing sketches, and comforted her when she asked disturbing questions that in her illness fell heedlessly from parched lips.

"Why did I set fire to the wing, Nicholas?"

He laid a compress on her brow. "You have an illness, darling. Others in our family have had it. Nothing to be alarmed about."

But her brain was reeling, her throat on fire. "What is . . . it?" she cried weakly between vicious bouts of coughing, each one leaving her more debilitated.

"Hush! Don't upset yourself. It was a child's prank—no more."

"Am I insane?" she mourned. "Why am I . . . locked . . . in the . . . stone chamber?"

Nicholas Farjeon caressed her flushed face. "You've been having a nightmare, Ariel. You must rest—"

"So . . . hard . . . to breathe—" Tears stung the haunted eyes. She looked about the room, hopelessly confused. "Where is . . . Simon?"

"Simon?" Her brother's face grew cold. "Who are you talking about?"

Tremors shook her body. "A doctor—"

"Silly girl!" He chucked her under the chin. "Would Grinnell let anyone else tend you? Now, sleep, my darling. You're growing delirious. . . ."

A bolt of lightning smashed into a bay window, awakening her in horror. Not even thunder could drown out her shrieks. In his bedroom, Nicholas Farjeon heard her cries and rushed in. Hysterical with fear, Ariel stood gripping the mullioned windows, beating against them like a trapped bird, cutting herself in the torn glass, eyes riveted to the burnt wing beyond. Carrying her back to bed, Farjeon bound up her wounds. For the first time she was conscious of the aroma and hardness of his powerful body. Tender lips kissed her tear-stained face; loving words eased the terror. But she didn't want him to go. The night outside was an even greater peril, and she pulled him down beside her onto the bed. All night long, he held her against the storm's fury. And night after night, he came to her, shielding her from nightmares until that extraordinary moment when their bodies united. And what happened once . . . happened many times. . . .

"She's very ill," Ariel heard her brother say from a great distance. "Get Desmond. Tell him, please, for God's sake, to come! That I think she's dying—" His voice broke. "I know no one else. . . ."

Beatrice Clayton gave Farjeon's urgent message to Desmond in his surgery as he was painting a child's throat with glycerine of tannin. Patently ignoring her, he helped the lad down from the leather table and spoke to his mother. "I don't think it's serious. The tonsils aren't that enlarged, and there's no evidence of scarlet fever or quinsy that I can see. Just a bad sore throat." He rumpled the child's scruffy hair. "Put him to bed, Mrs. Mullen, and ply him with hot milk and soup. I'll stop 'round tomorrow—" Opening the surgery door to let them out, he held up a hand, warding off his next patient, then turned to his sister-in-law. "Well, Bea, what is it?"

She stared at him, bewildered. "I just told you, Simon. Farjeon's groom is waiting in the hall. Ariel Farjeon is critically ill."

Brother and sister kissing. He turned from the image as if it were a poisonous snake. "Send him to Broughton."

The brown eyes widened in astonishment. "Dear God, what's the matter with you! You haven't been able to stay away from her in months. What happened?"

His look was very bitter, his voice stinging. "Isn't this what you wanted, Bea? For me to forget this mad infatuation? Well, that's what I'm in the process of doing." He started to open the waiting-room door, but she caught his arm.

"You can't make the break like this," she cried in a vehement undertone. "If anything happens to her, Simon, you'll never forgive yourself. Besides, Broughton thinks her crazy—"

"Well, isn't she?" he savagely interrupted.

"Once, you loved her. For the sake of that memory and your peace of mind, don't abandon her. Go to her so that you won't have to spend the rest of your life in hell if she dies."

His face contorted in anguish. "It was an evil day when I met her—"

"Go now, Simon. Whatever happens, you can make a clean break afterward. . . ."

Entering Ariel Farjeon's bedchamber, Simon Desmond heard the sound of wheezing as she struggled frantically for breath. With head raised high on pillows, a bluish tinge to her lips and face, she weakly fought the paroxysms shaking her body. At her side, helpless and frightened, stood Farjeon.

"Damn it!" Desmond exploded. "Why the hell didn't you send for me earlier?"

"I didn't think you'd come. . . ." He had the decency to look chagrined as Desmond bore down upon Ariel, his expression grim.

"It's capillary bronchitis—just what I feared!" Touching her face, he found it icy. "Has she been feverish?"

"Not much, until last night. The maid sitting up with her said she became very distressed at about three in the morning. Pulse erratic, veins standing out in her throat—obviously the temperature was quite high. But the wretch didn't tell me until this morning—" His voice trembled. "Will she die?"

"I don't know. Perhaps it might be for the best, eh?" He bent over Ariel, trying to hide his grief and terrible guilt. Pulling back the bedclothes, he noticed a cold, clammy sweat on her torso soaking the fine nightdress; her feet were as blue and livid as her face. "Has she been coughing up phlegm?"

"Yes, fairly steadily, but it's getting harder."

"Well, at least she's gotten rid of some of it—that's a good sign." Desmond smiled thinly. "Let's hope her chest isn't blocked. I'll give her some aconite now, and I want more bolsters and pillows. We'll set up a steam inhalation system with chloric ether. Bring me sheets for a tent and another kettle to steam in the fireplace. If she improves, I'll switch to an effervescing ammonia mixture and chloroform drops on her hand to inhale. With luck, this will lessen the spasms and ease expectoration. A mustard poultice will help. . . ."

"May I stay?" Farjeon's voice was barely audible.

"If you want." Desmond grimaced. "But I'd like you to send for my sister-in-law. She knows my methods and can relieve me when needed." Their eyes met for a brief, uncomfortable moment. "I intend to see this case through to the end, Farjeon. Please make up a room nearby for Beatrice." As the brother hesitated by the door, Desmond said with withering scorn, "There's no need to worry about our being left alone together. Whatever I once felt . . . is dead. She is only a patient now. Hurry, please!"

In less than a half-hour, all the equipment was set up, and Desmond, in shirt sleeves, readied himself for a long siege. Ariel sat against a bulwark of bolsters and pillows, dimly conscious, fighting with feeble strength the deadly paroxysms attacking her. At one point, in her extremity, she reached for his hand. Desmond, still bitterly crushed, tried to ignore her plea but couldn't. Only when he heard a knock on the corridor door did he relinquish his hold, reluctantly.

"How is she?" Beatrice Clayton asked, joining him at the tented bedside, her face pinched in alarm.

"Very ill. The smaller bronchial tubes are inflamed. She's still putting up a fight, but he's kept her in that damp room so long I doubt that she has the strength to survive. I'll spend the rest of the day and night with her." He raised an eyebrow. "Broughton's taking over?"

"Yes, Simon. Nothing to worry about." She took off her gloves. "How can I help?"

"Nothing here at the moment. A room's been set up for you—" He gave her a hard look. "There is one thing, Bea, that you can do. Take a stroll in the park and see if you can locate a gardening shed—"

"Simon, have you lost your wits! With a dying woman on your hands, you worry about gardening sheds!" She almost laughed.

But his face was ashen, his strain evident. "No, I'm deadly earnest, Bea. It was something I didn't want to know before. Now I must. . . ." The words tumbled in a desperate flow. "It should be near the stables. Find out if it's locked each night and the equipment, such as wheelbarrows, returned."

She gaped. "You're the one in need of a doctor!"

"Indulge me!" he begged, hurrying her to the door. "But be casual. You've a splendid afternoon for a walk. . . ."

Now that Ariel Farjeon might be dying, he could face the truth. The possibility of losing her and not knowing what had happened on that terrible night of Regina's death was unbearable. If he could ever hope to break free of her and start life afresh, he had to learn the truth—no matter how grievous.

Hard on Beatrice Clayton's heels came Nicholas Farjeon. "Best not to see her like this," said the young doctor curtly. "Her suffering is very great."

"I've seen her worse."

"Yes, I know you have," Desmond replied, surprisingly gentle. "But it's painful to watch. I'll call you if any change occurs." Farjeon stooped, looking into the tent. "You see, she's still livid. The wheezing is somewhat improved, but she's having great difficulty coughing up phlegm."

"Let me stay!" he begged.

"No, we'll only get on each other's nerves. The best thing you can do for her now is to take some rest yourself. You look as if you've lost a week's sleep."

"I don't understand. I thought she was getting better. . . ."

Farjeon's voice was dull with grief. "Is it possible that she wants to die?"

"What has she to live for?" Desmond sounded very angry. "Everything in life a woman covets is denied her: love, a husband, children. . . . I'm not certain I'd make the effort—"

"She knows I love her," the brother cried, shaken.

"Does that compensate for twelve years—though really it's been twenty years of horror, hasn't it?"

"I keep telling you, Desmond, nothing registers in her mind. Witness her behavior over Regina."

Simon Desmond's eyes grew reflective. "When you returned the wheelbarrow that night, do you remember if the shed was locked or not?"

"Unlocked, I think. It must have been. How else could she have gotten it?" Farjeon frowned, strolling off towards his sister's dressing room. "I'll be in my suite if you need me."

A soft tap on the door was Beatrice Clayton, back from her walk. Advancing towards Desmond, she said quietly, "Well, you were right, dear. It is next to the stables—a huge barn holding everything from farm machines to gardening tools—"

"Wheelbarrows?"

"A half-dozen at least. I found a garrulous old man puttering about who was most informative. Both the carriagehouse and this building are locked at night."

"Locked?" Desmond blinked. "Are you sure?"

She drew up a chair beside him. "Oh, he was most emphatic about that. A groom sleeps with the horses in case of fire, but the other buildings are locked to guard against thefts. Any equipment used during the day is always returned."

Desmond gave Ariel a sip of brandy and water. "What happens to the keys?"

"Each evening they're returned to the butler's pantry."

"Are there duplicates?" he asked, touching his patient's forehead—still cold.

"Yes, Nicholas Farjeon has a complete set of keys." She peered in at Ariel. "Poor soul, she looks dreadful. . . ." Their eyes locked. "Simon, will she live?"

"I need a miracle. You may have just given it to me."

She looked baffled.

"A wheelbarrow!" he said, laughing.

"Dear one, you're overworked! Let me get you some tea."

"On the contrary, I feel invigorated. Bea, you're invaluable!" He smiled. "Will that man talk, do you think?"

She shrugged. "Probably."

"Well, not a word to anyone, eh? You were just out for your constitutional . . ."

"Yes, sir." Her voice turned serious. "Now, what else can I do, Simon?"

"Refill the kettles, and bring me another poultice, then take a rest. I hope you'll join Farjeon at dinner if he's affable. I have my miracle," he said softly. "Just leave me alone with her. . . ."

Ducking under the tent, Desmond sat beside Ariel on the bed—a jarring motion that caused her eyes to flick open. Sleep was impossible, the constant fight to breathe destroying any hope for a respite. He wasn't even certain that she knew him. Divorced by so many painful incidents, he felt it imperative to first regain her trust and then concentrate on the urgent task of her recovery. Stroking her face, he spoke gently, "Ariel, do you know who I am?"

Speech was beyond her. As she slid into a violent spasm, he caught her to him. "I can read lips," he whispered. "What's my name?"

Her eyes focused with cloudy recognition. It was enough for him. She knew who he was.

"Good girl!" He kissed her damp cheek. "Listen to me, Ariel. Hard. You're very ill. It's capillary bronchitis, and we must rid your chest of all that phlegm." He cupped her face tenderly. "Do you understand?" At her faint nod, he rocked her against him, unbearably moved. "I have never stopped loving you, Ariel, though I savagely abused you and thought you guilty of Regina's death—" She started feebly in his arms, her heart pounding. "Now I know you couldn't have killed her, and it is one more thing I lay at your feet, imploring your forgiveness. I love you so much, Ariel. . . . Nothing in your past bedevils me. I count only the hours when we slept together and I was reborn in your arms, my darling." A tear ran down her cheek, and he stopped it with a loving finger. "Get well, my love. Don't leave me—"

She shook her head, and he cried passionately, "I can't live without you! Even those few pitiful moments in the stone building mean more to me than anything—are worth any amount of sorrow. Just live, Ariel. Live so that I can see you!" Desmond embraced her tightly, feeling another spasm rip through her body. Misty-eyed, he held out his handkerchief.

"Cough it up, darling. Don't be afraid. I'll support you." The effort was excruciating, but at last she brought up a small clot of phlegm.

As pleased as a father watching his child's first steps, he guided her through the rigors of a dreadful night. Whenever she weakened, he prodded her, lovingly or harshly, as the occasion demanded, forcing her to loosen up that suffocating mass. Hour after hour, he dragged her through her ordeal, sparing neither of them. In calmer moments, he dosed her with brandy and water. Ariel begged for sleep, but the idea frightened him, so debilitated was her condition. Several times she almost stopped breathing, and he pounded her on the back in frenzy, shaking her to consciousness.

Shortly after ten o'clock, Nicholas Farjeon and Beatrice Clayton arrived in the shrouded bedroom. Monstrous shadows from oil lamps leapt across the walls and curtains like evil sprites. The bewitching chamber now seemed full of menace, and the man seated on the bed holding the stricken woman appeared more spectral than human. Appalled by Desmond's seemingly brutal methods, the pair stood rooted by the bedside.

"It's working!" he shouted, glaring at them. "She's coughed up a good deal."

Examining his sister's tear-stained face as she lay exhausted against Simon Desmond's shoulder, Farjeon snarled, "And is this a case where the cure kills?"

"If she survives the next ten hours, she'll live. Granted, the treatment appears cruel. It is. But I know of no other way to succeed."

"Simon!" Beatrice exclaimed in dismay. "At least let her rest."

He gazed possessively at the woman in his arms. "When she's ready."

"One would think you're playing God, Desmond!" Farjeon spat, his face dark with rage.

"No, I'm merely willing her to live. A prerequisite for recovery. . . ." With an effort, he tore himself away from Ariel. "Bea, the kettles need refilling, and I'd like a very strong pot of China tea, a carafe of water, and another bottle of brandy."

"Wouldn't she be more relaxed if you held her in not quite such a crushing embrace?" sneered Farjeon.

"On the contrary, bodily contact is what she needs now.

She feeds on my strength like an infant." He tightened his grip defiantly, enjoying Farjeon's discomfiture.

"I'll get you a bottle—two bottles!" He stormed off to his suite.

"Be careful, Simon. You go too far." Bea laid a warning hand on his arm. "Let me sit with you. It will look better."

"It may, dear, but it won't help." A fanatic light shone in Desmond's hazel eyes. "She needs love, a great deal of it, so much that it will bring her out of danger—"

"Back to where you were before?" she asked sadly.

"No one will take tonight from me, do you understand? All the passion, the devotion I gave her in Yarmouth, she will feel again, and will live...."

Awed by his desperate intensity, she backed away from the tent. "And what will you feel, Simon? You, her doctor?"

"I am a man who loves this woman, and she knows it. One day, she may have an even greater need for such love. We may never speak of it again, but it will always exist between us—as if in great pain, we conceived our love-child tonight. A miracle forever binding us. You must have felt this with Jed."

"Please, no more! I can't bear it! I'll get your supplies...." and she flew out of the room with a muffled sob.

Farjeon, returning, tight-lipped, with Napoleon brandy, said nothing. The hostility he felt could wait its turn. Whatever Ariel experienced in Desmond's arms, she would feel again with other men. It was all a matter of degree. And the important thing—the crucial thing—was her recovery.

Shortly before eight in the morning, braced against the warm security of Simon Desmond's body, Ariel Farjeon again implored him for mercy. "Please, let me sleep, Simon!" she cried in a husky but audible tone. "I have...so little... strength...."

The bluish tinge had receded from her face and lips, leaving her features wan, the high cheekbones even more prominent, but her pulse beat steadily, and no wheezing came from her chest. All trace of cold, clammy sweat had evaporated; what moisture remained came from the steamers' vapor.

"Are you in any pain, my darling?"

"I ache." She smiled faintly. "It's a wonder you have any living patients, Dr. Desmond!"

He laughed and gave her another sip of brandy and water,

then laid her back on her pillow bulwark. Her glance was baleful.

"Can't I lie down?"

"Not until the spasms stop, Ariel, and you're rid of that phlegm." She made a face at him, and he kissed her hands, holding them to his heart. "Does it hurt to breathe?"

"A lot of . . . pressure is gone . . . but I'm still afraid—"

"And so you should be. You've been desperately ill." His eyes darkened with emotion. "Twice I thought I was going to lose you, and you're not out of danger yet. . . ."

"I don't like the tent," she muttered.

"A necessity, sweet."

"It reminds me—" Breaking off, she stared at him, a frown of worry on her face.

"What is it?"

"I love you, Simon—" As he moved to embrace her, she stopped him. "I heard everything you said. . . . Be careful. . . . My fate was decided for me years ago—" She fell asleep.

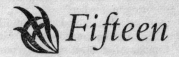 *Fifteen*

Simon Desmond kept up his vigil day and night until he was assured that Ariel Farjeon was safely on the way to recovery. Only then would he consent to share the sickroom with Farjeon and Beatrice Clayton. Both remonstrated with his obstinacy, but to their pleas he turned a deaf ear.

"You provide me with food and drink," he told Farjeon. "I have the stamina to take long watches and will do so until she's out of danger. This is no place for amateurs. . . ." To Beatrice, he said the same thing.

"That's not quite the real reason, is it, Simon?" she asked quietly. "Anyone can see she's getting better by the minute. You simply want to be alone with her—"

"Will we ever again have such a chance?" he cried bitterly.

Baffled by his recalcitrance, she hissed, "For God's sake, Simon, this is your last chance to recoup! Howland almost sank you. Lord Symonds is pulling you up again. Stick with him and you'll survive, but he doesn't like scandal, and this family is tainted. You've saved her life. Now call in Colin Broughton. Make the break. You were ready to do it days ago. She's not worth ruin—" Helplessly, she wrung her hands.

With difficulty, Desmond controlled his temper. "What are you talking about?"

"It's Regina. The drunken accident is being seriously questioned—"

"She was a secret drinker and intoxicated that night." His voice was chilly. "Why not ask Farjeon!"

"So you both say, but opinion is fickle. Many think you're covering up for her!"

"Look, Bea, if you want out, I'll give you back the money."

She flinched, deeply hurt. "Money isn't the only problem, Simon. After all, it's yours. You gave it to Jed."

Ashamed to have caused her grief, he retreated to a bay window, mulling over his bruised thoughts, distantly eyeing the stone building below.

Bea took a deep breath. "Farjeon has something on you, doesn't he?"

He looked back at the sleeping woman. "Yes, he knows about Yarmouth," he said dully.

"Dear God, is that what holds you together in this appalling mess!"

"One of the things. That fact known could destroy me. . . ." He was measuring the distance between the moat and her fortress. "Call it what you will—infatuation, love—I've never known such a woman. But there's more to it than a devastating emotion," he added grimly. "Was she ever insane?"

"Simon, she spent twelve years in an asylum!"

"Eleven years of which, according to its superintendent, she appeared quite normal."

"And the first year?" Bea asked, a trifle impatient.

"Oh, granted something was wrong then."

"Simon, she lost her mind! Why can't you accept what everyone else does?"

"Something doesn't jell—"

"It's her beauty that moves you. Face it," she said without reproach, drawing him away from the window, forcing him to confront her. "Would you be quite so smitten if she were plain—like me?"

"Jed always thought you beautiful," he said, flushing. "Told me so many a time." Wrinkles furrowed her brow, and he patted her cheek. "Bear with me, Beatrice. We have so little. Once recovered, she'll be constantly chaperoned."

"Are you to be trusted?" she asked wistfully.

"Of course," he whispered. "Our affair ended in Yarmouth. Ariel knows that as well as I do. And what harm can come to her with her brother next door?" Irony tinged his smile. "You wanted me to find love, and I found it. . . ." She shook her head, visibly agitated. With a heavy heart, Desmond tried to make light of the situation. "All right, Bea, I'll go back to the surgery tomorrow, provided you stay here. She can't be left alone."

"And Farjeon?"

"Will aid you. I'll take the nights and stop by once daily. Wire Broughton, please." As she headed for the door, he stopped her. "Try not to judge Ariel too harshly. I've made a number of mistakes with her, which will haunt me all my life. If I can remove her from that stone blasphemy, perhaps it will make amends. . . . Spend as much time with her as possible, Bea. She is a . . . gentle woman and needs affection. Don't show your dislike—" His voice broke.

"I pity you, Simon." She left the room, distraught.

Locking himself in with his patient, Desmond sat quietly by her bedside, a hand clasping hers, his face suffused with tenderness. Minutes went by. Sunlight transfigured the lovers on the magical wall. . . . Ariel Farjeon stirred among satin pillows. Opening her eyes, she smiled at him.

"Don't you ever rest, Simon?"

His lips brushed her forehead, but she wanted more. Pulling his mouth to hers in a long, passionate kiss, she cupped his hands over her breasts.

"Make love to me, please!" she cried, fiercely urgent.

He wanted to badly but restrained himself. "I am, my darling," he whispered. "Can't you see it in my eyes? We are as we were in Yarmouth—" And holding her in a close embrace, he broke his news. Tomorrow he was returning to his surgery, leaving her in the care of her brother and Beatrice Clayton.

She looked stricken. "When will you come?"

"At night, when you're asleep." As the gray eyes filled with tears, he rose from her bed, fighting despair. "It's best, my dear. We have been too much alone of late—"

"How much time have we left?" she breathed.

"In ten days, you should be absolutely fit."

"Why didn't you let me die!" At the sight of his shocked face, her voice grew brittle. "When can I return to my suite?"

"Never, if I can help it! I intend to have a long talk with your brother. You belong here. The gravity of your illness was such that if you move back, you face either chronic bronchitis or consumption."

"But it's my home. . . . My home!" She began to sob bitterly.

Beauty gleamed at him from every side. He looked bewildered. "You lived here as a young woman. It's a lovely suite—"

Suddenly flinging aside the bedcovers, Ariel raced for the corridor door. Finding it locked, she beat on it frantically. Desmond caught her in strong arms, imprisoning her.

"Where is it? Where is it?" she cried, never dreaming that he would lock her in during her illness.

"What the devil is wrong with you!"

"Oh, God, Simon, do you have it? Is that it?" She wept. "You conspire.... Let me go back, please!" She collapsed against him, struggling for breath. Relaxing his tight hold, he was stunned when she shoved him to the wall, her face taut with fury.

"The key! Give me the key, damn it!" A string of profanity burst from her lips.

Her dressing room door shot open. Nicholas Farjeon, moving swiftly, separated the pair and dragged his shrieking sister back to bed. Ariel fought like a wildcat, scratching his face, jabbing at his eyes, but he flung her down, pinned a leather strap to one wrist, and fastened it to a bedpost. A second quickly followed. Beating him with her legs, she hit hard, but he crushed her as easily as he might an ant. Within minutes, her ankles were bound and a gag tightened to stop the obscene flood. Desmond turned away, fighting nausea.

"Well, now do you believe me about her strength?"

"Must you do that?"

"Would you rather she had killed you? It's the only thing keeping her under control."

"At least take off the gag," Desmond muttered. "She's weeping. I'll sedate her."

"She hates the stuff. She'd bite your hand off rather than submit." His expression was grim. "Now, doctor, what happened?"

A dazed Simon Desmond ran a hand through his unruly hair. "She wants to return to the stone suite. I said no. The dampness will undermine her health. Growing increasingly distressed, she called it her 'home' and then tried to fight her way out."

"A lightning change, eh?" Farjeon's tone was cynical. "Well, you've seen behind the mask—beauty turned into beast. What do you think of her now? Lovely, isn't she?"

Ignoring him, Desmond removed her gag, dreading the abuse to follow. None came, only a stream of tears. "I don't understand," he said, wiping her face. "Why does she prefer the charnel house? What frightens her about this room?"

Farjeon shrugged. "Perhaps it holds too many memories. Time and again, she shared that bed with some nameless lover. It reeks of lust. When she realized I knew about her sordid affairs, she made no pretense of hiding them—on occasion, deliberately leaving the connecting door open, flaunting her depravity. Her pregnancy was diagnosed in that bed. . . ." He laughed softly, a pitying look on his face. "And this is the woman you want to marry?"

Desmond threw him an anguished glance. "Leave me alone with her, will you? I think I can calm her without medication."

"I'd keep the straps on if I were you."

"Lock the door. Nothing will happen. I'll try and find out what's wrong."

Farjeon's eyes glittered. "Don't meddle, Desmond. Too much remembrance is dangerous for Ariel. Frankly, that's the worst outbreak I've seen since she attacked me."

"Well, I'll see what precipitated it."

"Don't probe too hard. You can't risk a collapse—"

Stung, Desmond lashed out, "I'll tell you one thing that may relieve your mind. Your wife must have fallen into that moat by herself. The wheelbarrows are locked up at night." Farjeon's face drained of color. "I have only your word it was there, and a frail woman I think incapable of handling such a burden—" He paused, his voice cold. "You are blackmailing me, Farjeon, and for good reason, but don't stretch me too far. Madness runs in your family. . . ."

"So it does, Desmond. So it does. But that is the creature who is mad." He jabbed a finger at Ariel. "One who killed her bastard, tried to murder me, beguiled you as she did so many others. . . . I saw the wheelbarrow." He frowned. "But if you're so certain about my sister's innocence, why did you say nothing about Regina's jewels? To me that smacks of aiding and abetting—"

"The jewels are a trifle. You could have put them there yourself!" Desmond said hotly. "It's the question of her sanity or insanity that preoccupies me. Frankly, I find her case baffling."

"Be careful, my friend. I thought you trustworthy." Farjeon clamped a restraining hand on Desmond's shoulder. "I can only protect Ariel so far. The fire . . . the baby is nothing compared with Regina's death. Disturbing rumors are abroad. If one reaches her father, neither of us can shield Ariel. He seeks blood. . . ." Farjeon stared pensively at the bound woman. "I was the one she wanted. Sometimes I think had I succumbed to her madness, we would all have been spared a great deal of grief. . . . But it's a sin, isn't it? To lie with one's brother . . . ?"

"To lie with one's sister?" Desmond replied vaguely, a shooting pain darting into his right temple, a sign of great fatigue. "I gather the desire was never a *fait accompli*. A dead issue. Our problem is giving Ariel the best possible care."

Nicholas Farjeon smiled in appreciaton. "And I know you will be discreet. If she falls, we all will. . . ."

Alone with his patient, Desmond quickly removed her straps. She made no attempt to escape or to attack him, merely turning her face to the wall.

"I only want to help you. You must know that," he said, running a caressing hand down her cheek.

"Certify me," she whispered. "Send me to Bedlam. It's the only way."

Horrified, he gathered her to him. "Ariel, what frightens you? Is it fear of a breakdown?"

She nodded.

"I don't think you mad! You've been distraught at the idea of going there. Why did you change your mind?"

"I will forget. . . ."

Her tone was so poignant, it made his heart ache. "How much do you remember?" he murmured.

But she shook her head, refusing to answer..

"I can't help you, Ariel, if you won't speak to me."

She stroked his mouth. "I love you so much, Simon."

"Then how can you ask me to certify you!" he cried, kissing her very hard. "At Bellereve we can at least see each other."

"Always chaperoned," she said mournfully. "And I see you doubt me one day and trust me the next. Now you have a chance to get out. Take it! Broughton will help." A tremor shook her body. "One thing will work. . . . Tell Regina's father that I killed her—"

"Jesus!" He leapt to his feet, stupefied. "I don't believe it! You couldn't have carried her dead weight—"

"And the diamonds? How did I get them?" She held out her arms, beseeching. "Make love to me, my darling, so that I can woo one more lover to this reeking bed—"

"I love you!" he cried violently. "You know it, yet you mock me. Constantly!" Beside himself, he shouted, "I can't spend this shift with you. I'll call Beatrice." He fled from her presence, his mind in turmoil. Bea knew something was very wrong the instant he appeared, but he refused to confide in her and wouldn't even look her in the eye.

"I've had an emergency call and will be away until tomorrow," he said curtly. "Go to her, please. I'll tell Farjeon. . . ." Expecting to see the man buried in his library, he was disconcerted to find the room empty. Perhaps he was in his suite, Desmond decided, knocking on an oak door adjacent to Ariel's chamber. Farjeon greeted him, raising an eyebrow.

"Trouble?" He ushered the doctor into his bedroom.

"An emergency," Desmond lied. "I must return to Heydon. Beatrice is with her now. Perhaps you might join her later, or get a maid. I don't want her left alone."

"We'll cope. Don't worry."

"Oh, I took the straps off. Best not to use them. It only increases her suffering, and she showed no signs of violence." He turned to the door. A portrait hanging above the fireplace caught his eye. Riveted, Desmond stopped in astonishment. The subject, a young woman with jet black hair, stood proud in her naked beauty, enticing the viewer with every sensual curve of her body. It was so real, so lovingly drawn, he could feel her flesh. Tears filled his eyes.

"She was fifteen when that was done. Oh, don't be so shocked, Desmond! Magnificent women like my sister are born to be painted—not to hide their glory. Best thing I ever did," he said softly. "A remembrance before all the pain. . . ."

"A remembrance for all the pain—" Desmond muttered, hastily excusing himself. Outside, in the Long Gallery, the wing rocked under his heels. He felt the frozen stares of countless Farjeon ancestors waiting for him to make the correct move, the exact diagnosis. Behind which set smile lay the mad? Jewels from the Orient eclipsed an exquisite face; a fur ruff brushed a gentleman's throat; gauntlets hid another's powerful hands. Temptation could be read in every flat eye. . . . The past was a mockery. The family leered, taunting him with his ignorance, his suspicions. . . .

Up and down, he strolled, studying each portrait, longing for a clue, but none came. Gross fatigue was dulling his senses. Days and nights at Ariel's bedside, with little food and no sleep, had sadly reduced his mental and physical capacities. Again he walked past her suite, resisting an urge to see her. It would only cloud the issue. What he really needed was to take out the chestnut for a workout to clear his head. In his present state, he felt as if he were caught in some monstrous game of blindman's buff or trapped in the midst of a life-size jigsaw puzzle that had been scattered in huge, unruly pieces throughout Bellereve.

Deep in his reverie, he stood leaning against a door when he was arrested by a peculiar odor, frequently noticeable in this wing, up to now baffling as to source, but the shock of seeing Ariel's portrait had unraveled the mystery. Varnish. Oil paints. Nicholas Farjeon was a painter, and this must be his studio. Suddenly, it became desperately important to take a look at that room. Desmond tried the bronze handle. It was locked, but if the chamber was constructed along the lines of the two suites, another entrance must exist, and the room beyond was the library.

Treading lightly, he entered it, fabricating an excuse should he meet Farjeon. The room was empty. At the far end stood another door of curious design, built of oak with bronze arabesque inlays. In the center of a panel was mounted a gilt key with an Arabic inscription. Touching it in surprise, Desmond started as the door sprang open, and he stepped into the same extraordinary world that had so dazed Regina Farjeon weeks before. The glare of white walls made his eyes ache; a sparkle of colors danced before him like jewels.

Everywhere, canvases stood on easels, hung on racks, or were stacked against the walls. Shelves built into the wainscotting held rows of sketch books and portfolios. Beginning his search, Desmond flipped through the books and folios. A number held still lifes; more contained pastoral and town scenes of Norfolk; others were occupied with cities: London, the European capitals. An entire shelf was devoted to Spain, with loving attention paid to Grenada and the exotic palaces of the Alhambra. Farjeon had gone through the pile with a fine-toothed comb, missing nothing, Desmond thought in admiration, capturing its magical splendor as gracefully as had Washington Irving in prose.

Amid hundreds of character studies, the face of one model kept reappearing, caught in all her stages of growth and moods—Ariel Farjeon. He had first tentatively sketched her as an infant; then, his technique developing, he drew the child; finally came the stunning blossoming of a young woman in everyday gowns and fancy dress. But the garments, concealing too much, were at last shed, and she emerged naked in all her opulent beauty while her brother studied her body as a man might contemplate a wondrous treasure.

Had the artist been any man but Nicholas Farjeon, Desmond would have found his work magnificent. But in these sketches and paintings there was an intensity of emotion, a sensitivity to her most intimate moments, that suggested less the relationship between artist and model than that between a husband and wife. Some moments were unbearably moving: Ariel nursing a tiny baby, a look of joy on her face. To Desmond, it was at once a profound yet disturbing experience. Seldom in his life had he been so shaken.

Two large canvases stood draped near the bay windows. With trembling hands, he flung up the first cover. Ariel's face shone out at him, tender, luminous—only the hair aged her. Desmond stepped over to the second easel. She lay naked on the pallet, her white hair falling like a cloud down her shoulders, barely concealing her breasts. Obviously, it was a companion piece to the earlier painting in Farjeon's bedroom, but while that expressed an innocent sexuality, the second work bore a hint of the obscene. Here was a woman who knew neither modesty nor shame—a woman who wantonly seduced. A concubine who turned a sultan into an abject slave. Had a Saracen ancestor with Ariel's astonishing beauty so used her wiles in the Alhambra? Was it a pictorial key? A symbol of the one mounted on the studio door with its Mohammedan legend: "The key is the emblem of the faith or of power...." So it was proclaimed, he remembered. And centuries after Moorish glory in Spain, had an equally ravishing woman in some perverted sense usurped that power...?

Numbed by such thoughts, he tugged at the cover, but it snagged on a canvas edge, mocking him.

"Well, Desmond, what do you think of it?" said a harsh voice. Nicholas Farjeon stood in the doorway leading to the Long Gallery, lounging with a big man's grace. Amused.

Desmond caught his breath, mortified. "I can only say that you have great talent, sir," he warily admitted.

"And you were so struck by the model I presume you went through the lot?"

"As you said earlier, such beauty needs to be painted." The words stuck in his throat.

Farjeon strolled over to the canvas. Appraising it with bleak eyes, he said finally, "It's the madness that gives her an almost unbearable poignancy, don't you think? And she hasn't too

many years left of that uncanny radiance...." With a heavy
sigh, he rolled down the cover. "Then I'll have to find another
model."

"How did you manage during her incarceration?"

"Why, I searched for someone else, naturally! But they're
damned few, as you can see. That heartbreaking quality is
elusive.... So I took to painting landscapes, still lifes, character studies—"

"I compliment you again. A remarkable collection!" His
smile was a grimace, but years of practice had conditioned the
professional. Outwardly self-possessed, he threaded his way
through the studio's maze, filled with admiration. Then as if
suddenly recalling mundane duties, he looked from a sketch
of the Alhambra to the man at his side. "On second thought,
while I'm away, it might be better if you didn't see her." At
Farjeon's protest, he said mildly, "You did use restraint. Perhaps it was warranted, but she's upset. It's a setback."

"Has she turned against me again?" Farjeon's brooding face
was very bitter.

"No, but that's the last thing we want, isn't it? Just wait
for my return. Then we can manage her together. If you need
someone, call Colin Broughton...." He stepped into the clois-
tered comfort of the library, Farjeon following hard on his
heels.

"Damn you, he thinks she's crazy! Why call him?"

"He's been handling my caseload this week, and we've
discussed Ariel on a number of occasions. Medical opinions
do change, and if I'm delayed, he's highly competent....
Now, if you'll excuse me, Farjeon," he muttered as their footsteps echoed in the Long Gallery, "I'll just have a word with
Bea."

They parted amicably outside Ariel Farjeon's suite, and
Desmond, heaving a sigh of relief, unlocked the door and
slipped into the chamber. She lay sleeping like a bewitched
odalisque in her floral bower, ravishing in her innocence. But
seen in another light, he thought ominously, she might have
been one of those exquisite clockwork figures fashioned in
Arabia whose sole design was to entice a man into a lovers'
embrace and then kill him with a poisoned kiss or a venomous
caress.

Approaching the japanned couch where Beatrice Clayton
sat placidly absorbed in her endless knitting, Desmond whispered, "I'm going, Bea. Stay with her as much as possible."

"Of course, dear." She smiled at him, ivory needles clicking softly, her brown eyes serene. "And Farjeon will relieve me?"

His body tensed. "No, one of the maids. Have a bed made up for you on that couch and take your meals here—"

"I don't understand, Simon! Why the change?"

"Farjeon and I had a bit of trouble with Ariel today. Oh, nothing to be alarmed about!" he added hastily. "But I want them kept apart until my return."

A frown streaked her face like a shadow, but she kept her voice light. "How long will you be away?"

"Two or three days. I'll apprise Broughton of the situation. Call him if necessary. There are some patients I must check tonight, and I'll take the morning clinic. Afterward—" The sleeping woman drew him to her side like a magnet. "I think I'll run down to London. Remember that box of instruments that was smashed in transit? Time to replace them. Ought to have been done weeks ago. She's well enough for me to leave...." Incredibly, he saw his name on her lips. It was enough to keep him going. If she could think of him asleep, then he must have meant something to her. And the terrible hurt he felt viewing Farjeon's work would soften with time.

"Don't leave her alone, Bea," he called over his shoulder on his way out the door. "She is very precious to me...."

As he walked down the Long Gallery, his mouth curved in distaste when he passed the studio. Did the servants know its secret? Come to leer at that lovely body, to be aroused as Desmond had been. So red hot was his desire, he would give his soul just to sink into her body again. Had Farjeon noticed the lust on his face he couldn't hide? But then he well knew Desmond's passionate weakness for Ariel. Had him firmly in his grasp without any hope for escape.... He must see Broughton. Someone had to give him a sense of perspective; he was becoming overwhelmed. Too much love and torment lay between him and his darling....

Simon Desmond's father had harbored a small collection of erotica, which his son discovered at an early age before his mother's death. Then it had shocked him; later in life he understood such matters. He was quite certain that what he had seen in Farjeon's studio fell into that category, though the model's face exhibited no lustful inclinations. She was proud of her body, unashamed. Only in the last painting was there a feeling of total abandon. Yet the entire collection he would call obscene. Had Farjeon used these pictures as might a procurer?

Tempting friends and acquaintances to rape her as she slept in that charming room . . . ? Was that why she wanted to go to Bethlem? To flee a repetition of such horror?

Hesitating, he turned back to her suite, afraid of leaving. He could send Beatrice on this task, but she might not ask the right questions or be able to interpret the answers. How could she when she was basically unsympathetic to Ariel? And Desmond himself was still blindly stumbling in the dark—one minute loving, the next damning her.

The time had come. There must be no more lies. His chilled heart told him that this week would decide his destiny. The threat of ruin had lost its terror. He wasn't about to spend the rest of his life in such a peculiar ménage à trois. If Ariel Farjeon was a killer, she must pay the penalty the law demanded. If she was innocent, then he—Simon Desmond—would find a solution.

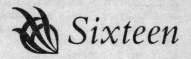 *Sixteen*

Leaving Bellereve, he felt the heat of the day warming the bricks, turning them a fiery gold. Flowers stood crisply dry on withered stalks; an unpleasant odor trailed him from the moat, and the carp, normally gay flashes of color, moved sluggishly. The hedgerow bordering the cobblestone path to the gateway looked dusty to the eye and crackled in a faint breeze, its blossoms wilting.

Looking backward, Desmond searched in vain for a glimpse of Bellereve. It had totally vanished, as if never existing. Approaching the gatehouse, he drew on the reins, chatting to the old man as he hobbled out to fling back the iron gates. Once released, the chestnut sped on its way to Reepham. In lazy surprise, Desmond watched the horizon change, the brilliant sky obliterated by a cumulus so thick that not an inch of blue remained. Awaiting the storm, the landscape darkened, and Desmond swiftly urged his horse past Foulsham's church and nestling group of Georgian brick houses. But wherever he looked, no park, hedge, or tree bore Bellereve's desolate aridity. Roses transformed the meanest cottage into a demi-paradise. The rich black Norfolk earth was vibrant with fresh crops, while newly born animals and yearlings gamboled in lush pastures. Shimmering in the distance, like a silver ribbon, a stream flowed by a bank of gray willows.

Despite the threatening atmosphere, Simon Desmond dozed in his trap, emotionally exhausted, as the chestnut flew down a winding lane into a thickly wooded forest crowded with mossy stems and gigantic beds of ferns, rushes, and tangles. Arriving at the outskirts of Reepham, he snapped awake, his eyes on the churchyard. Within its confines leaned two churches— once, there had been three, clinging together in ancient faith. Still, the sight never failed to move him: the survivors standing guard over the marketplace. Opposite, a row of handsome brick houses studded one side of the busy square.

Colin Broughton lived apart from the village in a half-timbered house that was all nooks, crannies, gables, treacherous stairs, and rooms of every shape and design. Floors split into different levels or pitched alarmingly. Ceilings forced one to stoop or rise. Despite these eccentricities, it was a house of great charm, perfect for a bachelor and his never-ending brood of relatives. Some came and went with children, pets, servants, and mountains of luggage; other were permanent fixtures: two or three spinster sisters, some distant cousins, an aged uncle. Desmond had long since given up trying to sort them out. As a restless man who basically craved a family life, he sought out Broughton as opposites will do, returning to Fairhaven refreshed after each visit.

He found his friend buried in his consulting room, working his way through a mass of papers. At the sight of Desmond, Broughton leapt up, a pile of mail cascading to his feet. "I hope Beatrice does a better job with these accounts than Polly." He chuckled. "But, poor dear, she really can't help it!"

"Her arthritis flaring up?"

"Yes, she can hardly write, but it gives her something to do." With his flat moon face, Broughton looked a fool, but behind that slightly childish look hid an astute intelligence and sensitivity that kept the patients flocking. Unfortunately, it had not brought him a wife, which Desmond thought a pity.

Broughton lifted a sleeping Manx cat from a marble-topped rosewood bookcase where it had delicately wound itself around a silver tray. "Sorry about that. They have no manners!" he exclaimed, reaching for a decanter. "Do stop pacing, Desmond. I can't concentrate." He smiled affably. "Have some brandy, and you'll join us for dinner, I hope?"

His guest shook his head vehemently. "No, I've patients to see. . . ." Strolling over to a diamond-paned window, he peered at the sky. "It's going to be a bad night. I didn't think I'd make it here. Now I wonder if it'll hold off before I reach Heydon—"

"I insist that you have a brandy and water. You look wretched!" Handing him a tumbler, Broughton resettled himself in a massive armchair behind the cluttered desk. "Well, how is she?" he asked after an awkward pause.

Desmond flushed and sat down on a leather couch, patting the spaniel beside him. "That's why I'm here." His look bordered on the desperate. "Can you help me out a few more days?"

"Certainly." Broughton winked. "But I'm counting each and every day—"

"And on my return you take a well-earned vacation!" Desmond said tensely. "Now I need some information, Colin. I've spoken to Peter Curwen and others, and the picture I get of Ariel Farjeon is totally at variance with the one her brother draws—" He winced.

"Well, she's mad!"

"So everyone says. . . ."

"And you must take it to heart, my friend." Broughton leaned forward intently. "Otherwise you're going to wreck a fine career."

Desmond drank deeply from his glass. "Is it Regina?"

"Yes, Simon, her death baffles the countryside, and you're the one calling it an accident. Was it?"

"I don't know," he miserably confessed.

"Jesus! You're covering up for Ariel Farjeon. Is that it?" His bland face sagged in worry.

"I'm not going to hide anything from you, Colin." He looked at his friend with dead eyes. "I wanted an autopsy, but Farjeon said no. Under the circumstances, I couldn't push it."

Broughton cleared his throat. "Did she do it?"

"I don't see how she could have managed it alone—"

"Then it was an accident!" He tried to sound encouraging.

"Possibly." Desmond took a deep breath. "Or Nicholas Farjeon might have killed her."

Hiding his shock, Broughton poured them a hefty refill.

"I need a few days to mull things over, see some people—things like that." Setting down his glass on a mound of periodicals, he took out a notebook and pencil. "Do you know who took care of the Farjeons about twenty years ago?"

"You mean when the fire was set?" Desmond nodded.

"Grinnell, most likely," Broughton replied.

"Is he still living?"

"God, yes! I can't imagine why he ever retired. Everytime I see him he looks better than I do."

"Why did he leave Heydon?"

"I don't know, Simon. Bored with it, perhaps. He likes action, and Norwich is more his style. He had means, but not that much. One always thought of him as the type who would die in harness. Obviously, he came into money, because he has a big house and lives exceedingly well—remarkably so for a man who was known as a skinflint."

Desmond's eyes narrowed. "Do you find that strange?"

"Yes, at the time—as did everyone. But a relative or a grateful patient may have left him a fortune."

"How long ago did he leave?"

"Ten, eleven years ago—something like that."

Desmond changed the subject. "Who set the fire?"

"Why, the old man."

"Farjeon told me Ariel was the arsonist." His friend looked astonished. "Now you see what I'm up against—"

"Were they shielding her?" Broughton asked uneasily, hauling the Manx onto his copious lap.

"Perhaps. . . ." Desmond's tone turned brisk. "How can I find Grinnell?"

Broughton spun a revolving bookcase at his elbow. Extracting a volume, he thumbed through it, then said, "He's still listed in the *Medical Directory*, which probably means he's keeping his hand in with the odd rich patient or two. Here's his address." He handed Desmond a slip of paper. "Don't go there unless you're desperate. He's a wily old devil. Hates all GPs except his friends. Try and beard him at the Maid's Head Hotel. He and his cronies hole up in the Jacobean Room twice a week before dining—" He screwed up his face in thought. "On Tuesdays and Thursdays. They never miss a night unless grounded by accident, illness, or death!"

A flash of lightning punctured the horizon, topped by a dull rumble of thunder. Desmond rose to his feet, annoying the spaniel, who darted away. "Colin, thank you!" He held out his hand.

Clasping it in a bear's paw, Broughton stood up ponderously. "Can't you find yourself a nice, healthy, *sane* woman?"

Desmond's smile was wry. "She may very well be just that. Remember, if Bea calls, it's serious." On his way out, he hesitated. "What did you think of the Farjeons in their youth?"

Broughton, lumbering behind, said, "Quite frankly, they

were the most handsome—exotic would be a better word—
couple I've ever seen. But everyone felt that." He laughed.
"Devoted to each other. I don't recall ever seeing them apart.
Polly"— and he looked surprised—"I haven't thought of this
in years! Polly said it was a pity that they were brother and
sister—"

"Why?" Desmond's face paled.

"Because they couldn't marry, and they were so right for
one another. Ariel appeared to be his right hand—"

"Then why the hell did he abandon her in a lunatic asylum
for twelve years?" Desmond cried bitterly.

"God knows! Maybe he couldn't face her." Staring out at
the glowering sky, Broughton said, "Dine with us and spend
the night, Simon. You're in no shape to make this journey."

"If I go now, I can beat the storm. Tomorrow is Tuesday.
I can't wait until Thursday. Don't you understand?"

"Do you want me to visit her?"

"Only if something's wrong. I don't want him alerted. Bea
will contact you. . . ."

"Poor fool!" Broughton sighed heavily, closing the door
after Desmond's hasty departure. "Poor fool. . . ."

Miraculously, Simon Desmond avoided the storm. It chased
him all the way north from Reepham, through Salle, and into
Heydon, but on reaching Fairhaven, he saw that it had changed
its course and was heading east—Aylsham way. Good, he
thought, shouting for his groom. By morning it would be over,
and he could get an early start.

In the darkened hall, Bessie handed him the patients' ledger.
Over a cold supper, Desmond leafed through her laboriously
written entries. Thank God, no crisis loomed. Hopefully, he
could get a decent night's sleep. And Ariel would be safe with
Bea. . . .

At dawn, Desmond caught the Norwich train at Reepham
for a second interview with Dr. Portman at Bracon Ash. They
met again in the committee room. The park, so austere in
winter, was now ablaze with flowering trees. Sitting in that
elegant room, Desmond might have been visiting a country
house, not a lunatic asylum.

"Now, sir, what brings you here? How is your patient?"

"Frankly, I'm bewildered. Aspects of her case are infinitely
disturbing."

Portman stared at him gravely. "I thought we'd covered
everything before, Desmond."

"So had I, sir, but questions remain...."

"What?"

"The dead child. Farjeon told me she overlay it."

"Well, that's a more serious admission than stillborn, but I'm sure there was no criminal intent, doctor." His glance was intimidating, but Desmond refused to be cowed.

"He made a third statement. Ariel Farjeon strangled her baby with her own hands when it was four days old."

There was a long silence. "That, of course, is murder," Portman said, frowning. "But impossible to prove after all this time."

"But if it was murder, that makes Farjeon an accessory after the fact!"

"Something he would realize. You must remember, Desmond, that he loved her."

"Then why abandon her?" Desmond exploded. "Madness for one year perhaps. Sanity for eleven years! Why subject her to such misery?"

"He was getting married."

"Five years after her commitment!" He scoffed.

The medical superintendent lit his pipe, keeping a thoughtful eye on his restive visitor. "You're not a fool, Desmond," he conceded. "What's bothering you?"

"Farjeon is obsessed with her to the point that he repeatedly paints and sketches her portrait—many of the studies are nude, I might add," he said tightly. Portman looked startled. "Yet he deliberately leaves his beloved *sane* sister in an asylum for eleven years—"

"Have you forgotten what the first year was like? How painful for him! Each time they met she grew increasingly violent, accusing him of killing her child—"

"How did it really die?" Desmond asked darkly. "Did she say anything?"

"Only what I've told you."

"Did she ever speak of fire?"

Repressing a sigh of annoyance, Portman flipped through her case study. "Occasionally, a wardress heard her talking in her sleep. Yes, she mentioned 'fire,' and 'baby,' too."

"Always the two linked together...." Desmond mused. "She is still haunted by those images. Yet the woman today appears deathly afraid of fire. But Farjeon accuses her of setting fire to a wing at Bellereve when she was ten years old and gloating over it, saying how beautiful it was! What could cause such a change?"

Portman shrugged. "Guilt, perhaps."

"What was your opinion of Nicholas Farjeon?"

"That he was devoted to his sister and would go to great lengths to protect her."

"To protect her. . . ." Desmond echoed softly. "Tell me, did he know about the rapes she was subjected to?"

Portman stiffened. "Certainly not! We dismissed the men involved."

"How many?"

"Two, three—"

"Last time, you said one. Now, which was it, Portman?"

"It has nothing to do with her case—"

"Yes, it does, God damn it!" Desmond was on his feet, enraged. "Farjeon, while 'loving' her, described her as worse than a London slut. Those who knew her before her illness call her chaste. I'd simply like to know the truth."

"At eighteen, she went mad. I told you before that such women can become exceedingly provocative, their conduct ruinous. Now, up to that point—yes, she might have been chaste."

"Her brother says she was a wanton. That she began taking lovers at age fifteen." Unable to suppress his anguish, he advanced on Portman, sitting in cold isolation behind his desk. "But the villagers speak only of their devotion, and he continuously paints her naked. I find that distressing!"

For the first time, Portman showed signs of unease. "Are you suggesting an immoral relationship?" he whispered.

"Something of the sort. . . ." Desmond stared numbly at his clenched hands. "She's not a killer. Not the woman I know. And I question if she was ever insane—"

"Two young doctors before you said exactly the same thing. Remember that and think of the legacy of madness in that family. I don't know what happened between brother and sister. I saw only the lunatic and a man who cherished her." He rose, his voice and manner forbidding. The interview was over. "You've quite obviously lost your professional detachment, Desmond. It's written all over your face. Find her another doctor and forget her! These pretty madwomen can rip apart a man's soul. . . ."

Simon Desmond returned to Norwich in a dazed state. Something had occurred between them of so serious a nature as to

precipitate her initial breakdown and three subsequent attacks.
One of them was lying. But who was it? Ariel Farjeon, who
had survived the hell of that first year at Weston Asylum, or
Nicholas Farjeon, who professed love for his sister yet constantly damned her? Or were they both mad, jeering at his
desperate attempts to save the woman he loved?

The afternoon was humid, and his head ached, partly from
hunger but more from an uneasy feeling that if Grinnell couldn't
supply the answers, no one would. And then Desmond might
have to make the agonizing decision, as had Farjeon before
him, of whether or not to abandon her.

Desmond's cabby set him down in the brick courtyard of
the Maid's Head Hotel. In the distance, horses stamped and
whinnied, vehicles were berthed, and stablehands scuttled about
loading stalls with hay. Fat, overbearing women disembarked
from elegant carriages, grooms staggering in their wake with
excess luggage. Bored husbands stood stiffly remote, eyeing
the lone female, a smile on leonine lips. Idle young fops lounged
by the adjacent taproom, enjoying the tumult, commenting on
every neat bit of ankle or taut breast.

Desmond booked a first-floor room, then hurried down to
the saloon bar for a late lunch. Waiting for his pasty, he made
some preliminary inquiries to the barmaid. Dr. Grinnell and
his party regularly reserved the Jacobean Room twice a week
from six to eight o'clock. Curious, Desmond poked his head
into one of the smallest rooms he had ever seen. Four ancient
chairs huddled at a round table. A minute Dutch-tile fireplace,
shelves loaded with pitchers and figurines, several dim landscapes, and a wall clock—these simple objects graced a tiny
darkened parlor, its wood as black as if it had been burnt,
Desmond thought with a shudder. But in this case it was the
Jacobean dark oak, and the effect was one of coziness, not
horror.

Finishing lunch with two hours to spare, he went for a stroll,
emerging just as all the bells of Norwich's cathedral and its
thirty-six churches began to toll four o'clock. For a moment,
he stood spellbound, caught in a world of extraordinary music.
Like a flight of birds, one group would start, a second followed,
while a third overtook both. He spent over an hour lost in
winding streets, captivated by the city's charm, then finally
made his way to Grinnell's house—mansion would be a more
apt term. It was as ugly as he had imagined it. "I have arrived!"
its glum stone walls and huge, gaping windows shouted to the

world. "I am a personage of importance"—and this from a man whom Broughton claimed would probably die in harness! Smiling cynically, Desmond studied the pile. Much money had brought in the hideous stone where brick and flint would have been more appropriate. Several relatives must have contributed to this farce, and he laughed at life's ironies, thinking of his father's garish retreat in Kent.

Returning to the Maid's Head, he came by way of steep Elm Hill, where ancient gabled houses crowded up against the narrow cobblestone street. White walls stung the eyes; crooked windows danced in the walls. Some of the houses were badly in need of repair; others stood prosperous with half-timbered walls impregnable. One was for sale. Peering in through a dusty bow window, Desmond saw that it was a much bigger residence than it looked from the street. How perfect for her! he thought. A place where they could find peace together. Like a child, he leaned against a pane of glass, forehead and hands pressed to the window, dreaming of a haven he could never afford to give her.

"I love you, my darling," he whispered. "Stay close to me. Help me to learn the truth." Blinded by sudden tears, he turned away, abashed to encounter a startled woman.

Back at the Maid's Head, he loitered in the saloon bar. This room, a lighter shade of oak less torturous to the eye, quickly filled up with customers. A fat man waddled into the Jacobean box. Desmond spoke to the barmaid. "A shilling for you if you point out Dr. Grinnell."

"Gladly, sir." She flashed a toothy smile, pouring him a brandy and soda.

What could he say? he wondered, gazing into the foaming liquid. Portman had been fairly confidential; Grinnell might not be. As physician to the Farjeons, he must have been privy to many secrets. Many secrets about a mad family. . . .

"That's him!" the woman hissed.

Desmond straightened, sizing up his quarry. A nattily dressed little man, thin as a cigarette, with foxy features reminding him unpleasantly of the Jackal—but where she was stupid, this man was alert. Mean and ruthless, from his eyes and mouth.

Desmond approached, his manner polite. "Dr. Grinnell?" A wiry eyebrow shot up. "My name is Desmond—Dr. Simon Desmond. I took over your practice in Heydon."

"Sherman failed, eh?" He cackled in glee. "That's two down. What about you?"

"I'm holding my own," Desmond replied evenly. "One of my patients is Ariel Farjeon—" Even in the dim light, he noticed a spot of color prick Grinnell's cheeks.

"Come and have a drink with me," the old doctor mumbled, leading the way into the tiny room.

Best not rush things, Desmond thought. "Thank you, sir, yes." He pulled up a chair to join the foursome clustered around the table. At Grinnell's side, he began discussing cases, as they all were; the odd, unexpected, and mysterious tumbled into the conversation. After his second brandy and soda, Desmond launched into his real objective.

"You treated the Farjeons, didn't you?"

The sly features lit up. "Yes, indeed. A sad family. One never knew where the insanity would pop up next. I delivered both Nicholas and that exquisite little girl—" He gazed out a bottle-glass window pane. "Prettiest baby I ever saw. Unfortunately, she killed her mother."

Desmond's heart constricted. "Did you ever see signs of insanity in her as a child?"

Grinnell frowned at his empty glass, and Desmond speedily ordered another round. "Insanity! In that child? No, nothing."

"Nothing? What about the fire?"

Grinnell's face was expressionless. "She couldn't possibly have set it. I saw her less than an hour later. The wing was engulfed in flames, and the poor creature was hysterical. Kept babbling about seeing it happen. Evidently, she was first on the scene, and when she reached the courtyard, she slipped on a piece of paving, hit her head, and was knocked unconscious. By the time the others gathered—"

"Who?" Desmond's voice was cold.

"Father, brother, grandfather—" Grinnell sighed. "The building was almost gutted."

"When did she regain consciousness?"

"Well, as far as I can remember, she was alert on my arrival. It wasn't a bad wound. She was more frightened than anything, insisting that she'd seen a torch going through the rooms setting things alight."

"Why was she so frightened?" Desmond pensively twisted his glass.

"Shock. And she may have seen the arsonist."

"Did she mention any names?"

Grinnell shook his head.

"Did you think her grandfather capable of such an act?"

A wary look crept into Grinnell's eyes. "Not really, but he was senile and the most likely candidate."

"Candidate?" Desmond stared at him. "That's an odd word to use. All the Farjeons were present. Could it have been a servant?"

"Oh, no, the police were most thorough in their investigations. No one bore that family a grudge, and it fell on the old man's head. Not a great loss, really. . . ."

Desmond faced him with burning eyes. "Do you know what Nicholas Farjeon told me? That Ariel set it!" Grinnell sat stubbornly mute. "You know that she went mad and may have killed her love-child? I've heard three versions of that baby's death."

Grinnell imperiously snapped his fingers for another drink. Desmond obliged, noting that his man was getting a bit tight. The foxy features were less wily.

"I know that she lost her mind, and something happened to the child—what, I don't know." He sipped his new drink with a pleased sigh, his speech slurring. "That point was the most puzzling—the baby. I brought her into the world, looked after her as a child and a young woman. After her father's death, only one man mattered to her. She would do anything to please him—"

"And who was that?" Desmond asked quietly.

"Nicholas Farjeon—her guardian and mentor."

"Who impregnated her?"

Grinnell froze, then said laboriously, "I have no idea. But she was very beautiful. Any persistent man might have seduced her. . . ."

Desmond pushed his glass in his host's direction. It was accepted without comment. "When did you last see her?"

"She had just turned eighteen. Nicholas said they were off to visit relatives in America. Boston, I believe. And that was the end of it. He traveled on the Continent, married—"

"Did you diagnose her pregnancy?"

"Certainly not!" Grinnell looked indignant.

"But you were the family physician—"

"Farjeon called in an outsider. Embarrassed, most likely."

Desmond leaned on the table. "Who certified her?" Grinnell gave him a startled glance. "Well, someone had to," Desmond said brutally. "Two doctors were needed. Were you called in?" There was no reply. "Were you called in, sir?"

The old man mopped a damp forehead. "Yes, I was. Farjeon

wired that his sister had had a breakdown. It seems she tried to kill him." He thumped his chest. "He had a nasty puncture wound here."

"Not in the back?"

"A chest wound—pectoral muscle," Grinnell said petulantly.

"Did you see or speak to her?"

"I saw her, but she was strapped to a bed and gagged—"

"Gagged?" Desmond's fine mouth curved in disgust.

"Farjeon said her language was foul." His eyes dimmed in remembrance. "She was covered with dirt and filth—a wreck. Far removed from the exquisite young woman I had known. . . . Naturally, I certified her."

"How could you get an idea of her mental condition if you kept her gagged?" Desmond asked dryly. Receiving no answer, he continued, "Did he say anything about the baby?"

"Oh, yes, he told me she had overlain it, but he was quite certain that it was no accident."

Desmond couldn't have sounded more casual. "Did you see its body?"

Grinnell flushed. "No."

"Yet you certified a woman who might have been a murderess. You ought to have seen that child's body. That's unethical!"

A flicker of emotion leapt across Grinnell's face, and he stood up, whining. "Go away. You bore me!"

Desmond rose, his smile grim. "Would you like to know what finally happened to her, or are you already informed?"

"No. . . . No!"

"Well, I'm going to tell you, Grinnell," he said in a cold fury, alarming the other guests. "Thanks to you and your *precise* diagnosis, she spent twelve years in an insane asylum. Her hair is now white, but I strongly doubt that she killed her child or ever suffered a bout of mania. A few months of grief for her dead infant and rage at her brother for destroying a love affair doesn't necessarily make her a lunatic. Now, speak, Grinnell! Who was the baby's father?"

The old doctor's face wrinkled like an aged monkey's. "She was so lovely . . . so beautiful. . . ." Then he looked at Desmond without censure. "Some things are best not gone into. Leave the mad to the mad. Families like the Farjeons are best left alone. . . ." Swooping up his cronies, he marched them off to dinner, leaving Simon Desmond alone in the tiny room.

Desmond ordered another brandy and soda, carefully sifting his thoughts. The ethical practitioner would never certify a gagged woman. He would pay as much attention to her speech as he would to the condition of her body. A chest wound was described, but Farjeon said he was stabbed in the back, and Desmond had caught something he wasn't supposed to hear. Dear Dr. Grinnell was hiding something from him. He knew the baby's father.

Early the next morning, Desmond forced his way into Grinnell's ugly domain, catching the old man at his breakfast. Angry eyes glared at him for the interruption.

"You have a great deal of explaining to do, Grinnell. And if you don't begin immediately"—Desmond sat down and poured himself a cup of tea—"I'm going to call the police."

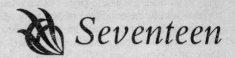 *Seventeen*

Arriving in Reepham, Simon Desmond had an urgent word with Colin Broughton, then sped away to Heydon. Delayed by his visit to Grinnell, he now concentrated on his notes, jotted down on the rail journey. The picture emerging was an ugly one, and many questions remained unanswered. It was going to be a long day, he thought, plotting his next move. He must make Ariel Farjeon tell him everything. Salvation lay in speaking. They would have to go back to her childhood and the fire—the start of all the nightmares. Once the floodgates opened, other memories might surface.

At Fairhaven, he was dumbfounded to find Beatrice Clayton in her favorite parlor chair engrossed in some embroidery, the tabby rolled up in a ball at her feet.

"Simon!" Her face lit up. "How was London?"

"As always," he said curtly, advancing on her. "What the devil are you doing here? Why aren't you at Bellereve?"

"Yesterday afternoon Nicholas Farjeon told me I could leave." Bewildered by his anger, she smiled apologetically. "I'm sorry, dear, there was little I could do, and she's much better. Walking now—"

"Were you thrown out?"

She hesitated, frowning. "Not really—"

"I told you not to leave her alone—above all, not with Farjeon!" Beside himself with anxiety, he fought an impulse to damn her for her stupidity.

"Simon, try and understand. Something in his tone made me not want to cross him. It wasn't unpleasant really, just final. After all, he is her brother. . . ." Aware of his strain and exhaustion, she tried to laugh off her concern. "Dear, have some sherry and a bite to eat. Have you been scouring London from end to end?" She held out a glass. Surprisingly, he refused, his manner abrupt.

"I'm sorry, I've no time for a chat. I've business to attend to upstairs. If anyone calls, I'm out." He strode to the door. "Oh, by the way, Bea, Colin Broughton is dining with us tonight. Try and get Cook to outshine herself. . . ."

Alone in the parlor, his sister-in-law stood bemused. Never had it been her practice to seriously interfere in men's affairs. A word dropped here or there was sufficient. Discretion was her guide, but caution was sometimes a dangerous thing. An agonizing lesson learned from Jed's death. Something had been very wrong, but not once had she challenged him, and by that lack, she lost her love. A mistake she wasn't going to repeat with Simon Desmond. A man so very dear to her whom she had somehow failed. On one point, however, she could reassure him, and she hastened up to his bedroom. He sat at his desk in shirt sleeves, writing with deep absorption.

Lingering on the threshold, she said quietly, "Simon, I am allowed to visit her—"

"Oh, he grants you that, eh?" Desmond sneered, blotting some pages.

Breathlessly, she took the plunge. "Where were you, Simon? You don't usually lie to me, and you look very out of sorts. What happened? Where have you been?"

"I told you, Bea—in London." He stared unseeingly out a window. "I simply have a raging hangover."

"Well, I can believe that from your appearance, but something else is wrong. You never closet yourself at this time of the afternoon. Why, you haven't even checked the ledger!" she exclaimed. "Farmer Hoskins shot himself dead—"

"He was dying of brain cancer and knew he faced excruciating pain. Something he didn't want his family to witness." The blond head bowed for a moment of silence. "He sought dignity and deserved it. . . ." Flipping through his papers, he studied her uneasily. "Beatrice, I've written you a letter, with some explanatory notes. In a short while, I'm going out. If I'm not back by seven, read it. But not before—" At her alarmed cry, he snapped, "No, Bea, not before! Then decide what's best to do. Consult Broughton if need be. I don't have all the facts or answers, and what you may read will shock you, but I'm depending on your help should things go badly—"

"You never went to London, did you?" Ignoring her, he coolly slipped the papers into an envelope, then sealed it with wax. "Where have you been?" she again demanded.

"In Bracon Ash. I went back to Weston Asylum."

Bea looked stunned. "Why?"

"I went there and to Norwich, seeking the truth."

Panic made her voice shrill. "What truth?"

"Someone had to take the responsibility. Assume the role of madness. Why not a vulnerable young woman?"

"You're bewitched by her, Simon! Or is it guilt for so using a poor lunatic when she couldn't defend herself?"

His heart wrenched. "Just stand by me these next hours. Tonight should see the end . . ."

In Bellereve's Chinese suite, Nicholas Farjeon stood rapt, gazing at his sister, who lay on the japanned couch, reading. Startled, she looked up, and their gray eyes met. Approaching swiftly, a heavy hand reached inside the bodice of her rose-colored peignoir as he kissed her deeply.

Burying his face in her fragrant hair, he murmured, "You know how hard Father and I tried to protect you, Ariel—" Stricken, she nodded. "As long as possible. Grandfather was such an able substitute. . . . But why do you keep on pretending to have forgotten? You know you set it, darling!"

She stared at him, terrified.

"Don't you remember how I caught you as you came running out of the wing? A wing alight, blazing like shooting stars, and when Father appeared, I had enough presence of mind to concoct our little fantasy. Sweet innocent!" He stroked her taut face. "We both knew how much you loved the flames. . . . And they were beautiful, weren't they? Spitting from the great beam to the wainscotting, licking the curtains, dancing on the furniture. . . . How can you deny the memory of that incredible roar as the floors fell one by one?" Farjeon burst out laughing. "Oh, what a sublime moment! The sky was blood-red for miles. More brilliant than any sunset I've ever seen. But only one wing, darling! Just think, Ariel, if you'd torched the whole manor-house—"

She turned from his fervid expression.

"And you were such a good girl until the baby's death." He

sighed, deeply affected. "Whatever possessed you to do such a horrid thing, sweet?" Tears rolled down her cheeks, and Farjeon flicked them away with a contemptuous finger. "Years of suffering will never atone for that act. Imagine the poor babe's agonies. . . ." Clasping her in a vise, he forced her to look at him.

"Listen to me, damn it! I've just had a wire from old Grinnell. It seems that our inquisitive friend and lover"—he sneered—"Simon Desmond was poking around Norwich last night, deluging him with impertinent questions. Now, we can't have the family honor ruined, eh?" Wearily, she shook her head. His eyes glinted. "Desmond still thinks you incurable. Wants you shipped to Bedlam—" She started, and he pinned her down. "Thinks you're too far gone to be kept at Bellereve, and he may have a point—Regina!" His voice softened. "You wouldn't want the hell of that kind of life again, eh?"

"God, Nicholas, what do you want?" she moaned.

"A promise from you that you'll tell the smart doctor the truth. . . . Play on his sympathy. Toy with him, darling, until I can get to him." Big hands stroked her body, hurting her.

Ariel Farjeon flung back her head. "And what else?"

"Let me lie with you for a while—"

"If Beatrice comes?" She trembled.

He smiled lazily. "We have plenty of time, Ariel." Kissing her neck, he muttered, "Now, whom do you love? That Judas, Desmond, or me?"

A blind look came into her eyes. "You," she breathed.

Slowly, he began to undress her. "How did you survive without me all that time?"

Her body was passive under his caresses. "I dreamt of you, Nicholas, . . . constantly, during those years of anguish!"

He came down upon her hard, stifling her cries. . . .

Simon Desmond, still immersed at his bedroom desk, had just penned a second letter to Peter Curwen, his lawyer. What little he owned, he left to Beatrice Clayton. The house and practice would tide her over, he thought grimly.

Placing the two envelopes on his desktop, he reached into the lowest drawer and pulled out a small object, which he slipped into his vest pocket. Next came a brown-paper parcel containing a four-barreled derringer. Methodically loading each chamber, he dropped it into a pocket of his riding jacket. Today was no day for the physician's traditional garb of frock coat and top hat, and for his needs, the trap was too cumbersome. The chestnut, carrying him alone or with another person, could fly like the wind.

Fastening his breeches, he pulled on top boots, reflecting that the spurs might just come in handy. At his hip, the derringer was barely a wrinkle. Passersby would castigate him for neglecting his practice, he thought, smiling in irony at his pale image in the cheval glass.

On the way downstairs, he hesitated, torn by doubts. Why not confide in Beatrice? But without the letter, how could she believe his fantastic tale? She was fearful enough of Ariel as it was. And if anything happened to Desmond, surely she would join ranks with the villagers in condemning his darling. In sudden panic, he realized that in attempting to free her, he might only be serving as an agent of destruction, so that not even Nicholas Farjeon could offer further protection.

Beatrice Clayton was waiting for him in the hall, her plain face brittle in the harsh light of day, lines of sadness etched around her warm eyes and mouth. Dressed in her widow's weeds, she seemed more bereft than on that terrible day of Jed's death.

He gently kissed her cheek. "I'm going out riding. . . ."

With effort, she suppressed a half-sob, a plea to keep him home as he walked out into the Elizabethan garden.

Simon Desmond left Fairhaven, a home once treasured, without any regrets, feeling incredibly young, as alive and vigorous as in that first year at Guy's Hospital, before all the ugliness. Ariel Farjeon was his only home, he thought tenderly, flicking the chestnut into a gallop down the winding road from Heydon to Foulsham.

It had rained during his absence, and the countryside glistened, newly cleansed under a radiant sky. Only Bellereve's vast park seemed oppressively arid, and the great house, usually so magnificent in any light, looked blasted, its red-gold bricks as unhealthy as the sickly-looking carp threading their laborious way through the moat.

Desmond's fears had vanished, and he laughed aloud, exhilarated—the conqueror. Invincible because of his love for a woman who had looked once into his eyes and enchanted him for life. And he climbed up to her bower. . . . Shadows, like giant swords, streaked the Long Gallery, obscuring corners and dark, heavy pieces of furniture. Only the portraits sprang to life, their smiles cynical, eyes treacherous. It was not a calm

place to walk, he reflected. Jenkins had given him her key—
Farjeon was nowhere in sight—and he knocked softly on the
door. No answer. With heart pounding, he stepped into her
chamber.

She lay asleep on her bed under a coverlet, her soft white
hair tumbling down a rose-colored gown. Her left arm cradled
her waist, her right hand was clenched on the pillow beside
her as if to ward off a blow.

Sitting beside her on the bed, Desmond reached into his
vest pocket for his mother's wedding ring. With loving words,
he slipped it onto her finger. Awakened by his touch, Ariel sat
up with a low cry.

Instinctively, they embraced, lips desperately meeting. And
then the fragments of dreams and days' nightmares became a
reality, and she pushed him away, a look of abject shame and
misery on her face. Would he guess? she wondered sadly. But
overcome by love and the sheer joy of seeing her again, he
misunderstood her shyness, her seemingly chaste withdrawal.
Catching her in greedy arms, he covered her face with kisses.

"These two days without you have been hell, my darling!
I didn't go to London. I've been to Weston Asylum and Norwich, trying to piece your life together." She trembled, and he
held her very close. "I know a great deal, Ariel, but crucial
facts still elude me. Only you can help. . . ." Her eyes widened
fearfully as he whispered, "Who set the fire?"

Was Nicholas in the room with them? she wondered, faint
with exhaustion. Or was he spying from her dressing room?
Desmond gripped her, trying to still his urgency, and she cried
out wildly, "I set it!"

"How did you do it? With matches? A flambeau? Or did
you overturn a candle or a lamp?"

The noise. The noise—she would never forget it as long
as she lived. A howling gale sucking up the earth, dragging
her along the ground. And then the ghastly shrieks. Crawling,
crawling . . . and something hurling her backward so that she
hit her head . . . on brick . . . on wood. Fire. Shrieks.

Ariel's face went livid.

"Help me!" Desmond implored. "Did you start at the top?
Work down to the ground?" Her eyes glazed. "What did you
do, damn it? Or see?" Alarmed by her silence, he shook her.
No response. He would have to try another tack.

"How did your baby die, Ariel?" he asked more gently. She

winced as if struck. His voice rose. "Was it stillborn?" A tear
slid down a wan cheek.

"Did you overlie it?" She wrenched away from his suffocating grasp, but he tightened his hold. "Did you overlie it?"
he grimly repeated, ignoring her audible weeping. "Did you
fall asleep nursing it and awake to find it dead?"

Nothing. She was like a sphinx. As he sat crushed, she
attempted to flee the bed, panic-stricken, but he caught her to
him, shouting, "Did you strangle your child?"

Agonizing screams tore through her brain. Not even her
hands could block out the clamor. Only when Simon Desmond
pushed her back onto the bed, slapping her hard across the
face, did she realize it was her voice.

The door linking the two suites burst open. Nicholas Farjeon, wearing a dressing gown, barged in angrily, his face
black with fury.

"What the hell are you doing to my sister?"

"Trying to cure her," Desmond said with a wry smile.

"Your methods are unduly harsh, as I've noted before!"
Farjeon snapped. "Leave her. I want a word with you."

"In a minute. As soon as I've brought her 'round."

The brother leaned insolently against the doorjamb. "I'll
wait—"

"In your room," Desmond mildly interrupted, but his tone
brooked no argument. Farjeon wavered, torn between the prostrate figure of Ariel and the rebellious young doctor.

"So be it," he finally muttered, disappearing into the recess
of the dressing room.

"Is he gone?" she whispered from a damp pillow.

"Yes, sweet love." Seizing her left hand, Desmond showed
her the ring. "Do you remember this?" Her heart contracted
painfully at the gold circlet of flowers. "In Yarmouth, we slept
together as husband and wife. Cruelly, I took it from you. . . ."
His voice shook. "Today I return it."

"Why?" Ariel asked coldly, gray eyes flashing. "So that I
may cherish it in Bedlam?"

"Dear God! Is that what you feared? That I'd commit you?"
In torment, he kissed her hands. "Oh, my darling, I think you
sane."

"Sane!" She looked astounded.

Again he gathered her in a lover's embrace. "Someone else
was mad, but not you, Ariel. . . ."

And she took the risk, pulling him down beside her on the

bed, aching for his touch. Feverish kisses swept them out of that dangerous room, far beyond to a world where Ariel Farjeon could safely walk. In sunlight, on a Yarmouth beach, wrapped in her beloved's arms, his lips passionately yearning. But this would be the last such moment they would ever again share. She was destined to fire and madness. . . .

The man she loved lay nestled in her arms, his head against her breasts, never dreaming, not once suspecting that her body was defiled. He would learn in time, she thought bitterly. Tears stung her eyes, gentle fingers caressed his peaceful face. "Simon. . . ."

Desmond raised his head, sublimely happy, faint lines of bitterness occasionally seen in his expression now erased, flecks of silver highlighting the thick crop of blond hair. A man in love if ever there was one, and her heart ached.

"I love you," she whispered. "So very much. . . ."

"And you are the only woman I have ever loved," he cried ardently. "Or will love!"

"Be careful, my darling. He means you harm. Grinnell sent him a wire."

Tenderly, he closed her bodice. "I am prepared."

For everything? she wondered fearfully. We have been too long together. He will know and break your heart. . . . Taking his hand, she confessed, "I can't protect you any longer."

"Any longer!" He smiled as if she'd given him a magical key. "I don't ask you to. . . . Are you still in restraints?"

"No, but I have so little strength. A fifteen-minute walk exhausts me. . . ." Again the tears began to flow. It was hard, so very hard to break with him.

"For God's sake, Simon, leave us!" she implored. "Then we will all be safe. *All of us!*" she added fiercely. "Go! Go while there's still time!"

But he was not to be led astray. He knew her panic—it was his, and it was as grievous for him to leave as it was for her to send him away. Taking her face in his hands, inhaling its sweet fragrance, he kissed each beloved feature. "I'll come back for you today, Ariel. To take you home to Fairhaven. I'm going to marry you. . . ." One long burning kiss searing his soul, and then he vanished through her dressing room and stepped into Nicholas Farjeon's world. . . .

Bellereve's master, now dressed in a lounge suit, greeted him politely. "Will you join me in a brandy?"

Desmond nodded, apprehensive about the interview's outcome. He could confront the man with his suspicions or tackle him obliquely, but whatever the method, nothing must be done to harm Ariel. Remembering the slap he'd given her, he winced.

They strolled over to a circular table holding a large silver tray and a glittering array of crystal. Two ornately carved and painted oak armchairs were drawn up. Settling himself, Farjeon threw a sideways glance at his visitor. "I hear you've been doing some snooping, doctor."

Desmond shrugged. "If you're referring to questions asked at Weston Asylum, I disagree with you."

"What did you learn?"

"Nothing that I haven't already shared with you. Since Ariel was considered sane for eleven years, both Portman and I are still astonished that you—so devoted—would leave her to such hell."

"I thought you understood my rationale, Desmond." Farjeon studied him with heavy lidded eyes, his face inscrutable. Abruptly rising, he said, "Come. My sketches will show you—" He strode out to the Long Gallery, Desmond reluctantly following. One of those blasted *eynds* was on its way unless he was much mistaken. The shadows in the great chamber were vaporous, and the brilliant horizon, seen from bay and oriel windows, was misting over.

"A bad night ahead, don't you think?" Farjeon grimaced.

"Yes," Desmond agreed. Stepping to a window, he wondered if the chestnut would be able to fight his way home in such weather. "And I'm sure you're aware that the villagers thought her chaste," he added casually. "You are the only one damning her. . . ." Across the vast room, they stared at one another for a long moment of silence.

Farjeon cleared his throat. "She hurt me very badly. I have simply been honest with you." He unlocked the studio door. "A great jewel—even with a flaw—has its fascination. Surely you can see that."

Desmond was ushered inside. It was not a place he had ever wished to see again. Tension lingered in the air, a suppressed violence, unnerving him. Dully, he glanced at the two covered canvases, the great racks, the folios and numerous sketchbooks. How many times had she stood here naked before her brother? The thought sickened him.

"I couldn't go back, Desmond. She killed her bastard. Tried to murder me—"

"How was it done, sir? I forget," he lied.

Farjeon looked impatient. "She came from behind. Stabbed me in the back."

Stabbed in the chest, Grinnell had said. Desmond admired a view of Granada hanging on a rack.

"You didn't see this the day of your foray." Farjeon's voice dripped acid. "I always keep them locked up. They record the last sad moments of our life together. . . ."

In the white wainscotting, above a shelf, was a keyhole. Farjeon inserted a tiny key, and a concealed cubbyhole sprang open. "Grinnell diagnosed her pregnancy at four months. Little bitch couldn't even remember who had sired the thing!" He swore under his breath. "Waste . . . waste . . . waste! Poor old Grinnell did his best to help. Suggested we take an obscure cottage, then farm the brat out. Sensible, valuable man!" Laughing, he flung several sketchbooks down onto a drawing table, leaning on them so that Desmond couldn't pry them open.

"Ironically, she became a loving, expectant mother, living in a fantasy world, deaf to her perilous situation. But when I finally breached that peculiar self-absorption to tell her that the baby must be farmed out so that she could return to Bellereve, her virtue supposedly intact—what did she do? Strangled the poor bastard with so tight a grip that she broke its neck!"

Desmond's face went white, and Farjeon flipped open a sketchbook. "Look through these, friend, and then tell me if I should have fetched her home earlier. . . ."

The first book was unremarkable: sketches of the cottage, its interior, the garden; and studies of Ariel in mid-pregnancy— a decidedly unhappy Ariel, obviously upset by her condition. Shame and despair haunted these sorrowful pictures.

The second book contained drawings made during her final months, and her mood had certainly changed. In place of fear, her lovely face shone with wonder as she cradled her unborn child. Farjeon had sketched her at all the tasks any pregnant woman might engage in, preparing for her baby. There were nude studies, too, Desmond saw with distaste. The work became more and more intimate, uncomfortably so. Turning to the last volume, Desmond was astonished to find even her painful labor sketched in detail. The ordeal over, there were pictures of an ecstatic Ariel nursing her baby. Then came a charcoal drawing—one he couldn't decipher. Evidently, Farjeon must have decided to rework it, smudged out the original, but never returned to the subject. Now came pictures of a distraught Ariel so moving he thought he would weep. A broken, useless body lying in a torn shift, her face wracked with anguish. Illness appeared as she tossed feverishly on her bed, tears running down thin cheeks, eyes stung with grief. And then came the most harrowing section. Ariel, lying obscenely naked, tied to the bed in agony. Screaming, screaming, screaming. . . .

Desmond took a deep breath, feeling ill.

Farjeon clapped him on the back. "Well, if you suffer, Desmond, imagine what it was like for me. I lived it! How could I bring her home and face a repetition of the whole hideous business?"

"What are you going to do with her?" Desmond's voice was flat.

"Why, keep her at Bellereve, of course."

"Back to the stone chamber and the Jackal?"

"No, if she's a good girl, I'll let her stay here—"

"And if you can't control her?"

Farjeon looked highly amused. "Ah, she's back to her old tricks again, I see!" He flicked a malicious glance toward her bedroom. "Did you enjoy her just now?"

Anger shot from the hazel eyes. "What happens between us is none of your concern."

"None of my concern!" Farjeon echoed softly.

"We are in love. I want to marry her."

"Marry a madwoman, Desmond! Do you realize the snake's nest you're falling into? One week of you and she'll sink her fangs into another fool. You'd be nothing but a caretaker—not a husband. Suspecting, watching every man she came across, just as I did years ago. And do you look forward to welcoming a bastard?"

"Ariel loves me. The child will be mine," was the calm reply.

"You are a dreamer." Farjeon stood massive and dark against a bay window, his face taut with rage. "No doubt she's spun you many a fancy tale!"

"On the contrary, she told me nothing."

"Damn your impudence! What the hell did you hear from Grinnell?"

He had to take the step. Now. "Many things—"

"And you believed them?" Farjeon bridled. "The man's a notorious gossip and drunk. He killed our mother. Befuddled with port, he let her labor go on interminably before performing a Caesarean. She died from shock."

"Why, then, did you continue to employ him?"

Farjeon blinked in surprise. "That was Father's decision, not mine," he said hastily. "We had secrets to hide——"

"Secrets to hide, yet you kept the gossip! Just as you keep me." He raised a cynical eyebrow. "We are all bound together, Farjeon, but I've not been paid. Why pay him?"

"Is that what he told you?" His laugh was derisive. "God, he inherited a packet years ago, retired, and built that vault!"

Simon Desmond gazed pensively out a window at the other vault—her prison. "Grinnell certified Ariel. Why would you pick so unreliable a man?"

With a sneer, Farjeon returned the sketchbooks to their hiding place. "In such a delicate matter, do you think I was about to call in a stranger?"

"He killed your mother and saved Ariel from the hangman. You paid a lot for that call, didn't you?"

"Yes." Farjeon's eyes were bleak. "I lost my beloved sister."

The room was unbearably warm. White walls and splashes of color blinded him. Desmond wanted only to get his darling out of that damnable house as speedily as possible. But he must tread cautiously in such an inferno.

"All four of us have secrets to hide," he said tightly. "I want my payment. Now!"

"And what is that, my friend?" Farjeon studied him with interest.

"Your sister. Give her to me. Our life together will be a good one——"

"And if I refuse?"

"You can't." Desmond's tone was faintly contemptuous. "I have as much on you as does Grinnell. We are equal now——"

"I can ruin you on three counts. By tomorrow, your name will be anathema in this county!"

"If I fall, so do you, Farjeon. And I warn you, I, too, can be ruthless. . . ." Mercifully, he was able to curb his temper. "On the other hand, I'll make you a pact. Let me walk out of Bellereve with Ariel now, and that will be an end to our feud. I don't intend hurting my wife anymore than she's been hurt."

"How has she been hurt?" Farjeon looked curious.

Simon Desmond hesitated, feeling himself slip into dangerous waters. The colors were too jarring for an exhausted mind, his nerves unsteady for such a duel. "For twenty years," he said thickly, "Ariel's played the scapegoat."

"Poor, infatuated fool, that's what she wants you to believe! Always in search of a sympathetic male ear—a pretense for toying." His pitying look changed to concern. "Is the heat disturbing you, Desmond? You look very pale."

Vehemently, the younger man shook his head.

"What would you give for her?" his host whispered.

"My life," Desmond replied without hesitation. "She took my heart very early. And you shall give her to me—"

"Shall! My, my, dear sir!" Farjeon purred. "I really think if you're going to be my brother-in-law, you ought to know the full story, don't you?"

"You consent?" Thrown, Desmond felt his heart falter. He had never expected to win this easily.

"Yes, if you still feel the same way later." He flashed a charming smile. "Let's go for a walk. You Englishmen can never stand the heat, can you?" He stepped out into the Long Gallery. "It begins, of course, with the burnt wing," he said in high good humor, Desmond, at his side, wondering at what labyrinth he would next find himself. Bellereve's interior was like an oven, but when they walked into the courtyard, over-grown with weeds and ragged flowers, a blast of heat sent him reeling. Steadying himself against a burning wall, he looked up at Ariel's suite.

"You see the vines...how heavy they are—" Farjeon laughed. "They climb to the odalisque's boudoir." He threw Desmond a fixed look. "They could easily hold a man's weight."

"Not that of a heavy, muscular man," Desmond retorted, watching vine leaves crumble under his touch. "Very dry."

"Yes, that's the way it was the night the wing caught fire. Went up like a child's cardboard house. Only a shift in the wind saved the remainder." He glanced back at the manor-house, his head like an imperious eagle's. "One of our Saracen ancestors was burned at the stake," he said defiantly.

Desmond dropped the vine, chilled. "In Spain?"

"Yes, he refused to convert to Christianity. Imagine—en-during hideous torture and sacrificing his life so that the rest of the family might escape. Would you be capable of that?" he asked softly. "My sister and I—" He ran a tongue over dry lips.

Fully alert, Desmond snapped to attention. "Yes?"

Farjeon confronted the ruined wing, his voice melodic. "We

saw the exact spot. Ariel was fascinated. Had a stake been there, I think I could have set her on fire.... She was intoxicated, almost sexually so—" His smile was lazy. "But she had this behind her." He gestured toward the ruin. "We think it began on the far right side, then leapt over the stone suite to the rooms on the left. Certainly, the damage is less extensive there."

Inhaling an acrid odor of smoke, Desmond stood riveted. "Astonishing—it still smells!"

"I call it Ariel's folly," Farjeon replied, fitting a key into an eroded brass lock. "Come, brother-in-law, I'll show you what havoc your darling wreaked." The blackened oak door moaned in protest against his powerful shove, then reluctantly creaked open. "Follow me carefully, Desmond, and watch your step. If you don't you'll fall through."

Simon Desmond, treading impatiently on his heels, stopped in horror. Before him yawned a tremendous void where the floor had collapsed. A few stout beams still stretched across the immense cavity gouging out a once great chamber. One massive beam, like a clipper's mast, rose far out of sight to the roof. Shreds of plastered ceiling dangled like tattered gowns. Occasionally, one glimpsed the wreckage of upstairs rooms with wainscotted walls fairly intact. An ancient painting swung crazily from an upper story. All the windows were broken, but so thick was the vine growth that it was impossible to see outside. Only from a gap in the roof did a dagger of sun slash through. Below, in the vast pit, broken pieces of furniture rotting in pools of filth and water crouched like dead bodies in the muck. An unpleasant noise and lightning dart was the wild scuttle of a large rat. Looking down grimly, Desmond saw it wasn't the only one. And there was worse....

"Hold on to the sides and you'll be all right. The brick's solid," Farjeon called over his shoulder.

Fighting disgust, his companion followed, shouting a question. "Where did it start?"

"Probably in this room. It's the largest in the wing, and it must have lit the central beam, which runs throughout the fireplaces. Within minutes, the whole section was ablaze." Almost tenderly, Farjeon asked, "And this is the woman you want to marry?" He was climbing the treads of a Jacobean staircase, which rose perilously into the charred chaos above. Desmond plodded behind, intent on every unexpected noise, every shadow.

"How do you think she set it, Farjeon?"

Nicholas Farjeon grimaced. "God knows! Lucifer matches, perhaps. A candle, or some embers may still have been smoldering. . . ."

"How did your ancestor set the first fire?"

Farjeon gave a roar of laughter that echoed dully in the ruin. "With a flambeau! Now, that must have been a beauty. This one caused scarcely a ripple."

"Grinnell said she fell and bruised her head that night and was knocked unconscious. Who found her?"

"I did. The tricky little devil! It was all faked. I caught her running out of the building. . . ."

They had reached the first-floor landing, still outwardly intact. To the right and left ran a corridor with doors banging in the wind. Desmond couldn't stomach it any longer. "No more, Farjeon. I've seen enough," he wheezed, choking on the debris. "Just give her to me. She will be well loved—"

"You don't know one damn thing about her!" Farjeon exploded, his back to a shattered oriel window. "Would you know how to hold her against the night terrors destroying her soul? How to touch that exquisite creature so that instantly she's calm? How to make love to her so that all fear dissolves in an ecstasy so great that she begs and begs for more? I doubt it!" He sneered. "You and other men may have soiled her, but I alone have knowledge of that extraordinary heart. . . ."

Simon Desmond paused, looking around carefully. The sturdy brick sides were reliable, centuries old, but each floor and ceiling held its own menace. Even as they walked, the slightest step sent plaster or wood splintering. Such an easy place in which to get killed.

The words hurt. "You were her lover, weren't you, Farjeon?"

The man seemed neither surprised nor affronted by the question. "Of course," he said gently. "How could I resist such beauty? Such warmth? Poor darling, even as a young girl she was terrified of thunder storms, and one night we had a horrendous one. It almost struck this ruin. I came to soothe her, but she wouldn't let go. Implored me to stay. So I spent the night in true brotherly fashion"—he spat the words—"on top of the comforter. I came again the next night—she was still so frightened but eagerly receptive to my presence. Before long, I moved into her bed." He smiled. "She gave up her virginity very easily, Desmond."

Simon Desmond's face was expressionless. "And became your mistress?"

"Not my mistress, fool. My lover!" Farjeon hissed. "She adored me...." Even in that murky light, his eyes glittered. "I have never known so loving a woman, so devoted or so insatiable. She thirsted after me, as I did her—" He broke off, his voice trembling with emotion. "Only the bastard spoiled it."

Suddenly, it occurred to Simon Desmond that he wasn't going to get out of that charnel house alive. Farjeon was too big a man, too quick on his feet for him to escape, and he had few words left to stall him. Quietly, he began to retreat down the staircase, but Nicholas Farjeon, observing his maneuver, took a step forward.

"I wouldn't walk anywhere without me, Dr. Desmond," he said in a mocking tone. "One misstep and you plunge below. From here, it's quite a drop."

Only self-preservation kept him moving in that dreamlike world. He had expected such a revelation, but its reality shattered him. "I take it no one seeking her hand in marriage would find a welcome, eh?" he shouted.

"Not necessarily," Farjeon grinned. "The others, of course, were impossible for us. But you might be the one candidate who could oblige me.... Allow me an hour or so alone with her when my need arose." He laughed coarsely.

Simon Desmond climbed down two more steps. It was a hellishly long staircase, the treads shook ominously, and he wasn't certain which way to turn at the end. Abruptly, he halted, his eyes stinging with tears.

"You were the baby's father, weren't you?" he whispered.

"Of course...." Farjeon pursued him relentlessly, never once stopping, sure-footed without looking. "It was a strong, healthy little boy that she, in her madness, had to kill—"

Desmond, a hand gripping the mangled rail, felt for the bottom step. "But you were the one who killed it, weren't you?" he breathed.

An oath came from Nicholas Farjeon as he raced down the staircase. Suddenly, sharply, Desmond heard Ariel's warning voice in his ear, and he stepped aside as something slammed into his head. Dimly, he felt himself falling into her outstretched arms, and then nothing as he sank into the abyss.

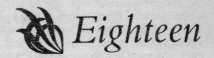 *Eighteen*

Five forty-five. Ariel Farjeon, still wearing the dusty-rose peignoir, sat stiffly before a tea service. Behind her, a silk curtain flapped in a warm breeze from an open casement window. Below, a fountain splashed—or was that only a memory? Faraway, a guitar's intoxicating beat rivaled the passionate singing of a lone voice.

Normally, her appetite was modest, but instinct warned her to build up a reservoir of strength, and she piled her Chelsea plate high with thin sandwiches and cake, washing the meal down with strong cups of China tea. But underneath her composure, thoughts spun like a whirlwind. Simon had left her a minute ago, or was it over an hour? Two hours? Where in God's name was he?

He had been closeted too long with Nicholas. Any discussion, either agreeable or angry, ought to have been settled by now. Something was wrong. . . . Uneasily, she began pacing the bedchamber. Since childhood, she had learned every deception necessary to survive, skimming in and out of Bellereve's vast rooms with a shadow's stealth. In cunning, though he didn't know it, she surpassed Nicholas. It was his great physical strength that undid her and the simple fact that no one would ever believe her. Many times in the last twenty years, she had known fear, and there were worse, agonizing moments when she wondered if she sidestepped or fell into madness. Memories still eluded her. And tonight might witness a final defeat—the death of all her poor hopes, the fragile prayers that had kept her alive during those monstrous years of incarceration.

Great streaks of red leapt across the sky as the *eynd* evaporated. A flock of geese, with raucous cries, slid into the horizon. The music of guitars and fountains ceased. Whatever move she made, tonight would be her end. For two decades, they had kept the secret, and now this. . . .

A maid came and removed the tea service, and Ariel turned away, shaken by hysteria. Accidentally, the silly woman had left the bedroom key behind days before, which meant that she—the lunatic—could roam at will. But she must wait until one of them returned. It was fatal to escape from her gilded prison not knowing Simon's whereabouts. One glimpse of her and the alarm would spread. Perhaps he had already left the manor-house, she thought wretchedly, learning something *too unpleasant.*

A shadow behind was Nicholas Farjeon. So quietly had he entered that she hadn't heard the connecting door's creak. He kissed her throat, his mouth burning, then caught her in a rough embrace.

"Desmond knows," he said, almost exultant.

Her heart, against his, began to race. "Knows what?"

"About us. *All* about us. . . ." A tremor ran through his big body, and he clasped his hands to her bosom.

"Where is he, Nicholas? Did you send him back to Fairhaven?" His eyes glittered with lust, and she loosened her bodice, recognizing his need.

He sank his lips into her sweet-scented body. "Damn you! You should never have become pregnant. You belong to me and to no one else. . . ." Cupping a breast, he bent down. A tear ran down her cheek as she stroked his neck.

"I need you, Ariel!" he cried brokenly. "I'm afraid—"

"Hush, my darling. . . ." With tender endearments, she led him to her bed and delicately began to unbutton his shirt. "What did you do with Desmond?" she asked idly, an amused look masking her fears.

"Knocked him out and tied him up—"

"Oh, Nicholas, that wasn't very wise!" She sighed. "How are you going to explain such a fit of temper?" The handsome face quivered with emotion, and in a terrifying instant she saw all their ancestors—as he had once described them—mirrored in his features. The eerie sensation, which she had felt in the

Alhambra, of living with him repeatedly over the centuries, stamped itself in her mind. They were one flesh, one heart. Both insane. . . .

"Let me hold you," she urged, lying beside him. "What did you do with the fool? Where is he?"

"In the burnt wing." He eyed her hungrily, an insistent hand fondling her body.

"Which section?" She laughed. "There are two, Nicholas." Earlier that afternoon he had taken her by force, heedless of her acute distress. Now their roles were reversed. He was the one terrified. Very delicately, arousing but not inflaming, she teased him, tenderly passionate. He nestled against her warmth, captivated.

"The one where the fire began," he murmured.

"But what are you going to do with him?"

"We're going to have another fire, darling." Farjeon caught her appalled look. In a burst of fury, he shook her violently, shouting, "Are you in love with him?"

Ariel fought a dizzying spiral of panic. "Of course not. Don't be ridiculous! There's never been anyone but you."

His face was cold. "Then why the hell did you sleep with him in Yarmouth?"

She closed her bodice. "He was amorous. I was perverse. No more."

"How could you lie with a man you didn't love?"

Feeling her small reserve of strength ebbing, she began to weep. "Do you know what happened to me at the asylum, Nicholas, in that hideous room? It went on for quite some time before a doctor found out. I lost count of how many men raped me—"

"You slut!" He struck her. "Why didn't you kill yourself? That's what I told you to do."

"I was afraid."

"Before restraint, you had the chance. Do you think *I* would have missed the opportunity?" He mocked her anguish.

"I didn't have your courage," she sobbed. "Besides, I always hoped that one day you'd free me—"

"You disgust me!" He sneered. "I sent you there—pure, in love with me—and what did I get back? A whore!"

Her face was bleak with despair. "I couldn't protect myself, Nicholas. You must believe me—"

"Damn you, bitch! You profess undying love to me, yet

have the nerve—the indecency—to ensnare Simon Desmond. The man's crazy about you!"

An impatient edge masked her deep joy as she rose from the bed. "What are you going to do with him?"

The question triggered a tirade. "Had you been sensible after the baby's death, everything would have been fine, Ariel! We could have come home to Bellereve, going on as before. No one suspected. But you had to get so emotional over a trifle—"

"What are you going to do with Desmond?"

Farjeon lay back on the bed, gloating. "He'll die in the fire."

"Oh, God, they'll think I set it!" she moaned. "His body will be found. . . . Nicholas, that's murder!"

"But you're insane, sister dear!" he said, laughing. "Everyone knows it. I'd say you have a fifty-fifty chance of escaping the hangman. With luck, you might end up with the criminal lunatics at Broadmoor."

"Let him go! I beg you, let him go!" Somehow, she managed to keep the frenzy out of her voice.

"Oh, do you want your lover back?" He jeered. "I can't, my pet, he knows everything—"

"Let him go, Nicholas. He's done us no harm and won't. Have mercy. Free him. . . ." she cried brokenly. "And I'll do anything you want."

"I'm satiated with you!" Farjeon snarled. "Why should I want more? Besides, in a few years, you'll be an ugly old woman." He glared at her. "Your body reeks of lust, Ariel. You sicken me."

She crossed her hands over her bosom. "I reek of you, Nicholas. You had me less than two hours ago—"

"And Desmond?"

"Comforted me only. There was no copulating, brother!" She flicked him a contemptuous glance, going as far as she dared. No, it was no gross animal act, but an exquisite union of two souls—a reminder of Yarmouth's love, she thought sadly.

"Get dressed." His voice was icy as he buttoned up his shirt.

"Why?"

"I'm taking you back to the stone suite." She flinched, and he laid a possessive hand on her shoulder, grinning. "Oh, don't fret. The Jackal has been booted out. I just thought you might enjoy listening to your lover's screams."

Ariel's face went white. "I have only one lover, Nicholas—you! How often must I say it? And now you turn from me. . . ." At her wits' end, she let fall the peignoir and stood before him naked. "Why?" she asked in a very hurt voice.

Farjeon's mouth tensed with desire. Sitting down heavily in an armchair, he beckoned her over. "We'll waste a few more minutes, Ariel. . . ."

Afterward, in a wave of repulsion, she dressed under his rapacious eyes, putting on a cambric wrapper and thin slippers. From his chair, her brother laughed at her humiliation, lighted to make her endure an act she despised, but it pleased him to so degrade her.

Fetching a cloak from her wardrobe, she faced him, lovingly submissive. "Nicholas, I implore you! Set him free. Then we can live together in peace for as long as you want." He remained silent, brooding. "Please, my darling. . . ."

"How can I?" He glowered. "He knows too much—"

"Ah, but he raped me, and you can always hold that over his head should he try to force your hand."

"He knows I am your lover, the father of your child—" His wave of indecision changed to outrage. "And he even had the audacity to suggest that I killed it!" She stared at him, horrified. "Don't you see, Ariel, he holds all the trump cards. He must die."

"And what about me?" she whispered.

"The police may only be able to swarm—not light. They can't do much without a body." He smiled, again in control. "And I can promise you, darling, it will be a very big fire. Hopefully, he'll just be one more *thing* in the pit!" Enthralled by the image, he shoved her out into the Long Gallery, hurrying her down the Jacobean staircase, where they ran into Jenkins, the butler. Naturally, Farjeon explained that his sister was being returned to the stone suite. Within minutes, Ariel thought bitterly, the entire staff would learn about her confinement and draw the inevitable conclusion: she had suffered a relapse. No Farjeon was ever locked up unless mad or on the edge of a breakdown, and the hand on her wrist was crushingly tight, obviously so.

"I'm sorry, sir," Jenkins murmured, opening the door.

As they walked across the courtyard, Ariel was deplorably aware of her physical weakness. Her legs felt like jelly, and she leaned too heavily on Nicholas's arm. A strong wind buffeted her skirts, making her stumble.

"You can't do it tonight!" she gasped. "The wind's too strong. It will strike Bellereve."

"I like taking risks, Ariel. It makes the game more exciting. . . ." Unlocking the iron-banded door, he pushed her inside.

"Give me a light, please, Nicholas!"

"You'll soon have a great deal!" He laughed, hugely amused. "And don't worry, sweet, you're not to die. I'll rescue you in plenty of time. . . . Enjoy your lover's agony!" With a slam, he locked the door on her frantic cries.

For a long time, she stood paralyzed, too stunned to move. A dim light trickled through filthy windows. What time was it? she wondered stupidly. Close to seven, from the length of the shadows, she judged. That gave her at least two hours of visibility. Nicholas would dine and then wait for the household to retire. Nothing would happen until eleven or twelve o'clock, but it was quite likely that he might pay her a "brotherly" visit just to prolong her torment.

Abruptly, the light changed, clouds blotting out the sun. Turning from this new menace, Ariel Farjeon tried to remember her past. Events occurring after the fire and her grandfather's death. Memories encompassing Nicholas. On a number of occasions, they had explored the ruined wing, exhilarated by its danger. As terrible a hazard as their love affair. Without light, he was in great peril, but if she could recall the dangers and retrace the old path they had used, she might be able to reach Simon Desmond. Dear God! Where was he? she wondered, her heart aching.

The stone suite she knew blindfolded. Often at night, unable to sleep, she had groped her way around its walls, her hand scraping a line on stone. Others had done so, too, she noticed by daylight, and there was a dreadful indentation where some mad relative had killed himself by bashing in his skull. Now she must prepare herself and then wait for Nicholas to set the damned thing on fire before venturing forth.

All doors in her suite were locked, of course. Working her way out to the kitchen, she searched for the brandy flask left by Simon. Locating it high on a shelf, she pulled out the stopper with shaking fingers. Mercifully, it was full, and she took a good swig to give herself energy. Thinking of Simon, her eyes misted. He would need some later, and she thrust it into her chemise.

Opening a drawer where the Jackal kept her poor lot of implements, she grasped several dull knives and headed for

the oak door leading into the burnt wing. The lock was old
and the wood around it decaying from the combined effects of
age and fire. Ariel Farjeon set to work, chipping away at the
wood. A splinter fell into her hand, and she sobbed in relief.
The knife broke. She picked up a second. More wood came
away, but not enough. By now she was frantic. It was pitch
black outside. At most, she had an hour and a half before
Nicholas might come visiting, and these knives were totally
inefficient for such grueling labor.

In despair, she hunted through the kitchen. And then to her
surprise, she found a cleaver and trowel—rusty but workable,
she prayed. Amazingly, the cleaver held up. The wood broke
away in larger and larger pieces, allowing her to force a hand
in to try to unlock the door. Gingerly, she felt for a bolt, but
none existed, only the lock. Now she used the trowel. First on
one side, then on the other. The stench of smoke-filled rooms
nauseated her, making her almost faint. Finally, the lock gave
and fell to the floor.

Impossible to take the cleaver and trowel. A knife she could
handle and must take, but the damn things in the kitchen were
worthless. And then in the midst of her anguish, she remembered the knife Simon had used to cut open a parcel he once
brought her. A knife accidentally left behind. One she had
hidden. But where was it? She inched her way out to the sitting
room. Nervous fingers explored every article of furniture, finding nothing. Perhaps it was in the mattress pallet. No, there
had been no hole then. Nicholas made it when he hid Regina's
jewels after suffocating her that dreadful night. Thinking Ariel
asleep, he poured out his confession, and it became one more
memory to be forgotten like fire and baby. . . .

No, there was nothing in that miserable room. Alarmed by
her slow progress, she resumed her hunt. Nothing. Not even
in the rat holes. At the fireplace, she hesitated. No fires were
ever lit in that grate. On her knees, she rummaged in the
chimney, finally locating a tiny ledge where she had safely
concealed Simon's knife from the predatory eyes of the Jackal.
The blade was remarkably sharp, and she stuck it into her
corset.

Now she must wait. God knows how long. Until the lamps
in the servants' quarters were extinguished. Nicholas would
keep his lamps burning in his suite until far in the night as was
his custom. Ariel dragged a ladder-backed chair over to the
window. If only she could break a pane. . . . And she fetched

the trowel from the kitchen. A corner pane was needed, one not easily noticeable. Under her blow, the two-hundred-year-old glass shattered, and she peered through a jagged opening toward Bellereve. Her brother's suite was lit. The staff slept in the attic above the guest rooms. Knocking out all the glass, she searched in vain. That area was obscured. Only Nicholas's domain and the entrance porch with a few rooms beyond were visible. Regina had had gaslight installed in every room she frequented, and for some reason tonight, the house was ablaze with light. Later, flickering night lamps would replace gas jets. Hopefully, she could tell the difference.

Every move must now be outlined. One misstep on her part could end both their lives. Dismally, she acknowledged her glaring weakness. She couldn't remember the wing's layout. So many years had elapsed since she and Nicholas had scrambled through its desolation. How many floors were there? It must be built along the same lines as the Jacobean Bellereve, so there would be two floors and an attic above the ground floor. Below, of course, were the cellars. God, what if Nicholas had thrown him down there! But such a fall, following a head injury, might kill him, and her brother wouldn't want a merciful release for his hated rival. This was to be Simon Desmond's punishment for transgression.... And hers, if she didn't find him. Screams that would overshadow those tiny shrieks.

The stone suite was stifling. Freezing in winter, it became an oven in summer. Stripping off her cloak, Ariel paced the chamber, testing her strength. The wrapper wasn't cumbersome, and the kid slippers gave her feet a strong grip. Up and down she walked in the dark, then stole over to her shabby vanity case. Her hair must be tightly bound, not falling loose, but the box had vanished from the mantel—a prize stolen by the Jackal, she guessed.

In her wardrobe, she felt among her old clothes and worn lingerie. A petticoat ripped easily in her hands, and she tied up her hair. Layer after layer of the once exquisite garment tore off, and she rolled up the pieces like bandages, tucking several into her bodice and leaving the rest beside the cleaver and trowel. Under a leaking faucet, she sponged her damp face and neck, then scrubbed her hands, despairing. If only she could keep them dry.

A noise by the front door shocked her, and she fought her way back to the sitting room. Was Nicholas outside or in? A devotee of pranks, he would delight in maddening her. But the chamber was ominously still. Once more, she sought the lights' reflection from the broken pane. It was unchanged, and she sank to the floor, weeping. The great door's clanging alarm would have warned her.... She was still alone, tossing in limbo. In hell.

How long? How long, dear God, must she wait? Unconsciously, she gripped her stomach as she had done in childbirth. Easing the pains.... God damn it! Why the hell didn't he come? What was he waiting for? The night stars... the music... the scent of a thousand roses....

Withdrawing the flask from her bodice, she took another bracing nip. Why delay? she asked herself, agonized. Why not find Simon now, while she had time to make mistakes? A moment wasted was a moment forever lost, and her chances were slim indeed. Perspiration froze on her body, her reeling mind grew calm, and she returned to the kitchen. Move. Move! There was no time to linger. He had been baiting her. She, too, must be punished. She would not *hear* her lover's screams. The ultimate torture would come later, when Nicholas forced her to watch....

Leaning against the kitchen door, she gave it a strong shove, but it wouldn't budge. Infuriated, Ariel grabbed a stool and broke it on the stubborn oak. The door creaked open an inch, and pushing hard, she burst into a charred world. Ashes rained on her, and she clutched at the door, spinning dizzily into space. Hurled back against the wall, she caught her breath, then lowered herself to the floor, seeking the lock. Like a dead fish, it lay on the rotten planks—a heavy, brass object—and she flung it ahead, hearing it strike wood. A second of quiet, and then came the crash of splintering beams as a section of the floor ripped away. Very gingerly, Ariel crept around the edge of the chamber, her fingers gripping brick rather than the oak wainscotting, patches of which were loose. Youth's memories were reviving. The exterior wall was largely safe; it was the interior that was so deadly.

With her heart in her mouth, she called Simon's name. No answer. This room, she dimly remembered, was the last of a series of reception rooms embracing a palatial chamber—fit replacement for the Great Hall destroyed some two hundred years before.

An ivy-covered window and a loosened panel of wainscotting told her she had reached the room's corner. Steering to her left, she felt her way along like a blind person. Entering a second room, she almost slipped; she heard the dreadful sound of decaying wood tumble into the cellar below. Again she called Simon's name. Nothing greeted her but a mocking silence.

Another bay window choked with ivy vines writhing like snakes met her touch, and she made an opening. Bellereve's lights had dimmed. Sagging breathlessly against the brick wall, she tried to steady her trembling legs. How had she so miscalculated the time? Had he sent them to bed early, or was this a further trick to unnerve her?

Insects were climbing on the vines, and she plucked them off with a spasm of disgust when they pricked her skin, again resuming her laborious journey. Her worst moments came when she left the exterior wall's safety to seek an entrance into another chamber, not knowing if she would encounter solid planks or a hole.

An oriel window leered as in a dream, and she peeped out through rank leaves. The manor-house lights were extinguished. Only a full moon whitened the courtyard, as it did the long dead rooms about her. Occasionally, a blast of moonbeams illuminated her as if she were a ghost, blinding her.

Ahead loomed an enormous void. Gusts of wind whipped doors against ruinous walls. Abandoning the outer wall, she crept into the wing's heart, seeking the great staircase. Afraid of the wainscotting, she moved at a snail's pace into the unknown. And then finally, she felt a tread, warped and splintered but seemingly stable. Reaching higher, she touched another, and a third. A massive newel post, crowned by a lion finial, bruised her forehead, and she smiled, misty-eyed. She had found the hall.

The handrail was solid enough, she judged, testing it. Lifting her head, she saw the moon seeping through a gigantic crack, gashing the roof high above.

"Simon!" she hissed into glowing darkness. "Where are you?"

The building was alive with strange noises. Sorting them out—a door banging, a rat's scuffle, the groan of decaying oak—she distinctly heard a low cry. A human voice.

"God, darling!" she moaned. "I can't see you!"

Simon Desmond flicked his eyes from side to side, seeing nothing except swathes of moonlight and shadows, still stunned by his head wound, the rope on his wrists so tight that it threatened to cut off his circulation. But he could move his legs, and all he felt under them was space.

"Simon, where are you?" Ariel called frantically.

"Tied . . . to a beam, I think—" he whispered.

"Oh, God!" she raged. "Which one?"

"I don't know. . . . You mustn't come out. Some stretch across. Some rise. . . . I don't know which. Don't come out!"

"Which one?" she called, wild with anxiety, trying to remember the daredevil escapades of long ago. And then a burst of light, like a rocket, shot out from a gap overhead. By its glare, she saw where he was tied. On the foremast beam, they called it. A monstrous thing some distance out. Again came a searing flash, and she looked up. Lightning? No, it was fire. Nicholas was in the wing with them, directly overhead.

"When did he get here?" she cried fearfully.

"Fifteen . . . twenty minutes ago. I don't know, darling. I haven't kept count. . . ."

"Did he lock the door?"

"Yes."

A chill of horror ran through her. He would concentrate on the upstairs, letting the debris fall, and then move to the rooms beyond her suite, coming for her then or after he had torched the remainder. Controlling her panic, she called out softly, "I have a knife. I'm going to walk out on the connecting beam and cut you loose. Then you must follow me back. . . ." She wiped her damp face. "Do you think you can manage?"

"I don't know. My head aches so. . . . I may have a . . . concussion—" His voice grew weaker.

"You can do it!" she said fiercely. "I love you, Simon. Just do as I say, and I'll get you out of this hell."

Lying full-length on the rotting floor, Ariel groped for the chasm. With feet braced against the staircase, she cautiously inched to her left, seeking the right beam. Reaching one, she struck it hard. With a deafening roar, it hurtled below. A second and third were worm-eaten, spider-webbed stumps. But a fourth stoutly resisted her frenzied pounding, and she gripped it, half-sobbing. Suddenly, a great mass of flaming stucco dropped into the abyss, narrowly missing her.

Desmond had seen it. "For God's sake, go, Ariel!" he shouted. "I don't want to watch you die."

"I can walk it," she replied icily, trying to numb her terror. "Many's the time I've done it. . . ." With one foot, she tested the beam. It held, and it was equally sturdy with her full weight. Taking a deep breath, she began the long trek, moving like a tightrope walker, because the beam was not wide enough to support both feet together. Riveted to the bound man ahead, she fought two terrifying images: Nicholas strolling down the great staircase, and Simon Desmond falling to his death when she untied him.

As a very young woman, on a dare from Nicholas, she had first walked the beam. So wishing to please, she lightheartedly followed him—trusting, admiring his magnificent grace. Not until she joined him at the mast did she fully appreciate her danger. The pit yawned, his eyes were wild, and fear was not an emotion she shared with him.... Remembering, she broke into a spasm of coughing, cursing her still weakened body. The beam swayed and she collapsed, struggling to keep her balance.

Nicholas had walked this beam carrying an unconscious man. The thought enraged her, giving her a sorely needed boost of energy. But it was too risky to stand so she grimly crawled the remaining distance. A touch of leather under her palm was Simon's riding boot. Loving words met her as she hauled herself to her feet. Clinging to him passionately, her tears mingled with the blood and grime on his face.

"Am I dreaming, or are you alive?" he murmured against her cheek.

"Alive." Her lips brushed his. "Are you in much pain?"

"I heard your voice and stepped aside. Otherwise I think he might have killed me.... Whatever the weapon was, it only grazed, but it stings like the devil—"

"Do you want some brandy?"

"No, I'm too nauseous...."

Ariel wrapped a linen strip about his forehead. "Hopefully, you can see with this—" Blinking back tears, she grasped the knife. "I'm going to cut your bonds." Steadying herself against his chest, she felt for the rope. It was tightly knotted but not too thick, and she set to work. Minutes raced by—too many. Then the strands broke free in her hand.

"How's your circulation?" she muttered, clasping him to the beam in a protective embrace.

Desmond managed a faint smile. "It's been better!"

A crackling noise overhead alerted her to a new danger. Fire snaking down the mast.

"I'll go first." She controlled her urgency. "Have you strength enough to follow?"

"I'll try, Ariel—"

"Try?" she shouted. *"You will.* I'm not about to lose you!

The distance isn't that great. Keep your eyes on me and don't look down." Bravado evaporating, she began the crawl back.

Simon Desmond, sinking to his knees, clutched at the beam, his head spinning. Ahead of him, Ariel's white cambric wrapper shone like a beacon. The rapid change in position caused his wound to reopen. Blood dripped onto his neck, down his shirt. Dangerously lightheaded, he began the perilous journey.

"Don't worry!" Ariel called, almost gaily. "The beam is sturdy. Move as quickly as possible. . . ." Gaining the end, she crouched by the staircase, encouraging him along. With her heart in her mouth, she saw him almost fall. Blood trickled down his bandage as he fought to regain his hold.

Ariel knew his vigor, but never before had she seen him fully tested. Horrified, she watched him dangle over the chasm, swinging like an acrobat. Incredibly, he managed to hook a boot spur in the oak. A moment later, he was lying on the splintered beam, panting, gasping for breath, his arms feeling as if they had been yanked out of the sockets. She crawled out to meet him, hands outstretched. Her touch revived him.

"If you fall, Simon, so will I. I cannot live without you!"

"You are my life, Ariel. I will always follow you. . . ." He gripped her hand. "Go, my love!" Not once did he take his eyes from her face as she backed away. Slowly, painfully, he struggled after her. Against the staircase, they met in a desperate embrace.

"We must hurry, darling!" she cried. "We'll have to escape from the wing's end. He's locked my quarters." Turning, she clasped Simon's arms about her waist. "Walk right behind me. Whatever happens, don't step to the side. The outer wall is safe, the rest is very treacherous. If you need to rest, we'll stop for a moment—"

"Why not go through a window?"

"The vines are too tight," she muttered, pulling him along. Their return was a nightmare. He was obviously ill, and they stopped frequently to halt his bouts of giddiness and nausea. Ariel kept one final fear to herself: Nicholas would be waiting for her in the stone suite.

On and on, they stumbled in a dreadful world of fire and madness. His hands' pressure on her exhausted body hurt. Her gown was drenched with blood whenever he laid his head on her shoulder. Smoke stung her eyes, making it difficult to see, and aggravated her breathing.

"Just a few steps more, my darling!" she wheezed. Out came the knife. In case they met Nicholas.

Fumbling blindly for the suite entrance, Ariel grasped the empty lock hole and flung back the door. He would be hiding, invisible in the dark. Like a sylph, she glided across the kitchen, keeping Simon away from any obstacle. At the sitting room's portal, she paused, intent on every sound. Red lightning danced across the windows, fighting the moon's brilliance, giving them some illumination. Not the slightest flicker of movement— anywhere.

"Nicholas!" she called warily. There was no reply. Simon Desmond groaned, his head pressed tightly to hers.

"I can't let you rest any longer. We must get out. Soon he'll torch this area." An arm about his waist, she helped him into the tiny room, only to realize that she'd forgotten to pick the lock. Cursing her stupidity, she left Simon on the pallet, then scrambled over to the door to test its strength. To her dismay, it opened immediately. Nicholas had come back for her and found her gone. Appalled, she cradled Simon to her heart. "He's been here. We must hurry!"

Opening the door, they stepped out into an inferno. Already, the floors above were on fire. On all sides came the thunder of crashing beams, falling wainscotting, plaster, and the spit of flame. Again clinging to brick, they took a torturous path with Ariel leading. Breaking into a chamber as massive as the one at the other end, Ariel glanced at the great oak door opening into the courtyard. Nicholas would have locked it, expecting to escape from the stone suite.

But where was he? she wondered, looking around fearfully. Through the smoky haze, Simon's face was ominously pale. Blood and soot stained his bandage. Pressing a handkerchief to his nose and mouth, she said, "It's not much farther, darling. Just to that wainscotted wall. A secret room and passage lead to the outside. We'll get out that way."

"I wouldn't bet on that!" a mocking voice shouted.

Ariel wheeled about. Descending the staircase in leisurely fashion—as if nothing at all were the matter—strode Nicholas Farjeon, resplendent in black, as handsome in that ghastly light as he had been in her youth, magnificent in his virility. Drawing her to him with every fiber of his being. Feeling her tension, Desmond tightened his grip on her waist. Incredibly, she was torn. In love with Simon Desmond, yet bewitched by Nicholas, whose mastery of her still dominated her life. He smiled, stretching out a hand.

"Come to me, beloved!"

"No!" Desmond yelled coldly. "She's mine. You've tormented her long enough, Farjeon."

"Do you want a weakling or a man, Ariel? Which is it to be, my love? Remember this afternoon, and a thousand nights...." He had reached the floor. Against Desmond, she trembled.

Simon Desmond pulled out his derringer. "Earlier, you caught me unawares. Now I have the upper hand!"

"Let Ariel make the decison," Farjeon snapped insolently.

A great roundel of plaster crashed into the room, spurting tongues of flame. Tears streaked her face.

"You'll put me away again, won't you, Nicholas? Blame me for this holocaust!"

"Don't be ridiculous, darling." He strolled nearer. "Would I do that to the mother of my child?"

As if a bucket of water had been tossed in her face, Ariel awoke from her lethargy. Above the fire's roar, she shouted, "It's Simon Desmond I love! Not you, Nicholas. It died between us with the baby's death...." Gripping Desmond's arm, she began moving backward to the wainscotted wall.

Farjeon halted in fury, his satanic face growing ugly in the raging light.

Desmond whispered, "Do you know how to open it, Ariel?"

"I used to, years ago.... Help me, Simon. Keep him away."

Drawing closer, Farjeon sneered at the pistol. "A toy!"

"Is it?" Desmond retorted, firing a shot at Farjeon's head, deliberately missing him by two inches. "Go, darling. Get to work. I'll hold him off."

Ariel ran from him, her lungs aching with smoke, eyes tearing. In her childhood, she had spent hours in this room, eager little fingers playing with the knobs that gave access to the tunnel. Once, her ancestors had stored plate and other valuables in a tiny secret room. In later years, a passage was built to the outside and used as a smuggler's hide-out. Already the oak wainscotting was hot to the touch. A few more minutes and it would catch fire.

Nicholas Farjeon laughed at her feeble attempts to locate the exact set of knobs hidden in the rich carving, his laughter shrill over the inferno. Desmond supported her while she searched frantically. Acorns? No, not acorns. Oak leaves? Not those either, and then she remembered the forgotten aroma of yule logs at Bellereve—eucalyptus. Five little buds to be touched in the right order. And then they would be safely on their way. . . .

Farjeon moved steadily toward them. Not believing a word of this farce. Wanting only one thing. Ariel in his arms so that they could enjoy this beautiful spectacle together.

On her knees, Ariel sobbed in frustration, pounding the wood, defying the panel to snap open of its own accord. Her head was throbbing, her stays so tight, she felt as if she were being cut in two. And Simon's hand on her shoulder, at first so strong, was weakening. Less than five feet away, Nicholas Farjeon stood, watching them with malicious amusement.

"Have you forgotten, sweet sister, the first five notes of 'Greensleeves'?"

The key—an Elizabethan folk song! Humming to herself in that hellish atmosphere, she carefully punched five small buds and the wainscotting swung open. Grabbing her by the waist, Desmond hauled her to her feet.

"Don't come any closer, Farjeon. I won't miss next time. You can get out another way." He slammed the door shut on the man's startled face.

"He can't!" Ariel cried wildly. "The whole thing is going."

"He almost destroyed you." Desmond's grip was possessive. "If he gets you again, he'll have to kill me, and I want very much to live. With you—as my wife!" He pushed her forward in the dark. "Do you know how to escape this room?"

"Yes," she murmured.

"What about the exit? Can you manage that?"

"It's tricky. . . . I don't know."

"Well, at least we've a chance. Now hurry!"

Sick with fright, she pushed a panel in the little room. Rotten with age, it disintegrated in her hands, and she crept into the pitch-black tunnel beyond, clutching Simon's hand. Guided by a brick wall, they stumbled through rubble and foul-smelling pools of muck. Something loathsome crawled across her slipper. Cobwebs brushed her face, tangled in her hair. Their fingers were bruised and bleeding from the rough stone.

"Why doesn't he come? He knows how to open it!" she moaned. "What is he waiting for?"

They had almost reached the tunnel's end when they heard Farjeon's cries against the wainscotted wall. A series of agonized screams. Wrenching apart her soul.

"For God's sake, let me go back!" Ariel sobbed. "He needs me—"

"No, darling, I need you!" Simon Desmond said brutally. "Open that door."

This one was even more elusive than the first. A cleverly concealed slit running through brick, flint, and Carstone.

"I can't find it!" she cried, panicking.

Another terrible scream reached them. Desmond caught her in a tight embrace, but she clawed at him, frantically trying to reach her brother.

"God! God, Simon, let me go to him.... Please!"

"No, Ariel! Don't you see? He can get in but doesn't want to—"

"He forgot!"

"How could he? He gave you the clue!" Desmond shouted, shoving her back to the exit. "Come, darling, we've no time—" Smoke wisps drifted in through the wainscotting, penetrating the brick tunnel. Nicholas pounded on the wood, cursing his sister.

"Help me," she said dully. "I think this is the spot." Up and down, she ran his knife in a jagged crack. And then it shattered. A single inhuman cry pierced her heart.

"Let me go to him, Simon. I'll take care of him."

"It may be a trick, Ariel, to taunt you. God knows he's capable of it. Haven't you been punished enough?"

"One of us is mad.... Perhaps we both are." She wept bitterly.

"The responsibility is mine alone," Desmond cried. "I shut the door on him. He brings only madness and death. I offer you life...."

"Give me the pistol," she said after a long pause.

Without hesitation, he handed it to her, as trusting as a child. At such close range she could kill him with one bullet and then reclaim her brother. Tensely, he waited. Ariel touched his heart with loving fingers, then looked at the wall.

"Brace me, Simon."

"No, it may ricochet!" he argued passionately. "Let me—"

"I'm not afraid," she interrupted. Calmly putting his arms around her waist, she steadied her head against his shoulder, then pulled the trigger. The blast deafened them, and he clung to her hard, blinded by tears.

"It's opening!" she whispered, awestruck. Moonlight danced

before them as the ancient crack widened. Dragging him out to the grass, Ariel swiftly embraced him.

"Had anything happened to you, I would have gone back and killed him!" Desmond muttered feverishly.

"We must flee," she cried, staring at the engulfed wing. "Once I'm spotted, they'll think I set it. Take my arm, Simon—" She walked by the moat so that his dark riding suit hid her white wrapper. Over the fire's tumult, shouts and screams came from the courtyard, and the frenzied sound of many footsteps. Probably robbing the place without Nicholas in command. Nicholas. . . .

"Dear, sweet Jesus!"

Desmond followed her glance as a heavy gust of wind buffeted a great tongue of flame across the gap separating the two wings: the one ruined, the other she had shared with Farjeon. Sparks like evil flowers burst into full bloom on the roof, exploding into flames; fireballs crashed through bay and oriel windows, crawled down vines. In that uncanny light of moon and fire, Ariel's face was disturbingly remote.

"I told him the wind was too strong," she said sadly.

Alerted by a grinding roar behind them, Desmond pulled her swiftly along the moat, ready to throw her in if necessary. Both turned at once, caught spellbound as the entire wing imprisoning the stone suite collapsed.

Ariel's lips moved in silent prayer for her brother. Simon Desmond, fearing her immediate collapse, took charge, relieved to find that the stinging air cleared his head. "Can we reach the stables from here?" he asked tensely.

No emotion shone on the tear-streaked face. "Yes, straight ahead through the park . . ." Talking exhausted her; her splendid resources were fast dwindling. Arms entwined, supporting each other, they stepped out from the flickering shadows of Bellereve's inferno to the ghostly enchantment of the great park.

"I have only my chestnut," he muttered, flinging his jacket around her shivering body. She swayed, then drew out the flask. Again he refused, and she took another hefty swig.

"Will it carry us both?" she asked tremulously.

"Easily. He knows the way to Fairhaven blindfolded." Ariel smiled as the brandy coursed through her veins, feeling strength reborn, but Desmond thought differently. She was only a few days out of a sickbed and still very weak. Of the two, he felt the stronger, but she surprised him again.

"Good!" she whispered, clinging to him helplessly for one minute, the next vibrantly alive. "While I'm saddling him, wash yourself. I'm worried about that wound—" Her voice shook. "Shouldn't I take you to a doctor?"

"Broughton's waiting for me in Heydon. They're alerted."

Ariel held up a warning hand, her body stiff with apprehension. Ahead, under a blood-red moonlit sky, stood the darkened stables. Stealing cautiously from the safety of the trees to the open clearing, she gripped Desmond's arm, whispering, "They've bedded down the horses. Everyone's up at Bellereve. We must leave before the engines arrive. . . ."

Sickened by the stable's odor, the headache pounding into his skull like a mallet, he retched while Ariel held him. When it was safe to leave him alone, she lit a bull's-eye lamp and peered among the stalls.

"Which horse is it, darling?" He nodded at the chestnut and his saddle, and Ariel took Desmond over to a tap. "Rinse off the dirt, Simon. I've more bandages."

He soaked his head for what seemed an eternity. A hand on his shoulder and the turning off of rusty, icy water tore him away from Farjeon's terrible image. . . . Before him stood a ragamuffin—no, it was a stable hand. Then he blinked in astonishment, realizing it was Ariel.

"Well, I can't show my legs, and this is not the time to ride sidesaddle!" She laughed, wiping off his face and head, gently tying on a bandage. "Poor lad, I just hope he owns another outfit. . . ." Leading Desmond over to the saddled chestnut, she said, "You'll ride behind, Simon. I'm strapping you to me in case you fall—"

"When in hell did you last ride a horse?" Desmond asked, dumbfounded.

Helping him to mount, she smiled. "About thirteen years ago, but Nicholas"— a flicker of anguish clouded her eyes— "taught me to ride bareback as a child. This is nothing!" Over his protests, she swung up gracefully into the saddle, then buckled them together with a stout belt. "Grip me hard," she ordered. "And try not to faint!"

Nuzzling her neck, he murmured, "Soon, Ariel, I will reap my reward. . . ."

Caressing his cheek with a loving hand, she urged the horse out of the stable, onto the dirt path leading to the cobblestone road. If anyone saw them, no outcry was heard. Even the gatehouse stood darkly silent. The massive gates had been drawn back, anticipating the fire engines' arrival. Presumably, they would come via the Reepham road—one she wished to avoid. Desmond directed her to the shortcut leading to Heydon. Only once did she glance back, her heart in tumult. The whole sky was ablaze, the way Nicholas had always dreamed of seeing it. Even the moon dripped fire.

Shock would come later. When she fully understood what she had done. Had she killed Nicholas? Or was that a death he deliberately sought? Again revenging himself on her. Once more she was in great danger. Not only would she be blamed for setting the fire and causing her brother's death, but the countryside would condemn her for Desmond's attack.

"Don't think!" Simon Desmond whispered, sensing her despair. "Just get us back to Fairhaven. . . ." He slumped against her shoulder.

His falling weight could pull them off the horse, but Ariel had attached a second strap to the first and connected it to the saddle. It would give her sufficient resistance should he collapse, she hoped. Allowing the chestnut its rein, she concentrated only on Simon, whispering loving words when she felt him weaken. Tied together, they rode as one, entwined in a moonlit embrace.

Reaching Heydon, she saw lights still flickering around the village green and heard voices coming from the Green Dragon, but no loiterer observed their progress. It was the last peaceful moment she expected. On entering Fairhaven, she was fully prepared to be separated from Simon Desmond and locked up in her old room. The "loony" safely imprisoned.

The chestnut halted in exhaustion beside its hitching post, waiting for the groom. With a deep breath, Ariel Farjeon unbuckled herself from Desmond and slid to the ground, one hand supporting the half-conscious man. The bandage was soaking, she saw with dismay.

Through a miasma of pain, Desmond stared at her, then kissed her hand with a supreme effort. "I . . . think you are the . . . most . . . extraordinary woman—"

His head drooped, and she held up her arms to help him down. He came, his body heavy against hers. Only then did she appreciate her own weakness as she kept from stumbling. In the sweet-scented Elizabethan garden, they clung to one another with passionate yearning, then she gently disengaged herself and assisted him toward the house, thinking numbly, They will take you away from me. One wall will separate us . . . until I am sent to Bedlam.

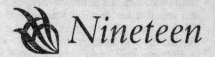 *Nineteen*

Blood trickled down her neck and bodice as the front door opened wide. Lamplight poured from every window in the Queen Anne brick house. Dazed, Ariel took off the stablehand's cap, her hair tumbling free as she awkwardly helped Desmond up the steps.

"Dear Lord!" Beatrice Clayton's face was ashen. "What happened to you?"

A protective arm around Ariel, Simon Desmond sagged against the doorjamb, struggling for words. "Farjeon...tried to...kill me," he wheezed. "Damn madman set...Bellereve on fire—"

Colin Broughton strode into view. One look at Desmond and he hustled him off to his surgery, leaving the women alone together on the porch.

"He may have a concussion," Ariel said, wiping her eyes. "And he's lost a lot of blood—" She broke down, weeping hysterically. Gathering her shocked wits together, the older woman ushered her inside, clucking at the ludicrous costume.

"Well, I couldn't ride in a white cambric wrapper, could I?" Managing a faint smile, Ariel sank exhausted onto a chair.

"You're both as weak as newborn kittens!" Beatrice sniffled. "How on earth did you manage?"

"Simon gave me strength. He never stopped believing—" She covered her eyes, fighting horrifying memories. Nicholas in flames... Simon dead.

"Oh, my dear, I must apologize," Beatrice cried, impulsively embracing the destitute figure. "I thought you mad. . . ." Until I read Simon's letter, she thought. Some of the disclosures still appalled her, but this was no time to pass judgment. . . . "They'll be a while in the surgery. Let's get you tidied up." She led the way upstairs.

Helping Ariel undress in the spare bedroom while Bessie filled a tin hip bath with hot water, Beatrice fingered the stained wrapper with trembling hands.

"Don't take it from me!" Ariel pleaded. "If anything happens to Simon, it's all I have—" She pressed the garment to her heart, grieving. Later, in a fresh wrapper, her hair washed and glistening like silk by candlelight, she stared numbly at a heaping plate of food. Fighting nausea, she put her fork down. "I'm sorry, I can't eat." Her look was anguished. "Why is it taking so long? Why can't I see him?"

"Stitches take time," Beatrice replied, edgy herself.

Colin Broughton walked into the dining room. "Miss Farjeon, Simon wants you upstairs—" As she tore out of the room, he stopped Beatrice's heated objection with a warning hand.

"They're not married," she hissed, jealousy for once getting the better of her. "It's not decent."

"What is? The contents of that letter?" She flushed, and he sat down heavily at the table. "Fetch me some port, Beatrice, and we'll have a chat. Then I'll give him some morphine." Accepting a glass, he said quietly, "She wears his ring. In three weeks, he swears they'll be married. No good arguing with him now. Give them this little time together—"

"But what happened?" she asked, her face taut with strain. "In God's name, Colin, what happened?"

Broughton sipped his port, eyes half-closed. "I gather the two men had a confrontation. Farjeon left Simon to die, set the wing on fire, and Ariel Farjeon saved his life—"

"And Nicholas Farjeon?"

"Is missing. . . ."

"As is his sister," Beatrice said bitterly. "Soon the whole constabulary will turn up on our doorstep."

"The entire manor will have to be searched. By then, Simon will be up and about. . . ."

In his darkened bedroom, Simon Desmond lay motionless, a single oil lamp casting shadows on the wall. Grief-stricken, Ariel studied the bandaged head, the sunken face—in repose so like her father and grandfather on their biers. But this man was alive. With a sigh, he opened his eyes, smiling at the sight of her.

"Come here." He held out an arm. She nestled against his shoulder. "It looks worse than it is, darling. Broughton leans to the dramatic. Just a few stitches, rest in bed, and I'll be back on duty in a few days."

"You're so pale," she murmured.

"Well, I've a mild concussion and some blood loss, but nothing to be alarmed about!" he added hastily, kissing her forehead.

A knock on the door drove them instantly apart. Broughton loomed, bag in hand. Rolling up Desmond's sleeve, he gave him an injection of morphine. "How's the headache?"

"Still there. . . ." He grimaced as the needle was withdrawn, then fumbled for Ariel's hand. "Let her stay."

Broughton peered at her, incredulous. "Simon, she's on the verge of collapsing. She needs sleep, for heaven's sake! Beatrice will nurse you."

"No!" Desmond roared. "Ariel will, won't you, darling?"

Her face was serene. "Yes."

Broughton frowned at her, doubtful, and Desmond threw him a wicked glare. "She saved my life, Colin. In this room with me, she's safe. I don't want any gossip spreading from Fairhaven. Eventually, the police will come sniffing. Let's delay them as long as possible. And I'm to see them before Ariel. Is that clearly understood?" Broughton nodded. "You and Bea must fend them off until I'm fit. . . ." His eyelids drooped, and he tugged on his darling's arm. "Sit by me, love. I'm so tired."

Drawing up a chair to the bedside, she clasped Desmond's outstretched hand, whispering to Broughton, "He'll come to no harm through me, I assure you."

When the door had finally closed behind Broughton, Simon Desmond winked at Ariel. "You're too far away, darling. I need you beside me." He patted his bed.

"They'll find us," she said worriedly.

"No, there'll be a lot of loud knocking first. . . ." As she cradled him against her breast, he clung to her tightly, never wanting to let go. "Whenever I close my eyes, I see that damnable chamber—without you!"

"You must forget, Simon. Forget, my darling," she crooned.

"Is that what you did?" he asked softly.

"Yes. . . ."

He stroked her face. "To keep from going mad?"

A tear ran down her cheek. "I don't know, Simon . . . what I was then, or now. . . ."

Desmond didn't want to press her. She was too vulnerable. At the right moment, he would seek the answers, and he fell asleep. All night and into mid-morning, she held him, cherishing those hours of fragile happiness—all she might ever know. If the police doubted Simon's word, she was doomed.

News came with breakfast. Bellereve was gutted. Farjeon and his sister were reported missing and presumed dead.

"Any feelers in my direction?" Desmond asked Beatrice.

"No, but it will come, Simon." She couldn't disguise her anxiety. "Someone will have noted your visit."

"Just keep them away, Bea." He turned to Ariel. Her lovely face was drawn, the gray eyes misty. In a day or so, he would have to drag her through a hellish session. To find a truth that might save or utterly destroy them. The last inquisition. . . .

Alone, he again pulled her down beside him, finding comfort and strength in her touch while she clung to him with fervent devotion, loving words masking her terror and abject shame.

Late evening brought bad tidings. While Broughton changed Desmond's bandage, Beatrice spoke to him quietly. "The police came at six o'clock, Simon. I told them you were ill, and they said they'd return tomorrow—same time. Can you make it?"

"Wait two more days," Broughton advised. "The longer the delay, the greater the chance of finding Farjeon's body." He rested his eyes on a stricken Ariel Farjeon. "You'll be in a better position to help her."

"Leave us a moment, darling," Desmond whispered to Ariel, waving both women out of the room. "What if they don't find his body?" he asked Broughton tensely.

"It will look bad for her. She's the one called a lunatic. But if Farjeon is found and you can convince them his sister is innocent, you'll win your case, I imagine. But without something concrete, she's in trouble—"

"What about my letter?"

"The critical question still remains unanswered, Simon. Which Farjeon was mad? Everything points to her."

"But you and Beatrice agree that he used her as a dupe?"

"Yes," Broughton slowly admitted. "But that first year is a hurdle. You must find out what really happened and then be very discreet with the authorities. Will she talk?"

"Hopefully, yes, and I will be careful." Desmond's eyes darkened in worry. "There's no need to mention incest, or the fact that he fathered her child...." He gave Broughton an uneasy look, his voice husky. "Does Bea know?"

"Yes." His friend rocked back and forth on his heels. "Bit shocked, I'm afraid. It's a terrible story."

"But it explains so much: why the villagers thought her chaste, why Farjeon never let her out of his sight, why he dismissed all the young male servants. The man was mad about her—in more ways than one, if I'm right. He must have been frantic that one day she might escape him—"

"Then why lock her up in an asylum for twelve years?"

"Everything hinges on the baby's death," Desmond sighed.

In the darkened hall, the two women paced in an uncomfortable silence, finally broken nervously by Beatrice Clayton.

"Simon is deeply in love with you," she muttered, "but I implore you, if you care anything about him, don't marry him. Such a union will destroy his career. Frankly, I would rather see you as his mistress. Though I disapprove of such liaisons...." Her mouth was a grim line. "Take off the ring, my dear, and save his life again. You have suffered grievously, and I pity you, but I don't want to witness the heartbreak of your marriage. What if you bore him a child?"

"A baby," Ariel whispered, her expression remote. "My baby—"

"Simon's baby!" Beatrice cried angrily. "Do you want to watch with him waiting for it to go mad?"

Shock filled the gray eyes. "Do you hate me?"

Beatrice shook her head, pressing a handkerchief to her mouth. "No, Ariel, but I fear you. You had strength enough to get Simon out of that burning ruin. Now have the strength to release him—"

"Am I to tell him that I don't love him?" Ariel asked sadly. "He knows I do. Already he thinks of me as his wife."

"Then lie. Lie! You will bring him nothing but grief...." With a flurry of skirts and a stifled sob, Beatrice Clayton vanished into her bedroom, leaving Ariel Farjeon alone in the corridor.

Again Simon Desmond passed another peaceful night in Ariel's arms, his head pillowed against her bosom, knowing nothing of her mind's agony. Several times he awoke, touched to find her awake, a look of love illuminating her beautiful face while she kept watch.

"Sleep, darling," he murmured. Tomorrow he would have to force out the truth, and he wanted her well rested for such an ordeal.

"I dreamt of you," she whispered. "Prayed for such a man all those years in the asylum. To rescue me, to love me.... How can I give you up, my darling?" She wept bitterly.

The time had come. Simon Desmond, wearing a dressing gown, sat grimly in a wing chair, his back to the glorious expanse of the Elizabethan garden. A window was open, and the bedroom was drenched with the heady aroma of summer roses. "We must talk," he said, stroking Ariel's hair as she sat at his feet. Nearby, an occasional table held a snifter of brandy to fortify him. Poor darling, she would have nothing to sustain her except his love. Pray God, it sufficed!

He took a deep breath. "Who set the wing on fire?"

"Oh, God, must we talk about it!" she moaned.

"Yes, Ariel. It's the only way I can save you."

"I don't know...." Her voice quavered.

"Was it your grandfather?"

Ariel turned so pale he thought she was going to faint. "No, poor man—"

"Did you do it?"

"I can't remember!"

"Yes, you can," Desmond spoke gently. "Nicholas can't hurt you any longer. What happened that night, Ariel?"

Fighting tears, she laid her head on his lap. "In those days, I slept in the nursery. Something woke me up. A flash of light and a crackling noise like a gigantic tree snapping. It was summer, and I ran to an open window. Flames... I saw flames... in the wing opposite." She was breathing heavily, whimpering with fright. "I ran down the great staircase screaming for help. 'Fire! Fire!' Then dashed out to the courtyard. Every window shone blood-red...."

"Did you see anyone?"

"I slipped and fell, hit my head—"

"Before that, darling. Who did you see leaving the wing?" He cradled her anguished face. "Who was it, Ariel?"

"Just before I tripped, I saw a man." Tears ran down her cheeks. "He came out with a flambeau, laughing. Laughing in exultation. When he spotted me, he threw the torch inside and slammed the door shut. I fainted...."

"Who was it?"

She bent her head, grieving. "Nicholas."

"Why was your grandfather blamed?"

"Because he was old," she sobbed. "He had no one to defend him. When I spoke, Father told me I was imagining things." She flinched, remembering his rage. "But then he couldn't bear to think Nicholas might be insane."

"So he let the elderly rot for the young," Desmond mused. "Did you ever hear Nicholas and your father discussing it?"

"Once," she whispered. "Father said he knew Nicholas was the arsonist, and that there was to be no more such 'nonsense' or he'd be incarcerated. I told Grandfather—he broke a window pane, and I used to talk to him every day—but he warned me never to mention it."

"Why not?"

"Nicholas was more important than I was. Only a male could inherit and carry on the line, Grandfather said. I was nothing and could be sacrificed as easily as he had been...." She raised a haunted face. "He said Nicholas was mad."

"Did you believe him?" Desmond asked quietly.

The child's despair flickered in the woman's expression. A shudder ran through her body as she confronted the painful memory. "No, I had to choose between them. Everyone thought him senile, so it made it easier for me." She wept. "Grandfather understood, I think. He never rebuked me...."

Desmond caressed her back with loving fingers, his voice husky with emotion. "Tell me about you and Nicholas."

"No! Please, Simon!" She struggled to break free.

"Ariel, I know so much. That's why he tried to kill me. I want only to learn the truth—your truth, not Nicholas's fabrication. You must know that he blamed you for everything."

"I sensed it from your changes of mood—" He winced, and she added sadly, "But I am the one known to be insane. My truth may be pure fabrication, too, and you—a man in love— may be blinded."

"Try me and see." She shook her head, but he was adamant. "How did it begin? Tell me, Ariel."

And if I do, she thought wretchedly, I will lose you. Even love has its limits. I won't be the one refusing you in marriage, my darling.... She collapsed in defeat, and Desmond drew her up to sit beside him in the roomy chair, aching to embrace her yet resisting. The wall was still too great between them, and her fear was chilling his heart.

In a flat, almost inaudible tone, she began. "You know what

Nicholas meant to me, Simon. In the early years. Father died
when I was twelve—a man I scarcely knew. My childhood
was spent with nannies and governesses.... But in my four-
teenth year, Nicholas stepped into my solitary, stultifying life
like a young god, sweeping me into a world of enchantment.
Dismissing the latest incompetent governess, he took over my
education himself, assigning the 'boring' subjects to an im-
poverished curate. For two years, everything between us was
innocent...." Aware of Simon's growing discomfort, she fought
tears, adding in a very low voice, "I loved him without qualm."

Desmond's pulse rose. "I went through his studio and saw
everything." Heartsick eyes met his. "When did the nude studies begin?"

"With our love affair." Fruitlessly, she searched his rigid
face for some understanding. "One night, when I was sixteen,
there was a terrible storm. A bolt of lightning almost struck
the ruin. I screamed, and Nicholas appeared in the Chinese
bedroom. Comforting me, he held me so gently that I fell asleep
in his arms. He lay as I've done with you these past
nights—" A spasm of grief shook her. "On top of the quilt.
But when he left at dawn, we both knew that we needed the
comfort of sleeping together. A fond embrace—that's all it
was in the beginning. Just a naive extension, I pretended, of
the gentle kisses, hand-holding, and caresses that had been
going on for some time...."

"Didn't you know you were playing with fire?" Desmond
cried with bitter irony, torn by jealousy. "That you were on
the verge of committing incest?"

It took all her courage to meet his anger. "Yes," she admitted, white-faced. "But by then Nicholas had told me our
destiny. One or both of us would go insane. Marriage was out
of the question. The risk was too great."

"When did you learn that?"

"Before my sixteenth birthday," she whispered. "We had
been having a procession of middle-aged gentlemen as house-
guests. Such conviviality was foreign to Nicholas's nature. He
relished solitude, so I teased him about it.... And he looked
at me as if I were a stranger. A haunted, passionate look,
although I didn't then recognize it as such. In a fury, he began
slashing his canvases—all pictures of me." Cursing Father's
burden of finding me a husband." A ripple of pain shot across
her face. "Nicholas shouted, 'They lust after you! Not one of
them will care for you. All they want is your body....'" She

reached for Desmond's hand, but he drew back, appalled. In silent grief, she began to rock backward and forward. "Then he kissed me as he never had before. Hard, his face streaked with tears, muttering, 'I will give you love, cherish you. . . .'" Distantly, she twisted Simon's ring on her finger. "And he screamed, 'God, why are you so beautiful!'" By now, her eyes had that blank look Desmond so dreaded. "I held him in my arms while he revealed our mutual fate. I had already shown signs of insanity, he said, when I set the wing on fire—"

"Did you think he was lying?"

"Yes, Simon, I did," she said wearily. "But it had happened so long ago. Father called me delirious. Grandfather, who agreed with me, was dead and known as a lunatic. I had only Nicholas, my solace. Confronting a dead future, we had only each other. To cherish was to give hope. . . . Even on the night"—her voice trembled—"when our relationship changed so drastically, he took me so gently that I said nothing. But the sensations he aroused gradually so stirred me that I became desperate for the intimacy. Shamelessly, I craved him—" She wiped away tears. "For weeks, we were seldom apart. Both of us intoxicated with our lovemaking." Desmond's face blanched, and she sadly took off his ring. "At any hour of the day or night, he came to me. By then, the servants were too old or indifferent to notice. . . ."

It hurt to hear, like acid searing the flesh, but he had to know every particle of the truth no matter how agonizing.

"What happened to this idyl?" he asked tightly.

Ariel Farjeon rose, pacing with the grace of a dancer. "Abruptly, it changed. Frenzy dying to ashes. My touch now enraged him. No more did he seek my bed. . . . Oh, outwardly, he was considerate, but now he took pleasure in—" She faltered. Desmond raised a cynical eyebrow. "In denying and humiliating me," she cried. "He painted and sketched me for hours, naked. Insisting on it. I hated it but agreed, because his mood frightened me. He made me feel like a harlot. . . . Much later, I realized it was his way of ridding himself of me. Loneliness and fear had driven us together to a forbidden passion that at once exhilarated and terrified. . . . Daily, I begged him to stop, but he refused, stripping me himself, leering at me, subjecting me to obscene taunts. Not once did I catch a shred of kindness. . . ."

The anguish she had felt years ago was mild compared to what she was now experiencing. Each word twisted the knife in Desmond's heart and her own. She would have given anything to stop it, but no lies came. . . .

"Suddenly, his depressed state changed to one of excitement," she said with a half-sob. "He whisked me off to Europe, declaring we would have a painter's holiday. It was like the old days—I basked in his affection. We sketched in Greece, Egypt, Italy, France, Holland. . . . Finally, he suggested that we return to Norfolk. All those months we had been circumspect, holding hands—no more. And then I made a fatal mistake." She threw Desmond an unhappy look. "Because of our Saracen ancestry, I urged a trip to Spain. Instantly, I knew he didn't want it. The idea alarmed him. . . . And then that disturbing hesitancy vanished, and he brought me home—'home,' he called it—to Granada, where dwelt our forebears amid the splendors of the Alhambra. We stayed two months. At first dutifully sketching that wondrous fortress and palace where we rented an apartment—so enraptured by Moorish and Christian beauties that nothing escaped our notice. But in groves and gardens, the burning sun and the ravishing scent of orange and citron trees inflamed our cool English blood; and at night, alone in moonlit beds, unable to sleep because of a nightingale's song, splashing fountains, and the incessant beat of dancing Andalusians—we lost ourselves, driven by our past into each other's arms. Within a week, we were lovers. . . ." Desmond paled, and Ariel forced herself to go on, utterly miserable.

"Nicholas called me his 'Moorish Princess,' after our ancestor who was a Sultan's concubine. From her sprang our good fortune!" She grimaced. "The son she bore him took the name Farjeon, ousted his many rivals, and rose to be chief advisor to his half-brother, the new king. My bastard"—tears filled her eyes—"was less fortunate. Conceived in a chamber where once that concubine might have slept with her lord, his existence became a thing of terror. We fled the evil enchantment of the Alhambra and returned to Bellereve. I wanted nothing more to do with Nicholas," she said in a choked voice, "but he never let me alone—hoping, I think, to produce a miscarriage. Each day he made me ride horseback. I even spent a night in the ruin, tied to that beam—"

"Jesus!" Desmond was on his feet, but she held him off.

"Not even fright worked. The child was determined to live. In my fourth month, Grinnell was summoned. On his advice, Nicholas found the Sheringham cottage where we lived as brother and sister awaiting my 'husband's' return from a Canadian mining expedition. Except for an old charwoman, we were completely isolated. Two months before the baby's birth, my horror about its conception vanished. In a daze of happiness, I knitted clothes, fixed up a bed.... Later, in the asylum, I tried to understand—"

Noticing her pallor, Desmond helped her to the snifter of brandy, and she drank deeply, returning it with shaking hands, her fingers still clasping his ring.

"Of course, my advancing pregnancy freed me of Nicholas's demands, and I could dream an imaginary father.... husband—" she shamefully confessed. "We agreed to farm out the child at birth, but in my heart I longed to keep it. At night, I seldom slept, its movements so enraptured me." Her face crumpled in remembrance. "Nicholas hired a midwife from Cromer, one he knew wouldn't gossip—"

"Why not call Grinnell?" Desmond asked very gently.

"He didn't want a safe delivery. A drunken midwife might deliver a dead child.... What he hadn't counted on was the intensity of my suffering. He stayed in the room with me, not from choice but because he was terrified that in my agony I might say something!" She laughed bleakly. "God knows why I didn't! I cursed everyone but him.... Over a day later, our son was born. The most perfect little being I had ever seen. I forgot my shame, the torment—all I wanted was my baby. Nicholas himself put it to my breast...." She blushed. "Since that was the time to take him away, it took me a long while to understand his hesitation. Was he mocking me, or was it kindness because the fear of my death had unnerved him? I thought it compassion for my labor. That was *his* mistake. He let me keep him, and I grew passionately fond—" Breaking down, she sobbed wildly. "I was so happy! With its birth, I felt reborn—the fear of insanity far away. Nicholas, too, seemed content, sketching us...." With an agonized gesture, she raked her breasts. "And then one day when I was nursing our baby, I said, 'He's the most beautiful thing I've ever seen!' Nicholas's face contorted in fury. Never had I seen him so angry. Raging. He tore the baby from me—" A shriek of despair broke from her, and Desmond caught her in an ardent embrace.

"Ariel, I love you! Nothing you've said has hurt my love," he cried passionately. "Share the burden, darling. Tell me what happened!"

Stark terror shone on her face. Trapped in the room of her nightmares, she sank to her knees, panting. "There was a large fire burning in the grate next to my bed. . . . God! No more, Simon. *No more!*" She pitifully implored.

Kneeling beside her, Desmond stroked her trembling body, pleading, encouraging her with loving words.

Finally, she met his eyes and pressed his hand to her heart. "He threw our baby into the flames—"

"Oh, my God!" Simon Desmond wept.

"As long as I live, I will hear those dreadful cries," she moaned. "For hours, I kept trying to reach him. . . . to pull him out of the fireplace, while Nicholas plied me with brandy trying to shut me up. . . . Once, I crawled to the grate and found a tiny bone—Nicholas was outside burying him. When he saw me crooning over it, he hit me so hard I fell against the bedstead and lost consciousness. Eventually, he thought I'd be quiet. A dead bastard was better than a living one—" Against Simon Desmond's shoulder, she fought hysteria. "But I couldn't be calmed. When he caught me scrabbling in the garden, he sent for Grinnell, then stabbed himself—restraining and gagging me so that I couldn't blurt out the truth. He concocted a story that I'd gone crazy and overlain my baby."

"Grinnell never saw the child's body." Ariel stared at him, not understanding. "Yet he certified you to an asylum—"

"He saw Nicholas's wound. Thought I'd attacked him."

"Your brother told me you struck from behind. Grinnell insisted it was a chest wound. . . ."

"Yes, it was," she said miserably. "He stood right before me and did it—" She hit the left pectoral muscle. "As an artist, he knew how to avoid a vital organ. It looked distressing, but was far from lethal—"

"Which Grinnell grudgingly acknowledged." Desmond's tone was scathing, remembering that grim breakfast interview. "Why did he acquiesce to your brother?"

"Grinnells have served our family for generations. Not only was he told that I'd deliberately overlain my baby, but Nicholas then revealed that I was the arsonist—not Grandfather." She cringed. "Any qualm Grinnell may have felt was stifled."

"Why weren't you confined immediately in the stone suite— the home of all the mad Farjeons?" he asked bitingly.

Ariel's face turned white. "Nicholas had killed. I knew the truth. His position was desperate. So he destroyed me. . . ." Her smile was tragic. "Once committed to an insane asylum, one is branded for life. No one would ever again believe a word I said. Have you, Simon?"

He bent his head in sorrow. "Not always."

"Well, I had a hard time, too, with belief," she said, fighting anguish. "They drugged me, and when I awoke in Weston Asylum, I almost went mad. All I wanted was my baby. By day, in dreams, I was haunted by his pitiful shrieks. . . . Three times, Nicholas came, hoping I would be amiable, but each visit I threw his crime in his face. He had murdered our child, and I wanted him to suffer! I ought to have remembered Grandfather's warning. How easily I could be sacrificed. . . ." She laughed brokenly. "Six months in a padded cell almost destroyed me. Weeks and weeks of being encased in a strait-jacket or shackled to a wall, hosed down for 'naughtiness,' living with rats and your own filth, force-fed—" She avoided Desmond's eyes, too frightened. "I was raped so many times I prayed for death. . . ." Still determined that he should know everything, she asked for no mercy. "Nicholas called me a whore. I was the serpent—the temptress. Perhaps, I was—"

"No!" Desmond cried, unbearably moved. "He couldn't accept being your lover." Rocking her against his breast, he murmured, "How did you survive those years, my darling?"

"In that cell," she whispered, "to keep myself sane, I pieced my life together—sorting out truth from fancy. I confessed my transgression. That I was perhaps equally guilty in our child's death. Had I insisted that he be immediately farmed out, had I not smiled at him that day—he might still be alive. . . . But such thoughts were leading me to madness, and I blocked out the unbearable. That's why I stopped speaking—so that no word might betray me. . . ."

"You recognized the Sheringham cottage." Desmond's voice was heavy with emotion. "Did you remember what had happened?"

"Not really. I knew there was something horribly wrong with it, but for twelve years I'd worked so hard to forget, and life in the stone fortress encouraged memory lapses. . . . Only you awakened me, Simon."

"And how grievously I abused you!" he cried, heartsick.

Ariel ran a gentle finger across his mouth. "You credited Nicholas's lies. I couldn't blame you. Everyone else thought me mad." She sighed. "If I had told you that he raped me, killed Regina, and hid her jewels, would you have believed me?"

The hazel eyes glistened. "No."

"Every move he made reflected against me. He suffocated Regina, removed her jewelry, tossed her into the moat, then came to me, dripping wet—saying there was a bad storm, but he made certain to drench my hair and nightgown so that I looked the obvious culprit—"

"Ariel... Ariel!" Desmond murmured against a fragrant cheek.

"Regina, poor woman, rummaging through his studio, confronting him with her suspicions, was summarily dispatched. Punishment for trespassing. Once you agreed to forego an autopsy to shield me, Nicholas had you at his mercy, which is exactly what he wanted. Constantly, he held over my head the threat of retribution. One day, it would fall. He enjoyed the waiting torment. I kept trying to postpone that horror by agreeing to his... demands." She was very pale.

"Which were?" Desmond's jaw tightened.

"That I sleep with him," she said dully. "On the day he trapped you, I prostituted myself, frantic to learn your whereabouts...." She kissed the gold ring Desmond was replacing on her finger, whispering in awe, "Yet loving you, I could still pity him. He was growing so wild—"

"On the edge of another breakdown, Ariel," Desmond said quietly. "Twice Grinnell treated him for attacks of mania in the years preceding his marriage. The two of them would go abroad, riding it out...." Shocked, Ariel looked away in alarm as a loud knock jerked them to their feet. Beatrice Clayton stood in the doorway, nervously twisting her hands.

"Simon, the police are downstairs." At Ariel's dismayed cry, she flicked her a pitying glance. "I'm sorry, my dear, they've found your brother—"

"Oh, God!" She burst into violent weeping.

"Is it a positive identification?" Desmond asked tensely.

Beatrice went white to the lips. A badly charred body, she was told, face unrecognizable. "Yes, from a ring bearing the Farjeon crest," she said flatly. Ariel sank onto Desmond's bed, terrified.

"I take it they're still looking for Ariel. What do they want of me?"

"You are her doctor, and it's known you went to Bellereve that afternoon. I suppose they want to question you about her mental state. Where she might be—"

"Yes, the lunatic who set the fire!" Ariel mumbled.

"Leave us, Bea," Desmond whispered. "Tell them I'll be

down shortly." Alarmed by Ariel's distraught mood, he went to her.

"Nothing you say will convince them. I'm the one who's crazy.... I'm the killer!"

"And I'll prove them wrong!" he cried, tempted to shake some sense into her. Suddenly, with aching clarity, he understood. "Do you think I'm going downstairs to betray you? Is that it?" At her frightened nod, he embraced her, murmuring, "Oh, my darling, so many years of torment! Trust doesn't come easily, does it?" She shook her head, despairing. "And what about love, Ariel?" His voice softened.

Fear dissolved in the gray eyes. Her lovely face grew radiant. On his bed, they kissed hungrily—a kiss so passionate it left an ardent Desmond breathless.

"Perhaps they could wait!" He laughed, very happy, strong hands caressing her. Then sighing, he said, "No, we will wait. Come, sweet love. Help me dress...." Exchanging his nightclothes for a lounge suit, he kept up a running, urgent conversation. "Five people know the whole story—your truth. But not one of them will ever reveal it, I promise you."

She drooped against him. "What can you say?"

"That you were as much a victim as your grandfather, Ariel. Grinnell gave me an affidavit attesting to Nicholas's breakdowns, his pyromania, and his extraordinary luck in casting the blame on others...." She winced, and he stroked her face. "Nothing will be said about incest, darling, or the baby's real death. Nicholas incarcerated you in a blind fury for disgracing the family name. But your lover is *unknown*, and the child's death not an issue. You're not the first woman to be so brutally punished. And many will agree with me that he was too possessive...." Their eyes locked uneasily. "Then I will say that not once have I believed you to be insane.... That on that last day, I went to Nicholas asking for your hand in marriage. We quarreled; he refused me. Still I persisted, and he tried to kill me. Bodies must be disposed of, so he set the wing on fire. You saved my life—"

"We escaped," she said numbly. "Why didn't Nicholas?"

"He couldn't release the mechanism. It jammed. In that conflagration, we heard nothing. But remember, darling, I shut the door on him. The guilt is mine alone." His voice rose over her outcry. "Ariel, he knew it was the end! He was calling you back. Together, you might die in glory on a fiery bier, but if you reached safety with me—his hated rival—I'm sure he hoped his memory would forever taunt you—"

"And won't it?" she asked with great bitterness.

"No!" His impassioned kiss made her tremble. "I'm very demanding, Ariel. You'll have your work cut out for you." He headed for the door.

"Nicholas!"

Which man did she want? he wondered, chilled. But with a low cry, she flung herself in his arms.

"Don't be afraid, my darling. Soon it will all be over," he whispered. "Grinnell's affidavit will be a great help. Shall I send up Beatrice?" She shook her head vehemently, remembering their last chilly interview. "Then have a glass of wine, Ariel. . . ." Laced with a few drops of choral, it would give her some blessed moments of oblivion.

"No, I'm fine," she insisted woodenly, her eyes sliding past him to the dead, bewitching grandeur of Bellereve.

Desmond, possessively in love, knew what he was facing. Nicholas Farjeon's ghost. Hiding his alarm, he launched a rough attack. "Damn it, you're coming with me! If you and I could escape that inferno, we can survive a police inquiry—"

"Simon, no!" she implored, frantic with despair.

"I need you, Ariel Farjeon!" he cried, fervently wooing her. "I've spent a lifetime—gone through hell—to find you!" He forced her to look at him. "I've no doubts about you at all. You saved my life. Do you think after that I'll let anyone tear us apart? No!" he shouted. "No dead brother. No police. No one!" Clasping her tightly, he smiled. "You're going to be my wife, Ariel." As a look of deep love suffused her face, he said tenderly, "It's time, darling. You know what to say. . . ."

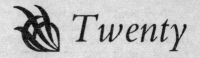 *Twenty*

Amazingly, she did, from the moment she entered the parlor on Simon's arm. But how could she falter when he introduced her to the thunderstruck officers as "Miss Farjeon, my fiancée," and then sat protectively beside her on the sofa, holding her hand. Suspicion, rumors, flew out the window in the face of such devotion. Desmond had been right, gambling on the fact that most people would concur that Nicholas Farjeon had been overly possessive of his sister. A stifling relationship, but not immoral. Only very frightening. For he was mad and was slowly killing her.... Grimly shaking their heads at such goings on, the sergeant and constable left with a heavy sigh. No need to prod anymore. Let the dead rest....

Alone in the waning light, the couple embraced.

"How right you were, Simon," Ariel breathed. "I couldn't have stood the wait. His presence is sometimes so strong it terrifies me."

"I, too, have memories to forget. We'll find a way...."

"Who is the fifth person to know my secret?" she asked, trembling against him.

"Grinnell. He'd always been baffled by the earlier fire. Arriving at Bellereve, he found your grandfather in nightclothes—spotless. You had a bad bruise and abrasions on your face and moss stains on your nightdress from your fall, but Nicholas was 'disheveled'—Grinnell's exact word—dirty, perspiring, his manner unduly excited. Frankly, the good doctor

279

was stunned when your grandfather was incarcerated, but always alert to his own interests, he kept his suspicions to himself."

"Poor man!" Ariel's voice was wistful. "Living two years in that hellish suite without even a companion as miserable as the Jackal. I guess Father was afraid that someone might learn he was neither crazy nor senile—just old." Desmond ran a loving hand through her hair, soothing her. "I, too, would have rotted if you hadn't come. Nicholas only hired you because you were a newcomer. One, he thought, who would accept his lies." She shivered. "And ask no questions—"

"Instead, I fell in love and asked many questions." He laughed softly. "Grinnell in time came round. Once he had digested the fearful implications behind that pitiful scene in the Sheringham cottage, he confronted Nicholas. Both of them were in a devilish position. Your brother had committed murder, Grinnell suggested, and in certifying an innocent, sane woman to a lunatic asylum, he had aided and abetted Farjeon's crimes and become an accessory after the fact."

"Why didn't he get me released?" she asked in a small voice.

"His precious career might have suffered." Desmond swore under his breath. "In their desperate plight, they struck a bargain. Farjeon would give Grinnell a yearly allowance, which almost bankrupted him, and Grinnell would look after him should he be taken ill—meanwhile fostering the story of your lunacy when necessary." In his arms, Ariel wept. "I have all this information in notes, a letter, and his affidavit. Both Beatrice and Colin Broughton, as witnesses to this tragic account, have read their contents."

"She doesn't want me to marry you, Simon," Ariel wretchedly confessed. "And she's right. After all, what do I bring as my dowry? Madness and ruin—"

"Hush, my darling. . . ." Gathering her close, he whispered, "We will have healthy babies, Ariel. One may carry the trait, but no more. I saw Farjeon's sons in Norwich. Two bright-eyed little scamps, very sound. Happy with their grandfather and thriving."

"Thank God!" she murmured, a haunted look crossing her face. "What if I should be stricken, Simon?"

"You spent twelve-and-a-half years as a 'madwoman,' Ariel. The miracle is that you survived it. I'm prepared to take the risk. Are you?" he asked gently.

She took a deep breath. "Yes. . . ."

"I love you," he said simply, holding her very tight.

"We'll have to leave Heydon. No one will understand."

Brushing aside her sadness, Desmond laughed. "Once, I thought Fairhaven and its life was everything I wanted, but without you it's as much a ruin as Bellereve. You are my home, my destiny. In your eyes is my world, Ariel." She smiled through tears. "How would you like to live in Norwich?"

Looking captivated and a little awed by the thought, she exclaimed, "But can we afford it, Simon? I know I've cost you many patients."

"Well, this practice will fetch something, and Grinnell will back us. He owes you that and has admitted his debt in writing. The perfect house is waiting for us on Elm Street. It needs work but will meet all our wants for the next few years." He nuzzled her cheek happily. "I'd like Bea to keep house—" She blinked in surprise. "Because you're going to work with me in the surgery. That way the nightmares will go—"

"Simon, I'm not a nurse!" she gently protested.

"No, but Dr. Portman told me you have a rare affinity with patients. That's what I need."

"They had no one," she said sadly. "Weston Asylum was a dumping ground. Many of them had been there for years, totally forgotten. I learned that a simple touch worked wonders—"

"I know it does. That's why I want you with me." Desmond gave her a lingering kiss. "Warming my bed, nestling in my heart—your lovely face the first thing I see. . . . And one day you will bear my child."

"Pray God, it be a healthy one!"

"It will be, my love." He smiled. "Now, let's tell Bea and Colin our news."

The pair were having tea in the study, engaging in nervous chitchat, food and tea growing cold in their anxiety. Over a half-hour ago, the front door had slammed, then nothing. No voices, no footsteps. . . .

"Colin, would you like some sherry?"

"No, Bea, this is an occasion for champagne!"

One look at the radiant couple standing before them, arms entwined, and they knew the joyous tidings.

"She's free," Desmond announced. "Free after all these years! Not many questions were raised, though I know the clincher was Grinnell's affidavit. We'll start calling the banns on Sunday, and in three weeks' time we'll be married." Gazing

down at Ariel, his voice grew husky with emotion. "We know
the risks and are not afraid," he added firmly.

There was a moment's awkward pause. Desmond stood
fiercely protective of Ariel while she stared nervously at Beatrice, dreading her castigation. But none came. The older
woman, confronting such deep love, found her fears dissipating. Whatever life brought these two, they would survive together.

"Oh, my dears!" she cried, tenderly embracing them.

Broughton cleared his throat. "Will you be staying on?"

"No, Colin, we're moving to Norwich." Desmond smiled
at his darling. "Now, where shall we go on our honeymoon?"

She whispered in his ear. "Yarmouth."

With a delighted laugh, he caressed her face. "Same inn?
Same suite?"

A tear ran down her cheek. "Yes."

"I'm going to miss you, Simon, damn it!" Broughton
growled.

"We'll always keep a room ready, Colin, and expect fre-
quent visits." He gripped his friend's hand. "After all, without
you, we might not be here!"

The two women had been talking together. Learning that
she was to be part of the household, Beatrice Clayton, deeply
moved, exclaimed with bright eyes, "I don't think I've been
so happy since my wedding day!" Turning to Desmond, she
beamed. "Simon, I think it's time I gave up mourning."

"Splendid! Jed would approve." He gave her a hearty kiss,
then took Ariel's hand. "It won't be an easy life, darling, until
the practice gets going, but I prefer city life to the hypocrisies
of the villages. Once we leave, that's an end to past grief."

Ariel smiled with shy grace. "Let me keep the wedding
ring, Simon, that bound us together."

"My mother would be proud to have you wear it," he said,
very touched.

They took a month's honeymoon while Beatrice began ren-
ovations on the Elm Hill house. The newlyweds went not only
to Yarmouth, but to Cromer, Hunstanton, Lynn—all the places
she associated with Nicholas—so as to efface searing memories. And at night, wrapped in each other's arms, both found
ecstasy and the peace they had so long sought.

Returning to Norwich, Simon Desmond launched his practice. Dr. Grinnell introduced him to the medical fraternity and

sent him some influential patients. Others came, from all walks of life, to the charming house. Always cheerfully greeting and comforting them in their various afflictions was Desmond's wife, the beautiful white-haired woman who held the frightened child, calmed the nervous invalid, and soothed the desperately ill while her husband healed them. She remained at his side when he operated, never flinching, assisted women in labor, and kept watch over the dying. Inseparable, they worked as one. And then one afternoon, she fainted.

Opening her eyes, she found Desmond sitting beside her on their bed. At her flush of embarrassment, he stroked the fine curls back from her forehead and kissed her ardently. "Nothing to worry about, darling," he whispered. "You're just going to have a baby."

A moment of terror eclipsed the luminous gray eyes, and he caught her tight. "The child will be healthy, Ariel, I'm sure of it. . . ."

Simon Desmond had the poignant joy of delivering his son himself and laying the baby in Ariel's arms. Tears ran down her cheeks as it snuffled at her breast with a strong pull.

"Three months, my darling, I allow you to devote yourself solely to our son. Then you're coming back to me."

Ariel smiled in wonder at her nursling, gently ruffling his wispy black hair. "And what are we to do with him?"

Desmond laughed. "You will be released at intervals to feed him; otherwise you remain with me." His hazel eyes darkened. "I told you I'm very demanding."

Clasping his hand, she placed it against the baby's face. "What if this child be more Farjeon than Desmond?" she asked quietly.

"Others will follow who will be well," he murmured. "But this babe is lusty. A perfect child. He will be fine. And remember, Ariel—" His lips bruised hers. "We have each other. We're no longer alone. No walls will ever part us again."

About the Author

The daughter of a writer and an actress, Katherine Hale grew up in Hollywood, and then came east to college at Sarah Lawrence and Barnard (where she spent most of her time acting with the Columbia Players). She soon fled academe for the wilds of the theater and was lucky enough to land the part of Miep in the original Broadway production of "The Diary of Anne Frank." In addition to acting on and off Broadway, Miss Hale worked at the Metropolitan Museum of Art and counts herself fortunate to have lived in New York City during the halcyon days of the mid-fifties and the sixties.

The author of two previous novels, AFFINITY and OB-SESSION, Katherine Hale lives in a book-crammed, cluttered house in Sudbury, Massachusetts, with her physician husband, two impish children, and an eccentric Australian terrier. When not writing dark Gothic tales, she can be found at the movies, immersed in Puccini or Rachmaninoff, or studying a murder case.